"You want another reason to go after the Sharks, Senator? Try revenge."

"I would say that you're fairly adept at manipulation yourself, Ms. Davis." She colored nicely at the soft accusation.

Gregg hurried into the gap. His words laced with the old power. "Hannah, I have to be certain that all your facts are correct and verifiable before we move." He was certain as soon as he said it. Gregg was not a particularly devout man: call it God, call it Fate, call it Destiny, call it Accident. Whatever, Gregg had been handed a Gift. He'd been given back a portion of what he'd once had, and he intended to use it. "Hannah, I *will* take care of this. It is very, very important to me."

Hannah gave him the first smile he'd seen from her.

It was what he would have told her anyway. But now conviction lent strength to the words. This time he meant them. Tomorrow, he'd start things rolling.

After all, now he had something to prove.

This is your chance, Greggie. This is your one last chance to get it all back. If Hannah's even halfway right, you can redeem yourself.

He wasn't going to blow it this time.

Marked Cards

A Wild Cards Mosaic Novel

edited by:
GEORGE R.R. MARTIN

assistant editor:
MELINDA M. SNODGRASS

and written by:

STEPHEN LEIGH   WALTER JON WILLIAMS

WALTON SIMONS   SAGE WALKER

VICTOR MILÁN   LAURA J. MIXON

LEANNE C. HARPER   MELINDA M. SNODGRASS

MARKED CARDS: WILD CARDS

Copyright © 1994 by George R. R. Martin & The Wild Cards Trust

"The Color of His Skin," copyright © 1994 by Stephen Leigh,
"Two of a Kind," copyright © 1994 by Walton Simons,
"My Sweet Lord," copyright © 1994 by Victor Milán,
"Paths of Silence and of Night," copyright © 1994 by Leanne C. Harper,
"Feeding Frenzy," copyright © 1994 by Walter Jon Williams,
"A Breath of Life," copyright © 1994 by Sage Walker,
"A Dose of Reality," copyright © 1994 by Laura J. Mixon and Melinda M. Snodgrass.

A Baen Books Original

Baen Publishing Enterprises
P.O. Box 1403
Riverdale, N.Y. 10471

ISBN: 0-671-72212-3

Cover art by Barclay Shaw

First printing, March 1994

Distributed by
SIMON & SCHUSTER
1230 Avenue of the Americas
New York, N.Y. 10020

Printed in the United States of America

to Julius Schwartz

who made it all possible

(and should have published my letters)

The Color of His Skin
by Stephen Leigh

Part 1

"Ms. Davis, I promise you that I take the concerns of the jokers very seriously. I will do whatever needs to be done."

Gregg Hartmann ushered the attractive and intense blond woman from his offices, sliding her out the door with a perfect blend of smile and frown. *Yes, I understand the importance of what you've just shown me,* his expression said. *You've made the right decision. Really, you have . . .*

"Hold my calls, Jo Ann," he said to his secretary after the outer door closed. A soft, strangely inflected "Gotcha, boss" followed him as he closed the mahogany doors to his private office. The way she said it made him look back, but Jo Ann only smiled at him. Jo Ann was a minor joker, a woman whose only visible affliction was that her skin was as green and warty as a fairy tale witch's—and her tongue as sharp. Gregg had always had joker secretaries; it was expected of him.

Gregg sank into the leather caress of his chair and contemplated the cardboard box of transcripts, tapes, and photos Hannah Davis had given him. His right hand

1

throbbed achingly, but when he looked down there was only the dead plastic mockery of the prosthetic resting on the chair's arm—a dead weight whose ironic, crude symbolism didn't escape him. The inner voice that had begun to nag him more and more over the last several months spoke again.

You took Tachyon's hand with Mackie Messer and Herne's hounds returned you a just revenge. Don't complain when you bear only a tithe of the pain you've caused over the years, Greggie. An eye for an eye . . .

Shut up, he told the voice. Left-handed, he touched the speed dial on his phone system and punched in two numbers. He listened to the phone ringing and picked up the receiver as the line clicked open.

"Pan?" he said. "Gregg Hartmann."

"Gregg, so good to hear from you." The voice on the other end sounded entirely normal. Gregg heard nothing in the soft accents he hadn't heard before, and Gregg *knew* Pan Rudo, or at least he once had. He'd known him very well indeed. "In fact, I've just learned that the new WHO funding sailed through the Senate untouched, thanks largely to the lobbying you've done on our behalf. Thank you."

"You're entirely welcome, and Jo Ann should have my invoice to you tomorrow, but that's not what I'm calling about. Pan . . . well, I need to talk to you. In person. I'm also calling Brandon van Renssaeler. . . ."

"She is truly a most persistent woman," Pan said.

The director of the World Health Organization placed the sheaf of transcripts back in the box on Gregg's desk and sat back in his chair, as elegant and composed as usual. Rudo shook his graying head slowly and let out a deep sigh, glancing at Brandon van Renssaeler, who sat silently next to him with his gaze directed on the shuttered windows behind Gregg, his jaw muscles bunched under his grim frown. Brandon had flushed brightly when he'd seen Lamia's transcript; since then, he'd said little.

"But then, fanatics often are persistent," Rudo continued. "I should have guessed that she'd come to you eventually, considering your reputation."

"I felt you both deserved a chance at private rebuttal before I did anything. Since we all know each other, and since you're both mentioned in the material, I thought I might as well talk to the two of you together. But I have to tell you, Pan, Brandon, this stuff here ..." Gregg frowned. "I'd hate to think there was any truth in it."

"There's none," Brandon grunted suddenly. "Not in what was said about me, anyway. Gregg, we've known each other a long, long time. I consider us friends as well as colleagues. Pan and I certainly know each other well, and I've done work for him through the firm, but to suggest that I had something to do with the assassination of Robert Kennedy ..." He shook his head. "My ... *wife* was never exactly a stable person, Gregg. You knew her then. You were at the damn party she talks about in this transcript, where I supposedly became involved with Ms. Monroe. Gregg, I really hope you're not planning to do anything about this."

"You're denying it, then."

"Yes," Brandon said emphatically. "All of it. And believe me, if I hear a word of it in the press or anywhere else, I will slap a lawsuit on this Hannah Davis and whoever is with her so fast ..." Brandon pressed his lips together. "We're both attorneys, Gregg. You can see as well as I can that all Davis has are the imaginings of a neurotic woman who probably blames me for the failure of our marriage. There's no photograph, Gregg. There never was one. I believe world-spanning conspiracies are best left to comic books and the tabloids. I understand why you feel you had to ask, and I appreciate that you called before doing anything Davis wanted you to do, but I resent the fact that I have to defend myself against anything so ludicrous, even to you." Brandon released a long, heavy exhalation after that. He ran fingers through perfectly clipped hair. He was so obviously angry that Gregg simply nodded and turned to Rudo.

"And you, Pan? I take it you're denying all this as well?"

Pan smiled, and Gregg once more felt the sense of frustrating interior blindness that had afflicted him for the last five and a half years, since that terrible night in Atlanta. Once, Gregg could have deciphered the emotional matrix behind that smile. Once, Gregg would have known exactly how Rudo was feeling, could have twisted and pulled on that emotion until Rudo writhed in his chair in fury or disgust. Rudo had been a puppet like a thousand others—not one Gregg had ever used much, but pliable and interesting in his own way, with odd quirks that made him ... *tasty.* But Puppetman had perished in the black chasm of Demise's gaze, and the power had gone with him. Like his lost hand, the vestigial remnants of the ability still ached, mockingly useless.

"Gregg, my friend, I would prefer to talk with you alone, if that's possible."

Brandon cast Rudo a sharp glance at that, and the two men locked gazes for a second. Once more, Gregg regretted the loss of his power. There was something going on here that he was missing, some unspoken communication between the two men. Like Rudo, Brandon had also been a puppet—and like Rudo, one not much used. He regretted that; it seemed he might have missed something.

"Fine with me," Brandon said. "I'm supposed to be at a Chamber meeting anyway. Gregg, is there anything else?"

Gregg shook his head. "No. I think you've told me all I need to know."

"Good." Brandon put his hand on Hannah's cardboard box. "Give this stuff back, Gregg. Give it back or just burn it and be done. That's the best advice I can give you, both as a professional and as a friend. Don't get involved in this insanity."

"I hear you, Brandon. Thanks for coming."

Brandon nodded to Gregg, then looked again at Pan before taking his coat from the rack and leaving the office. As the outer door closed behind the man, Rudo rose stiffly from his chair and went to the side window of Gregg's office.

Gregg had sent Jo Ann home at five. Brandon and Pan
had arrived around seven, within minutes of each other.
A few office lights in the old building across the alley
gleamed outside Gregg's windows. Scant blocks away,
hidden behind the brick flanks of Broadway and 44th,
Jokertown was awakening, rising as the sun set. Now more
than ever in its life, J-town was a place of night and shadow,
a land where the only normality was abnormality.

And if what Hannah Davis had told Gregg was even
partially true, then the person sitting before him was
responsible for much of that. *If it's true, then I wasted
a glorious puppet ...* And with that, the voice scolded:
*Be glad. It was that much less pain laid at your feet, and
Hannah has given you a chance for atonement.*

"Do I deny it?" Pan repeated. "Gregg, how long have
we known each other?"

Gregg shrugged. "I don't know.... Ten, twelve years,
I guess. Since you hooked up with WHO."

"Have I ever indicated to you a particular hatred of
jokers in that time?"

*A party at the Lindsays' ... there were several promi-
nent jokers in the crowd, and you radiated such revulsion
that Puppetman awoke. I never had the opportunity to
use you that night, but Puppetman's hunger drove me
out into the street afterward, seeking pain. I remember....* "No," Gregg told him. "Nothing overt, anyway.
Nothing that stands out."

Pan nodded. "Then let me tell you the truth, Gregg.
I *hate* the wild card virus. I loathe it. And there *is* an
organization known as the Card Sharks."

"Oh my God ..." Gregg sucked in an involuntary breath.
He blinked, startled by the unexpected, quick admission
and not certain how to react to the vehemence in the
man's voice. *Yes!* the voice inside him exulted. *You've
wanted to erase the horrors of Puppetman. You've
wanted to make amends, and the way has been handed
to you ...* "Pan ... Pan, I—"

"I know," Pan said. "You asked me here because you
were certain that it was poppycock, that I could dismiss
this so-called evidence of Ms. Davis's with a shrug and

a laugh, and you could forget about it and her. Well, as much as I hate to admit it, the woman has done all too good a job. How's the saying go? A little knowledge is a dangerous thing. This is a fine example of exactly that."

"Pan ..." Gregg had no words. He almost laughed in surprise and shock. "Brandon, too? Is that what you're saying?"

Rudo grimaced, waving a hand. "Brandon has done some legal work for us, work done under my own name, but he ... let's just say that he told you the truth as he knows it. Not everything Ms. Davis has surmised is true."

"Pan, do you realize what you're telling me? You leave me no choice but to call the authorities and go public with this."

Rudo looked out at the city. Gregg watched Rudo's wavering reflection in the glass, trying to see a demon and only seeing the image of a man. "Let me finish," Rudo said. "Ms. Davis has it half right, Gregg. We're not the hidden viper she imagines. In fact, I believe you would be sympathetic to our aims."

Rudo turned back into the room. His eyes were alight, his face serious. "I'm not going to give you the recruitment speech, Gregg. We both know that nothing about the wild card is simple. The issues are complex. There's no black or white, just endless shades of gray. That's where Ms. Davis has found her delusions. We can both agree that this alien virus is a scourge, a plague that is best eradicated. For every hundred it infects, it horribly slays most, curses nearly all that survive with disfigurement or worse, and leaves one person, *one* out of that entire hundred with a small gift in exchange. Hardly a fair trade, I would say. And that's without mentioning the social chaos that has resulted from the virus, the thousands upon thousands of secondary deaths from misunderstanding and prejudice and outright hatred. *That's* the legacy of the wild card, and I believe very strongly that anyone who *doesn't* despise the virus is truly insane."

Rudo stopped. His hands, frozen in the midst of frantic motion, suddenly dropped to his side. He gave Gregg a self-deprecating smile. "I see that I've given you the speech anyway. Forgive me, it does spill out at odd moments. But let me add the second part, the part Ms. Davis has forgotten or has chosen not to see. I—we, the Sharks—hate the *virus*. Not the people infected with it: they're utterly blameless. They are sad, innocent victims. The Card Sharks—I must complement our dear Hannah. She's even ferreted out the pet name we once gave ourselves—do *not* exist to terrorize or kill jokers. We have pledged to end this modern plague by finding a cure: a treatment to halt the disease in those already infected, a vaccine to inoculate those who haven't yet been exposed. We are not a cabal; we are not terrorists. We are, very simply, a private research organization, funded by several wealthy and influential people who prefer that their efforts remain anonymous."

Rudo spread his hands wide, like a performer taking a bow, like the pope blessing the multitudes.

"Am I supposed to applaud now, Pan?" Gregg asked. "I can't. All this . . ." He gestured at Hannah's box. "You can't erase everything with a few well-chosen words." *You should know that more than anyone, Greggie. . . .* "This Dr. Faneuil, infecting the jokers with AIDS—"

"We've made mistakes," Rudo said. "Kenya was a terrible one. I'll admit that freely. We'd manufactured a retrovirus, an infection that would rewrite DNA the way the Takisian virus does. We had hopes that it would reverse the process and bring an infected body back to its original form. We thought we were on the right trail; we were wrong."

"You experimented on jokers," Gregg said. *Why do you sound so composed? Where's the heat? There's no rage, no fury in your voice. Here's someone dancing around to justify a horror. "It's not really my fault."* The same thing you *used* to say . . . . "You used *people* as laboratory animals."

Rudo pressed his lips tightly together. "We experimented on jokers who were dying already, from drought and neglect, from horrible prejudice directed at them from their own people, and from the wild card. We did it in the hope of saving them, and if we'd been successful

we would have been heroes. As it was . . . the wild card
infects no other animal besides us, Gregg. Once the lab
tests were done, Dr. Faneuil had no other way to know."

Under the urging of his inner voice, Gregg started to
protest, but Rudo shook his head once more. "Let me
bring us to the bottom line. Gregg, my good friend, the
Card Sharks had nothing to do with the incident that
precipitated all this and brought Hannah Davis into the
picture in the first place—the tragic fire at the church.
You're a lawyer: I will wager that there is not one *shred*
of hard evidence in your box pointing to that, not one.
I've spoken with Ms. Davis and she admitted that to me.
Nor have we ever threatened Ms. Davis's life or attempted
to silence her, as she claims. For an organization that's
supposed to be as huge and powerful as she's contending,
it would seem that we're remarkably inefficient at carrying out death threats. Brandon already gave you his
answer to the assassination of Robert Kennedy; I'll tell
you that we also had nothing to do with the assassination
of President Kennedy. We never tried to burn down Jokertown; we never sabotaged the X-llA space program, we
weren't part of the witch hunts of the fifties. Gregg, the
woman's prime piece of evidence is a talking *hat*. I'm
afraid that Hannah Davis is paranoid and delusional. A
very intelligent and a very attractive woman, but unfortunately mentally unbalanced—and that's a diagnosis I can
give you from my own field of expertise, as you know."

Again, the faint, uneasy smile. Rudo seemed to be
trying to gauge Gregg in some way; Gregg remained
silent. *Shout! Get angry! Point out the inconsistencies!*
the inner voice railed; but Gregg ignored it.

*Fascinating. All the time this was festering inside Pan
and I didn't know—*

"Still," Rudo continued, sitting once more, "if the contents of that box were to become public knowledge, we
would find it embarrassing and costly. We'd rather that
didn't happen. Gregg, you're known as a friend of the
jokers. I appreciate that. I admire your dedication, the
way you've sacrificed your own ambitions for a higher
ideal. I also know that fate hasn't been kind to you. This

office—it's expensive enough, but not exactly upscale. You've had to sell property and assets you once owned to stay solvent. You're in your mid-fifties, you have no hope of recovering your political career, and frankly, in a country that elected the Barnett/Zappa ticket, your views are hardly popular anyway. How does this sound? I would like to hire you as a consultant for our research facility. Name your own salary, whatever you need. Write your own job description, as well. Maybe you're right. We've kept our work secret because we wanted to leap-frog over the tangles of legislation and regulations, because we wanted to move as fast as possible, and Gregg, I will tell you that we are closer than we have ever dreamed. A few more puzzle pieces . . . Maybe with your help and contacts, we can bring our work to comple-tion—in the mainstream."

"You're offering me a bribe, Pan."

"Bribe is an ugly word. I am offering you compensa-tion for decades of effort. I'm offering you a chance to *continue* your good work. I am offering you a chance at redemption for the unfortunate failures in your life."

Redemption . . . "And if I say no? If I tell you that the implications of the Davis material disgust me and I can't in good conscience condone it by silence?" *Because you don't believe this artful deceit. You don't believe it at all. You can look at him and see that's he's lying, Greggie. . . .*

Rudo *did* smile now. He chuckled—a cultured, con-trolled amusement. His long, delicate fingers steepled under his chin. "Am I supposed to threaten *you*, to say 'then we will be forced to eliminate you?' Gregg . . ."

The laugh came again, then Rudo's face fell into seri-ous lines as he leaned forward. "If you say no, I walk out of your office believing you have the sense to look at your 'evidence' and realize that you have nothing actionable beyond a few tall tales and the musings of a deranged woman. And if you still go public with this, then—" Rudo smiled again. "Then I contact Brandon and my other lawyers. There, *that* is a threat worse than death."

Rudo laughed once more, and Gregg found it hard

not to smile in response. Gregg drew Hannah's box to him and glanced at the contents. *He's lying....* "Pan, I don't know. This 'research organization' of yours.... You're operating totally outside the legal system. A cure for the wild card virus would be a wonderful thing—a damn miracle, in fact—but this.... She didn't sound deranged to me."

"They rarely do, at first. Think about it, Gregg. Mull it over. Check out this Davis woman and her conspiracy theory. If you'd like, I can arrange for you to meet with Ms. Monroe—she's still in town. I invite you to ask her version of what happened the other night. Ms. Davis's tale is so compelling because it *is* an artful blend of truth and delusion, fact and fiction. If you decide that there's anything *evil* about me, well, do what you need to do."

"That's exactly my intention."

"Good." Rudo uncrossed his legs and stood. He strode quickly across the room to the office door and paused, his hand on the brass handle. "Thank you for calling me first, Gregg. I appreciate that. And keep my offer in mind," he said. "Tell me what you need, and we will get it for you."

No! You can't just let him go like that! But Gregg found himself nodding. Rudo gave a short inclination of his head in return, and left.

... A chance at redemption ...

So what are you going to do? What are you going to do?

He still prowled Jokertown—not as Puppetman, no longer looking to feed on rage and fury and hatred, but searching for more mundane, more *human* solace.

So poor Gregg Hartmann can't get it up with normal women anymore. So you only really get off on jokers. Why should you be surprised? That's your penance, too, Greggie....

She called him "Jack," though Gregg knew that she must have recognized him—one-handed ex-senators whose faces were occasionally plastered all over the various media weren't exactly plentiful. Over the last year he'd picked up this same woman a half dozen times. *Her* real name Gregg neither knew nor cared to know. On the J-Town streets she was known as Ichor-bod. Her pores oozed a translucent jelly that coated her like a second skin. Her short dark hair was perpetually slicked down like a twenties movie star, and her clothing—what little she generally wore—was stained as if it'd been dipped in Vaseline. If one could have turned off the internal tap, she might have been pretty; as it was, her features were obscured and smeared with gelatinous perspiration.

She reclined on the bed naked, her legs sprawled carelessly apart, the glistening effluvium of her skin already staining the cheap sheets, the triangle of pubic hair matted with it. She watched him undress with an expression of bored impatience. "What's the problem, Jack?" she asked, her gaze low. "Oh, that's right, I remember. Jack likes it hot. He likes it hot and slick and wet."

She crawled across the bed toward him. Kneeling, she kissed him from navel to nipple, leaving a glistening trail across his abdomen as he gasped. Her hand caressed him. Where she kissed, where she touched, wherever the strange substance from her body came into contact with his skin, there was a tingling, growing heat—another attribute of Ichor-bod. She cupped his scrotum in her other hand, and the sudden warmth seared upward in his groin, just on the edge of pain. Her breasts were twin fires on his belly.

Gregg closed his eyes, moaning.

. . . *Peanut moaning as Puppetman pumped his libido and lust to unnatural levels, as the unbidden, frightening erection split open his scaly, inelastic skin, melding glorious pain with the pleasure.* . . .

. . . *Mackie Messer, gleefully dissecting the living Kahina before the horrified eyes of Chrysalis and Digger Downs as Gregg leaned against the wall outside the room and gorged at the feast.* . . .

. . . *Ellen tumbling down the flight of stairs, and Puppetman reveling in the death-throes of the child dying*

*inside her womb—the child possessed by Gimli (and it
was Gimli, no matter what the bastard Tachyon said). . . .*

"Yes, now that's more like it," Ichor-bod crooned
below him. Gregg felt her slip a condom over his length,
and he suddenly pushed her down, falling heavily on top
of her as his hips lunged forward helplessly.

Afterward, he took a long shower.

Gregg could feel her watching as he dressed, as he
settled the Leo Barnett mask over his face. Somehow it
felt right to wear the face of the man who now held the
position Gregg had once coveted. If Ichor-bod noticed
the irony, she said nothing. "Here's another fifty," Gregg
said, dropping the bill on the nightstand. "A tip."

Ichor-bod shrugged on the bed. "Whassa matter, Jack?
Feeling especially guilty about humpin' a poor joker
tonight?"

Gregg didn't answer. He left her room without another
word—he'd learned long ago that whores didn't expect
good-byes. On the way down the stairs of the apartment
building, he slipped on the gloves with the sewn-on extra
fingers: just another joker in the night.

Just another victim.

"Senator!"

Gregg jumped, his heart pounding. The voice came
from the alley between the buildings. A shape moved
there: a massive, cloaked form. The steel mesh of a fencing mask glimmered in the light of the street lamp.
Gregg slowly relaxed. "Oddity. How did you—"

"Someone needs to talk to you." Oddity beckoned back
into the shadows. The slurred voice sounded like Patti's,
Gregg's favorite of the menage de'trois trapped inside
the powerful, misshapen body. Oddity groaned as shapes
moved under the cloak. Gregg remembered Oddity's
eternal agony of transformation, too. That pain had fed
Puppetman all too well.

"Patti, I—"

Oddity stared at him. "I hate that mask, Senator, on
you of all people. You shouldn't mock yourself that way.
Please, Senator. This really is important."

"All right." Gregg followed the joker into the alleyway.

Oddity too had been a puppet, one of the jokers close to him during his years of power. Oddity's great strength and loyalty had aided him numerous times. He told himself there was no reason to be apprehensive, not with Oddity.

"You went immediately to the goddamn enemy."

Gregg peered through Leo Barnett's eye holes into the shadows of the alley. A woman stepped out from under a fire escape, shaking blond hair from under a paisley cap. She was dressed like the night: black jeans, a black sweatshirt on the front of which was lettered in red: THE ROX DIDN'T DIE.

"Ms. Davis . . ." Under the mask, Gregg's mouth had dropped open. *She knows. How . . . ?* Then it struck him: *Jo Ann. She's a member of Father Squid's church. A bug . . .* The other voice, the one he hated, spoke as well: *Hey, Greggie, no reason for you to get pissed. The woman's right—you're a slime.*

Hannah stood in front of him like a sullen Valkyrie, hands folded under her breasts. She didn't look like she'd slept much in the two days since he'd last seen her. There were dark circles of fatigue under her eyes; her face was drawn and pale. She seemed dangerous, nervous, and there was the unmistakable bulge of a handgun at her right hip. Gregg felt the first beginnings of panic. "Pan Rudo and Brandon van Renssaeler visited you not four hours after I left. Did I make another mistake?" she asked him, cutting off his halting protest.

Tell her, Greggie. Tell her how you're about the worst choice she could have made. . . .

"Have you decided to take Rudo's bribe?" Hannah continued, raging. She came up close to him, though she was very careful not to touch him. The scent of her shampoo wafted around him, contrasting strangely with her fury. "How much, Senator? How much are you charging for your 'consultation'?"

The worst thing is that you know that she's right. You're scared. You're scared of Rudo and the Sharks, and scared because you know Hannah's right. Gregg Hartmann

*doesn't have the balls to atone for his sins, to do what
needs to be done. Not any more. . . .*

"Just shut up," he told the voice.

She blinked at him. "Shut up? Shut *up*?" Hannah
backed away a step, giving a mocking laugh of disbelief.
"We came to you for help, Senator. I need to know if
you've already betrayed us."

Not yet. But you've been thinking about it. . . .

"I don't have to listen to this," Gregg said. He started
to turn, but Oddity's hand was on his shoulder. He
looked up into the mismatched eyes hidden behind the
fencing mask.

"I think you do need to listen, Senator," Patti said, and
though her voice was gentle, there was steel in her grip.

"Patti, I don't know how you three got involved in
this, but you know *me*."

"Yes, we do, Senator, and I'm sorry," she said. "We're
involved because Father Squid asked me for help. We're
protecting Hannah—Quasiman isn't exactly reliable right
now."

"She's got a damn gun for protection."

"She's also had people shooting at her. She needs all the
help she can get. She needs you." Oddity groaned again,
and the hand clenching his shoulder tightened briefly.
When Gregg looked at it, the fingers were no longer Patti's,
but a black male's. "I've been telling Hannah that she's
wrong, that you were just being careful. Evan's told her
the same thing, and John's a lawyer—he says you were
obliged to talk to the other party. But Hannah—"

Gregg looked back at Hannah, standing with arms
crossed as she glared at him. *Tell her how after Rudo
left, you sat there staring at the box like it was going to
bite you, how you kept trying to believe all that crap
Rudo fed you.*

"John's right," Gregg said to both of them, clutching
at the proffered excuse. "You can't expect me to go public with what you gave me without first talking to Rudo.
Since you've obviously bugged my office, you also know
that I told him what he did was wrong."

Hannah sniffed. Her sneakers scuffed at the dirty

pavement. In her eyes, he found only scorn, as if she were contemplating a turd on a tablecloth. "I'm *so* damned impressed. He told you that he'd been directly responsible for infecting hundreds of jokers with AIDS, and you gave him a tongue-lashing. My, my. I'll bet you'll turn him over your knee if he kills Father Squid or me. Maybe even send him to his room without supper."

She started to turn away from him. *Once I could have broken you like a stick, you bitch. . . .* Gregg reached for her. "Listen . . ."

Hannah whirled around and slapped his hand aside contemptuously. Reflexively, Gregg raised his hand to strike back. Hannah pushed him and Gregg stumbled, staggering backward. His head slammed into wet, soiled brick. For a moment his vision blurred as interior fireworks splattered and burst against his eyelids.

She looked down at him, sagging against the filthy wall. "I should have known better," she said. "You're a fat, old, powerless man living on memories."

Anger filled him with that, a searing denial that rose from deep inside him. His head roared, drowning out the voices and the pain, and the blood-red tsunami battered against unseen, five-year-old walls in his mind, foaming and tearing. *A fat, old, powerless man . . .*

From beneath the fury, something rose. Gregg almost felt dizzy with the presence. He stood, drawing in a deep breath and confronting Hannah's ridicule with sudden honed steel in his voice. He pulled off the Barnett mask and threw it to the ground.

"I won't let you insult me that way," he said. And the words *burned*. They nearly lit the darkness. "Not after all I've done for the jokers. Over the years, I've nearly died for the wild card: in Syria at the hands of the Nur, in Berlin to terrorist kidnappers, in Atlanta to a crazed joker, during the invasion of the Rox to Herne. Everything I've done has been in the best interests of those infected by this damned virus. You have *no right* to question my intentions or my methods."

Yes! Gregg's voice had gone resonant and deep, the way he'd sounded when Puppetman filled his speeches with conviction. He felt young, powerful. The words flamed, and Hannah looked suddenly uncertain. Gregg pulled the glove from his right hand and held up the prosthesis in front of her face, turning it so she could not escape the vision. "You want to compare scars, Hannah? Here's one of mine."

Oddity growled wordlessly in the background. Hannah stared at him wide-eyed, as if seeing Gregg for the first time. For a long second, she held his unmasked gaze, then the resistance in her collapsed. "I—" she began, and stopped. She paced to the back of the alley like a caged beast, one hand beating against her thigh. Gregg saw the back of her sweatshirt: IT JUST FADED AWAY.

Gregg wanted to shout, to scream in delight. It was torture to simply stand there. Under his shoes, molded plastic crackled like dry fire.

My God, I thought it was lost and dead, but I've found it again! The power . . . And in response: *Don't you see, Greggie? It's been returned to you as a gift, a tool to allow you to atone for your sins, a way for you to make up for all the pain and misery you've caused. A gift . . .*

Gregg marveled.

When Hannah came back to him, the bristly defiance was gone from her voice. "Senator . . . I . . . well, I guess the only thing to say is, I'm sorry." Her hands fluttered up from her sides, fell again.

The apology was so sweet it almost made him grin. Instead, he simply nodded. "I understand. You've been under an enormous amount of pressure. Your apology's accepted, of course. And please, can we drop the formality, since we're on the same side here? I'm Gregg."

"Gregg." She glanced quickly away from him, biting her lower lip. "Umm, did I just make a total ass of myself?"

"No. You just reminded me again how important all this is." Gregg allowed himself a small smile. He tried to project some of his newly returned ability into the gesture, feeling—*tasting*—her passion. He touched her shoulder with his left hand, wanting to take her as he used to take puppets, to make the full psychic connection.

He felt nothing. He couldn't do it.

The charisma, the conviction was back in his voice, but this was not Puppetman. Gregg couldn't find the strings of her emotions, couldn't follow them back to their sources and make her dance the old dance. He could only tug gently at her feelings, not shape them completely. Hannah wanted so badly to believe him; that was the only thing that had made it possible.

Still, even this truncated power, after having it all vanish for so long, nearly took the breath from him. He nearly missed her question.

"Did you hear Barnett's speech tonight?"

"No. I was—"

"—occupied. We know." Hannah's look was almost shy, but it still made Gregg look aside for a moment. *Ashamed, Greggie? Ahh, too bad—well, you should be. . . .*

"Barnett called for mandatory blood testing for anyone who is currently in or is applying for a public service position," Hannah told him. "That's every doctor, every nurse, every health care worker, every police officer, every firefighter, every last government worker. 'The great majority of decent people have a right to know if the person treating them is infected by this horrible scourge.' That's what Barnett said. He's promised to sign the legislation as soon as Congress puts it on his desk. Zappa's already stumping for support, and you know how effective a speaker the vice president can be. A coalition of senators and representatives has pledged to introduce a joint bill in session tomorrow. It's starting—all the controls and oppression you oppose. First, it'll be the testing, then. . . . That's why . . ."

Hannah stopped, biting her lower lip. She was glorious, the emotions cascading from her like a fountain. So attractive.

So very, very attractive.

"Senator . . . Gregg—we can't wait any longer. My God, all the hidden manipulations, all the strings they pulled."

Manipulations. Strings. You remember those, don't you, Greggie. . . . Hannah nodded toward Oddity, watching them silently near the mouth of the alley. "Patti suggested something the other night: look at what happened to *you*, in '76 and again in '88. Doesn't it make you wonder? Who would the Sharks have been most against having as president? If they were willing to assassinate the Kennedys, what would they have been willing to do to you?"

Christ! Gregg couldn't speak, couldn't answer. *Of course! I missed Rudo. I could have missed others. Could Tachyon . . .?* His other voice seemed equally stunned. *You see! There it is, Greggie: redemption, redemption for it all!* "There was nothing in what you gave me to indicate that, Hannah," he heard himself protest automatically.

"No," she admitted. "But the Sharks were there. Given their ideology, they must have been. You want yet another reason to go after the Sharks, Senator? Try revenge."

"I would say that you're fairly adept at manipulation yourself, Ms. Davis." She colored nicely at the soft accusation. Gregg hurried into the gap, his words laced with the old power. "Hannah, I have to be certain that all your facts are correct and verifiable before we move." He was certain as soon as he said it. Gregg was not a particularly devout man: call it God, call it Fate, call it Destiny, call it Accident. Whatever, Gregg had been handed a Gift. He'd been given back a portion of what he'd once had, and he intended to use it. "Hannah, I *will* take care of this. It is very, very important to me."

Hannah gave him the first smile he'd seen from her. Behind her, Oddity was nodding.

It was what he would have told her anyway. But now conviction lent strength to the words. This time he meant them. Tomorrow, he'd start things rolling.

After all, now he had something to prove.

This is your chance, Greggie. This is your one last chance to get it all back. If Hannah's even halfway right, you can redeem yourself.

He wasn't going to blow it this time.

Two of a Kind
by Walton Simons

She was beautiful, the kind of woman men killed or
died for. The gabardine suit wasn't tailored to show off
the exquisite contours of her body, and her hair was
pinned back. It didn't matter. One look into her crimson
eyes and any man was lost, swallowed up in the promise
of a single, sensual glance. Seeing her made coming into
work every morning a pleasure.

"Is he in yet?" Jerry eased himself onto the corner of
Ezili's polished mahogany desk. Everything in the offices
reflected taste and wealth. From the plush carpeting and
deco fixtures to the location itself. Ackroyd and
Creighton took up half a floor of the most expensive
office space in Manhattan.

"Yes. He actually came in early, I think. I hope there's
no trouble at home." Ezili smiled, a look that went
beyond mischief into a kind of unconscious predation.

"I don't think there's much chance of that. Hastet
would never allow it." Friendly as she was, Jerry couldn't
help being intimidated by Jay's wife. But then, she was
a Takisian.

Jerry rapped on the smoked glass of the door, right
under the painted letters which read:

JAY ACKROYD, PRIVATE INVESTIGATOR

"Come in," Jay said. Jerry stepped inside and closed

19

the door behind him. Ackroyd straightened a stack of papers against the desktop and put them in a drawer. "How are you today? Ezili keep you up late again?"

"That's off and on, you know that." Jerry sat in the chair next to Jay's. "I want to sit in on the next meeting. The one with Hartmann."

"Hmmm."

"What does that mean?"

"It means *hmmm*," Jay said. "Jesus, now you've got me quoting the movies. I don't know. He's a big fish and I don't want to spook him."

Jerry tapped his fingers together. He didn't buy Jay's excuse, but that wasn't the real issue. "I'm a full partner. I want to be treated like one."

"You are treated like a full partner. Your fake name is as big as mine on the office stationery." Jay held up a piece of paper. "See. Ackroyd and Creighton. You never did tell me why you chose such a weird *nom de snoop*."

"It was Lon Chaney Jr.'s real first name." Jerry's Creighton face was a cross between Chaney Jr. and Bogart, craggy, but with sharp features and knowing eyes. "Stop trying to change the subject. You keep me away from all the really big cases, Jay."

Ackroyd rubbed the side of his head. "It's too early in the morning for anyone to be giving me this kind of headache."

The intercom buzzed. "He's here," Ezili said.

"I'm staying," Jerry said, settling as deeply as he could into the leather chair.

Jay sighed. "I guess you are." He pressed the intercom button. "Send him in."

Jerry stood as Hartmann walked into the room. His hair was thinning a bit, and his eyes had a touch less sparkle, but he still looked the part of a senator. He extended his prosthetic hand quickly and awkwardly to Jay. The real one had been mangled by some kind of demonic dog during the war for the Rox. "Mr. Ackroyd."

Jay held back for a second, then shook Hartmann's hand. "Senator, this is my partner, Mr. Creighton."

Hartmann turned and placed his prosthetic hand in

Jerry's. Jerry shook it tentatively. They made brief eye contact. There was an intensity about Hartmann that Jerry couldn't quite classify.

"Nice to meet you, Mr. Creighton."

"A pleasure," Jerry said. "Please, sit down."

Hartmann clumsily unbuttoned his tailored blue coat and seated himself, his briefcase in his lap.

"What is it exactly we can do for you?" Jay was giving Hartmann a look he usually reserved for thugs and lousy waiters.

"I've come across some information recently which, if true, could have major implications for wild cards everywhere." Hartman pulled a sheaf of papers from the briefcase. "In here is a list of individuals I need investigated. I want everything done in the quietest possible manner. Some of them are very influential, so I'd advise you to be circumspect."

Jay extended a hand. Hartmann handed the papers over. Jay began flipping through them, and shook his head. "Pan Rudo, Étienne Faneuil, Philip Baron von Herzenhagen, George G. Battle . . ."

"George G. *Battle*?" Jerry said the name much louder than he'd intended.

"Yes," Hartmann said, "you know him?"

Jerry cleared his throat. "We've met."

Jay handed the papers back to Hartmann, shaking his head. "What is the reason for these investigations, Senator? What are we looking for?"

Hartmann glanced away from Jay, toward the windows. "I'm afraid I can't divulge that. At least, not at this point."

"Then I'm afraid we can't be of any help to you," Jay said.

Hartmann arched an eyebrow and sat back in his chair. "Really? Why is that?"

"Well, if you're correct about how powerful these people are, we could be placing ourselves in real jeopardy if we go poking around." Jay shrugged. "Besides which, you're holding out information on us. I just don't like the way it smells, Senator."

Hartmann took the papers and tucked them back into his briefcase, then stood and gave Jay a tight smile. "I know your reputation, Mr. Ackroyd. You're not afraid of danger. Still, your reasons for refusing are your own. I trust you'll keep the nature of this meeting entirely confidential?"

Jay nodded. "That goes without saying, Senator. Goodbye."

Hartmann nodded and glanced over at Jerry. "Nice meeting you, Mr. Creighton." He brushed a piece of lint from his coat and walked imperiously from the office. If Hartmann was disappointed, it didn't register in his posture.

"You must not care for politicians," Jerry said.

Jay grinned. "Some I do, some I don't. Sascha?"

An eyeless man stepped from behind a partition in the corner. Sascha was one of the agency's key operatives. He was a skimmer, could pick up on a person's surface thoughts, though the depths were as much a mystery to him as anyone else. He'd been a bartender at the Crystal Palace until it burned down. Like Ezili, he'd become one of Ti Malice's mounts. They'd both done some pretty twisted stuff while under the little monster's influence. Jerry hadn't even known Sascha was in the room.

"Hartmann believes that the person who gave him this information is on the up-and-up. Her name is Hannah Davis, for what it's worth. I don't think he's convinced it's true, though." Sascha smoothed his moustache. "I don't think he likes you much either, Mr. Ackroyd."

"Nobody likes me. That's why I had to get married." Jay rubbed the back of his neck. "That's all we need for now, Sascha."

The eyeless joker walked in measured steps to the doorway, paused a second, then left.

"I'm always afraid he's going to send me to the cornfield," Jerry said, exhaling.

Jay laughed. "Yeah, he told me. You jumped a little high at Battle's name."

"Yeah," Jerry said. "Well, since he almost got me killed, I think I'm entitled."

It was true. When Jay was on Takis, Jerry had assumed his identity to get a little practical experience as a P.I. Battle had recruited him for a covert assault on the Rox, assuming he was the real Popinjay. Jerry managed to get caught in a flood in the caverns under the Rox, and had escaped by turning into the Creature from the Black Lagoon. He'd almost lost his mind, clawing and paddling his way through the dark waters under the Rox. The experience had terrified him on another level. Whenever he changed into something inhuman, he had to fight for control of his body. It had been a close thing as a gill-man; a slightly weaker will and he might be living in the East River, eating rotting fish.

"He sounded like a typical spook to me, just took a few more chances than most." Jay put his feet up on his desk. "You're not thinking of going after him on your own, are you?"

Jerry squirmed up from his chair and moved quickly to the door. "Of course not."

"Never hold out on your partner. It's the fifth rule of detective work."

"What are the first four rules?" Jerry asked from the doorway.

Ackroyd grinned. "Tell me the truth and I'll clue you in."

"You know I never lie," Jerry said. "Well, almost never."

Jay shook his head. "Have it your way."

Ezili was on top. Her *café au lait* skin was electric under his fingertips. Jerry looked into her red eyes. They were wild and unfocused, as if she were seeing some great truth far beyond either of them. He grabbed her shoulders hard and pushed upward. She leaned backward and bared her teeth. They were perfectly formed and perfectly white. Perfect, like every inch of her. Jerry closed his eyes and came. There was noise, almost inhuman. He thought Ezili must have made it, but wasn't sure. Ecstasy lingered a few moments, then passed, like the sun on a cloudy day.

He felt Ezili roll off him and he opened his eyes. She looked down at him, the wildness gone from her. Jerry got the feeling she was going to ask for something.

"How would you like to rub my feet?" he said, making a preemptive strike.

Ezili smiled and ran a finger down his calf. "Very well. Later will be for me." Her finger reached the bottom of his foot and she ran it lightly up to his toes.

"And if I don't?"

"Then I'll bite off one of your toes. It would make a fine necklace."

Jerry ignored the threat and sank into contentment. "Okay. Later is definitely for you. Do you think Jay respects me?" The question revealed more than he'd wanted it to. Abandon had its drawbacks.

Ezili looked at his feet. "If he did, it would not show. Mr. Ackroyd always seeks the advantage. Old habits die with their owner."

"Interesting twist on that old adage." Jerry pulled one foot away and offered the other. "I know better than to ask if you respect me."

"You get what you want from me. I get what I want from you. Is respect better than that?"

"Good question. You're full of them tonight."

Ezili took his feet out of her lap. "Now for me. Something unusual."

Jerry lifted his head up and bit his lip suspiciously. "What?"

"I want you to be a woman for me."

"You can't . . . I mean, that's not exactly playing to my strength."

She smiled her Ezili-will-have-it smile. "Get up." She took his hand and led him over to the bedroom mirror. "I want you to watch yourself do it."

Jerry lusted after many beautiful women, but right now he couldn't think of a single one he wanted to *be*. "Where should I start?"

"Here," she said, running a lacquered fingernail over one of his nipples.

Jerry concentrated. Breasts formed on his chest. Big,

but not as large as Ezili's, with dark nipples. There wasn't
much hair on his chest, but he got rid of it anyway. Ezili
glanced down at his crotch. Jerry sighed, then watched
his pride and joy disappear and shift into a female organ.
An image of a young Julie Newmar crept into his mind
and transformed his flesh. He/she had a wanton look that
might be a challenge even for Ezili.

"Satisfied?"

Ezili nuzzled Jerry/Julie's ear. "Aren't you glad I don't
just fuck you because you're the boss?"

"If you ever tell Jay about this, I'll kill you."

Ezili laughed and pulled her lover into the bed. She
positioned her head between Jerry's legs and blew lightly,
then extended her tongue. Jerry felt a ribbon of pleasure
knotting inside.

"The sweetest," Ezili said, then flicked her tongue
across him again.

"Yes," Jerry whispered. "The sweetest."

In spite of the fact that it was hell on his eyes, Jerry
did his computer work in the dark. He liked being alone
with the phosphor glow of the CRT while he prowled
through a system. He'd had a few of the local hackers
teach him system breaking, and in return provided them
with top-of-the-line equipment.

He was after George G. Battle. Jerry hadn't liked being
drafted by him, hadn't liked the way Battle looked or
spoke, or the company he kept. Jerry wouldn't be surprised if Battle were involved in some anti-wild card plot,
in spite of the fact that George G. had employed aces
in his covert team. Jerry figured Battle was one of those
people, who, the better you know them, the more you
despised them. Finding out more was his top priority
right now.

He always started with a person's credit record. Almost
everybody had one, and the systems were fairly easy to
get into and around in. He'd tried two, but so far no BAT-
TLE, GEORGE G. Jerry stretched and made his way over to
the red light on the coffee-pot, then poured himself half

a cup. He'd already put away most of the pot. If he didn't slow down, he'd be typing from the ceiling.

Jerry sat back down and tapped into the next system. He typed NOBODY, his superuser ID. Jerry started the listing with Battle, G, and began paging slowly through.

"Bingo," he said, locating his target. Jerry punched into the general history screen and started printing. He rubbed his moist palms together. There was always an adrenaline surge when he found what he was looking for, but this was something else. Maybe it was just the coffee. Then again, maybe it was that he thought George G. Battle might be a bad guy straight from the movies. There were four pages of material on as many screens, with plenty of base information. Jerry jumped out of the system as soon as the last sheet of paper slid up from his printer.

He turned on the lights and flipped through the pages. There was a lot to go on, home and secondary address, phone numbers, SSN, drivers license number. It was a good starting point.

He leaned back in his chair and sipped at his coffee. If Jerry's theory about Battle proved out, Jay was going to have to eat a heaping helping of crow for not taking the case.

Which would be just fine with Jerry.

Midtown traffic had been a snarl south of Central Park and Jerry was late. There wasn't a line of people waiting to get into Starfields, which was not too surprising, given the public's current level of paranoia and the fact that Starfields was run by a Takisian. Hastet.

The decor was different enough to be alien, but also had a curiously homey feel. Jerry took a few deep breaths and tried to relax. Although the food was superb, Hastet scared the bejesus out of him. Like Tachyon, she had a way of looking right through you. Unlike Tachyon, she didn't mince words. Jay had a bowl of something turquoise in front of him when Jerry walked up.

"Evening, partner," Jerry said, sitting down.

"Hi. You should try some of this soup, it's fabulous."

Jay motioned to a waiter, who immediately walked over. "A bottle of your best red wine."

"I didn't think Hastet liked you to tie one on," Jerry said, opening his menu.

"She doesn't. I'll have a glass or two. The rest is for you." Jay smiled. "I'm going to get you drunk and have my way with you."

Jerry set down the menu and looked hard at Jay. "You still think I'm after Battle, don't you?"

"You just may make a detective yet," Jay said. "You wouldn't keep it to yourself unless you had some ideas about the guy."

"You're right. If you'd accepted the case, we might have more than my ideas right now, but you didn't." Jerry shook his head. "Sorry, that came out a little sharper than I intended."

"I think it came out exactly as sharp as you intended." The waiter arrived with the wine, opened and poured it. Jay took a sip. "Wonderful, just what I had in mind. We'll need a couple more minutes before we order." The waiter nodded and left.

Jerry ignored the wine. "Hastet doesn't have that *thing* here tonight, does she?" Jerry didn't much care for Hastet's pet. It reminded him of some of the things he'd run into under the Rox, and it always looked hungry.

"Changing the subject on me?" Jay paused, as if on the verge of pursuing his line of questioning, then slowly exhaled. "I promise you'll be safe as long as I'm around. It's never even drooled on you."

Jerry gave in and took a sip of wine. It warmed, caressed, and soothed all the way down. He wondered why in hell Jay had taken him on in the first place. His partner had plenty of other operatives, and with his wealth from Takis, he certainly didn't need Jerry to bank-roll the agency. Maybe it was just plain guilt. Jerry had almost died trying to help Jay out. "Why don't you put Peter Pann or Topper on me to find out if I'm after Battle?"

Jay shook his head. "I can't waste them on anything

so stupid. You need a stable woman in your life, Jerry. Get you to toe the line. Whatever happened with Beth?"

That one still hurt. Beth had moved to Chicago and Jerry had refused to go with her. New York was the only place worth living as far as he was concerned, and he had been sure he could convince her to come back. He was wrong.

"Irreconcilable differences, I suppose. And anyone who speaks ill of unstable women should spend a few nights with Ezili. However, there is one thing I know we can agree on."

"It's time to eat," Jay offered.

Jerry set down his menu and signalled the waiter. "Common ground at last."

" That's why we're partners."

It was perfect weather for a drive. The October air was crisp and cool, even in the full sunlight. The pictures of Vermont in the fall didn't really do it justice. No photograph could capture the movement of the red, gold, and brown leaves against the blue sky.

He was driving an ash-gray Ford Taurus. He'd rented it under the name Anthony Carbone, one of a half-dozen false identities he'd created. His hair and skin were dark, and he had a small scar on his chin. If someone spotted him at Battle's house, they might figure he was Mafia. Battle could easily have enemies in the mob, or at least someone who might hire a hit.

Jerry pulled down the sun visor. He'd made a map of the area on a Post-it-note. If he had navigated right, Battle's place was only a couple of miles away. The area was still rural, with most houses out of sight of their nearest neighbors. That's what Jerry was counting on anyway.

Battle spent most of his time in DC, so the Vermont place was a logical starting point. There would be security, but he'd planned for that. He'd phoned earlier in the day and gotten a generic recording. He planned to have the house all to himself.

Jerry turned off the main highway and onto a narrow

asphalt road. It turned into gravel a few hundred yards in and Jerry saw a yard bordered with a high stone wall. He pulled the Taurus as far onto the shoulder as he could and killed the engine.

Jerry stepped out of the car and looked both ways before trotting across the gravel roadway to a wooded area by the wall. He jumped and caught the edge with his fingertips, then swung a leg over and hoisted himself up. Jerry paused for a moment, listening, then dropped over the side. Evening was coming fast, and Jerry crept toward the house, using trees for cover. The house was two stories of wood and stone, not formidable, but not friendly looking either.

Jerry made his way around back to the power and telephone lines. One thing he'd learned was that his body responded to electric current by converting it to mass. For the few moments his body was in flux, he could discharge the current; otherwise it became a part of him. At that point it became a little trickier to get rid of. He pulled out a knife and cut carefully into the power and telephone lines. He caught the juice from the power line and waited a moment then discharged a portion of it into the house's main line. He reached over to the phone line and gave it the rest of the juice. He figured the electricity had tripped every breaker in the house. The phone equipment should be fried too, so even if a security system was working, it still couldn't contact anyone on the outside.

Jerry walked over to the nearest window. It was heavily bolted from the inside. Jerry pulled out his glass cutter, and removed a section big enough to get his arm comfortably through, then unbolted the window and lifted it.

The trophy heads stared glassy-eyed down at him from the walls—deer, elk, what looked like a grizzly bear in a particularly bad mood. The temperature was low, not as cool as it was outside, but Jerry still figured there hadn't been anyone there that day. He walked over to a heavy oak desk and tried the drawers. Locked. Jerry took a couple of deep breaths and put the end of his first finger against the keyhole in the top drawer. He softened the

tip of his finger and pushed it inside, tearing his skin.
Jerry hardened his finger and turned carefully. It hurt
like hell, but he felt the metal give and swivel. Jerry
pulled his damaged finger out. He'd have to learn how
to pick locks the old-fashioned way someday.

Jerry rifled through the desk quickly. His fingertips
were smooth to avoid prints. He pushed aside the bank
statements and appliance warranties, and pulled out a
file marked "October Surprise." He opened it, then took
out a pocket camera and carefully photographed each
page. There were three unmarked blueprints. Jerry had
no idea what they belonged to. He could worry about
that later. He put the file back into the drawer and
checked out the rest of the desk, but didn't find anything
of interest.

Jerry stepped carefully out into the interior hallway.
He saw a motion detector at ceiling level, but its lights
were obligingly dark. If the system had a backup battery
it was dead. Jerry stopped at the phone stand and popped
open the answering machine. He lifted out the mini-
cassette and dropped in a blank one he'd brought along.
He'd planned more than usual, ultimately wanting to
impress Jay.

He reached the end of the hallway and stepped into
the living room. More trophies. There was a thick-legged
table in the center of the room surrounded by several
uncomfortable looking high-backed chairs. Jerry decided
to head upstairs. He'd only taken a couple of steps when
something caught his ankle and he pitched forward,
smacking his forearm onto the hardwood stair. He
crawled back down and fingered the ankle-height wire.
It had pulled out several inches.

Jerry heard loud barking from alongside the house. He
bounced up off the stairs and ran to the living room
window. The two mastiffs saw him and bared their teeth.
The wire must have triggered a physical mechanism to
set them loose. Battle had a military mind, and was
nobody's fool. He planned for every contingency.

He backed away from the window. He'd been feeling
lucky and hadn't brought a gun on this trip. Next time

he'd ignore his instincts and pack something. There was no choice but to run for it. Jerry crossed into the front of the house and unbolted the door, then opened it and sprinted toward the wall.

The dogs were on his heels before he made it twenty yards. Jerry fashioned his fingertips into claws and turned to face them. The first mastiff was already in the air, jaws open, going for this throat. Jerry brought his arm around as fast as he could and tore into its neck. It yelped and fell. The second animal hurled itself at him before he could get his arm back around. The mastiff slammed into his chest and knocked him to the ground. Jerry grabbed the dog's throat with a clawed hand and dug in. The animal shook its head violently, trying to break free. Saliva fell on Jerry's face, then blood. The mastiff collapsed on top of him, snapped its jaws, and was still. Jerry dragged himself from under the dog, fighting for breath. The other animal was still alive, lying in a pool of blood. Its eyes were peaceful, almost sad. Jerry looked at the blood on his clawed hand and gritted his teeth. The wound was fatal. There was nothing he could do.

He returned his hands to normal and staggered to the wall. It took him two tries to grab the top, and all his remaining strength to haul himself up. He checked his pockets to make sure the camera and mini-cassette were still there, then dropped heavily to the ground on the far side.

His silver Ford reflected golden in the sunset. Jerry jumped inside and power locked the doors, then took time for a few deep breaths. He started the car and did a quick U-turn. It was getting cold and he flipped on the heater. The main highway was clear, and he pulled out and sped away.

He noticed the car about a mile and a half later. It was black or dark blue, Jerry couldn't tell which in the fading light. There were two men in the front seat. Jerry changed lanes to let them around, but they stayed right behind him. Jerry didn't panic, but he wasn't calm either. Maybe they worked for Battle and had heard the dogs.

Maybe they'd driven by the place earlier and seen his car. Maybe they just liked tailgating. It didn't particularly matter, Jerry wanted them gone. A high speed chase was out of the question. His driving skills were only adequate at best. He would drive until he found a restaurant or something, pull in, and change into someone else in the bathroom. He'd done it before.

It was like they read his mind. The dark car pulled up alongside. Now Jerry had them on one side and a nasty incline into the trees on the other.

"Shit," he said.

The car veered over and slammed into the side of the Taurus. Sparks flew and the tires squealed and smoked. The impact knocked him onto the shoulder. Jerry hit the brakes, hoping they would sail by him, but the other car moved over again and caught his front fender. There was nothing but big trees in front, and Jerry threw up his hands.

There was a noise like styrofoam being cut, only a hundred times louder. The air bag hit him like a heavyweight with a grudge. His wrist crashed into his lip, splitting it. Jerry smelled fuel. He clutched for the clasp on the safety belt and ripped it loose. The passenger side of the car was facing down, so he opened it and dropped out onto the ground.

Jerry knew they might be watching from the road, so he limped away from the wreck in the opposite direction as fast as he could. There was a flash of heat and a concussion from behind. He was knocked further down the hill, tumbling until he landed against the bole of a tree. Jerry felt around behind him. The back of his shirt was in tatters. The pain wasn't that bad, yet. He knew with a burn it sometimes took awhile before you could really tell. Something to look forward to, if he managed to get through the night alive.

He heard tires squeal above him. Jerry looked up and saw taillights twinkling in and out as they receded through the trees. He was suddenly very cold. Jerry clambered up the hill, pulling himself along on bushes and low hanging branches. He could see a fair distance down the road. There was a single headlight approaching. Jerry took a breath and thought Austrian. His jaw went square and his hair shortened. He bulked up his entire body and lost a few inches of height in the process. He took a few steps to the center of the road and held up his right hand, motioning the approaching vehicle to stop.

The motorcycle slowed from a thrum to a putter. Jerry couldn't see anything of the driver, because of the glare from the headlights.

"I need your jacket, your boots, and your motorcycle." The accent was perfect. Jerry had been practicing it for months.

"Jesus, Mr. Schwarzenegger?" said the cyclist. His voice was shaky.

Jerry walked around and looked the driver in the eyes. The man looked to be in his early twenties, and was on the thin side. "Wrong, osshole."

"Uh." The man unbuckled his helmet and handed it over. "No boots." He looked down the hill at the burning Taurus. "Emergency, huh?"

"Get off the bike, dickweed," Jerry said. The cyclist dismounted. Jerry caught the bike before it fell over. "The chacket."

The man tugged the leather bomber jacket off and handed it over. Jerry slipped it on. It was wonderfully warm, but tight. He could fix that in a few moments.

The man put his hand on Jerry's shoulder. "It's only a Honda."

Jerry smiled thinly. "Hasta la vista, baby." The first phone he saw, he'd call the cops. That would take care of the motorcycle's owner. He accelerated off into the night, feeling more like something from *Pee Wee's Big Adventure* than *The Wild One*.

He'd had to pay the cab driver a hundred dollars to take him to the clinic. But then, it was the Jokertown Clinic, and almost nobody went into Jokertown anymore unless they were looking for trouble. Jerry told the cabbie that the police had been making a point of being visible, at least during the day, and it was noon at the time.

That, plus the money, had finally convinced the hack to make the trip. Jerry could have had Jay pop him there, but then Jay would have started prying. He didn't want his partner to know he was going there to have his burns looked at. Jay was too smart for any story Jerry could make up; besides, he'd never been on the receiving end of Jay's ace. It might be something he wouldn't enjoy. Jerry was disoriented enough without Jay's help.

The corridors were crammed with jokers. Some were trauma victims, some were sick, some were likely just trying to get in off the streets. Jerry tried to overlook the fact that they were different, deformed. He'd impersonated jokers plenty of times, and seen the way they were treated. But it was different for him. He could turn back whenever he wanted. They had to wait for the next life, assuming there was one.

Jerry saw Doctor Finn from halfway down the hall. Finn was a centaur, and a handsome one at that, so he was easy to pick out of any crowd. Even the one here.

Finn glanced Jerry's way and flashed a quick smile, then continued his conversation with a nurse. Jerry walked up and waited a few feet away from them. He didn't recognize the nurse, and he knew most of the staff. She was pretty enough that in contrast with her surroundings she looked positively beautiful. She was blond, pushing forty, judging by the lines around her eyes, but her overall bone structure was model perfect. If she was a bit overweight, she carried it well. Jerry thought of Ezili. He hoped his adventures with her hadn't spoiled him for other women.

"Mr. Strauss," Finn said, his conversation with the nurse apparently finished. "So good to see you. You always manage to show up on one of our slow days."

Jerry laughed. "Actually, I've been waiting for a day and a half. Uh, can I see you in private for a few minutes?"

"That will be no mean feat, but I'll see what I can arrange." The centaur moved carefully through a knot of people and unlocked a door. He motioned Jerry inside.

Jerry stepped in quickly and Finn closed the door behind them. "What can I do for you?"

"First, this." Jerry handed over a check for five thousand dollars. Finn took it and tucked it into a breast pocket. Jerry carefully unbuttoned his shirt and peeled it slowly off. "Then, this." He turned around and showed Finn his back. Jerry wondered why he couldn't heal the wounds himself. Maybe it was that he could only control healthy tissues, not dead or damaged ones. Then again, maybe the pain just made it too hard to concentrate.

"Umm," Finn said, testing the area carefully with his fingers. It hurt, but Jerry stayed still. "Would you like to tell me how this happened?"

"No. Just tell me what to do about it."

"Okay," Finn said, noncommittally. Jerry heard hooves on the floor. "It's bad, but not terrible. You won't need any debridement, and I doubt there will be any scarring. Still, I want to put you on a course of antibiotics. Keep an eye on it. If the pain gets too bad, I can prescribe something."

"It hurts a lot," Jerry said. "Can I put my shirt back on now?"

"Of course." Finn walked around in front of Jerry, busy scrawling on a pad. He tore two pieces of paper from it and gave them to Jerry. "Fill these ASAP. Get started on the antibiotics immediately. The pain reliever is codeine based, not very strong, but it should let you sleep. I want to see you again in a couple of days."

Jerry slid his shirt gingerly over his reddened shoulders. "If only the women in my life had your attitude."

Finn smiled and cocked his head. "Be sure to get an injection from Nurse Moffat before you go. More antibiotics. Get you started."

Jerry made a face. "A shot. I hate shots."

Finn wagged a finger. "Doctor's orders. Besides, you won't mind, she's cute. And her nickname around here is 'Painless.' "

Jerry's shoulders slumped. Might as well get it over with, but god he did hate needles. "Do I get a sucker on the way out?"

Finn opened the door and motioned Jerry out with his pen. "Back in two days."

"Yes, sir."

Jerry walked slowly down the hall, eyeing the doorway to the nurse's station like it was the gateway to hell. He stuck his head inside, hoping to find it packed with patients. A short, scaly joker pushed past him, leaving the room empty except for the nurse.

"Hello," he said. "Nurse Moffat?" She turned around. It was the nurse he'd seen talking to Finn a few moments before. Jerry straightened his shoulders and walked in.

"Yes," she said. "Is there something I can help you with?"

"Dr. Finn said I need an injection." He handed her the paper with the antibiotic prescription. "This stuff, I think." ·

She looked at the paper and gave it back. "No problem. Get that shirt off and have a seat." She indicated an aluminum chair with cracked red vinyl upholstery.

Jerry did as he was told. "Didn't Dr. Tachyon have a treatment that caused tissue to regenerate? Sure would be useful now."

"I don't think so. That lovely bit of technology gave us Demise. Besides, since Dr. Tachyon left, all the experimental equipment is locked up. Dr. Finn inventories it now and then, but otherwise we leave it be."

Jerry heard the sound of a needle going into a bottle cover. "Do they really call you 'Painless?' "

She walked around in front of him, holding the hypodermic. "Them what speaks of me at all." She put a hand on his shoulder and bent down. "Now think of something pleasant."

Jerry closed his eyes. To his surprise he found himself thinking of his nurse. "I'm as ready as I'm going to get." He waited a few seconds, then looked.

Nurse Moffat smiled at him. "You're done. They don't call me 'Painless' for nothing."

Jerry sat up straight and reached for his shirt. "Wow. You're great. You're going to have to do all my injections from now on." He stood, tucked in his shirt and walked to the door, then turned around. "What's your name? I mean, other than 'Painless.'"

"Emily Moffat. What's yours?"

"Jerry Strauss."

"Well, pleased to meet you, Jerry Strauss." She smiled again, and motioned with her hand. A joker scuttled into the room. "Drop in again anytime."

"I will," he said. "I will."

The answering machine cassette from Battle's house had one message on it, a female voice saying, "The Halloween party is on. Expect you to bring the treats. See you then."

Jerry figured that whatever the "October Surprise" was, the payoff was coming on Halloween. The pictures had survived the wreck, too, but the blueprints didn't mean anything to Jerry. He knew somebody that might have a better idea.

Ernie Swartz had been the archivist at the Department of Public Works for the past twenty years. He was the antithesis of the absent-minded clerk. He could carry on three conversations and simultaneously do whatever task was currently at hand. Jerry had done some architectural research for a period film set in New York. The movie was a pipe dream, but it had given him the opportunity to meet Ernie.

The office was relatively quiet today. There was actually one of the staff who didn't have a handful of documents, or a phone glued to his ear.

Jerry walked up to the unoccupied clerk, a young man nursing a large mug of coffee, and indicated Ernie's office. "He in today?"

"Today and everyday." The clerk's phone buzzed. He rolled his eyes and picked up.

Jerry made his way down an aisle between the rows of desks and rapped on Ernie's door.

"Come in."

Ernie had a sheaf of papers on the desk in front of him and his "in" box was overflowing with more. He looked up, saw Jerry, and smiled. "Jerry. Made your *Citizen Kane* yet?" He took Jerry's extended hand and gave it a warm shake.

"No. I think I'm either too young or too old to be a cinematic genius." Jerry sat down in the chair opposite Ernie, tapping the envelope with the blueprints against his pants' leg.

Ernie pointed to the envelope. "You got something else for me?"

Jerry handed it over. "There's some old blueprints. I don't even know if they're New York. I thought maybe you could tell me what building they go to."

Ernie slid the photographs out and pursed his lips. "Might be Manhattan. Hard to say. You need this in a hurry?"

"Well, if you don't find out before Halloween, it probably won't matter."

Ernie tossed the blueprints into his desk drawer. "That's less than a week. I'll see what I can manage in my copious free time. No promises."

"Great. I'll get you into a couple of Knicks games, regardless." Jerry stood and fished in his pocket for an agency business card. "Oh, and if you can't get in touch with me at home, call this number and leave a message for Mr. Creighton."

Ernie's phone buzzed. He gave Jerry an "OK" sign and snatched up the receiver. "Swartz."

Jerry nodded and left.

Ezili was standing by the door when he stepped in. "Mr. Ackroyd wants to see you first thing. You should make time for me later."

Jerry smiled at the thought. "Sounds good. I'll let you know."

She returned the smile and walked slowly back to her desk, rolling her hips just enough to remind him what it was like to be with her. Not that he needed reminding.

Jay had his feet propped up on the desk, and was staring out the window. "I kind of miss the neon 'live nude girls' sign." He turned to Jerry. "Not that I'm against being more upscale. There's just too little neon in the world."

"Right. Now I know what to get you for Christmas. You wanted to see me?"

Jay walked over and slapped Jerry on the back, hard. Jerry tensed his shoulders, but managed not to scream. "I like you, Jerry. You know that."

"I appreciate that. I like you, too."

"So, it would be very depressing if you got yourself killed." Jay eased into his desk chair. "I know you're working on something right now. I know it's dangerous and probably has something to do with Battle."

"Hold it." Jerry lifted a hand. "If I am involved in something a little risky, and I'm not saying I am, then there's a damned good reason. And for Christ's sake, Jay, I'm not just a stooge out there. I can handle myself."

Jay rubbed his forehead. "You're just not getting the message here. It takes years to develop the instincts and techniques to be a good private investigator. I'm still learning, myself."

Jerry started taking deep, measured breaths. He didn't want to start yelling, that would only reinforce Jay's argument. "You're just going to have to trust me on this one. It's important."

Jay slowly formed his hand into the familiar gun-shape, then pointed it at Jerry. "I should send you to Takis, to worry Tachyon's ass."

"Yeah. I could change to look like you, go home and fuck your wife." Jerry leaned onto Jay's desktop. "But I'm no more going to do that, than you're going to send me to Takis."

Jay looked Jerry in the eye. "Don't bet on it. The only person I know as stubborn as Tachyon is you. Don't force my hand on this, I've got a business to run."

"We've got a business to run." Jerry walked to the door. " There are two names on the glass outside. Don't forget it." He shut the door and stalked out of the office.

It was Halloween, a little after three in the afternoon. The coffee shop at the George Washington was nearly

deserted. Jerry remembered a time when the place was
a real dive, but they'd done a few renovations, even put
in color TV. It was a weird place for Battle to be staying,
but that only made Jerry more certain something was up.

Tracking Battle down had been easier than he figured.
He'd called George G.'s office using Peter Jennings'
voice, said the network was considering doing a special
on the last days of the Rox. Battle's secretary had started
gushing as soon as she heard his accent. She explained
that he was out of town at the moment, but gave Jerry/
Jennings a phone number where he could be reached.
Jerry tapped into the phone system and fed it the number, out came the George Washington Hotel on Lexington Avenue.

His motorcycle was parked outside. He'd enjoyed
riding one so much, he'd bought one. It was an old Triumph, black and almost too heavy. He'd picked it up
under an assumed name, of course.

Jerry's look today was somewhere between James
Dean and Nicholas Cage. His dark hair was slicked back
and his eyes were bright with too much caffeine. He'd
made a couple of lightning fast trips to the men's room
earlier, but was sure Battle hadn't gotten out past him.
Jerry didn't really expect anything to go down until evening anyway, but better safe than sorry. He eased back
and ordered another cheese Danish.

Battle went past when Jerry was in mid-bite. His
quarry was wearing a gray overcoat and tan pants. He
seemed to be alone. Jerry tossed a twenty onto the
countertop and headed for the street. Battle was getting
into an old silver van when Jerry hit the door. Jerry
trotted down to his Triumph and kicked it to life.

The van was halfway down the block when Jerry pulled
out. He accelerated around a bus. The van was about
five cars ahead of him and one lane over. They stayed
on Lexington through Gramercy Park and then over to
Park Avenue South. Jerry maintained his distance and
tried not to get directly behind the van.

He heard sirens to his right, heading his way. The light
at Fourteenth Street turned amber and the van charged

through the intersection. Jerry gunned it, slicing between
the lanes of slowing autos. He was into the intersection
when the police car flashed in front of him. Jerry braked
and twisted the handlebars to the right. The tires went
out from under him, and the bike skidded sideways
across the rest of Fourteenth Street and onto the sidewalk. Jerry struggled to right the bike as passers-by began
to form around him. The cop car was long gone.

"I'm okay," he said. It was more or less true. His right
leg was a little torn up, but there were no broken bones.
"Just get out of my way."

Jerry bounced his bike off the curb and onto the street,
headed south. He thought he glimpsed a silver car top
ahead and began weaving through the traffic, closing in.
A couple of blocks later, he caught up. It was a silver
van alright, but it belonged to a florist shop. A light
turned red ahead. Jerry slowed the bike to a stop. He
rubbed his right thigh, which was beginning to throb. It
hurt almost as much as his pride.

He'd lost them.

He'd gone back to the George Washington in the hope
that Battle would show up, but that hadn't worked. Jerry's instincts were right about that. At this moment Battle
was doing something that could affect wild cards everywhere, and Jerry couldn't raise a finger to stop him. Jay
was right; he wasn't good enough yet.

He put on his Creighton face and went back to the
office. There was a bottle of Jack Black and a Gameboy
in his desk. Right now that was the only company he
wanted.

She was sitting behind the desk, filing her nails, when
he walked in. Ezili looked up and nodded. "I thought
you'd be coming back here."

Jerry shook his head. "I'm tired, Ezili. So tired even
the prospect of sex with you couldn't pep me up. If
tomorrow night's okay with you, I'll be more than happy
to do whatever you want."

Ezili smiled. "I didn't stay for that reason. A man

called. A Mr. Swartz. He said he identified the blueprints
you left him."

Jerry's brain was slow in taking the information in. He
thought for a second, then straightened. "What? What
did he say it was?"

"The Jokertown Clinic."

Jerry bent down and kissed Ezili, a kiss of gratitude,
not passion. "Thanks. You may have saved my career as
a detective. If I'm still alive tomorrow, I'll try to get you
another raise."

"Your energy has come back, I see. Save some for me
tomorrow." She moistened her lips. "No good deed
should go unpunished."

"It won't." Jerry dashed from the office, the pain in
his leg forgotten. Maybe his luck was changing. He'd
know soon enough.

No amount of money was going to get a cabbie into
Jokertown on Halloween night. There was no point in
taking his bike either. Somebody would rip it out from
under him long before he made it to the clinic. That left
the subway. When Jerry got on he was a nat with a Nixon
mask propped on the top of his head. As the train rum-
bled south the crowds began to thin. At the last stop
outside Jokertown, there were only two people left in
the car with him. One was a drunk, the other was a
transit cop. Jerry pulled the mask down and started
changing his face. He felt particularly ugly tonight, and
his features were going to reflect it. He extended his
mouth from just under one ear to the other and filled it
with large, yellowing teeth; he thickened his brow ridge
and skull. He didn't want anyone fucking with him in
the streets. It was several blocks from the subway to the
clinic, and he wanted to make it as quickly as possible.
Once there, he'd poke around. Battle couldn't hide the
way he could. Jerry should be able to spot him right
away.

The lights flickered and the subway car squealed
around a turn, then slowed down next to the platform.
A tentacle slapped up against the glass next to Jerry's

head as the car hissed to a stop. Jerry lifted his mask and gave the joker a baleful stare. She made a face and turned away. Jerry got up and slid through the door as it opened, then made his way up to the street.

A bottle broke at his feet as he stepped into the open air. There were screams all around him, some happy, some crazy, some from pain. A group of jokers was performing something resembling a dance in the middle of the street. Another knot was clustered by a warehouse wall, spraying it with cans of paint. Most of the crowd looked young to Jerry. A generation of "hideous joker babies" grown into their teens.

Jerry started making his way toward the clinic. He smelled smoke, but couldn't see any sign of a fire. Maybe it was just fireworks. He hoped the entire neighborhood wasn't burned to the ground by morning. Public sentiment being what it currently was, no one would care much if the fire department was slow answering calls to Jokertown.

Jerry walked with his hands in his pockets. He fingered the .45 automatic with his right hand. Jerry didn't much care for guns, especially handguns, but Battle played rough. He wasn't planning on being a martyr.

He felt hands on his shoulders from behind. Jerry spun around. A joker was extending a hand to him. His skin was the color of uncooked sausage and the top of his head was oversized and misshapen. "Help me out, friend?"

Jerry fished out a five and handed it over.

The joker smiled. As his face moved, it squeaked. "I think you can do better than that." He whipped out a knife.

"Okay," Jerry said. He pulled out the gun and pointed it at the joker's face. "Give me a reason."

The joker took two careful steps backward, hands raised, then turned and ran.

He put the gun away. This is all the public ever sees. They give the rest a bad name, Jerry thought. He watched the joker disappear around the corner, then trotted toward the clinic. He was close enough now that he could make it without getting winded.

He almost needed the gun to get into the clinic. Wounded jokers were everywhere. Jerry waded through the misery into the waiting area. Finding Battle might not be as easy as he'd first figured. The clinic was a big place, and Jerry wasn't sure what it was they were after. Arson was his first guess, but that seemed too small an operation for someone with Battle's ambitions. There was no point in trying to disgrace Tachyon in some way. The doctor was gone, and might never return. No. Jerry figured there had to be something here they wanted. His logic couldn't get him any further than that.

Jerry bounced up and down as he made his way down the hall. He was looking for Finn. He wanted to warn them that the clinic was targeted for trouble. At the top of one of his jumps he saw a familiar blond head. Emily Moffat was walking his way, moving with tired but purposeful strides.

He grabbed her by the arm as she reached his side. "Nurse Moffat, we met the other day."

"I'm sorry, I don't recall you." She looked him over. "You don't look too bad, you'll have to wait your turn."

Jerry paused for a second, not knowing how much he could really trust her. He leaned in and whispered, "I'm Jerry Strauss. I really need to talk to Dr. Finn."

She looked at him incredulously. "Who? I'm in no mood for jokes. Dr. Finn is in surgery, and I'm very busy."

"Sorry," Jerry said, grabbing her by the elbow and guiding her into a room. He pulled her into one of the bedspaces and closed the curtain. "Look at me." His appearance shifted to Jerry Strauss, then back to his joker facade. "Now do you believe me?"

She looked hard at Jerry for a moment, her eyes betraying nothing. "Okay. So you're probably Mr. Strauss. What the hell is going on?"

Jerry shook his head. "I wish I knew. The clinic is a target for something tonight. Is there anything around here worth stealing?"

"Hardly. Most of our facilities and equipment are practically antique. Except for the experimental stuff, of course. I can't imagine anyone would even know what to do with most of that."

Jerry noticed he was still holding her arm and let it go. "It's at least worth checking out. I can't think of anything else. Do you have access to that area?"

"Yes, but I can't—" she paused, conflict evident in her eyes. "What the hell. If you're right, something has to be done." She pointed to his face. "How long have you been able to do that?"

"A long time. Let's go."

They took the stairs to the basement. Emily punched a code into the keypad on the door. It buzzed and the lock clicked back. She opened it and stared down the dark corridor.

"I'll have to come with you," she said.

"No," Jerry whispered. "This is potentially very dangerous. Wait at the top of the stairs. Better yet, find Troll and send him down here to back me up, but tell him to keep it quiet. If you don't see us again in half an hour, call the police."

She took two steps up the stairs, then turned. Jerry motioned her to keep going. She sighed and continued her ascent.

Jerry slipped in and closed the door behind him. The darkness was almost complete, dotted here and there with small lights from the equipment. He pulled off his shoes and slipped slowly down the hallway, sliding his hand along the cold wall. He thought he heard something and froze, taking shallow breaths. He waited a minute. Nothing. He continued on his way. His hand found a door frame. Jerry fumbled for the knob and slowly twisted it, then stepped inside. He saw a small spot of light sweep over a glassed-in wall to his left. Whoever was holding the light was in the adjacent room. The light continued to roam about the room, lighting here and there, then moving on. Jerry's eyes had adjusted to the darkness well enough for him to make out a door between the two rooms. He walked slowly toward the door, sliding his feet. If he stubbed his toe now, it could be a fatal mistake. He pressed his body up against the door and pulled the automatic from his pocket.

Make your next move a good one, he thought. Make it count.

There was no way he could get through the doorway and still retain the element of surprise. His chances of dropping Battle and whoever he had with him before they got him weren't very good. While he was groping for a solution, the door opened slightly and light came through the crack. Jerry backed away, holding his breath.

They slid into the room and stopped, playing the light over the contents of the laboratory. Jerry was only a few feet behind them. In a moment they'd turn around with the flashlight and he'd be dead meat. Jerry moved forward silently and smashed his automatic into the side of one of the intruders' heads. He felt the shock of the blow up to his elbow, and heard the man crumple to the floor. Jerry crouched and foot-swept his other opponent. The man cried out as his legs went out from under him. Jerry scrambled forward in the near darkness, placed his knee solidly in the man's back and pressed the barrel of his gun into the captive's temple.

"Hands behind you," Jerry said. The man quickly did as he was ordered. Jerry pulled a pair of cuffs from his belt and snapped them on. He picked up the flashlight and pointed it at the face he hoped would be Battle's. The man wasn't George G. or anyone else Jerry recognized. He looked thirtyish and Hispanic, Cuban maybe. Jerry directed the flashlight to the man he'd pistol-whipped. This one could have been the other guy's twin, except for the bruise that was coming up on the side of his head.

Jerry figured there was nothing to be gained talking to either of these two. He pulled a glove out of his pocket and shoved it deep into the mouth of his conscious captive. Having cuffed him first, Jerry did the same to the one who was out. Whatever other reason Battle had for using these men, it wasn't for their personal hygiene.

They smelled like a garbage dump on an August afternoon.

There was a soft voice behind him. "Now, Bobby Joe."

Something closed around Jerry's wrist. His bones ground together and he stifled a scream. The gun clattered to the linoleum floor. Jerry twisted his head around and saw the giant form in the dim light. He'd seen this guy before—smelled him too. It hadn't been the Cubans. If only he'd remembered!

Bobby Joe, aka the Crypt Kicker, was dead. He looked worse than the last time Jerry had seen him, under the Rox. The Crypt Kicker was dressed in jet black, with a half-hood over one side of his face. The hood draped so that Jerry could tell a sizable portion of his skull was missing underneath it. There was a crimson cross over one eye, and the dead man looked like someone had used him for flamethrower practice. Jerry's jacket began to smoke where the Crypt Kicker was holding it. He tried to whip-kick the dead giant, but his foot glanced off without getting so much as a grunt.

"Make it look like an accident if you can, Bobby Joe. Keep it quiet. I'll be down the hall." Battle patted Jerry on the cheek and smiled. "Enjoy it."

A huge hand clamped over Jerry's mouth, searing his flesh with noxious chemicals. He started to change. As afraid as he was of being inhuman, he was a lot more scared of being dead. Lon Chaney Jr.'s wolfman was a sentimental favorite, but he'd seen *The Howling* recently, and that lycanthrope looked considerably more lethal. Jerry elongated his mouth into a snout and filled it with sharp teeth. Claws formed at the ends of his fingers and toes. He bit down on his enemy's wrist and began worrying at the dead flesh. Bits came off in his mouth, acid-sour and putrid.

Crypt Kicker tossed him in the air. Jerry brought his legs underneath him and landed on all fours. A coat of thick hair now covered him from head to foot. He could see better, too. His blood was pounding, and Jerry wanted the kill, wanted to feel his enemy's throat in his mouth and tear the life from it. He growled and charged.

The lumbering giant brought his fists down as Jerry leapt in, catching him on the shoulder and knocking him aside. Jerry pounced up on one of the lab tables and bared his teeth. Crypt Kicker lurched forward, arms outstretched. Jerry scrambled out of the way and launched himself onto the corpse-thing's back. He tore through the clothing and into the muscles in the dead monstrosity's back and shoulders, the flesh burning his lips and mouth. The giant, moving quicker than Jerry had anticipated, pushed himself over backwards and landed on top of Jerry. He felt a rib give way under the weight.

Jerry crawled away and looked around the room. This was a losing battle. There was no way he could kill someone who was already dead. He saw a freezer in the corner and ran for it. Jerry opened the door with a clawed hand, and turned to make sure Crypt Kicker was following him. He was. Jerry dodged into the freezer and crouched in the back, among cases of pharmaceuticals. The room was about twelve feet deep and half as wide. Crypt Kicker appeared in the doorway, ducking to get inside. He seemed unable to locate his enemy in the darkness. Jerry picked up a case with clawed hands and tossed it at Crypt Kicker, then darted out between the giant's legs. He slammed the door shut and brought down the heavy metal handle. A slow, heavy pounding began on the door. Jerry figured it would keep him there, for awhile anyway.

Jerry crept out into the hall and sniffed. Battle was still there, and close. He hunched down and walked down the hall, claws clicking on the cold floor. There was a different smell now. Fear. Jerry began salivating. Soon Battle would be his, screaming in terror as the blood pumped from his torn body. Soon. Jerry continued to creep forward, his broken rib searing his side. A shape appeared in a doorway at the end of the hall and there was an explosion of light with a muffled sound. Jerry felt something whine past his ear. He bounded forward, wanting nothing but the kill. No matter the cost. Light filled the hallway. Jerry squinted and kept going. Battle screamed and ducked out of the hallway into one of the rooms.

Jerry crouched down and let his vision clear, then started advancing slowly. A growl started at the back of his throat. He cut it off. No point in giving his position away.

He paused outside the room. Battle was inside. The man's heart raced, his breathing was shallow. He was terrified, but not yet ready to die. Jerry didn't care what Battle wanted. George G. wasn't leaving the clinic alive. He sprang into the room. There were twin stacatto bursts of light and sound, but the bullets missed. Jerry snarled and scrambled toward Battle, who fell over backward onto a lab table, shattering glass beneath him. Jerry swatted the gun from Battle's hand, leaving claw marks on the man's wrist. The man was helpless, it was time to make him pay.

"Stop." The voice came from behind him. It was the nurse. Troll stood behind her, his huge green body tensed.

Jerry could take her next, after the man. Troll would be more difficult, but Jerry could outmaneuver him. Just like the Crypt Kicker. Jerry bent down and took his prey's throat. He could almost taste the blood pulsing underneath the skin.

"I said stop." The nurse took a step toward him. "What are you doing?"

Jerry let go of Battle and curled his lips. The woman moved beautifully. Her eyes were bright with life. It would be sweeter to kill her last, but he wanted her now. Wanted her to come apart in his hands and mouth.

She stood in front of him, unafraid. Jerry leaned in her direction, ready to spring. She would never even feel it.

The pain in his side vanished. Jerry lowered his arms. The nurse moved closer and looked into his eyes. Hers were aqua. He couldn't see anything else. Just her eyes.

"Change back."

Jerry felt the mat of hair on his skin. It itched. He wanted it to go away. His teeth began to recede, and his face began to shift.

"That's it. Change back."

Jerry felt the world shifting underneath him. He collapsed to the floor, breathing heavily. "I could have killed you."

Battle screamed. Jerry turned at the sound, still light-headed. Battle was in convulsions. Emily moved in and tried to grab his shoulders, but Battle kicked her away. His body poured out of his clothes and onto the floor. The flesh shifted and changed color and texture, becoming yellow and brittle. Multiple legs sprouted from Battle's new form. His face became putty-like and his ears melted into dark globs. The thing screamed and backed into a corner. There was a crash from another room. Jerry heard steel thud heavily onto the linoleum floor.

"Jesus, the Crypt Kicker," Jerry said.

"I'll get him," Troll said, turning away.

"Look out for his hands," Jerry said. Troll nodded and headed own the hall.

"What the fuck happened to him?" Jerry looked over at Battle, who was cowering in the corner.

"You mean you don't have all the answers? Who was that to begin with?" She began to sift through the glass wreckage on the table. "Hello." She pulled out a broken vial, dappled with blood, and examined it. "Xenovirus Takis-A."

Jerry laughed. "A joker. He turned into a joker. There is some justice after all. Eh, George G.?"

"*Who the fuck are you?*" Battle screamed, curling his limbs protectively around his body.

"Nobody," Jerry replied, and smiled.

"What did he want here?" Emily tapped Jerry on the shoulder.

Jerry said nothing. He wasn't really sure, anyway. The pain in his side returned, worse than before. All the air went out of him and he crumped back to the floor.

"Sorry," she said. "I pushed you too hard. I still want some answers. We've got to get this wing sealed off, too."

"Come with me to visit a friend, and I'll tell you everything I know." He held out his hand. She took it and helped him back to his feet.

"Troll can handle anything else that might happen.

You'd better get the hell out of here before the police show. I have a feeling you aren't going to want to answer most of their questions." She picked up Battle's gun and pointed it in his direction. "Besides, I want your answers all to myself."

"He kept screaming, 'I'm not a joker. I'm not a joker,' when the cops took him away." Emily drained the coffee from the bottom of her cup.

Jay sat behind his desk listening to the story, stopping them once or twice to clarify a point. Jerry couldn't really gauge his partner's reaction. He'd left out any references to a conspiracy, or to himself as Mr. Creighton of Ackroyd and Creighton.

"Do you know what Battle was after?" Emily asked, then yawned.

"No. But we're going to check into it. You can count on that." Jay looked over at the half-empty coffeepot. "I think you're past the point of caffeine being a help. Want me to send you back to the clinic?"

"Yes." She rubbed the side of her head. "The explanation I left Dr. Finn with wasn't exactly adequate. And the cops want to talk to me again."

"No doubt," Jay said. "Thanks for taking care of Jerry here. He's a valued client. If you don't mind, either Mr. Creighton or I would like to buy you dinner sometime."

"Who's Mr. Creighton?"

"One of our best, Ms. Moffat. One of our very best." Jay made his hand gun-shaped and pointed at the nurse. "Get to sleep as soon as you can."

She nodded, then vanished with a soft pop.

"Another nurse," Jay said, raising his eyebrow. "An analyst would say you're trying to reenact your failed relationship with Beth and make it come out right. Ezili might not like it."

Jerry shook his head. "So I'm attracted to her. I don't think that has anything to do with Beth. I don't have any idea what's going to happen with any of the women in my life. Par for the course." He paused. "Well, aren't you going to let me have it?"

"What for?"

"Taking stupid chances, risking lives, mine included."
Jerry felt the fatigue in his body down to his bones. He
wanted to get this over with.

"Nope. You did take chances, but it turned out
alright." Jay grinned. "That's one of the keys. You're still
alive and still learning. I'll bet next time you won't be
such an eager beaver."

"That's for damned sure. If Emily hadn't helped turn
me back . . ." He shook his head. "All I wanted to do
was kill. It was scary. I owe Ezili, too. You just can't do
it all on your own."

"That's why I have operatives." Jay smiled. "And a
partner."

Jerry straightened in his chair. "That's all I want to
be. Are we really going to look into this conspiracy?"

"Might not be a bad idea. But it would be an agency
investigation. No freelancing." Jay stood and stretched.
"Let's get out of here."

Jerry pulled himself up out of the chair. "You going
to tell me why you don't like Hartmann?"

Jay fingered his palm. "If I could, I would, but I can't.
Have you had any dirty dreams about Emily Moffat?"

Jerry made a face. "You want something for nothing,
eh?" He opened the door and stepped out into the hallway. "It'll cost you dinner."

"A small price to pay."

Jerry was so tired he could barely walk, but he felt
good. Content. "You know, Jay. This could be the beginning of a beautiful partnership."

The Color of His Skin

Part 2

"What do you know about this Judge Sweeney, Sam?"

The city prosecutor—Samuel Hanley, in his mid-thirties and showing progressive male pattern baldness and perpetual bags of weariness under his eyes—shrugged at Gregg and adjusted his wrinkled Brooks Brothers suit. It wasn't much of an improvement. "Not a hell of a lot. Political appointment, probably has his eye on some cushy circuit. He's been fair enough in the cases I've had before him up until now." Hanley rummaged in his briefcase and pulled out the case file—the edges of paper bristled and curled around the manila folder. "I'm more worried about the guy van Renssaeler's firm has brought in: Fitzpatrick. That's a fed if I ever saw one."

Brandon van Renssaeler, at the table on the other side of the courtroom, was one of a quartet of lawyers retained by Battle and Puckett. He conversed earnestly with a tall man in a tailored dark suit. The bristle-cut hair and the lean, muscular body lurking under the expensive wool, Gregg admitted, seemed to shout "Federal agent." Fitzpatrick glanced over once at Gregg, nodded, and favored him with a faint smile that bordered

53

on a smirk before turning back to Brandon. The knot in Gregg's stomach tightened another notch.

Nothing about this case made Gregg feel good.

With the break-in at the Jokertown clinic and Troll's identification of Battle and Crypt Kicker as the two men responsible, Gregg had felt a surge of optimism. It had seemed fated, his path laid out in neon letters before him: *Here is the Way*. All the hazy plans Hannah, Gregg, and Father Squid had devised were quickly scrapped.

Armed with the information Ackroyd and Creighton had funneled to him, Gregg had gone to Hanley, the DA in charge of Battle's case. Gregg had convinced the man that this trial would be a fame-maker, something to bust open the whole conspiracy and (just incidentally) make everyone involved very, very visible. Expanded charges had been filed, bench warrants and subpoenas issued. Everything was moving so well for a week or so that Gregg could almost envision the headlines. It didn't matter that Battle and the joker known as Crypt Kicker had disappeared—in fact, that was in their favor. Let them run. Gregg had already put out tentative feelers to *America's Most Wanted*; their executive producer seemed interested, especially with Gregg's hints that there was a deeper plot behind the burglary. Gregg had begun outlining the way they'd pull the existence of the Sharks into the tale of the Jokertown Clinic Burglary. Hardly the forum Gregg wanted, but it was a start. He could almost imagine Robert Stack's intro. . . .

But Battle and Puckett had suddenly and unexpectedly turned themselves in to the authorities. A high-powered staff of attorneys had been hired, and the case had suddenly gone forward at a breakneck pace. Gregg pulled a few of the strings he still held: the DA had received permission to allow Gregg to act as co-counsel in the case. He figured a trial was almost as good as a television show. The onlookers were mostly press, and camera crews were waiting outside.

But Gregg didn't like the way Brandon smiled easily as he talked with his companion, glancing from Gregg to Hannah, who sat in the spectator's area behind the railing.

He didn't like the fact that after the bailiff announced Judge Sweeney's arrival, the judge immediately asked Fitzpatrick to approach the bench. The two were quickly engaged in a lengthy whispered conversation. The judge had a thin nap of salt-and-pepper hair receding from his forehead, and his small eyes were sharp and hard—he looked like someone who knew political expediencies; he looked like someone who would have been a tasty puppet. But Gregg could sense nothing but a smug self-satisfaction from the man, nothing more. Gregg cursed the limits of his new power.

The judge nodded as Fitzpatrick stepped away. "We will delay proceedings for an hour, gentlemen. I will be meeting with Mr. Fitzpatrick in my chambers immediately."

Hanley, followed a moment later by Gregg, leapt up from his chair. "Your Honor," the prosecutor said urgently, "the prosecution has the right and the obligation to be part of any discussion in this case. If there's something of import to our case—"

"I'm sorry, Mr. Hanley, but it seems that there are potential issues of national security involved, and I had been so notified earlier this morning, on a very high level. The precedent is clear enough; I don't have any choice in the matter. I will make the prosecution aware of the content of the discussion as soon as I can." Judge Sweeney nodded to Fitzpatrick, Brandon, and the others. "In my chambers, Mr. Fitzpatrick . . ."

Sweeney banged his gavel. Fitzpatrick gave Gregg the smile again as he passed their table, causing the dull embers of nervous pain in Gregg's stomach to burst into a full roaring inferno. He tried to reach out with the Gift, but again it did nothing but let him sip the sour taste of confidence in Fitzpatrick's mind. The voice scolded him: *"If I had Puppetman . . ." We both know that old lament, Greggie. Give it up. That's not the way to redeem yourself.*

Hanley shook his head, scooped up his files and dumped them in his briefcase again. He snapped the lid closed on the heap and shrugged at Gregg with a tired expression on his face. "Not a damn thing we can do about it right now," he said. "I'm going for coffee and a Danish. Join me? No? See you in an hour, then."

Brandon looked at Gregg. He shook his head almost imperceptibly.

"Gregg?" Hannah had come up from her chair. She glared at Brandon as he passed on his way out of the courtroom. "What's going on?"

"I'm not sure," he answered. "But I don't like the look of it. They've brought in some heavy suit from the government."

"*Damn* it!" Hannah burst out. "My God, the Sharks broke into Tachyon's lab for *some* reason—once they're brought to trial, everything we know can be brought out. *All* of it. . . ."

Hannah leaned heavily on the railing, intense, her fingers white where they curled around the polished mahogany. Now she sighed, and Gregg sensed the woman's weariness, her despair, and her idealistic fury. *She is truly incredible. I wish I had known her before . . .*

With Puppetman? the inner voice interjected. *What would you have done with her, Greggie? You would have dragged her through the slime like all the rest. You don't deserve her. Not until you've redeemed yourself.*

"These are lives we're talking about," Hannah continued, softer now. "People who happen to be jokers. People who laugh, and love—and hurt."

"Hannah," Gregg said quietly. "You're preaching to the converted."

That earned him a fleeting smile. "I know. It's just . . ." She stared at the door through which the judge and Fitzpatrick had gone. "I just wish I could *do* something."

"So do I," Gregg told her. *But you can't*, the voice answered him. *Not this way.* Gregg had the sense of being outmaneuvered, of being hemmed in by unseen forces behind the scenes. He could feel the Sharks' presence again, a hidden, sinister presence tugging on his line from below the surface. The sensation brought back strange feelings of yearning. *If only I'd known, back then. If only I'd stumbled across them before, with Puppetman . . .*

An hour later, Gregg heard the words he'd somehow

known he was going to hear as soon as he'd seen Fitzpatrick and van Rensselaer. Judge Sweeney cleared the
courtroom of everyone but the lawyers and himself. He
took a long breath before he spoke. "Mr. Hanley, I regret
this, as I can tell by the reams of paper that you've
stacked over there that you've done your usual exemplary
job of preparing your case. However, I must tell you and
your co-counsel that I have been informed of certain
mitigating circumstances regarding the break-in at the
Jokertown Clinic. I have already ordered the release of
Mr. Battle and Mr. Puckett from custody."

"No!" Hanley slapped his hand down on his briefcase.
Sweeney glowered at the prosecutor, but the judge's
attention snapped back to Gregg as he stood. Gregg
reached out with the Gift and felt the emotions within
Sweeney. He could sense a nagging irritation within the
man—evidently the judge had been looking forward to
the publicity this trial would bring him as well.

"Your Honor," Gregg began, letting the Gift lend his
words all the power it could, "surely the defendants are
not claiming that this was a matter of national security.
That's ludicrous. The Jokertown Clinic treats the poor
jokers of this city. It provides a badly needed service to
people who would not otherwise have it available to
them, and it has done that good work for decades. The
clinic is hardly a threat to the nation; in fact, it is quite
the opposite. There are no hidden agendas there, no
weapons, no secret laboratories, no threat to the public
welfare. There are only caring people and a dedicated,
caring staff."

Gregg could feel Sweeney's agreement, like an azure
sea deep within him, but the Gift would only let him
raise the smallest wavelets on that surface. He could also
sense something else holding back that agreement, a dam
of scarlet, nameless fear that made Gregg wonder. Puppetman could have raised a storm of certainty, a hurricane
of assurance that would have shattered that dam. With
Puppetman, Sweeney would have nodded and smiled and
spread his hands wide. *"I have never heard anything*

more convincing," he would have said. "*I have never been so moved. . . .*"

The words flared with the Gift. Incandescent, they battered against the dark fear and fell guttering into silence. Something inside Sweeney was stronger than the Gift. Gregg could sense the seed of compassion the Gift found within the man, but the seed was locked in stone, captured in a hold the Gift could not break.

What is it that holds him? Damn it! What use is this power if it doesn't work?

The voice chided him. *Accept it as it is, Greggie. Use the Gift correctly and it will become powerful.*

Sweeney was speaking. "Mr. Hanley, Mr. Hartmann, it is *done.* I have no choice. This court has dropped all charges against George G. Battle and Robert Joseph Puckett in the matter of the Jokertown Clinic burglary."

"Judge Sweeney," Hanley persisted, "Mr. Battle is known to be attached to the Special Executive Task Force. Are Mr. Fitzpatrick and Mr. van Renssaeler claiming that the burglary of the clinic was performed at the behest of the executive branch?"

Sweeney looked at Fitzpatrick, and then back at Hanley. "I have nothing more to say on the matter at all, Mr. Hanley." Sweeney raised his hand as Hanley started to speak again. "The matter is closed. One more word, and you'll be held in contempt. Mr. Battle and Mr. Puckett have been cleared of all charges against them. That is the ruling of this court. Furthermore, I must warn both of you to be very careful as to what you say to the press outside . . ." The judge was still talking, but Gregg heard nothing of it.

Brandon van Renssaeler snapped shut the locks of his briefcase. The sound was very loud in the room.

In the cab afterward, Gregg looked over to see tears gathering in Hannah's eyes. He was surprised, momentarily, to see the vulnerability in the woman. *She would have been a glorious puppet. She feels so deeply, so strongly. . . .*

"What now?" Hannah asked him. She stared straight ahead as the cab headed uptown. "We're sunk, right?"

Gregg reached over to her and touched her shoulder gently with his left hand, his real hand. Hannah shrugged away from him, glaring at him. "Hannah," he said, and he let the Gift, the power, touch the word. *Greggie . . .* the voice said warningly inside him, but he ignored it. "I'm very sorry."

The tears fell then, twin droplets tracking down either cheek. Hannah brushed them away angrily. The desire to use the power came on him. Even with this poor shadow of the old ability, he knew he could make this grief that so filled her overflow. He could take her in his arms and let her sob her despair, sheltering her, and once the tears were gone, she might look up at him and . . .

He was surprised at how much he wanted to do that. At how much he desired her. His hand was still out. All he had to do was touch, to say the right words garlanded with his new Gift.

He withdrew his hand. Set it on his lap and covered it with the prosthetic. That was very nearly harder to do than anything he'd ever done in his life.

She's angry and furious because this means that more people will be hurt. She cries for them, not herself. But you, Greggie . . . you're just disappointed. *You're feeling irritated because this means Gregg Hartmann won't get the publicity he wants. You're a sham. You're an ass.*

"We're not done, Hannah," he said, ignoring the voice. "There's another way—if you're willing to trust me."

"I still don't know you well enough to trust you."

"Father Squid tells me that you couldn't trust Quasiman in the beginning, either."

That nearly brought the tears again. "Poor Quasi . . ." Hannah covered her mouth with her hand, then wiped at her eyes as she looked out at the skyscraper canyon around them. "What is it you want to do, Gregg?"

"First, I have to know how much you're willing to risk," he said.

Hannah tossed her hair defiantly. "To expose the Sharks? Anything."

"This would be a true gamble. If it doesn't work, we'd have nowhere else to go. It would involve playing almost our full hand, laying it all out in the open. All or nothing. Either we cause things to break loose, or we find out once and for all that no one cares." *And just incidentally, it will also give me the most exposure. Yes! I should have pushed for this from the beginning. . . .* "On the other hand, with hindsight and the publicity from the break-in, I think it's probably the way we should have gone in the first place. What do you think?"

"You're saying that we go public anyway—just lay it all out for everyone to see."

"Yes. And I think I know how."

"I'm still listening."

"Great." Gregg smiled at her. "First I think we'll stop midtown and see someone. . . ."

"Are you ready, Mr. Hartmann?"

Gregg gave the floor director a grim-faced nod and a thumbs-up. He hadn't expected to be this nervous. He'd been on *Peregrine's Perch* a dozen times or more over the years, though the last time—a few months after the debacle of the '88 convention—had been an unmitigated disaster. Stripped of Puppetman, shamed by Tachyon's brutal mind-controlling, and unable to speak freely with Tachyon there on the stage with him, he'd only reinforced his image as a man with a few loose wheels.

He was ready this time. This time would be much, much different.

Through the thick stage curtains, Gregg could hear the audience settle into silence. On the backstage monitor, he saw the house lights dim. The band swung into "Peri's Theme" as a single spot plucked Peregrine's announcer out of the darkness. "From our studio high atop New York City, here she is: PEEEEERRRRRRegrine."

The announcer's spot flicked off. A trio of searchlights arced out over the open balcony of the studio, lancing the New York skyline with blue-white lines. In the intersection of the three beams, Peregrine appeared, the searchlights gleaming from her snow-white wings and blue-sequined flying costume. She soared into the applause, flying through the open studio windows and onto the stage as the audience roared. She smiled into their adulation and blew her traditional kiss to the back row.

As the applause died, Peregrine let her wings fold behind, no longer smiling but looking seriously into the front camera. "Thank you," she said. "Thank you very much. Tonight's format is going to be a little different. As you know, our original schedule had Elephant Girl, Tom Cruise, and Cosmos & Chaos. They've consented to appear on a later show because of the importance of what we're going to talk about tonight."

The stage curtains billowed open behind Peregrine, revealing the traditional set: a couch, Peregrine's stool—the Perch. Gregg was standing alongside the couch as the curtains opened. Peregrine offered him a hand and turned her cheek. He gave her a perfunctory kiss, being careful—as the makeup people had warned him—not to actually touch skin. "Gregg Hartman," she announced to the camera.

The applause that followed was polite but hardly overwhelming. Peri's live audience, at least recently, tended to be largely jokers. Since the rise and fall of the Rox, New York had lost much of its luster as a tourist city, and nats tended to stay away from anything having to do with the wild card. Hartmann's reputation among the jokers was mixed. To some he was still the saviour of J-Town; to others, he'd been tarnished by the '88 failure and his recent stand against the Rox. He could feel their coolness toward him, washing from the tiers of seats like a winter wind.

Not yet. They aren't ready yet.

Peregrine had wanted to tape the show. It was Gregg who had insisted on the live audience, knowing that he needed them. He nodded to them now: his tools. For the last four days, the network had been running teasers: a black-and-white still picture of Peregrine's empty set and the legend underneath: WARNING: WHAT YOU'RE GOING TO LEARN ON FRIDAY WILL SHOCK YOU. The secret of Peri's guest list held; speculation and curiosity had peaked. The promos and resultant publicity had resulted in huge lines for tickets to the show; it was estimated that Peri's Nielsen ratings would go through the roof tonight.

The newfound power inside Gregg ached.

In the last few weeks, he'd consolidated their information. Gregg had called everyone with whom he had a vestige of influence, asking questions with a growing enthusiasm, researching the erratic trail of the Sharks and uncovering a filmy web of deceit and ugliness that amazed even him. He'd consulted with Furs, once one of his campaign directors and now a media consultant, deciding with him, Hannah and Father Squid the best way to present their case. What they'd put together was powerful, powerful enough that even Gregg was moved by it.

He didn't hate the Sharks as Hannah did. He loved them. They were going to turn things around for Gregg Hartmann, and tonight, tonight was the beginning.

Peregrine took her perch. Gregg sat on the couch. "I don't think Gregg needs introduction. He's an ex-Senator from New York, a man who won the Democratic nomination for president before an unfortunate incident ended that dream, a man who has always been a champion of the rights of people of the virus."

Peri patted Gregg's hand—his left hand—and smiled at him. "And I find, Gregg, that I don't know quite where to start. What you've brought for us tonight . . . well, let's just say that it's nearly unbelievable."

"Unfortunately, it's all too real, Peri," Gregg answered. "My investigations have convinced me of that. As to where to start, well, let's begin with a fire."

Furs had chosen and edited the footage. The studio monitors flickered; an orange inferno, a harsh roar, and the camera pulled back to show a church steeple lost in hell, wreathed in flame and smoke as sparks danced toward the sky. The scene shifted to news footage from the next morning: destruction, the ruins of the church steaming in the mist, the street a snarl of firehoses and equipment, twisted and blackened bodies sprawled in rubble.

The video was at once horrible and fascinating.

"The Church of Jesus Christ Joker burned last Black Queen Night," Gregg's voice said over the film. "We all remember that disaster, when over a hundred innocent jokers were murdered by an arsonist who blocked the church doors and then set fire to the church while those inside were worshiping. The alleged arsonist was found, but not before he killed himself in an accidental explosion. The official explanation is that the arsonist acted alone. But that's not what the chief investigator of the fire believes. I'd like you to meet Hannah Davis, whose task it was to find the arsonist."

The tape faded, and the cameras swung to follow Hannah's entrance onto the set. Gregg had to admit that the woman managed to give Peri a run for her money, and she was perfect for the revelation tonight: pretty, yet vulnerable. Again, Furs had chosen the image and tailored Hannah to match it: a blond nat, just like the millions of other whitebread Americans watching—and that fact would give more credence to the story. Furs had insisted that Hannah rest, and makeup had done the rest. The dark shadows were gone from under her eyes, and she looked rested and attractive.

Like Andrea, Gregg realized with a start, or Succubus. The memory of those two caused a stirring inside as he gazed at Hannah, and the voice rose to scold him. *She isn't why you're here*, it said. *You're here to make amends.*

Gregg could feel Hannah's nervousness as she blinked into the stage lights and the audience's applause. "You'll be fine," he whispered as she sat alongside him. He let the power ride along with the words, and was gratified to see her smile in response. He sat back as Peregrine finished Hannah's introduction.

"I was called by my boss, Malcolm Coan, around midnight," Hannah began. Her voice was hesitant at first, but Gregg let the new Gift nudge her—a touch here, a caress there—and as Hannah fell into the tale, she spoke more forcefully. "The fire had just gone to five alarms and we realized that there was going to be significant loss of life. The NYFD had already reported the blocked exits ..."

Yes, very attractive ...

For the next forty-five minutes, Gregg and Peregrine, with Hannah's assistance, walked the viewers through the serendipitous discovery of the Sharks. The presentation was a careful mixture of live interviews, tapes, and stills of various photos and documents. Father Squid, to a tremendous acclamation from the audience, was brought on early to give his account of the fire and add his corroboration of Hannah's evidence. Dr. Finn had adamantly refused to go on with them—"Even if I absolutely believed in the conspiracy, and I don't, this isn't the way to go about dealing with it. And Hannah, Gregg *Hartmann*, of all people?"—but the AIDS outbreak at Dr. Faneuil's Kenya clinic was public knowledge and easily covered; Margaret Durand's role in the X11A tragedy was outlined; Cameo channeled Nick Williams' fedora to give the Marilyn Monroe connection; the Hedda Hopper documents indicting Hoover, Hughes, and others as Sharks were shown; the three failed attempts against Hannah's life were chronicled; Battle's connections with Iran, the Rox, and the botched burglary of the Jokertown Clinic were exposed.

Gregg kept one thing out: Brandon van Renssaeler and the assassination of Robert Kennedy. Whether van Renssaeler was directly involved with the Sharks or not, he was right about one thing—until they found Lamia's photograph of Brandon and Sirhan Sirhan, there was no hard evidence against the man. Lamia had seemed relieved when Gregg and Hannah had told her that they weren't going to ask her to appear..

And Pan Rudo—his name was never specifically mentioned, but Gregg knew that any reporter with half a brain could put together the connections of this mysterious, unnamed figure who kept cropping up in the tales. There would be people on Rudo's doorstep tomorrow. *"Leave the media with some mud to sling on their own,"*

Furs had advised them. *"Believe me, they're more vicious
than any Shark—it might also keep us out of a quick
lawsuit."*

It was ugly. It was brutal. It was extremely effective.

Gregg could feel it as they broke for the last commercial segment. The anger and disgust radiated from the
audience like a bank of infrared lamps. They were
primed now. Ready.

It was Gregg's turn.

The Gift that had been given him wasn't nearly as
strong as his old ace. His meeting with Ackroyd had
proved that, if his failure with Judge Sweeney hadn't. Jay
hated Gregg so much that Gregg's power was useless.
He could put the conviction in his voice, but the ones
he affected had to have the core of belief already in
place. It was only Creighton's odd reaction to Battle's
name that had enabled him to be successful there. Gregg
knew that if he tried to sway the audience before they'd
seen the evidence, he would fail.

But now . . .

The cameras zoomed in on Peregrine. "Gregg," she
asked, leading into the question they'd agreed upon,
"conspiracy theories are as old as humanity. We seem to
have a difficult time believing that things simply are the
way they are. Somehow it's strangely comforting to
believe that there is some force acting upon us, some
sinister group who controls all the hidden strings—I
don't know why, maybe that way we can evade responsi-
bility for our lives. The evidence you've all just shown is
certainly compelling, but you'd be the first to admit that
it's still very circumstantial. You ask for a certain leap of
faith if we're to give credence to the Card Sharks. How
would you answer those who say that the Sharks are just
another Illuminati?"

Gregg gave a slow, deliberate sigh as if bending under
the awful burden of what they'd just shown. As he did
so, as the cameras panned in on his face, he opened the
gates in his mind and let the Gift spill out. His words
found the emotions of those listening and followed the

threads back, strengthening them, deepening the flow, beginning the slow feedback between himself and them.

"Peri, I would tell you first that I've never earned your trust," he began, and heard the echo inside: *You're damned right about that* ... From some of the audience there came a soft protest, but Gregg raised his right hand, smiling at them sympathetically as the prosthesis glittered dully in the lights.

"No. I'd like to believe that I've made some small contribution, but—for whatever reasons, and I'm beginning to question just what those reasons might be—I've never accomplished all I could or hoped to do. I ask you this, first of all: please, *please* do not let my own failures blind you to the truth of what we've brought here tonight."

Gregg paused, looking back at Hannah, at Father Squid, at Peregrine and the others on the stage. He could feel the pulse of the studio inside himself, all the emotions beating in time to his own heart. "I don't expect you to believe because Gregg Hartmann says it's so," he continued. "We had people refuse to appear tonight because of my involvement, and I can sympathize with their feelings. They're right. Gregg Hartmann doesn't deserve that kind of trust. Instead, believe because you've seen and heard our evidence with your own eyes and ears. Believe because you've felt the hatred and prejudice yourselves. Believe because you've experienced the pain and now you look at Hannah and Father Squid, and you see your own pain reflected in their lives. Believe—"

Gregg stopped. The linked emotions of the crowd hammered at him, made him take a breath that nearly sobbed. He rose from the couch where he sat with Hannah, Father Squid, and Cameo. He felt the tears gather in the corners of his eyes. *Careful ... You can't let this be seen as another breakdown....*

He gestured, softly pounding a fist into the cupped palm of the prosthesis as if it were the top of a lectern. "Believe because everything good in you is crying out in outrage and fury. And with belief comes the next question: what do we *do* about it?"

Like a wave crashing against rocks, the question sent shattered anger flashing. There were shouted answers from the audience, but Gregg raised his hand for quiet again.

"Hannah had to face that question." Gregg gave Hannah a long glance, knowing that the cameras would follow his lead. He extended his hand to her; they touched fingers briefly. "Imagine this young woman's dilemma, if you will. Imagine uncovering something more vile and disgusting than anything you or I have ever imagined, and then finding that no one wants to believe you. Imagine having to give up your job, your home, the whole structure of your life, because that's the only way you can find the truth. And imagine, if you can, being hounded, reviled, threatened, and nearly killed for your efforts. Hannah—"

Gregg stopped, shaking his head, and he let the gift swell and build until the sympathy of the audience threatened to burst. "Hannah knew that if *she* came forward with this, she would not be believed. She knew that she didn't have the clout to force those in power to listen. At best, her hard work would be swept under the rug and buried. She also knew that if she waited too long, the Sharks would find her and her evidence, and they would . . . well, that's best left unsaid. So, in wisdom or folly, she looked for a voice who would speak for her. She came to me."

Gregg smiled at Hannah. She nodded back to him. Gregg held the pose long enough to know that the cameras caught the interchange, then turned back.

"I think Hannah thought she'd made a mistake there at first." Gregg gave the half-smile that had been the political cartoonist's icon for him over the years. "You see, like many of you, I couldn't just accept what she'd given me. I had to do some investigation of my own. I had to check and verify all the facets of her story. And I could do one thing Hannah couldn't. I immediately confronted the man whom Hannah's evidence cites as the current head of the Sharks. Why? Because, like you, I needed to get rid of that last little shred of skepticism.

I laid out what Hannah had given me, and I dared him to tell me that it was a mistake. I challenged him to refute the evidence. He did not. Instead—"

Gregg stopped. He took a long breath. They were hanging on his words now, leaning forward. The mingled emotions of the audience cocooned him. He was a chrysalis, waiting to break out of the self-made shell of years of failure. . . . *redemption* . . .

"Instead, he coldly admitted that it was true," Gregg finished.

The howl of outrage drowned out anything else he might have said, and the power of their anger surged back through his Gift, nearly too powerful to handle. Gregg gaped momentarily, open-mouthed, then clamped down on his ace, slammed the mental floodgates. *Careful* . . . This was not as easy to control as Puppetman's power had been. He felt like he was wearing mental mittens— he hadn't wanted the emotions to peak so fast. "Who *is* he?" someone shouted in the audience, too loud to ignore. Gregg cursed under his breath, shaking his head. *Too early* . . .

"We can't tell you that yet. Not until we have all the evidence we need to convict him," he answered. The answer was clumsy, out of sequence in the script they'd planned. Gregg was momentarily lost.

"Why this forum, Gregg?" Peregrine asked, saving him. One of her wings fluttered softly; a snowy feather drifted to the stage floor. "Why come here?"

"I can answer that very simply, Peri," Gregg said, finding himself once more. "First, I did it for safety, for the safety of all of us here tonight. Hannah already knows that these people will go to any lengths to stay hidden. If Hannah had been killed before she came to me, this whole mess would have stayed in the shadows, in the darkness it likes so much. Not now. Now it's too late to hide."

He turned away from Peri, letting his gaze travel over the audience as the gates of his power opened and touched the chord of their emotions. "And because we need help. We need the aid of all people of conscience, and we need the courage of those who have already been touched by the Sharks. Now that all of you know that the beast exists, we hope that more of you will come forward with your own stories, and more and more light will glare down until everyone can see exactly what horrors this prejudice and hatred bring."

The audience erupted into applause, and Gregg reveled in the sound, an orgasm of support. He let the power loose fully now, let it rip open the last restraints on them. *Now* . . .

"More importantly," he continued, "as a lawyer I look at what we have, and know that legally the only ones we can touch are the little people. I don't *want* the goons and the subordinates, because they mean nothing. That would be like trying to catch a lizard by the tail—all you'll get is the tail while the lizard scurries away to grow another. I want the *whole* creature. To do that, we need more; to get more, we need each and every one of you. We have to know that none, *none* of you here will forget. We have to know that you will not permit this to continue even one day longer."

A wordless shout of affirmation came from several voices within the audience, and the reverberation made Gregg lift his head and smile. *Yes* . . . he exulted, and echoed the word aloud.

"Yes. That's why we came here. Because true power lies within the people. Within *you*, and *you*, and *you*." With each word, he stabbed a forefinger toward the audience. Where Gregg pointed, people rose in support, shouting back to him, screaming. "With your help," he concluded, "we will snare the head of this beast, and when we do . . ."

They waited, hanging on his words, the power, this Gift of his redemption seeming to sizzle and spark around him.

"We. Will. Slay. It." He finished each word as a thundering concussion.

They roared, they shouted, they screamed back at him. Inside, another voice shouted over the din. *Remember what the Gift is for, Greggie,* it warned. *Remember that it's to be used for atonement, for penance, for redemption. Never forget that . . .*

Gregg nodded.

Redemption, it seemed, was very, very tasty.

Gregg could already imagine the headlines in tomorrow's papers: HARTMANN UNCOVERS CONSPIRACY AGAINST WILD CARD. HARTMANN INDICTS HIGH-LEVEL GOVERNMENT OFFICIALS IN PLOT.

The floor director was waving to him as he left the stage. "A phone call for you, sir," he said. Gregg took the proferred phone.

"This is Gregg Hartmann."

There was a click on the other end. He heard the popping hiss of a recording—a long low tone, then another a half-step higher: daaaaaahhhhhh-*DUM*. The sequence repeated again, then again a little faster and more urgent until it was a pounding, insistent rhythm. Gregg suddenly realized what the music was: the theme from *Jaws*. A sudden chill prowled his spine.

He hung up the phone as if something was about to leap from the receiver and devour him.

My Sweet Lord
by Victor Milán

Walking with great deliberation, conscious of his destiny, and the eyes of the world—in the form of half a hundred news cameras—upon him, the man in the saffron robe entered the space between the shouting, cheering mob, and the armored personnel carrier that barred its entrance to the joker quarter of Cholon. The morning sun that leaned upon Saigon like a surly giant pressed sweat to his face and highlights to his shaven skull. The news services usually stayed away from the anti-wild cards riots in favor of the more politically correct demonstrations before the Presidential Pad, but today they had been tipped off, and were out in force, jostling the rioters and poking boom-microphones at the monk like dung-beetle antennas.

A man burning himself to death live and in color was what TV news was all about.

The BMP's commander watched the Buddhist monk and his assistant warily from his seat, half out of the turret, in case they got frisky with the red plastic jerricans of gasoline the assistant carried. The monk ignored him as serenely as he did the mob and the ungainly, pale-faced newsfolk. Turning his back to the armored vehicle he assumed full lotus on the griddle-hot pavement.

Visibly torn between self-importance and dismay, the

71

assistant took the cans of gas one at a time and doused
the monk with them, being careful not to get any of the
fluid on himself. Then he stood to the side and drew
himself to his full height, which wasn't conspicuous.

"The holy monk Thich will now immolate himself,"
he announced in a reedy voice—and in English, of
course, the language of international news—"to protest
the continued invasion of our country by the foreign
monsters."

The Saigon mob was fairly well educated, as mobs go;
many of its components understood English, and the rest
caught the drift. The crowd roared anger, or approval,
or whatever it is that communal entities bent on mayhem
feel. For the slow in the street and among the viewers at
home, the assistant propped placards against the empty
jerricans, left and right of the monk and well clear. One
read NO MORE JOKERS in English. The other repeated the
message in Vietnamese.

The assistant took out a book of matches and began
to fumble at it. On his third attempt he got one to light,
singeing his fingers in the process. "Yi!" he yelped, and
flipped the match away.

Crowd and journalists caught their breath. The burning match happened to land in the clear puddle surrounding the monk. The gasoline went up in a *whoosh*.

For a moment the monk was obscured by an orange
wash of fire. Then the flame shot upward away from him
in a mushroom cloud, to surround the figure of a man
hanging in midair, two meters above the monk. For a
moment it blazed like a saint's full-body halo in a pre-
Renaissance religious painting. Then it collapsed inward,
to outline momentarily the head and limbs and body of
the man.

Then it vanished.

"Ahh," the floating figure said, stretching its arms, "I
needed that." He was a small man for an overt Occiden-
tal, not much bigger than the Vietnamese norm, with a
narrow clever face and red hair. He wore an orange
sweatsuit and athletic shoes.

His cheeks pink with seeming sunburn, the monk was

staring upward at the interloper. "What is the meaning of this?" the assistant demanded.

"The meaning of this is, I'm denying your pal his cheap theatrics. Get him out of here and get him a shower."

"But—"

"Hit the road, Junior, before I scorch *your* tuchus." He sent a squirt of fire to the pavement at the acolyte's sandaled feet. The assistant jumped. Then he grabbed the monk by a skinny biceps and hauled him upright. With the supreme moment passed into anticlimax, flaming death didn't look so appealing any more; the monk allowed himself to be led away without protest.

The flying man settled into the pool of gas from which he had sucked the flame. A jet of fire from his fingertips reignited it. When it burned off, he was still standing there, arms akimbo, grinning like a fox.

"Jumpin' Jack Flash at your service," he told the assembled media. "Normally, as a good libertarian, I wouldn't *dream* of interfering with our little friend's right to light up anything he damn well pleased, himself included. But today I decided to make an exception, just to piss you people off."

The crowd was standing *well* back away from all this. The journalists grumbled among themselves. A couple shook their fists at the interloper.

"What about allegations that Vietnam is being overrun by jokers?" a British reporter shouted. The flying ace was, after all, a semi-official spokesman for the government of the Republic of Free Vietnam. He was rumored to be *like this* with its President. Perhaps anticlimax could be partly redeemed in embarrassing questions.

"If you brought all the jokers in the *world* here, they wouldn't make up five percent of the population," JJ said. "Get real."

"What about the way wealthy American jokers are dominating the economy?" asked a woman reporter for *Frontline*.

"At least now there's an economy to dominate," Flash said. "Even if that were true, which of course it isn't."

He cocked his head at her. "Didn't I see you do a feature a couple years ago, about how America was short-changing her jokers? Now they come over here, and you bitch because they've got it too good. Make up your damn *mind*, lady—"

He broke off because some of the reporters and the mob were trying to crane past the parked BMP, at something going on in the streets of the joker district. JJ Flash frowned. He wasn't used to being upstaged. He rose ten feet in the air and turned around.

An astounding cavalcade was approaching down the broad street of the former Chinese quarter. To the skirl of chants, chimes, and pipes, came a bevy of maidens of celestial beauty, hung about with flowers, and trinkets of ivory and gold: the sort of Indian gaud usually attendant upon Indian gods. So celestial was their beauty, in fact, that their bare lotus feet failed to touch the pavement as they walked.

Next up were a band of youths, boys and girls alike, dressed in the saffron robes of *sannyasi*, Indian ascetics. These were raising the musical din, clanging *kartal* cymbals, thumping *mridanga* drums with the heels of their hands, blowing wood flutes and singing songs of praise.

And behind came the evident object of that praise: a joker with an opulent belly spilling over a simple loincloth. His head was the head of an elephant, with one tusk. He carried a parasol in his trunk to shade himself. He rode a giant white rat whose eyes were the color of blood.

"Now, that's something you don't see every day," JJ Flash remarked to the air.

And way down inside him, a voice breathed, *Ganesha. Oh, wow.*

Oblivious, the cavalcade danced straight up to the flank of the BMP. The *Apsarases*—as JJ recalled the celestial babes were called—winged out to either side and froze into pretty curtsies, still in midair. Ganesha dismounted and danced up to the half-track.

"Please to vacate your vehicle immediately," he sang, "for I have no wish to put you at risk of harm."

The vehicle commander blinked down at him.

A fall of flowers rained upon Ganesha's elephant head, from a point in the air about three feet above the crown.

That did it. The President of Free Vietnam had made good on the hollow promise of the former Socialist Republic, turning Vietnam into a haven for the oppressed wild cards of the world—and damned near all of them *were*, by now. Cops who could not contain that customary Asian distaste for human deformity which animated today's mob had been booted off the force long since. So jokers did not particularly bother the APC commander. And he didn't know squat about the Hindu religion, so he had no idea he was being confronted by the spitting image of an actual *god*, offspring of Shiva and Parvati.

But flowers materializing in midair ... *that* got his attention. He yelped into his intercom and unassed his track right smart, followed in short order by the other two crew.

Ganesha smiled. "Know that I am the Remover of Obstacles," he sang in his high, pure voice. His acolytes cheered. The *Apsarases* beamed celestially. The rat sat on his haunches and cleaned his whiskers. His incisors were the color of the acolytes' robes.

Ganesha put forth his hands, pressed plump palms to the hot metal skin of the armored carrier. The vehicle shimmered and vanished. A gust of wind blew outward into the faces of the mob and the blank camera eyes. It smelled vaguely of sandalwood.

A single sigh rose up from the crowd on either side of the police line.

"I'll be dipped in shit," JJ Flash announced, "and fried for a corn dog."

Ganesha danced forward, through the space where the BMP had been. The rat waddled behind, and then the Floating Celestial Babes fell in, and the yellowrobe acolytes, singing and tootling up a storm. The crowd bolted away from the guru, front ranks battling those behind in their frenzy to get away from this apparition who could make fourteen and half metric tons of armored fighting vehicle disappear. Not to mention the rat.

Ganesha raised a plump hand, first two fingers extended. "Peace," he declared, in a voice both penetrant and musical. "Peace—and love. These are the tidings I bear you."

More flowers rained upon the mob. The protestors quit trying to escape, turned back to stare in wonder.

Ganesha strode into the crowd, straight up to a sullen man, big for a Vietnamese, who stood with his shirttail out, his bangs in his eyes, and a length of lumber in one hand. He had come prepared to crack joker heads.

"I am a joker," the guru sang, "and a holy fool. He who would harm any of the Lord Krishna's children, let him first strike me."

His merry eyes met those of the club-wielder. "Strike, my child, if that is what you will. No harm shall come to you."

The aspiring joker-basher dropped to his knees and began to weep. Ganesha laid a soft hand upon his head. The crying stopped

"My peace upon you, child," he said, and passed on, into the heart of the mob. It gave before him like the sea before a supertanker. Behind him, the Vietnamese man tossed away his two-by-four and joined the ranks of chanting faithful, clapping his hands and dancing clumsily, like a trained bear.

The camcorders were whirring, sucking the spectacle in through their optics. "This is where I check out," JJ Flash said. He darted down a side street and out of sight into a doorway.

A moment, and a figure emerged. A very different figure—gangly-tall and blond, with wire-rimmed spectacles before blue eyes that blinked at the vehemence of the Southeast Asian sun. He wore Western jeans and a blue chambray shirt with flowers embroidered on the pockets.

"*Ganesha*," he breathed. "Far *out*."

He moved quickly back into the intersection. Guru and company were making their musical way toward the center of Saigon. More of the protestors had broken away to join them. The rest were beginning to drift away, with hanging heads and slack arms. Their intention to harm had evaporated, like the Buddhist monk's resolve to burn.

Mark Meadows knelt, picked up a flower that had avoided being trampled by bare pious feet. It was a lotus blossom, red, heavy, and fragrant. He raised it, sniffed it.

The flower faded. It did not create a puff of breeze the way the BMP had. It simply melted back into the air.

"Madam President," the man in the suit was saying in sonorous American English. He had a nose like a flesh icicle that had begun to drip, and ears that consisted of bunches of limp pink tendrils that stirred with a feeble life of their own. He wore a blue pinstriped suit, well-tailored to his form, which was on the ample side. "We have come to bring certain matters to your attention."

The Saigon night, hot but none too black, tried to press itself in the tall windows of the French colonial villa the President's supporters had insisted she make her residence. Night was Moonchild's element. She could not bear the touch of the sun. The Republic's enemies—like President Barnett, and George Bush before him—made much of the fact.

Her audience chamber was the former ballroom, high-ceilinged, with an exquisitely polished floor of European hardwoods. Parachutes tie-dyed in firework explosions of color hung flanking her chair of state, which looked a great deal like a common camp stool, and was. To the dismay of her allies, she permitted no guards in the chamber with her, though there was one other person present tonight. But she was an ace, mistress of the martial arts, possessed of metahuman speed and powers of recuperation; if she encountered danger *she* couldn't handle, a handful of Vietnamese People's Army vets or expatriate joker kid-gang members from New York armed with Kalashnikovs wouldn't be much use.

The President of Free Vietnam gazed up at the joker

spokesman and felt guilty for her impulses. Which were to grab him by the front of his immaculate vest and shake him and shout, *Out with it, then, and don't waste my time mouthing the obvious, you pompous fat fool!*

She sighed. After two years of rulership she had never sought, and had no idea how to escape from, her soul was growing threadbare and grimy, like a rag in one of the tenderloin bars that had sprung back up aboveground with the fall of the communist regime.

"What might those matters be, Mr. Sorenson?" she asked.

He glanced at the others of his delegation: a sturdy man in a polo shirt whose collar was stretched almost to bursting around his muscular neck, and whose skin had the color and apparent consistency of none-too-well-dressed cement; a small precise woman with a yellow beak in place of nose and lips; and a handsome black man whose knees were articulated backwards.

"First of all," Sorenson said, "under increasing pressure from the Barnett administration, American wild cards—refugees—are arriving daily in ever-increasing numbers."

Moonchild nodded. She was a small woman, dressed in close-fitting black. The half of her face exposed by her *yin-yang* mask was Asian, and lovely. Black hair hung straight down her back, glossy as Japanese lacquer.

"I was aware of that," she murmured, and wondered when she had learned to be sarcastic. She who was so caring, so giving, so accepting.

Tock. At the sound the delegation stiffened, and its eyes fluttered over Moonchild's shoulder, past the hangings. Moonchild paid no attention.

"They, ah, they are being housed in quite intolerable conditions." After a moment's consternation Sorenson got his momentum back. "Shanty-towns, to be blunt."

"Are *you* living in a shanty, Mr. Sorenson?"

Tock-tock. Sorenson shook his head, his ear fringes wagging. He had begun to sweat, though the old colonial villa was equipped with excellent air-conditioning.

"As you must be aware, we are also receiving an influx

of Vietnamese refugees from the North. And, to be frank, the poorest of you American refugees is wealthy by Vietnamese standards. Most could find better accommodation more readily than their Vietnamese counterparts, if they were willing to do things such as share quarters with one another."

"And be gouged by landlords!" the beaked woman exclaimed. "You're permitting these Vietnamese to indulge in unbridled capitalism!"

"The Vietnamese are under the apprehension that their homes are their own." *Tock-tock. Tock.*

"And back home," the bull-necked man said, "we're protected against having to compete with people like these dinks."

"We can hardly erect trade barriers against the Vietnamese in Vietnam."

The *tock*ing sound really took off, like a machine gun in a jungle ambush. The delegation frankly stared past Moonchild at the rear of the ballroom.

Croyd Crenson stood by a window. In his current incarnation he was tall and skinny, with protruding faceted yellow eyes and black segmented antennae emerging from his unruly shock of black hair. He had his normal human left hand pressed, fingers splayed, on the top of a wooden table.

With the pointed chitinous foreclaw of his right he was stabbing the well-pocked surface between his fingers, moving from one to another with increasing speed.

The hard-shelled fingertip bit into the web between his first and second human fingers. "Fuck!" he screamed, waved his hand in the air and then stuffed it into his mouth to suck at the injury.

"Croyd," Moonchild said. "Please."

"Oh." He took his hand out of his mouth, examined it, giggled. "Oh. Sorry, your Excellency. Sorry. Heh-heh."

Moonchild turned her attention back to the delegates, who were eyeing Croyd as if he had produced a baby's leg and begun to gnaw it.

"Mr. Sorenson, if you are so concerned about the welfare of the less fortunate refugees, you might open your own purse to them. I understand you were able to get a great deal of your assets overseas before the freeze went into effect."

"But that's the government's job!"

"The Republic has made great strides economically in the past two years," Moonchild said. "Much of the ground has been gained with the assistance of wild card refugees, a fact which many of the Vietnamese people fail to appreciate. Nonetheless, this is a poor country, facing long recovery from decades of abuse. We try to help those who truly need it. But the able-bodied must shift for themselves."

They stared at her incredulously. "But we're *Americans!*" the black man burst out.

The room filled up with a gold glow and tinkling music, the scent of sandalwood. The delegates spun.

Ganesha stood in the doorway. The glow did not seem to originate from him. It simply surrounded him.

"I hope very much that I do not intrude—"

"As a matter of fact—" the beaked woman began pugnaciously.

"—my guests were on the verge of departure," Moonchild finished, in a voice like silk rustling over an ancient Korean *sulsa* knight's swordblade.

Croyd scrabbled the tips of his right fingers on the tabletop. "Want I should show you people out?" he asked.

The delegates could find their own way. Beaming, Ganesha stood aside to let them leave, and blessed them as they hurried past. Croyd went back to playing his game with his fingers.

Feeling an inexplicable tension at the pit of her belly, Moonchild said, "How may I help you, guru?" That cynical canker in her soul—or was it just JJ, bleeding through the increasingly porous barriers between personae?— answered, *money. Power. The usual.*

The guru tittered. "Already you have, by extending shelter to the wild cards, among whom is numbered my humble self. Now, it is I who must ask, may I help you?"

Moonchild studied him. He appeared harmless

enough, pale, fat, and jolly, like an Asian Santa Claus with a trunk. She had learned to put small stock in appearance. *Maya*, the Hindus called it.

"What manner of help, guru?"

"To bring peace to one who knows no peace, child."

Something about the way he said *one* made her look at him narrowly. *Does he know?*

She smiled weakly. "The Free Republic has many enemies, guru, some near, some far. If you can win us peace from them, you would do us a very great service."

"I will happily do what I can, my child," Ganesha said. "But the peace I am speaking of can only exist, or not exist—"

He extended his trunk and touched its tip between Moonchild's small breasts.

"—here."

The touch was so confident yet pure that she did not attempt to ward it off, and took no offense. She felt her eyes fill with tears. She lowered her head.

"If you can provide such peace," she whispered, "you are a miracle worker indeed."

"I—uh, I guess I'm intruding here, huh?" Croyd said. "Heh-heh."

Neither paid him any attention. He twitched his antennae and sidled out, chuckling to himself.

Moonchild felt the guru's warmth, smelled the perfumed oils with which his roly-poly person was anointed. "The gift is mine to give, my child," he said. "I am a *sat*-guru, a teacher of reality. Do you wish to learn?"

She jackknifed. The foreshocks of transition were upon her. *It never used to be this way.*

She jumped up, away from his outstretched hand. "I—I must beg permission to leave you, guru," she choked out, and bolted.

Mark came to himself in the bathroom off the parlor behind the audience hall, what he referred to internally as his changing-room. Moonchild had already gone to her knees on the cool tile, which saved him the risk of damaging them as he fell. He vomited into the chipped-enamel toilet.

When it was done and he felt a measure of strength return to his legs, he rose, went to the sink, splashed water in his face and rinsed his mouth. Then he raised his eyes to the mirror. He felt a visible resistance to *looking*, like a membrane stretched before his face. He made himself push through, and see.

The face was his own ... at least, it was the temporary face. The face he most often wore. Lined and haggard: the face of a tired specter.

"It's getting worse," he husked, his throat raw from puking. At least the voice that emerged was his own. He was getting regular aftershocks from the Moonchild persona now, talking in her voice even after the change, feeling her personality and thoughts swirling in confusion among his own for minutes, keeping him dizzy and unsure of his identity. It was the consequence of calling her too often.

But he had no choice. *She* was the President of Free Vietnam, probably the first who could be said to have been freely elected ever. He was merely her Chancellor.

She was an ace. And still, to most Central and South Vietnamese, a heroine. He was just a nat, whose own role in the Liberation was respected, but far overshadowed by Moonchild's.

He was her anointed spokesman. But in Asia appearance counted for much. For Moonchild to rule, to maintain a semblance of harmony among the tendentious and generally well-armed factions who formed her support base, she had to be *seen*.

What that was doing to Mark's mind and body ... He shook his head. He wanted to lie down and sleep forever.

In the audience chamber, serene, alone, and glowing, waited the guru. Mark felt a great longing well up within him, as great as the longings he had felt for his daughter during the years of enforced separation. Yet he could not bear to face Ganesha and his terrible calm.

Someone—French colonial official, American proconsul, Communist bureaucrat—had installed a phone in the bathroom. Mark picked it up, spoke in a frog voice to give instructions for the guru to be escorted from the hall and offered lodging for the night, and then lowered the toilet seat barely in time to collapse onto it.

Bent over a notebook computer held by a young joker in a colorful dashiki, Mark Meadows glanced up to see a man rolling through the bands of white sunlight sprayed onto the corridor walls by the windows at a purposeful amble that missed being a swagger by that much. He was much shorter than Mark, and a ways older, with a flamboyant seal-colored moustache with waxed tips, which showed far less gray than the hair cropped close to his squarish head. He wore a photojournalist's jacket over a pale yellow shirt, and baggy khaki trousers.

Mark smiled at the joker, sent him on his way with a thanks and a quick recommendation, then turned to meet the newcomer. "J. Bob," he said, smiling almost despite himself.

The man grinned beneath his moustache. "Guilty as charged. The minister without portfolio returns."

They shook hands. Because that gesture was inadequate for what existed between them, each man clasped the other quickly on the shoulder. Neither was comfortable with New Age touchy-feely rituals, though Mark felt somewhat guilty about the fact.

The two began to walk in the direction the moustached man had been headed, in the general direction of Mark's office.

"Have you heard the news?" Mark asked, his long face growing grave.

"Hartmann's revelations?" Major J. Robert Belew, United States Army Special Forces, retired, nodded. "JAL had it on the big screen as we were on final approach. Plane was packed with joker refugees out of Seattle, and there was much weeping and gnashing of teeth."

Mark looked at the smaller man. In many ways he represented everything Mark, the Last Hippie, had stood against since his stumbling into a kind of fitful political consciousness at the tag-end of the radical Sixties. This man—a palpable Green Beret Nam vet, conservative, authoritarian, militaristic, and self-describedly ruthless—was the most valued advisor to Vietnam's President, and her Chamberlain.

He was also Mark's best friend on Earth. Literally, with Tisianne—Tachyon—home ruling Takis.

"It's like you said all along, man. There is a conspiracy against us wild cards, and it reaches way up into the government."

"Given my experiences, it wasn't that hard to figure out: 'By their fruits shall ye know them,' to stay with Matthew." He shook his head. "At least the evil now has a name."

"Card Sharks."

Belew's moustache quirked to grin. "Got a ring to it, no? Ahh, I never thought I'd hate to be proved right. And by that limp liberal Hartmann, to boot."

"Gregg's a great man—" Mark began by reflex. Then he caught himself, rewound. "Well, he's a *good* man. The stress just got to be too much for him—"

"A man with good intentions, I'll grant," Belew said, "and recall what the road to Hell is paved with? Hartmann's a typical liberal politician. He looked to increase his own power by identifying himself with an ethnic minority, promoting its difference from mainstream America and its identity as a special interest group. That group happened to be *us*. And maybe he did the wild cards some good—but in the long run, the programs he helped push through gave Mr. Hardworking American Nat Taxpayer the impression that he was being bled to support a surly and uncontrollable super-race and an underclass of resentful monsters.

"That fractionalization of our society, which Hartmann so ably promoted and exploited, is one of the big reasons we're strangers in a strange land now, with planeloads more arriving each day. When you turn a nation into a collection of competing ethnicities, as the Welfare State has so ably accomplished, you generate *losers*. And we wild cards have duly lost."

Mark chewed on his lower lip. Reflex denials rose to the top of his throat and stayed there. He could take a look at Vietnam, before Liberation or after, and see the sick truth, that once a group became hipped on *ethnic pride* and *ethnic awareness*, it found it all too easy to slide on down the road to *ethnic cleansing*. Gregg Hartmann had made much of the common humanity of nats and wild cards; but the bulk of his actions had gone to emphasizing the difference.

He gave his head a small quick shake, like shedding water after a shower. *See what he does to you, man?* Belew liked to compare himself to Lucifer, and Mark could see the point; the master intriguer and shadow-operator could so easily lead Mark to stand his own most cherished beliefs on their head. It was why Mark could never *entirely* trust the man, for all that had passed between them.

"Unca Bob!" With a rainsquall patter of rubber soles on tile, a slim figure came flying down the hall to wrap Belew in a tangle of bare arms and legs and flying blond hair.

Belew was not a big man, but he was solidly built, thick through the chest, though he carried just the beginning of a paunch. The person who'd enwrapped him was several inches taller than he, and not light despite adolescent skinniness just beginning to fill out into adulthood. But he managed to absorb the happy impact without backing up more than two steps.

Mark looked on with a trace of wry envy. It was everything he could do not to go ass-over-teakettle when his daughter hit him like that. Sprout Meadows' mind was that of a four-year-old, perpetually, but her appearance was that of the fit and healthy seventeen year old she otherwise was.

With great gentleness Belew unwound the girl, who was smothering his face with kisses. She wore a white T-shirt with teddy bears on it, and cut-off shorts. "I'm happy to see you, too, Leaf. But let an old man breathe." She laughed musically and stepped away from him.

Leaf was his pet nickname for her. Sometimes it exasperated her, but she was happy now, and loved it.

"Where have you been?" she asked.

" 'Going to and fro in the earth, and walking up and down in it,' " he paraphrased. "Doing your Dad's bidding."

"Did you bring me something?" she asked.

He rubbed his chin, made a mouth, rolled his eyes as if at the effort of searching his memory. Sprout put her hands behind her back and tried not to writhe with impatience. Just when she was about to burst, Belew made a Groucho waggle of the eyebrows and stuck a hand into a pocket of his photojournalist's vest.

"I happened to run into this one day," he said, coming up with a palm-sized pink Gund polar bear arranged so that it appeared to be holding a box of Callard & Bowser's butterscotch in its lap. "She told me she belonged with Sprout Meadows, and would I please give her a ride to where you were. She had to twist my arm, but she talked me into it."

Sprout took the bear, hugged it to herself, kissed its forehead. Then she caught Belew's neck in a hug that would have choked a lesser man, and kissed his receding hairline. "Oh, Unca Bob! Thank you, thank you!"

Cradling the bear carefully between her breasts, she tore open the package. She offered it to her father, Belew, and the bear; politely refused by all three, she unwrapped a candy, popped it into her mouth, and began to suck on it with a blissful expression as she rocked her new toy.

"I wish you wouldn't give her sweets, man," Mark said. They set off again, Sprout swinging nonchalantly between them, cheeks concave. The whitewashed corridor had a hushed, cathedral quality to it, despite the maroon-tiled floors and a fair degree of traffic. A tiny wizened Nung woman with a scarf with penguins on it tied around her head looked up from her old-fashioned wringer-mounted mop bucket, nodded at Mark and smiled toothlessly as he passed. He smiled and nodded back. "I don't want her turning into a sugar junkie."

"Stuff. And nonsense. It's not as if she's getting loaded down with calories—she's almost as skinny as you are. Let the kid *live* a little."

Mark pouted. "Well—"

"And spare me the food-faddist 'ills of processed sugar' rap. You're a biochemist. You know perfectly well that sugar is sugar, just as a rose is a rose is a rose."

Despite himself, Mark chuckled. Had he truly objected to Belew giving his daughter candy, Belew would have cut it out in an instant. But chaffering like this was a standing routine, a way of bleeding existential tension from between two such unlikely friends and allies: the Last Hippie and the Last Cold Warrior.

"What did you find out?" Mark asked.

"Much of a muchness. The Canadians resent the Americans, but they buy into the 'aces, guns, drugs— scourge of our cities' rap almost as wholly as Barnett does. They'll vote against us at the UN, and try their best to honor the embargo if it goes through. The Japanese, on the other hand, think we're grotesque monsters, but that's not really all that far off how they feel about American nats. In any event, Japanese culture is to a large extent based on swallowing personal preference in pursuit of the bottom line, and naming that duty."

Mark started to frown, then grinned. Belew loved to make outrageous and sweeping generalizations, the more insensitive the better. At one time Mark would have responded with reflex liberal outrage. He wasn't so easily caught any more. Besides, Belew had a point.

"So the Japanese are smiling and nodding and making bland noises about how they have to 'consider the problem from every angle,' and stonewalling on the vote in the UN. Meanwhile, they're more than happy to trade with us—and that's unlikely to change if the embargo goes through."

"What about the Chinese?"

"The Dragon likes us, because we make Hanoi unhappy. As long as the Northerners are willing to bleed their populace to keep a million men under arms, the Chinese will do anything they can to keep a good percentage of those bad boys peering South. And they want the hard currency our economy's starting to generate, and they're big enough that they flat don't care what the rest of the world thinks. So there's a nice fat veto waiting for the embargo, whenever it hits the Security Council."

He raised his big, square hands. "The situation is far from ideal, I grant, but—"

They fetched up against a zone of humid heat like a force field trying to hold them back. The wall fell away to their right, opening into a courtyard garden ten yards square, with water singing down a pile of boulders into a mossy pool, and great-leaved plants crowded together amid a pervasive green smell. On a bench beside the pool sat Ganesha. He rose.

Belew froze in mid-step. "What're you doing here?"

"I am Ganesha."

"I know that. What I want to know is what you're doing here."

"Hey, ease off, man," Mark said, with unaccustomed sharpness, feeling tension pull his brows together. "He's my guest."

Belew made a mouth. "Is this another of your Sixties-nostalgia plunges? The guru you never had?"

Inside his head, a clamor of voices. Mark swayed. Sometimes it seemed he had a whole auditorium-load in there, instead of four—and another, hopefully buried so deep it would never surface again.

"He is my guest, Major." Mark's lips, Moonchild's voice. Not a falsetto, but an actual woman's voice, issuing from Mark's unquestionably masculine six-four frame. The others showed no response to the lapse. They had been coming frequently of late.

"You are the Minister, Major Belew," Ganesha said in his piping voice. "I have heard much of you."

From J. Bob's frown he turned to Sprout. "And what delightful creature have we here? Surely, it is an angel, all golden."

Sprout giggled. "I'm not an angel," she said, "I'm *Sprout*. This is my Daddy." She hugged Mark, laid her head briefly on his shoulder. "And this is my new pink bear. Are you a heffalump?" She always had trouble with the word, and fell back as usual on the *Winnie the Pooh* rendition.

"I am a man, little miss," Ganesha said to the girl. "But I am blessed with the head of an elephant."

"Oh." Her blue eyes lit. "Neat! Can I touch your nose?"

She reached a hand to the guru's pale trunk. It extended, twined once about her slim wrist to stroke the tanned back of her hand with its motile pink tip. She giggled.

"It is a wonderful child you have, Dr. Meadows," Ganesha said.

Belew frowned. Eyes and heart full, Mark could only nod.

"Rudo!" a voice bellowed. *"Ruuuuuudo!"*

Mark jumped. The sudden noise was like having a bulldozer crash into the Garden of Eden. He looked wildly left and right, one hand going around Sprout's shoulders, the other to the pocket that held the vials of powder in which resided his friends.

"Looks like Mr. Crenson finally switched on CNN," Belew remarked dryly.

Croyd appeared in the corridor, skidding slightly on the tile. Black taloned toes had burst through his shoes, and were interfering with his traction.

"That motherfucker," he raged. "I should have killed him. I'm *gonna* kill him."

Mark moved toward him. Croyd was far gone in the amphetamine psychosis of his waking phase's downside. His judgment was, to say the least, impaired.

"Here, man, I know how you feel," he said soothingly. "But are you sure you should, like, *rush into* anything?"

Croyd glared him back. "Don't try to stop me!" he shouted. "Don't give me any of your hippie-dippy love crap! Rip his fucking arms off and beat him to death with 'em—*that's* what I'm gonna do!"

"My child," Ganesha said mildly, "there is so much violence and misery in the world. Do you truly want to increase them? Would you be happier walking the path of peace?"

Croyd held out two fingers in a V. "Peace?"

He turned the fingers toward his face and stared between them at the guru with one burning yellow eye. "Peace on *you*, fatso! I'm outta here!"

"No, I don't want a drink," Croyd Crenson cackled to the pretty mahogany-faced stewardess as the Indonesian Air Lines 747 banked over the South China Sea. He had the anechoic cavern of coach virtually to himself; there was not much demand for flights leaving Saigon these days. "But if you got any *crank*—"

In his office in the villa he occupied to keep his people—Moonchild's people—happy, Mark had a desk. It was a fine old desk, exquisitely carved of oak, imported by some colonialist and well-cherished the last few years by some Party functionary as one of the perqs of life under revolutionary socialism. It wasn't unusually big, not like the half-acre Power Desks you'd find in corporate HQs in New York—or that he imagined you'd find there, anyway—but grand withal, definitely appropriate to his dual role as President and Chancellor of Free Vietnam. Mark chose not to sit behind the desk, but beside it, in a plain wooden chair, holding his forehead with thumb and forefinger.

The air-conditioning kept more than the awful Saigon heat at bay. It also muted the cries and chanting of the crowd of protestors outside.

Belew stood at the window with his hands in his pockets, gazing at the well-dressed mob without the walls. "That actor still hanging around?"

Mark nodded. A certain fading blond ingenue American actor with a penchant for trendy causes and socialist dictators had blown into town a few days before Belew. With so many of his old cronies unseated and facing indictment for things like murder and embezzlement on a Cyclopean scale, the last several years had not been kind to him. So he had come to identify himself with the dispossessed and downtrodden of Moonchild's regime: the former bureaucrats and Party members from the old days, who wanted their jobs and their privilege back.

Like a membrane around the protest stood a cordon of police in riot gear. They weren't there to keep the demonstrators in line. They were there to keep the much larger mob of Saigon citizens beyond from falling on the Party folk and beating the crap out of them.

"We have troubles enough," Belew said. "Maybe it's time to take up arms against them. Why don't you let me whack him, make it look like Hanoi did it. He hasn't made a decent movie for years."

Mark stared at him. Belew, half-turned from the window, regarded him with that studied infuriating blandness he displayed when he didn't intend to let you know if he was serious or not. Mark felt a stab of fury: *How dare he still test me, after all these years!*

And of course he felt instantly contrite. *It's the strain, man, I'm sorry.*

Mark, came JJ Flash's voice, gentle for once, *you didn't say anything. No need to apologize to the man.*

He shook his head. When he glanced at Belew again, the man's expression had gone from bland to blank. The older man was trying to mask pity and concern, and that pissed Mark off all over again.

"Forget it," he said with a wave of his hand. "The way the world media treat us, we'd get blamed for it even if Hanoi *did* do it, man."

Belew laughed. "There was a time when you'd have tried to talk me out of it on purely humanitarian grounds."

"Hanging around with you has made me worse."

"Something else that's getting worse," Belew said, "is our old friend Colonel Nguyen, up in the Highlands. He's starting to lean on the Montagnards and make noises about bolting to Hanoi."

"He wouldn't do that." To hang onto their own power in the face of the sucessful revolt of the South and increasing dissatisfaction in the North, the aging rulers of the rump Socialist Republic of Vietnam had resorted to increasingly savage repression. "They're like Nazis up there."

"Hitler was a socialist, after all. And Nguyen probably doesn't take their kill-the-wild-cards all that personally, since he's a nat in good standing."

"Yeah, but they're also liquidating anybody they even suspect of disloyalty. He *fought* against them. How can he expect they'd do anything but knife him, first chance they got?"

Belew laughed. " The capacity for self-deception in those who believe themselves practical men of politics is limitless. It's one of the great forces of nature. Besides, as I'm fond of saying, politics makes strange bedfellows; look at our other old friend, Dong, the ex-Saigon crime-lord. Since you bankrupted his racket by legalizing drugs, he's in the vest pocket of both the DEA and Hanoi, all the while running smack from the old Golden Triangle CIA plantations in Thailand."

"So you think he's serious?"

Belew shrugged. "He wants Moonchild to kiss him and tell him how important he is." Initially skeptical of Moonchild's leadership of the revolt, Nguyen had turned into a fervent admirer. He had spent the last couple of years growing progressively sulkier that his change of heart hadn't won him a look at what Moonchild had beneath that slinky black outfit.

"No way, man. I've gotta find something to do with all these refugees. And the violence keeps getting worse. A gang beat an Austrian joker to death on the street in Cholon last night."

Anti-wild card zealots were in a definite minority in the South; most Vietnamese, urban and rural alike, did not really love the jokers, but what they wanted first and foremost was to be left alone. Moonchild's regime gave them that, for the first time in at least a century.

But the really determined few were a nasty lot. They were getting open encouragement from Hanoi and covert help from America—and no doubt from the Card Sharks.

Belew nodded. "Somebody blew the doors off Rick's Café American with a hand grenade a couple of days ago." Rick's was a popular wild card hangout in down-town Saigon, off Freedom Street. "Just like the good old days. Look, why don't I make a trip up north, show the flag, lay down some law to our rambunctious colonel, reassure the 'Yards that we have no intention of letting the Viets beat up on them?"

Mark felt tension blow out of him in a gusty sigh. Not all of it. But some. "Yeah. Would you do that? Please?" He found himself almost pleading, eyes misty that someone was sharing the strain.

Belew started to leave, caught himself at the door, turned back. "There is something else."

Mark felt the muscles at the back of his neck go rigid. "Not Ganesha again."

"Listen to me. There's something very wrong with this picture."

"It's *okay*, man," Mark forced himself to say calmly, "really. He's just a guest of Moonchild. It's not like he's taking over my mind or anything."

"He's been thrown out of half the petty kingdoms in India," Belew said, "and all the not-so-petty ones. He won't show his face in Europe any more. He's *persona non grata* in Hong Kong and Singapore. There's something going on."

"What about America?"

Belew snorted a laugh. "He's not stupid, our Hosenose. He learned from the example of the Reverend Sun Myung Moon, the Bhagwan Rajneesh, and Dwight Gooden."

Mark raised an eyebrow at his friend. "Okay, man. Lay it on me. What do they have in common?"

"Got busted for being NIBCs, Mark," J. Bob said. "Niggers in big cars."

Mark made a face. "See, man? There's the problem there. It's prejudice, man. That's why he keeps getting chased out of places. You *know* how unpopular the wild cards are. The Sharks are probably on his case."

"Let's not get hypnotized, here; there'd be plenty of anti-wild card sentiment loose in the world without the help of a conspiracy."

"Ganesha's a victim of it. He's discriminated against because he's a joker."

"Not in *India,* Mark. If you draw an ace, it's because of good karma, and a joker means you're working off a mighty negative load all at once. Either way, you're holy. India's the only place in the Third World they don't treat jokers as kindling with legs. They *love* Hosenose there. He has upwards of two million followers scattered across the subcontinent."

"Don't call him 'Hosenose,' man. You're making fun of his disability."

" 'Disability?' Mark, he's the spit and image of a *god.* If there wasn't something funny going on, the Hindu kingdoms would all have put their little squabbles aside so he could rule them and lead them in squashing their Muslim neighbors."

"He'd never do that. He's a man of peace."

"He's a man of *something,* I'll grant you that." Belew shoved a dossier in a gray-green folder that lay on the corner of the desk toward Mark. "But I'm having Beelzebub's own time finding out just what. All I've gotten so far is a stack of press clippings. But I'm putting some inquiries out, to Interpol and some of my old buddies in the business. Of course, I'm having to be mighty roundabout, inasmuch as we're an 'outlaw regime' and all."

Mark pulled his head up. "Hey! Lay off him, man."

"I'm your national security adviser, Mark," Belew said evenly, "not to mention your chief bodyguard. You have a couple million bucks in prices on your head right now. When an ace with a mysterious past and even more mysterious powers starts hanging around the palace, it's my business to run a little background check."

"What do you mean, ace? He's a joker."

"So's Peregrine," Belew said, "but she sure can fly. Mark, he made a BMP disappear. I wish it had been that easy back when we were going *mano a mano* with the evil empire, let me tell you. And he surrounds himself with imaginary friends like the Apsarases, that you can see and talk to and even touch, and go away without a trace when he's through with them. What do you call somebody who can do things like that? David Copperfield?"

Mark's half-open hands waved in air, shaping vague clay. "He's, like, a holy man."

Belew sighed and sat on the corner of the desk. "You never had a guru, did you?" he asked with deceptive gentleness. "Back when the Beatles and the Who and everybody and his dog was trooping East for Enlightenment. You missed that scene, too, didn't you? You managed to get in on the peace-love-dope trip, back when everybody else was switching to burn-baby-burn. But you never did manage to jump on the old swami bandwagon."

"Stop it."

The words were spoken in a flat, hard tone, the way rapping a baton on the desk might have sounded. It was a voice Mark would never have believed of himself, before the last couple of years. Takis, Europe, the flight to the Nam, the war he had stumbled into leading. . . . He had seen many changes, in his world and in himself, and not all were for the better.

Belew's full lips worked briefly beneath his moustache. Mark watched him, feeling his anger-spike subside. Belew was a man who generally placed his words as he did his bullets, with precision and care; but it seldom took him so long to aim either.

"If he's a powerful ace, does that really matter?" Mark said, leaping in. "Or have you suddenly turned into an advocate of ace control?"

Belew slapped his hands down on his khaki-clad thighs. "For an old hippie burn-out, you turn in a fair imitation of a Jesuit, Mark." He stood.

"How would you know? You're an Episcopalian."

"But us High-Church Anglicans are Catholic wanna-bes, remember. We keep a close eye on the bead rattlers. You Methodists wouldn't know about that."

Mark laughed. Stopping going to church was perhaps the first of his few adolescent acts of rebellion. It was futile as the rest. When his father came home on leave from commanding a tactical fighter wing in Nam, he didn't even notice.

At the door Belew paused. " 'Fine words and an insinuating appearance are seldom associated with true virtue,' " he said. "There's Eastern wisdom for you: Confucius his bad self."

Polishing his wire-rim glasses on the hem of his shirt, Mark looked up at him. "With the Doc back on Takis," he said, "you're the slickest talker *and* the snappiest dresser I know, man."

Shaking his hand in half-mock exasperation, J. Bob shut the door and was gone.

Faces. Who am I?

Faces. Where am I? Where am I going? What will become of me.

In the swirling black there is no answer: only faces. K.C. Strange with her silver eyes. Durg at-Morakh. Starshine. Eric the Dreamer. Starshine. Colonel Sobel?

Why do you look at me? Am I you? Was I you.

"You killed us," the faces say, a growling chorus. They are joined by more, an infinity of faces, shifting, swirling, becoming one another in a kaleidoscope display: Takisian faces, Vietnamese faces, joker faces, nat faces.

"You killed us. And we are you."

No!

Other faces superimpose above the maelstrom, so close he can feel their breath: Moonchild in her black half-mask; JJ Flash; Cosmic Traveler's blue face, itself infinitely mutable, shadowed within the cowl of his cloak of stars; Aquarius' gray face, stolid, smooth, and disapproving.

"You have trapped us," Traveler says. "We are your victims too."

"You must release us to pursue our own karma," says Moonchild. "You must not hold onto us for your own selfish purposes."

JJ Flash says, "I wanna live my own life. Not be a sometime stooge for a burnt-out old hippie." Aquarius says nothing at all.

In the background, a clamor; familiar voices, vying for attention. He recognizes the chorus from the back of his skull. Aren't they already talking to him? He concen-trates, looks past the faces of his friends, which scatter

to the corners of the Universe with mocking laughter.
Beyond them he sees . . . their true faces?

A glimpse, no more; and then a giant fanged mouth,
yellow-orange with the flames of Hell and rushing toward
him with locomotive speed. He smells the stink of brim-
stone and corruption and turns to flee—

—He is caught up, swallowed, swept up and up and
up, till he towers two hundred feet above the ground,
and on his head are upswept horns, and thrusting from
his loins is a hard-on the size of a Greyhound bus, and
burning in his belly is the lust to slay and maim and
rape the world while it lies at his feet.

And at his feet lies Sprout, naked and cowering. He
bends toward her, erection quivering, stretches out a
hand with human meat decaying beneath black claws—

"No!"

—Mark sat bolt upright, wet as though he'd just
emerged from a swimming pool, throat hoarse from the
scream that woke him. Sprout, wearing a long T-shirt,
clung to his neck crying, "Daddy, Daddy!" He tried to
soothe her, but she could only sob.

Then he smelled incense and heard cool music, and
looked up. Ganesha stood above his bed, great ears out-
spread in darkness. He held forth a lotus bloom.

"Dreamless sleep," the guru said, "is the gift of the
gods. It may be attained as an elevated form of *samadhi,*
through meditation."

Slowly Mark unwound his clawed hands from the
sheets. He slid an arm around his daughter. He held the
palm of his other hand up to accept the flower.

"Can you teach me, man?" he asked.

The great head nodded. "I can."

"*Hold it!* Don't move!" A shout from the doorway,
Western and angular and strident after the lilt of Ganesha's voice. Belew stood there in nightshirt and skivvies,
holding his handgun leveled two-handed at the center of
Ganesha's back.

"It's—I'm okay, J. Bob," Mark said. "It was the dream
again."

"I gathered. What's he doing here?"

"Just trying to help out, man," Mark said, annoyed at his friend's obtuseness.

"Indeed. How'd he get *in* here? Your door's *gone*, Mark!"

"I am the Remover of Obstacles," Ganesha said placidly. He smiled at Sprout, who brushed back tear-sodden bangs to smile tentatively back at him.

"That's not much of an answer, my friend," J. Bob said, not taking the gun off him.

"Come *on*, man," Mark said.

The air around J. Bob was suddenly filled with fluttering brightness. He jumped back as they swarmed around him, lashed out with his pistol. The cold steel mass struck one. It fell to the wooden floor at his feet and lay, feebly opening and closing brightly colored, self-luminous wings.

"You need not react so violently, my friend," Ganesha said, "inasmuch as they are only butterflies."

A violet and yellow one landed on Sprout's nose. She giggled.

J. Bob stood for a moment, looking at Mark through the shifting, glowing cloud. Then he let the hammer down on his pistol, turned, and stalked off to bed.

A week later J. Robert Belew came back. Fatigue and the aching in his joints reminded him that he was not as young as he used to be. Nonetheless, he carried a glow of satisfaction in the pit of his stomach. He had reassured the Montagnards, chastised the colonel, and ambushed and destroyed a squad of North Vietnamese infiltrators. He had gotten out in the *field* again, and he still had his licks.

Then he came to the former ballroom which served Mark as his audience chamber, and stopped as if a Lexan barrier sealed the doorway.

J. Bob had never cared for the hippie hangings Mark affected to take the totalitarian edge off Moonchild's dealings with the public. They were nothing to what assailed his aesthetic sense now.

The room was the picture of Hindu Heaven, straight

out of a hopelessly garish mid-Seventies Hare Krishna broadsheet. It was all gaud and gold and ivory, well-bangled celestial maidens playing upon the flute, the *kartal* cymbals and *mridanga* drums; bright-pinioned birds and flowers everywhere of hues so bright it hurt to look at them. In the midst of it all sat Ganesha, fat and smug, with one of those beaded Indian elephant head-harnesses strung over his Indian elephant head. Next to him, eyes shut, Moonchild floated in full lotus, eighteen inches in the air.

"There are, my daughter, many varieties of *maya*," the guru was explaining. "In the latter days, after wise Shankara sought to reconcile Hinduism with Buddhism, *maya* came to be understood by many as meaning illusion, pure and simple. Yet there is an older meaning, woven through the *Vedas*, by which *maya* is the creative energy of nature and gods. And Nature, while it is real through the will and eternal presence of Brahma, is yet real enough.

"This is my poor power: a humble measure of the creative *maya*."

"So this world is not mere illusion, guru?" murmured Moonchild.

"It is, and it is not. Hold out your hand."

She did so. A yellow rose materialized in her palm. Her fingers closed around its stem.

Her eyes opened in surprise. A drop of red welled from the ball of her thumb where a thorn had pricked it. She sucked the blood away.

"The world is as real as that rose," the guru said. "If it pricks you, you bleed."

The rose vanished. Moonchild took her thumb from her mouth. A tiny drop of fresh blood ballooned from the puncture.

Belew stood leaning against the doorjamb with his arms folded over his chest. "So what?" he said. "So you can make her levitate. JJ Flash can *fly*."

Moonchild looked up with a start, then instantly dropped her eyes, as if in guilt. Ganesha laughed and laughed. Belew unfolded his arms and entered the room.

A slim figure in a saffron robe barred his way. The

features were almost Takisian in fineness, the hair shaved to a russet scalplock. Belew couldn't tell whether the figure was male or female.

"What do you want here, machine?" the figure asked in a lisping hermaphrodite German accent.

"I'm this woman's head bodyguard," Belew said, looking the yellowrobe over without evident favor. "Now I'm intent on moseying over to guard her body closer up . . . whether or not I have to walk over yours."

Ganesha giggled and waved. The yellowrobe drew back gracefully, with a graceful sneer of contempt. Belew mastered the impulse to tread on its toes as he walked into the room.

"Sandalwood?" he said, sniffing. "Isis, I thought Old Hippie taste was bad. But *this*—?"

"Isn't it wonderful?"

Belew sighed. "What's with the she-males?" he asked, gesturing at the wispy forms in saffron robes, draped artistically about the chamber. "Are they real too, guru?"

"My *sannyasi* are as real as you yourself."

"Some mornings," Belew said, digging in the many pockets of his vest, "I wonder."

"Guru is a teacher of reality," Moonchild said. "Perhaps he can teach you as well."

"Thank you, Madam President." Moonchild flushed and dropped her eyes from Belew's. She always found it difficult to look her Minister in the eye. "But Reality herself has taught me of her myriad ways, and a harsh schoolmistress she is."

He produced a cigar and a cutter, snipped the end, fished in a pocket again. "But what was that about 'machine?'"

"There are different kinds of *maya*, as Guru was just explaining," the door-keeper said languidly from behind Belew. "His *maya* is creative *maya*, natural *maya*. Yours is the *maya* of Western linear thought. The *maya* of the machine." The yellowrobe sniffed. "The true illusion. Special effects."

"Indeed." Belew produced an ancient Zippo lighter, gleaming and metal, held it up like a magician a card.

"Well, that's appropriate in my case—" Holding the cigar in his teeth he stuck his right thumb in the cigar cutter and nipped the tip off. Blood pulsed, flowed down his hairy wrist.

"—because I'm the ace of the machine." He stuck the lighter firmly on the bleeding thumbtip. It stuck. As if of its own accord, it opened its cover. Its wheel turned, striking flame. Belew bent forward and lit his cigar.

"Oh, *please*," the yellowrobe said. Belew turned and blew a cloud of smoke into its ethereal face. It doubled in a coughing fit.

A man-high sunflower swiveled on its stem, bringing its black face to bear on Belew. He turned back to Moonchild and the guru, bringing the cigar to his lips.

The sunflower shot a stream of water full into his face, extinguishing the cigar with a hiss and melting his moustache into sad wet-bird wings.

Ganesha and his *sannyasi* laughed and laughed.

Hot afternoon. Walking the corridor, face darkened by his thoughts, Belew caught a murmur of voices from the garden. He paused, and then without the least self-consciousness had edged to the beginning of the arcaded walkway that surrounded the garden, peered around the corner. As security chief, he was privileged to lurk as he pleased around the Palace.

Ganesha sat on the stone bench with Sprout arranged beside him, pointing into the water of the pool. "See the fish, with his veil fins, so colorful and lovely," he said in a singsong murmur. "So does *atman* swim in Nirvana, in perfect freedom and release."

Sprout clapped her hands together. "Pretty!"

"Now look, my child," Ganesha said. "Hold out your hands."

Sprout obeyed. A large plush stuffed fish like a rainbow-hued fancy goldfish materialized in air, dropped softly into them. She gaped, astonished, then hugged it to her cheek.

"Oh, thank you, Unca Neesha! Thank you, thank you!"

"Does it find favor, O jewel child?"

She set the toy down between them to gather him into a fervent hug. "Oh yes! I love it! I love *you*, Unca Neesha!"

A shudder ran visibly through the guru's plump body then. Watching around the corner, Belew marked the way Ganesha's eyes caressed the very grown-up breasts, swelling the girl's white T-shirt under pressure from his own chest. The line of Belew's jaw grew harder.

With obvious reluctance Ganesha pushed Sprout away. "Now, my child, observe once again the fish in his pond, serene. See how he changes color—"

Obedient, she leaned well out over the pond, then exclaimed delightedly again as the fish, apparently, performed as advertised. What she did not see was Ganesha twitch aside the hem of the white robe he wore today, pluck a stuffed fish identical to the one he had materialized from beneath the bench, and slam it into the place of the materialization, which duly vanished just as Sprout straightened.

A strange sensation came over Belew then—the sense of being *observed*, which he had learned long ago to honor. He ducked back.

From the far end of the garden, where the corridor moved indoors again, a figure in a yellow robe was watching Belew watch the guru. Belew straightened. He nodded to the *sannyas*, turned, and walked away, not too fast.

Inside, he seethed.

In his Spartan bedchamber, Mark sat lotus on his big colonial brass bed, rocking forward and back, pounding his thighs with knotted fists, tears pouring down his baby-red face.

"Oh, Guru, Guru," he moaned. "I've looked inside myself and seen what's there. It's *evil*. Ultimate darkness." He pounded his skinny chest. "In me."

He raised his head and looked at Ganesha through a cataract of tears. "Do you know what it's like, Guru? *Do you?*"

Ganesha's huge head nodded. "Yes, my son. I do."

Mark blinked, eyes as innocent as Sprout's. "And you overcame the darkness? You cleansed yourself of evil."

"I did," the Guru said. But his head turned away from Mark, ever so slightly, so that the pupil could not see what passed behind the master's eyes.

Belew had his own office near Mark's. It was modest in size, the walls hung with high-quality reproductions of paintings by Dutch masters: Rembrandt, macabre Brueghel, the vans Eyck and Dyck—but never Rubens, whom he considered too much of a good thing. His only presumption upon his status was a grand recliner chair, in which he could listen to music: Vivaldi, Verdi, or Van Halen, for his tastes were as diverse as his talents.

His fax machine was busy disgorging a stack of papers. He knocked the dottle from his pipe, filled, tamped, relit. Then he squared a sheaf on the table beside him, held it up before his face, and carefully settled a pair of reading-glasses on his occasionally broken nose. It was a pity, but the regenerative gift which was already budding out a new pink tip to the thumb he'd truncated as a parlor trick yesterday, could only buffer him against so many of the ravages of that old devil, Time.

He read for an interval. Then he set his pipe aside and read the pages carefully through once more. Then he set them aside, tilted his head back, massaged the bridge of his nose with thumb and forefinger.

"Was I fearing to see something like this," he asked the ceiling, "or hoping?"

Because he would not lie to himself, he silently answered *yes* to both questions. Then he rose and looked for his shoes.

The Vietnamese activist and the American joker spokesman stood in the audience hall and yelled at each other through interpreters. Moonchild stared from one to another in growing horror. She understood both languages well enough, yet she could not grasp what either was saying. It was as if she were trapped in a dream, one of those dreams when people look at you earnestly and mouth words, but all you hear are inchoate sounds, unintelligible as surf.

She glanced aside at guru, who stood beside her chair of state. He nodded slightly, smiled, and she felt warmth suffuse her.

He strengthens me with his darshan, *his presence*, she thought. *He reassures me that there are answers, even if I have to grope for them myself. . . .*

Yet she still felt that desperate dislocation. Still the disputants' words held no meaning. She felt *otherness* ripple across her like a shockwave packet from a distant earthquake, as the other personalities all threatened to burst the seams of her consciousness and come tumbling in at once.

Guru says there is a cure for that, too. The cure for all my—our—problems. I can make that sacrifice. Can the others?

You better believe not, an internal voice was responding, male and angry, when she looked up and saw J. Bob standing in the door.

"You seemed to be in something of a hurry to get out of there, Madam President," J. Bob said, standing in the corridor outside. "Not deriving the same serenity from the Presence as you used to?"

"I believe you wished to talk to me," Moonchild said coolly.

Belew nodded crisply. "This just came in. You and Mark might be interested in it. Mark especially."

Eyeing him sidelong, which was not her usual style at all, Moonchild accepted a sheaf of printout from Belew, began to flip the pages up.

"There's still not much concrete in there," Belew said. "No surprise; the money that flows into your pal's coffers from the faithful will buy a supertanker load of Third World justice of the blind variety, if you catch my drift. What's significant is that as much shows up as does.

"Especially since in India, frankly, they're pretty casual about sex with children. Holy men have near *carte blanche*. And at least Hosenose generally goes for early teens, not eight-year-olds. Have to give him that."

Moonchild glared at him. She tore the document in two with a petulant flip of her wrists.

"With a little practice," Belew said, watching the torn sheets flutter to the marble floor, "you'll work your way up to the Manhattan phonebook."

When his eyes found hers again Moonchild's anger was gone, replaced by sadness deep as arthritis. "I would not have believed it of you, Major Belew," she said softly. "But perhaps I should have expected it. Your fascist tendencies have finally gotten the better of you."

"Fascist?"

"To resort to such slander, simply because you feel threatened by Guru's antimaterialism." She shook her head. "There is much good in you, I still know that. Yet, as Mark might say, once a fascist, always a fascist."

She turned and vanished back into her audience chamber. Belew stood staring at the door for perhaps a minute. Then he laughed at himself for standing there like an adolescent left on the stoop without so much as a good-night kiss, and went up to bed.

Morning in the garden. Sprout stood on an inch of air. Her golden hair was caught in a ponytail. Her cheeks glowed like dawn.

"What I do, little miss," Ganesha was saying, "is create a layer of air beneath the soles of your lotus feet. Only it is not quite air, but something more substantial. And this do I add to, layer upon layer, until you, my little pretty one, are levitating." He knelt beside her on the white sand of the little path.

She smiled and nodded. Also fidgeted. She didn't really see the point to this. But her Daddy had taught her always to be nice, and Unca Neesha was always nice to her. She would play along for now.

"Sometime, perhaps, you would care to play in the evening," Ganesha said. "We could go somewhere outside the Palace—"

"Oh, I always go to bed at—" She briefly consulted

her fingers. "—at eight. Daddy doesn't make me. But it makes him happy."

Ganesha rose with a soft grunt of effort. "You are a dear child, to serve your father so well," he said. "Yet sometimes, well—what he does not know does not hurt him, don't they say, after all?"

"Learning to fly, Leaf?" a voice asked from behind them. The guru stiffened.

"Oh, Unca Bob," Sprout said. "You know my name's not Leaf. I told you."

J. Robert Belew slapped the side of his head with hand's heel. "Guess I forgot. Must be getting old." He grinned at her. "Feel like riding a horse, or would you rather hang there in midair?"

She clapped her hands together. "A horsie, really?" He nodded.

" 'Bye, Unca Neesha!" Sprout jumped down from her invisible pedestal and ran toward the soldier, who took her by the hand and led her away.

Ganesha, Remover of Obstacles, looked darkly after. Tiny malformed things appeared in the air, and flew buzzing around his vast-eared head.

For the next few days Belew stayed well out of Mark's way. He didn't stay out of Ganesha's. Whenever the guru contrived to get Sprout alone Belew appeared out of the woodwork with some new game or diversion.

J. Bob gave her a toy train and a six-foot panda. She enjoyed both gifts with a child's single-mindedness. But Belew, who was not as proud of the job he had done raising his own two children as he was of most things in his life, perceived that he could not bribe her.

On the other hand . . . it was clear that, throughout her life, she had never had as much of a father as she might have wanted. That was not to say that Mark was a failure as a father or a man; far from it. For all his hippie ways and New Age outlook, for all the fact that the first obstacle course he ran would be his last by reason of gasping death, Mark was a real man to J. Bob, who had an unfashionably archaic view of such things.

More, he was a real father. Mark had given everything for his daughter's sake that a man could give and still be able to draw breath. It was more, candidly, than J. Robert Belew had ever done in the role.

But like many another parent who would give anything for his or her child's welfare, Mark had never entirely known how to give *himself* to her. He loved her, cherished her. But he had never really learned to spend time with her.

Belew had never known how to spend time with his own children. But he wasn't too old a dog to learn.

As often as he interrupted Ganesha, he found himself observed by the surly yellow robed *sannyasi* who haunted the Palace. *Let them look,* he told himself. *Nothing they see will bring much comfort to old Hosenose.*

"Master."

The yellowrobes had been chased from the ballroom. The *maya* splendor was still intact, save for the Apsarases, who had been sent packing back into immateriality. This was a private occasion.

"Yes, my son."

"I—I would become your disciple. I would take *diksha,* and have my mantra from you."

"And do you understand what this initiation entails?"

"Renunciation, Master."

"And do you realize what you must renounce?"

"I must renounce the world, and my will."

"That is not all, my son. To become my disciple truly, you must become a *sannyas.* You must become celibate. You must give over choice and preference."

"I am prepared."

"You must give over the becoming what you call your 'friends.' You must put them all aside, and put them all from your mind."

Mark hesitated, hearing a defiant chorus in the back of his head. "And will I—will we all win freedom by my doing that, each of us to work out his or her own karma?"

"You shall."

"And I shall receive forgiveness? And ... forgetfulness?"

"All these things."

Mark bowed his head. "I am ready to receive my mantra, Master."

" Tomorrow."

Mark started to raise his head. The guru wagged a chubby finger. "No, no. You are surrendering your will entirely to God, through me. Remember?"

Mark nodded.

" Tomorrow it shall be."

" Tomorrow."

"And now, my son, there is something else I must speak with you about, something of the gravest concern."

The guru's high, musical voice seemed to catch. Mark looked up at him in wonder and dismay.

"It is with great sadness that I must speak to you of your friend J. Robert's unnatural and unholy interest in your virgin daughter, Sprout. . . ."

"Sprout. Sprout, now, settle down." The girl in the garden writhed and wriggled and laughed aloud at Belew's efforts to disloge her from his knee. "Sprout, this isn't dignified. And anyway, you're heavy."

"Am not. Am not. Unca Neesha says I'm slender as a willow branch. Whatever *that* means."

It means he's a disgusting tentacle-faced old pervert, Belew thought.

"Sprout," Belew said, trying not to be aware himself of the long, slim bare legs straddling his lap, or the full breasts bouncing around inside her sweater like puppies in a sack. "Sprout. You're a wonderful child. I—ouch—I understand that part of being a wonderful child is to be a brat sometimes, inasmuch as perfection is boring. But still, if you don't climb off Unca Bob's lap *right now*, Unca Bob is going to turn you over and tan your behind."

But Sprout was full of love and mischief this bright afternoon, and so she decided to act the way she'd seen grownups do, on TV and sometimes in person. She grabbed Belew by the head and planted a kiss full on his lips.

"Belew!"

Belew's hands froze to claws on the girl's biceps. He had never heard that rage-choked voice before. All the same, he knew it belonged to Mark Meadows.

Sprout was still giggling and trying to kiss him. For all her near-adult weight, he picked her up by the arms and set her to the side. She saw her father standing in the arcade with Ganesha, ran happily to them.

"Take her," Mark snapped to two of the armed jokers who accompanied him. "Take her someplace . . . someplace safe."

"Daddy?" she called as she was hustled away. "Daddy, what's the matter? Daddy, I'm *scared!*"

"Don't worry, honey," Mark said darkly. "You'll be all right now."

He turned a look of perfect loathing on Belew. "I should have known," he said. "What they said about you right-wing military types—it was true all along."

Ganesha laid a hand on his arm. "Do not judge him too harshly, my son," he said. "Sometimes the lust of older men for innocence comes to overpower their judgment. So it can be, when one has not learned to live without desire."

The six remaining jokers leveled their Kalashnikovs at Belew. He raised his hands.

"Just shoot me now," he suggested.

"Maybe later," Mark said, and turned away.

"Unca Neesha," Sprout asked, "where are we going?"

The elephant head swiveled left and right as the guru checked the hall. "Out to play, my child. Do not be afraid."

"But it's after dark. And Daddy told me to stay in my room."

He smiled at her. "He meditates. But he decided you could go with me. It's all right." The trunk tip chucked her beneath the chin. "You trust your Uncle Neesha, don't you?"

She nodded solemnly.

"Then let us go. It will be such a marvelous adventure."

* * *

"There is something damned well wrong with this picture," Mark's mouth said; and then his voice said, "Dammit, JJ, I resent you taking over control like that."

Somebody's got to get us back on track. We're all in this together, buddy. You can't just throw us aside, shave your head, and forget about us.

"I—JJ, I'm sorry. But this is driving me insane. I don't know who I am anymore."

We're always going to be here, came the waspish thought from the Traveler. *You can't get rid of us so easily.*

You already tried, *back when you were trying to be clean and sober to get custody of Sprout,* JJ Flash thought. *One worked about as well as the other.*

Mark sat on his bed, stork legs pulled up. He held his head in both hands.

"What happens if my mind just snaps?" he asked.

How would any of us tell the difference? Trav shot back.

Be honest with yourselves, JJ, Traveler, Moonchild said. *Have you never resented your imprisonment? Have you never wished you could be free of the confines of another's skull?*

You know it, baby, JJ Flash said.

Then why do you resist? Perhaps Guru can find a way to liberate us to pursue our own karma.

What if we don't have our own karma? JJ asked. *Remember how you couldn't understand Korean? The language you supposedly grew up speaking? What happens if we're just fantasy figments, or symptoms of the world's best-realized multiple personality disorder? What happens to us then?*

Perhaps we can be reintegrated into one whole again, Moonchild said. *Perhaps we can know peace.*

Yeah, JJ said with a sneer, *Nirvana. Smells like personal extinction to me, babe. That's what the Big Goal is, after all—flipping off the wheel of birth and death and getting to be nothing. Me, I'd feel cheated. I'd at least like to give the wheel a spin or two in my own improper person.*

"JJ," Mark said, "I'd switch places with you if I could. Really, I would. The stress, inside and out—I can't take it any more."

He beat his hands lightly on the bedclothes. "I'd accept nonbeing," he whispered, "in a minute."

What about the Radical? Flash asked.

"That was a long time ago. The human body replaces all its cells on a seven-year cycle; what was that, three bodies ago? And who knows how many lifetimes. Starshine's, for one. Maybe it's time to give up on that. I've never known if I even *was* the Radical, man. Maybe it's time to quit pretending."

Mark—Moonchild said.

"Yeah. I know. It's sad when dreams die." He stood up, paced around his small, bare room. "Or maybe I'll find the purity I've been lacking so long; maybe Guru can help me get the Radical back, and he'll be . . . greater than the sum of his parts."

The sound of half a mind thinking, JJ said, *is rationalization.*

"Call it what you will. Naming a thing doesn't change it." He shook his head. "I'm gonna check on my little girl. Then I'm going to get some sleep. And tomorrow—"

He paused with one bony hand on the door. "Tomorrow, my life begins anew."

He knew it sounded tacky. But he'd live with it.

Because he wasn't sure exactly what extremities he might need this night, he bit off the tip of his left little finger to take control of the door lock of the room he'd been imprisoned in.

His cell was on the third floor, in front. The window could not be locked from the outside, obviously, but there was no ready way down to the ground but surrender to gravity. Belew was confident in his abilities to say the least, but he knew he wasn't a movie hero, to scramble down the rain gutters, or whatever, three stories to the front courtyard, without falling and busting his fool neck. Besides, one of the sentries out front would likely spot him—and they were jokers, which meant their loyalty was to Mark first.

Like all machines, though, the lock was his to take. From listening at the door he knew that there was a bored pair of guards on watch. Piece of cake.

He opened the door and walked out. The guards were slouched against the walls, weapons slung, smoking illicit cigarettes. They gaped at him.

While they waited for their synapses to snap, he busted the nose of the right-hand guard with a backfist, then grabbed his sling and spun him around in a semicircle in front of him to slam into the other guard, who had actually come to life sufficiently to begin fumbling with his own weapon. The second guard sat down hard, losing his rifle in the process.

By the simple expedient of clinging to the sling as the first guard crumpled in a moaning face-clutching heap, Belew availed himself of an assault rifle. He proceeded to aim it at the pair.

The room had curtains. The guards had bootlaces, belts, a handkerchief, and socks. Of such things are rapid and wonderfully efficient field-expedient bonds and gags made. Belew was occupied less than a minute in securing the pair.

Sprout's room was a flight down, next to Mark's. Neither was guarded. Belew felt a terrible suspicion that certain trunk-overhung lips had dropped in Mark's ear a suggestion that most of the Palace guards should be elsewhere that night, like out front, or guarding the audience room, or keeping watch on Belew the putative child molester.

Belew's still bleeding pinky opened Sprout's locked door. The room was empty but for the immense stuffed panda keeping blind and futile vigil over the bed. Just as he feared.

He crossed quickly to the window, looked out into the back garden. Two figures, one with blond hair in a ponytail, one with an elephant's head, were riding a rising pillar of dirt to the top of the rear garden wall.

"Shit," Belew said, and ran.

* * *

"Where are we, Unca Neesha?" Sprout asked, hanging slightly back.

It was another villa a few blocks away, less grand than the one the President and Chancellor occupied, and dark. The grounds were overgrown, the shrubberies looming black ominous shapes.

"I don't like it here," the girl protested. "I'm afraid."

"There is nothing to fear," the guru said. "Not with your Uncle Ganesha here. Have I not the power of *maya*? Have I not magic?"

She bit her lip, but nodded. She was going to be brave. She had learned how a long time ago, when the bad people took her from her daddy.

He pushed the door. It opened. Inside, the house echoed to their steps, and smelled of mildew and the dust that swirled up to greet them as they entered.

The place had belonged to a ranking member of one of the former Socialist Republic's many and varied secret police organizations. Showing that wisdom Marcos owned, but Ceaucescu and Honecker sadly lacked, he had blown town before People Power came and nailed his ass to a light standard. The villa had suffered a little token vandalism and looting in the immediate aftermath of Liberation, but Madam President had made it known she Strongly Disapproved of that sort of thing, and it had ceased. The house had been closed up, and remained fairly undisturbed until the guru's *sannyasi* cased it.

They walked through the foyer and parlor to the great room. Ganesha gestured, and it became paradise. In this case paradise was dominated by a bed, canopied in fine silk and cloth of gold, lit by myriad candles and golden oil lamps, swaying from carved-ivory chains.

"We're going to go to bed?" Sprout asked, trying to hide her disappointment. She wasn't tired yet, and anyway the excitement of escaping the Palace had got her all awake.

"Here, my child, kneel upon the bed," the guru said, urging her onto it.

"I never sleep without my pink bear," she said, and then remembered to add politely, "and Mr. Fish."

"Sleep, my child?" Ganesha tittered. "Sleeping is the furthest thing from my mind. Soon, you shall truly know paradise. I can make you feel things your young body never knew it could experience—"

As he spoke, the tip of his trunk slid softly down her cheek. She smiled. It felt good.

His hands were on her, caressing. She tried to pull away. There was something wrong here, something her daddy had warned her about. . . .

The T-shirt vanished. Chimes began to play.

She gasped and hugged her arms over her white bra. "Stop it!" she wailed.

"Do not be afraid, my princess," Ganesha said. "I shall not hurt you, no. First I shall prepare you—"

He dropped a hand to her hip. The cut-off jeans vanished.

"And then will come the pleasure. Come now, my sweet, do not cringe away. Let me help you off with that."

He tried to reach her bra. She clasped her forearms in a tight inverted V before her and turned away. He tittered.

"No matter. That which I can touch, I can bring to nonbeing. As I can create, so can I destroy, though at not so long a range."

As he spoke, he got two plump fingers under the strap of Sprout's bra, pulled it away from her skin. She whimpered.

The bra disappeared.

"See? It is all so simple. Nothing to fear, nothing to worry about. I am your father's guru, but I would be more to you, precious child. Oh, so very much more."

"*Please,*" she said, unable to hold in the tears. "Leave me *alone.*"

"You will not wish that when you learn what I can offer." He ran his hand down her ribs. Her satiny skin was drawn up in goosebumps. He reached for the waistband of her panties.

A click from behind him, metallic and multiplex.

Deliberately Ganesha turned. J. Robert Belew stood in the door to the parlor, aiming his Para-Ordnance at the guru's broad stomach.

"Back off, Hosenose. Or I'll commence to let your *atman* leak out through your belly-button."

Ganesha sighed. "Truly, you are without wisdom."

His giant white rat materialized at Belew's right hand. Before he could pull the trigger it bit off his gun hand with a flash of orange incisors.

Belew gasped and fell to his knees as blood jetted across the room, spraying the magnificent canopy, Ganesha, and Sprout. Sprout crouched on the bed, looking wildly from Belew to Ganesha to the giant rat, which sat on its great haunches, demurely cleaning blood from its whiskers.

"Sprout, run!" Belew screamed. "Back to your father!"

The half-naked girl tried to obey. She started to jump off the bed, but the sheet rose up around her legs, tangling her and pulling her down.

The rat gave off cleaning its face to lunge again at Belew. Desperately he rolled aside, just avoiding its strike. The maneuver brought him into the corner, almost against the base of an old-fashioned floor lamp with a flexible neck. He pressed his spurting stump against its base.

The rat jumped for him. The top of the lamp slammed down right between its eyes, which showed maroon highlights in the candlelight.

The rat sat down on its haunches. The lamp struck like a cobra, cracking it on its snout. The rat chittered outrage and grabbed the lamp in its teeth. It bit down hard.

There was a blue flash, and a pop!, and a brief loud buzzing, accompanied by a stink of burning meat. The rat flopped over on its back, the broken lamp hanging from its convulsively working jaws, blue sparks flying like spittle from its mouth. It kicked around the room, tore the hangings from the bed, and expired.

"My rat," Ganesha said in tones of desolation. He had

trouble making himself heard over Sprout's screams. The sheet had completely entwined her long legs, turned her to a mummy lamia with an angel's face. "You have slain my sacred rat."

"You can build yourself another," J. Bob said, between pants, as he rolled to his knees and cast about for his sidearm. "Unless I miss my guess. What do you do, call virtual particles into being in the desired form? And if you need something really substantial, like a riding rat, it uses up a lot of your capacity, doesn't it? Thought I saw this LSD playboy pad of yours waver a few times there.

"And your little disintegration trick—you can suppress virtual particles, too, as well as call them into being, you rascal, you. Like the pions that carry the strong force—"

Ganesha shook his magnificent head. "You are lost in the *maya* of your machines—"

"Actually, I think it's the blood I've lost that makes me talk like this."

"—to concern yourself with how I do what I do, when all that matters is *what* I do."

And his mind caught the flames of the lamps and the candles, and drew them forth in bright strands into a roiling, roaring mass, and set them upon Belew. He fought, rolling on the floor to douse the flames, roaring as much in fury as in pain. But in the end, the flames had their way.

At last it was done, and he lay still.

For a moment Ganesha stood over his vanquished foe. The corpse was covered with a hard black charcoal crust, from which stinking smoke rose. The guru nodded and turned away.

"And now, my child," he said, going to the bed. The smell of incense filled the room, to banish less pleasant odors. "Let us continue where we left off."

Sprout stared at him with wide blue eyes. When he reached his trunk for her she struck at it with her fists.

"You hurt Unca Bob. I hate you!"

He reared, blinking back sudden tears of pain. He seized her wrists.

"I will not be denied any longer," he cried. Golden vines twined around Sprout's arms from the posts of the bed. They drew her down onto her back.

Behind Ganesha the smoking mummy stirred. Slowly, agonizingly, it stretched a foot toward the handgun lying near it on the floor. Handspan patches of blackened meat fell away like cheap plaster.

"Where were we, my child?" Ganesha asked when the girl was restrained. He dropped his hand to her belly, which was covered by the wound sheet. He patted it twice, and then the sheet disappeared. Before she could kick him, more vines seized her ankles.

The black crust over one big toe split open. Blood welled through the cracks. The mummy reached for the pistol with the toe. Clumsy in its coat of char, it nudged the weapon, which made a tiny scraping sound.

Ganesha spun, frowned thunderously. "So! You are hard to kill, Major."

He strode across the room with a speed belying his bulk, kicked the handgun away.

"And now," he said, "I fear that I must reach out and touch you." He held forth a hand as if to bestow a benediction, leaned forward.

The window exploded inward in a cascade of glass-shards and splintered wood. Ganesha looked up.

Moonchild drove a flying two-footed kick into his trunked face.

She touched down lightly. Ganesha flopped bonelessly to the hardwood floor at her feet. His great elephant head flickered once, twice, vanished.

In its place was the head of an ordinary Indian male, round, plump-cheeked, shaven in the priestly style. It lolled at an unnatural angle on a normal human neck, which was unmistakably broken. Protruding eyes stared at Moonchild like brown marbles.

She fell to her knees and began to scream.

J. Bob Belew's healing powers were not as those of ordinary men. By the time he was brought before Mark a few days later, he had enough skin, pink and new and fragile as a baby's, that he did not need to be kept pumped full of every antibiotic known to humankind to keep every known contagion from invading his body. He was still sadly deficient in the matter of hair and he preferred to wear bandages over his face and hands, to protect the sensibilities of others.

"Since I'm still not in possession of all my faculties," he told the Chancellor of Free Vietnam in his muffled voice, "I won't try to fight the impulse to say, 'I told you so.'"

Mark Meadows turned from the window to stare at him. His blue eyes were chill and pale as Arctic-circle sky. With the afternoon sun blasting in at his back his long features seemed skeleton-gaunt.

The audience chamber had been stripped to echoing bareness. Not only were Ganesha's tangible illusions gone, but the tie-dyed scrim as well. All that occupied the room was now the camp stool, the two men, a quartet of joker guards with their rifles trained on Belew.

"He was a fraud to the bone," Belew said. "You saw him, didn't you, at the end? *He wasn't even a joker.*"

Even during their days of privation and comradeship, in the fight for Vietnam, Belew thought he had never seen the skin so dry or parchment-tight over Mark's prominent cheekbones. Now emotion drew it tighter still, until it seemed the skin must snap.

"You've cost me a lot," he said. "Moonchild—I—killed my guru. Now I don't know if I can ever get Moonchild back. The last time I tried calling her, I went into convulsions, and then an hour-long coma. She was sworn never to take life."

Belew squeezed his eyes shut. "Mark. I'm sorry. There was no way for her to know his neck wasn't as strong as it looked."

"I've allowed myself to be manipulated by that agile tongue of yours for years, Major." He spread his hands. "Look where it's got me."

There was a response which might be made. Belew didn't make it. He stood erect, matched Mark gaze for gaze, and said nothing.

Mark drew a deep breath, let it slowly out. "I have spoken to my daughter. She appreciates what you did for her. So do I."

"I appreciate what you've done for me, too," Belew said. "You've seen I had the finest of care, in a country where care of any kind's still at a premium."

Mark cut him off with a sharp nod. "I did what I had to do. You've done a lot for me, more than any man or woman I ever met. You saved my daughter. That by itself is more than anything I can repay."

His features writhed briefly, set. "But I—I saw you with her, man. I don't know what really happened. I guess I never will. But all that I can give you now, is your life.

"One hundred thousand dollars has been deposited to that Swiss bank account you didn't think I knew about. And yes, I know you weren't skimming. You can have the transport of your choice, to the destination of your choice. But counting from this instant, you must be beyond the borders of Free Vietnam within twelve hours. And don't come back. Or I'll have you killed."

He raised his head. Though he held his face stiff, he could not hide the tears in his eyes.

"Have you anything to say, Major Belew?"

Slowly, painfully, Belew turned and shuffled to the door. Then he turned back, and raised a gauze-swaddled hand.

"*Ave atque vale*, Mark, my friend."

And he was gone.

The Color of His Skin

Part 3

Reality was cold water thrown in the face of dreams.

Gregg realized that listening to news reports in the days following the *Peregrine's Perch* show. The *Today Show* the next morning treated the story like it was headline material for *Aces* or the *National Enquirer*—just another cheap tabloid headline. The major networks placed it first or second in their newscasts the following evening, but focused mostly on Gregg's past. CNN was more serious in its commentary, but buried the story in the middle of its sequence and featured rebuttals by several government sources. Marilyn Monroe, in a widely-televised press conference, emotionally denied that she had met with Hannah and denounced the Hedda Hopper material as "entirely manufactured." Sarah Morgenstern wrote a scathing, sarcastic article for *Newsweek*. Rush Limbaugh, never a fan of "Liberal Loonie" Hartmann, was especially brutal in his usual searing jocularity, deriding this "theory of ex-Senator Gregg Crackpotmann, Hannah Bananas, and Father Sushi—the ultimate Three Stooges."

Puppetman's influence had always required live

interaction; his new Gift was identically limited. Gregg wasn't surprised that the viewing audience turned out to be more skeptical than the live audience. "Certainly the angry response of Peregrine's audience demonstrates that jokers experience far more prejudicial treatment than is either fair or just," Ed Bradley commented, then added, "but mistreatment hardly constitutes a conspiracy."

A Harris poll showed that only 12% of the general public (plus or minus 3%) bought into the existence of the Card Sharks, while another 17% thought that such a conspiracy was at least "possible." Among nats alone, the numbers dropped even further.

"This isn't what we'd hoped for, is it?" Father Squid said.

They were in the new parsonage, surrounded by boxes and clutter—gifts from the parishioners to replace what Father Squid had lost in the fire. The parsonage smelled of new paint and fresh-cut lumber; the small dining room through the archway was draped in plastic dropcloths. Through the windows, Gregg could see the rubble of the church, from which a new structure was slowly emerging.

Oddity—Evan—had made coffee. Gregg curled his finger around the pleasant warmth of the mug and sipped. "It's what I expected," he said.

"But after Peri's show, after that reaction . . ." Hannah leaned in a corner beside the silent bulk of Quasiman, who was in one of his fugues. The young woman stroked Quasiman's shoulder with one hand, and Gregg could sense Hannah's strong friendship for the joker radiating from her.

He found that he was almost jealous. *What does it matter?* the inner voice chided him. *After all, nat women aren't to your taste. Even attractive ones like her . . .* "Our audience there were the easy ones to convince, Hannah," he said. "The ones who live in Jokertown—they know already. But the nats, the whole rest of the country . . ." Gregg shrugged.

He could feel their doubt beginning to overshadow the hope. He began walking around the room as he spoke, letting the Gift touch each of them, letting it push back the darkness. He patted Father Squid's shoulder, hugged Oddity, crouched down beside Quasiman and touched the hunchback's knee.

Stood again looking at Hannah. He sent the Gift deep into her, and she smiled back at him. There was inside her an implicit trust of him, clear and unalloyed now with lingering doubts. Gregg could sense that melding of admiration and faith, and he sent the power down to that crystalline certainty, adding another careful new layer to it. *Stop it, Greggie!* He ignored the voice and touched Hannah's hand; she gave his fingers a squeeze in return.

"Listen, all of you. We accomplished what we needed to accomplish," Gregg said, looking at Hannah, then back to the others. "We made it safe for Hannah and Father Squid to come out of hiding—at least as safe as anyone in New York can be right now. We have the media digging for the facts, and if my experience is any indication, they'll be much more effective and thorough than we could ever hope to be. We'll let them investigate for us. The Sharks are going to be busy trying to hide their tracks or deny their involvement. If the joker that Battle's turned into is found, we'll start asking about the old burglary charges again. Monroe, Herzenhagen, Rudo—they'll all have the press camped out on their doorsteps for the next week at least."

"Until the next juicy story knocks us off the front page," Oddity commented.

"Furs said it would take a few days for the press to really get going, Evan," Gregg answered. "Let's give it that chance. And we're not done yet ourselves, remember."

"If people come through."

"They'll come through. I'm sure of it."

The use of the power had made him feel tired and old, as if he'd been working physically. He yawned, stretching. His muscles ached, and he suddenly wanted to be alone. Gregg left the room as the discussion continued, going outside.

He put his arms on the railing of the front porch, looking up to where the incomplete framework of the new steeple was etched against the cityglow of the sky. He heard the door open behind him.

"Are you as confident as you sound?" Hannah's voice, soft and low. Gregg could feel the warmth as she came alongside him, and he glanced over to see that her gaze, like his, had gone to the steeple.

Yes, he started to say, but couldn't. He found that he didn't want to lie to her. He didn't *need* to lie to her. "No."

"I thought so." For an instant, she smiled, still looking up at the steeple.

"I don't see that very often," he said.

"What?"

"You smiling. So why'd it happen?"

"I don't know," she said. She looked at him. In the half-darkness, her hair seemed to glow, and her eyes were only faint lights in the shadow of her face. "Maybe I like hearing you tell me the truth. Maybe it makes me trust you."

"And that makes you smile?"

"Yeah," she said. "Despite all the nastiness going on around me, it does. You're a good man, Gregg Hartmann. No matter what happens, I appreciate all you've done."

She smiled again, a flash of teeth, and went back inside. Gregg stayed out in the night for a long, long time.

"The Free Vietnamese government exhumed the reputed body of Dr. Etienne Faneuil two days ago," Gregg said. "We have here the documented report from the medical examiner, as well as a set of dental records from the corpse. As you can see, the dental records do not match those of Dr. Faneuil, and the skeletal remains show no evidence of the broken leg Dr. Faneuil is known to have suffered in 1972."

"Any dental records for Dr. Faneuil are extremely old. And, not to be prejudicial but Free Vietnam is not the United States. How can you be certain that the corpse they claim to have exhumed is indeed from Dr. Faneuil's grave, and can you be certain of the competency of the examiner?"

Mike Wallace managed to look smug. Gregg tried to smile into the camera lights. Gregg had been on *60 Minutes* once before for a piece on terrorism, and they'd interviewed him regarding his kidnapping in Berlin. Wallace's staff had initially been uninterested when Gregg contacted them regarding the Sharks, but in the wake of Peregrine's show, and with the promise that they'd be the first to reveal the findings of the exhumation, they'd agreed. The cameras and Wallace had arrived at Gregg's apartment that evening.

Hannah leaned forward toward Wallace. "We asked Chancellor Meadows to be certain that every step in the process was documented, and we'll provide you that documentation, Mr. Wallace. The body was taken from the grave in which Dr. Faneuil was reputedly buried. The Vietnamese medical examiner has a degree from Columbia and did his residency in Los Angeles; I don't doubt his credentials."

"But the dental records . . ."

"I've depended on dental records for identification many times in my work, Mr. Wallace," she said. "Fires don't leave much else. I'll admit that records for Dr. Faneuil are sketchy. Still, it's much, much easier to prove that records *don't* match than that they do. You have Dr. Faneuil's records in your hand. Look at the upper right incisor, here. As you can see, Dr. Faneuil had a crown put on that tooth in 1977." Hannah gave Wallace a set of X-ray negatives. "Compare those to this. The Vietnamese corpse doesn't have a crown on that incisor—in fact, the tooth was whole and healthy when the man died. No matter how sketchy the records, no one grows a new adult tooth where there was once a crown. I don't know who this man is. I *do* know that he is not Etienne Faneuil."

Wallace stared at the two sets of documents for a moment and then set them aside on Gregg's coffee table. "All right," he said. "Let's assume for the moment that you're correct. Dr. Faneuil faked his death and is conceivably still alive out there somewhere. What does that prove?"

"By itself, nothing," Gregg answered. "What's important is the reflection it casts on the rest of Hannah's evidence. Dr. Faneuil's death was the wall the Sharks threw up in Hannah's path when she began this. His death was supposed to end her uncovering of the Card Sharks just as it ended legal pursuit of the doctor in the first place. Hannah insisted that Faneuil was alive—and everyone ridiculed her. Largely because of that, the rest of her evidence was ignored or discounted. Well, Hannah Davis was right and everyone else was wrong."

"And thus she is right about the rest."

"Yes."

"And is Pan Rudo, Director of the World Health Organization, also the head of the Card Sharks?"

"We've not claimed that, Mr. Wallace," Gregg smiled. He glanced at Hannah; she nodded back to him. "We're still gathering evidence before we name the person. The rest is speculation on the part of the media. I suggest you ask Dr. Rudo that question, not me."

"We'd like to, but he won't talk to us. Ms. Davis, Senator, let me be candid with the two of you for a moment. I don't *want* to believe you. I don't *want* to think that there has been an ugly conspiracy on the part of some very important and influential people to discredit and even kill jokers. I don't want to believe that kind of horror, prejudice, and genocide is possible."

"It's happened before," Hannah said. "Not too long ago at all—when Adolf Hitler and the Nazis ruled Germany."

"Yes," Wallace admitted. " That doesn't mean it can happen again. Not here."

"I'd like to believe that, too, Mr. Wallace," Hannah said. "And if you in the media do *your* job, it won't."

". . . And if you in the media do *your* job, it won't."

The image of Hannah cut to that of Wallace on the *60 Minutes* studio set. "Well, we tried to do just that," he said to the camera. "We looked into several of the allegations made by Ms. Davis, and in each case, we found an alarming trend. Important records had been destroyed, crucial documents had vanished, people with vital pieces of knowledge had moved to parts unknown or had passed away due to accident or illness. Either Ms. Davis and ex-Senator Hartmann have managed to find the right combination of events to make things look suspicious, or there really is something or someone covering up their tracks. The Iranian hostage debacle is a case in point. We petitioned the State Department, the Justice Department, the CIA, the Pentagon, and the White House for documents relating to that incident."

Pictures of the request letters fell, one after another, on the screen. "Here's what we received back," Mike's voice said over them. New pages appeared, each pertinent section highlighted. "President Barnett's press secretary claims that the Carter administration documents relevant to that period are 'missing.' He promises to look into the matter. The Justice Department claims that it was 'not involved' and that any documents it might have regarding Cyclone's participation or non-participation in the operation are 'classified due to problems with his estate.' The Pentagon sent us reports which are, as you can see, mostly blacked-out and useless. The CIA has 'declined comment.' "

Cut back to Mike, looking seriously into the camera. "We would like to assure Ms. Davis that we will, indeed, 'do our job.' Our investigation will continue, and we will report back to you, our viewers, exactly what we find."

"*Yes!*"

The crowd of jokers and sympathizers gathered in Father Squid's new living room exulted as *60 Minutes* went to a commercial, hugging Hannah and clapping Gregg on the back. He grinned in the midst of the spontaneous celebration. "You've done it!" Father Squid roared at him. " Tell them, Gregg!" he shouted. Others joined in, urging him to speak: Jube, Dutton, Oddity, a dozen more.

Gregg rose, holding up his left hand, and the group slowly quieted. Someone snapped off the television set.

"I'll make this short and sweet," he said. "Yes, this is exactly what we were after," Gregg told them, and just for the pleasure it gave him, he used the Gift with the words, imbuing them with power and enjoying the feel of their reaction. Already primed, already wanting to rejoice with them, it was easy to stroke their emotions. "We haven't won. Not yet. But we've made a beginning. The Sharks are already running for cover. If we keep the spotlight on them, they can't escape. I'm just a tool in your hands, someone with the right contacts. You did this, all of you. So applaud yourselves."

They did so, vigorously, as Gregg sat again, wrapped in their silver joy.

You see, he told the voice inside himself. *If we can do this, we can do more—anything I want to do. God, it feels so GOOD!*

From across the room, Hannah caught his eye. She was watching him. For a moment, their gazes locked, and her smile went wide. She nodded. For a moment, he felt confused, as if her acknowledgment overrode all the pleasure of the moment. Then he grinned again and nodded back.

Doing the right thing for all the wrong reasons, the voice chided inside him. *Isn't that right, Greggie?*

To that, he had no answer.

Paths of Silence and of Night
by Leanne C. Harper

"The magic secrets of your forefathers were revealed to them by voices which came by the path of silence and the night."

—Popol Vuh
Sacred Book of the Quiché Maya

The movement caught her. The hawk, head turning in a search for food, fixed on the two men coming down the trail. Not villagers, not on the trail down from the mountains. The men of Chotol were in the *milpas* below the village. Neither the army nor the guerrillas would have been so foolish as to send only two men. Evangelical missionaries would have been coming up from the valleys. When they stopped, the hawk lost them amid the tangled mass of foliage. Suzanne Menotti shoved her thick black hair behind her ears as if it would aid her sight. She shared her vision with the black jaguar who stood at her side. They had been playing with the village children, making a game of learning Spanish. It was one of the reasons she was allowed to stay here. Now she let them play by themselves, chasing the dogs.

129

Listening, she heard nothing more than the quiet sounds of village life: maize being ground for tortillas and the tortillas themselves being patted into existence between the fingers of the women, the children laughing in their play, and beyond that the shrill bird calls that came from the jungle. The breeze that made life in the tropical heat bearable up here on the mountainside swept through the upper branches of the tall pine, oak, and cedar trees surrounding Chotol and down into her unbound hair.

Switching from one point of view to the next among her sentries in the forest, she watched the strangers approach the tiny Quiché Mayan village of Chotol. The eyes she used could tell her little about them at this distance. The eyes of her watchers were not adapted to see what she needed to know. The lead man avoided each trap set into the trail as if he had seen a map of their defenses.

When a coatimundi looked up from his meal and saw them twenty minutes from the village, Suzanne told the children to warn their mothers and grandparents in the eighteen thatched-roof houses surrounding the open center of the village. They did not hesitate, running silently with prematurely serious faces to follow a drill they had known all their lives. While they scattered into the tiny whitewashed houses, she went back to her surveillance of the intruders. As best she could tell, neither man was armed, but that was no guarantee. She called Luis, the eldest Ek child, back and sent him to warn the men farming the corn in the *milpas*. An unnatural quiet fell over the entire village as the adults and the children gathered food and weapons in preparation for evacuation. In a war zone, everyone learns their roles early.

The Eks were the village leaders. When Rosa Ek came out of her house fully armed with machete and ancient rifle, carrying both her youngest child and a bag of supplies, Suzanne explained the danger to her in the Quiché dialect she had struggled to learn. After a quick consultation, Rosa left Suzanne there to decide the intruders' fate and shepherded her charges to their jungle hiding places. It was a measure of the trust the people of Chotol had in her, and it never failed to make her proud. The danger was ten minutes away. Suzanne retreated into her own house to await its arrival.

When they left the jungle for the clearing around the village, the man who followed staggered as if, without the necessity of struggling through the fecund growth, he did not possess the strength to walk. The leader moved as slowly and deliberately here as he had through the jungle. Coming into the center of the village, he stopped for a moment before turning to face her home. His companion hauled himself to the edge of the well and began pulling up the bucket.

Now she could see them with her own eyes. The leader was Maya, in his late forties and already beating the statistics, a Cakchiquel she guessed from his embroidered shirt, although she was still terrible at determining tribal affiliations. Rosa despaired of her sometimes. Rosa could have told her precisely the village from which he came. To her surprise, his thirtysomething companion was white, as *norteamericano* as herself by the look of his sunburn. And a journalist, according to his filthy, many-pocketed vest and dangling cameras. By travelling alone with an Indian, he proclaimed himself a liberal journalist. Still, appearances here were at least as deceiving as they had been in New York. She saw no weapons other than the Maya's machete. They were travelling light, with only the white man's camera pack and the Maya's one red woven cotton bag. There was something wrong with her view of the Maya through the eyes of the margay perched high in a fir tree. The nervous little cat was difficult to control without taking over his mind entirely. Suzanne hated to do that.

She stood and walked out into the sunlight. Neither she nor the Maya spoke. The other man was concentrating on drinking his water, not even noticing her arrival. Sated at last, he looked up to meet blue eyes staring at him.

"Shit!" He tripped in his haste to back away. The weight of the swinging cameras destroyed his balance and he sat

down hard, hands splaying out behind him. But he did
not reach inside his vest. No gun. "Umán, there's a fucking jaguar over here." His Spanish was poor, mixing in
the English obscenity and rising in pitch. "*Jose . . .*"

"Don't move and you'll be okay. Balam, watch him."
The verbal order was for the reporter's benefit. Suzanne
used the jaguar's eyes to keep track of the journalist. Her
own eyes never left the Maya. Now she saw why the
image she had taken from the margay was so confused.
The right side of his body was human, but the left
explained his slow pace. He appeared to be made of
stone, a living stele from a dead Maya city, complete
with inscriptions and carved images. A joker, beautiful
and grotesque. But what took her most by surprise was
that the carvings seemed to change every time she
blinked her eyes.

She shook off her fascination to check the surrounding
jungle for more trouble through the eyes of nearby birds.
Everything was quiet. The men had gone directly from
the fields to the forest. The people were located strategically outside the village in hiding places established years
before her arrival. Even the children waited with the
patience taught by generations of people living under the
shadow of a would-be conqueror. It always impressed
her, this implacable patience under the worst of
circumstances.

The Maya before her gazed back with the same unwa-
vering stare, not insolent or even hostile, never subservi-
ent . . . just patient. The two sides of his face almost
matched, contemporary man and ancient king, for just
an instant before changing again. He spoke briefly in a
language with which she was unfamiliar. After the years
she had spent here, she could manage Quiché and her
high school Spanish had become near-fluency, but that
was all. She shrugged her lack of comprehension and he
switched to Spanish.

"We need to rest." He maneuvered his body by swinging it on the pivot of his left leg and gestured to include
his white fellow traveller. "We won't stay long."

"No, you won't." Suzanne stared pointedly at their bedraggled clothes. "Who's chasing you?"

The Maya's body shimmered as the hieroglyphs spun out their messages too quickly for the eye to follow. Almost idly, she wondered if he could read them and what the words held for him. His eyes moved to the journalist still seated in the dust before returning to Suzanne's.

"Are you an Evangelical or perhaps with one of the Catholic Action missions?" His question was asked with a lightness of tone that belied its importance.

"No, I'm not here to save any souls. Nor am I a misguided *norteamericano* liberal in Guatemala to help the rebels." Here, she deliberately looked over at the photojournalist. "I'm here because I love this land. It's my home now."

She thought but didn't say that, even in high summer, life in Guatemala beat the hell out of Central Park and steam grates in the Manhattan winter. Her eyes unfocused slightly as she flashed through the consciousness of innumerable creatures going about their lives throughout the forest, then came back hard to the intruders in her life.

"I'm here as a friend; the people are kind enough to let me stay. I avoid politics, *all* politics. I've found it's the best way to stay alive. Who's after you?"

"The Kaibiles." Before Umán could answer, the journalist spoke. "Josh McCoy, sometimes of New York."

"I can't say I'm pleased to meet someone leading the Guatemalan Army's finest counter-insurgency troops to my front door." Responding to the emotions coming through the two-way mental link with Suzanne, the jaguar growled softly as it continued to stare at McCoy's throat. Now the sweat streaming down his face was not due to the exertion or the humidity.

"Umán lost them. He says his blood told him which way they'd go. He was right." McCoy got up slowly, arms staying away from his sides, using his shoulders to readjust the position of his pack and cameras. "And I thought he was just another joker when I met him. I don't have any idea what you know about the Maya but he's a *chuchkajawib,* an *ajk'ij,* umm, a priest-shaman type. Sometimes they're called Daykeepers. You'd think I'd know better by now. You guys tap into things I never believed existed."

"What?" Suzanne was startled by his assumption and fiercely angered by the knowledge of her it implied.

"Look, Animal Lady, it's not exactly SOP for somebody to have a pet jaguar or use a taltuza as a living stole, right? In fact, you probably fall on the side of the aces. I don't know you, so you've kept it real quiet, but you're from up north." He looked around the tiny village with contempt. "It's a long way to run, but I've got to admit it makes a great place to stick your head in the fuckin' sand."

The pitch of the jaguar's growl increased as the rage she felt grew. More than a little of her anger came from the fact that she had entirely forgotten the taltuza, a little raccoon-like beast she had taken in and nursed back to health last winter. It had taken a liking to lying across her shoulders all day. She no longer even noticed it, it was so much a part of her. Her subconscious took in the information the taltuza provided as if it came from her own senses. Only the intercession of the Maya priest broke the tension between them.

"I'm hungry, I'm tired and I must cast the *tz'ite* seeds to find our path. Your village is safe for now." Umán blinked slowly in his exhaustion. His flat tone implied that he was more than slightly annoyed by their antipathy. Suzanne hesitated, staring at McCoy with the same hungry intensity as the jaguar.

"I'm Suzanne Menotti. Inside, there's food." She stood aside and waved them into her home of plastered and white-washed cornstalk walls with an exaggerated half-curtsey for McCoy. "It may be a trifle humble for your tastes. And watch out for the pit trap just inside the door."

"Lady, after Australian grubs, anything's an improvement." Skirting the jaguar who had moved to stand at Suzanne's side, the reporter followed Umán inside. Left outside, she scanned the surrounding jungle and then swept her left hand down sharply in a gesture meant to be seen by the village sentries who watched nearby. As she bent to enter, the people began to return to their interrupted lives.

The scent touching the nose of a peccary rooting for food brought Suzanne fully awake. As she rolled off the sleeping mat to her feet, she sent Balam, the black jaguar who had been her companion for two years, to warn the Eks, who would again oversee the evacuation of their village. They had agreed with Suzanne that the refugees could stay overnight but no more, and all traces of them had to be gone in the morning. The villagers were used to the disruption of the army patrols looking for rebels in their midst. She never would be. Years of living on the street had paradoxically made her as fiercely territorial as a jaguar.

Gunpowder and human sweat. Those were the smells she had caught through the peccary's sense. Soldiers. Or some guerrilla band. Scent could not tell her whether it was the government army or the Guatemalan Army of the Poor, or gods knew what other splinter group. Enemy or friend, it was best to hide first and determine the level of danger later. In either case, the strangers were likely to mean more trouble for the village.

"Up. Now." She nudged the Daykeeper Umán awake, then shoved the reporter hard. They slept under her roof because, since she had no family, she had the most room. And that way she could watch them. "We're leaving."

"We who, kemosabe?" McCoy helped Umán to gather his bag and clothing. She noted with some bemusement his patience with the elder Maya.

"I know the trails." She paused for a moment to use her other eyes, ears and nostrils throughout the nearby jungle. "I won't have you endanger these people. Umán doesn't know the area and he can't keep stopping to check the omens for every right turn. Come *on.*"

Suzanne threw a pair of black jeans and a couple of dark T-shirts into her backpack, followed by her maps and a flashlight. Two canteens of water were joined by a package of leftover tortillas, some chilis, salt and beans, wrapped in leaves. She was figuring on giving the men a day's lead over the army, then coming back by some circuitous route. Her machete and down vest hung by the door and she grabbed them as they left. She never carried a gun of any kind.

The night was bright and cold at their elevation. It was only a few days before a full moon. McCoy followed her out first. The shaman paused in the doorway, hieroglyphs dancing across his body. His eyes were closed and his right hand touched his left shoulder as if to confirm the message he felt internally. Last night, he had performed rites that he claimed would tell him more about how they would escape the army's net. He had not, however, been forthcoming about the specifics. The moment ended quickly. If Suzanne had not turned at that precise instant, she would never have seen it. She looked down at the jaguar back at her side. Balam would stay with the people as added protection. The taltuza had climbed back to its accustomed perch and would go with her. This could be an interesting day.

They had put kilometers between themselves and Chotol by the time she allowed them to rest with the coming of dawn. Umán amazed her with the steadiness of his progress. Despite his body, he had kept up with her. Even McCoy had managed to stay with the pace she set. She looked up from her wide-ranging reconnaissance of the forest to catch Umán's eyes on her.

"I think it's time I knew why an *ajk'ij* and a reporter are running through the Guatemalan Highlands in an attempt to escape from the army." Suzanne sat down with some gratitude herself, although she would never admit it to the others. She handed out one of the canteens of water. McCoy stopped cleaning the lens of his Minolta and glanced at Umán before continuing the operation with extreme concentration.

"A little trouble up in the *Altiplano*, further up in the mountains." He put the camera up to his eye and sighted. "Hard to stay out of trouble in the Highlands. Genocide brings out the worst in people, you know."

"I told you I wasn't political. If I wanted to play those games, I would have stayed in New York." Suzanne scowled out at the jungle. "I love this country, these people. I'd do anything for them, but I won't blindly follow anyone's party line. You *norteamericanos* always have some agenda—even if it is just assuaging your white liberal guilt."

"We *norteamericanos.*" McCoy barked a laugh.

"It is not a political question for us." Umán entered the conversation, ending his revery. "It is our survival, the survival of our traditions. You must know this."

"This is not answering my question. Okay, I know about the struggle, the defeat and murder of the Hero Twins at Nebaj last year, the destruction of the town, the imprisonment of most of the Maya separatists who weren't killed. It's not fair and it's not right. But why you? And why the Kaibiles?"

"There's a village in the *Altiplano*, like Chotol, but maybe four or five times as large. *Was* a village, until a week ago." McCoy had switched to English. He lay back on the ground and stared up through the dark green canopy of treetops toward the now light-blue sky. It was still cool. The heat would not come until the sun was higher.

"It was a little place, but pretty. Good people. Ixil Maya. Jokers, some of them. But, you know, I never saw jokers who were so accepted by their community. Doesn't happen in New York. I'd heard about Umán through some contacts of mine possibly associated with the EGP."

"So you are involved with the Army of the Poor?"

"Jeez, I know some people. It's my job to develop contacts. I'm not a freakin' Marxist, all right?"

"So you found a nice photogenic joker. Just the thing for a little *Newsweek* human interest piece? Oooh, maybe a cover story. That must pay well." Suzanne used English as well. Umán had looked up when McCoy began, but had not reacted since. Not all that many Maya spoke Spanish, let alone English. It was why she spent so much time teaching the children. Communication of the situation in their country was the only way she saw that could protect them from their ordained future. She dug into her pack and passed out tortillas and beans.

"Umán, did I come to do any harm?" McCoy appealed to the shaman in Spanish.

"He wanted to study our ways of time, past and future." Umán added salt and chilis to his food, as did she. McCoy ate his plain. "He is no anthropologist."

Suzanne smiled despite herself. Few Maya enjoyed the company of the graduate students in anthropology who threatened to overwhelm them every summer. She held up a bite to the taltuza, who snatched it away.

"Umán was able to use the ancient knowledge with rare accuracy. I was curious as to whether that was related to his joker nature. I have a personal interest in that." Suzanne looked over at him, but he did not explain. He had not said it with any of the hatred or revulsion she expected. His tone had been sad. Someone in his life was a joker. Or had been. "Anyway, I wanted to know more, and in my experience, the more light that can be shown on something and the more people who become interested, the more pressure can be put on the government from outside the country."

Suzanne glared out into the jungle. Casting her mind out over the land around them, she perceived no danger. She wished she knew what was happening in Chotol.

"So what happened last week?"

"The town was surrounded by the Guatemalan Army. So what else is new, right? But this time they brought a few new friends along with them. And a little experiment. They used their helicopter gunships to fog the town with some chemical, a biological weapon. Have you ever heard of 'Card Sharks?' "

"No."

"Well, they're pretty simple people to understand. They want you dead. Because you're an ace or something like it. But they're equal opportunity. They want jokers like Umán dead too." McCoy followed her gaze into the trees. " Their calculations were a little off this time. They killed everyone. Jokers, nats, kids, adults. Very effective. *Bastards.*"

"So how did you and Umán survive?"

"We were praying in a cave in the mountains, asking permission for me to study a little of Umán's knowledge. Umán felt something was wrong. We left the cavern and began hearing the howls of the people. But by the time we got back, it was all over. The bodies were covered in their own blood; it looked as though they had hemorrhaged through their skin. They were lying everywhere. Blood ran in streams in the street. The walls had the imprints of hands and bodies and even *faces,* where the dying had thrown themselves in their agonies. I've covered wars and natural disasters all over the world and I never before saw anything like *this.*" McCoy shivered, although the heat of the day had begun to penetrate their shelter.

"We hid on the hillside above the town. The army had already cleared it once. They controlled the roads, so they weren't looking for anyone else to get there. A few people actually survived the first onslaught. The Kaibiles shot each of them in the head. It must have been quick dispersal; they weren't even wearing gas masks when they came in. They thought there was no one left. But we were there and I had my cameras.

"I got the army officers, the Kaibiles, the bodies, the torching of the town and its final destruction by the gunships. And I got the most important shot of all. Etienne Faneuil. They used to call him the 'French Schweitzer,' you know—before the Kenya joker massacre. He's supposed to be dead. But I've got shots of him arguing with some Guatemalan general. The good doctor wasn't very happy. His trial had failed. This junk is just as deadly to nats as to wild card victims. All he wanted to do was get back to his lab."

Suzanne found herself staring at the man. Whatever she thought had made them fugitives, it wasn't this. None of the horrors she had seen or heard about since coming to Guatemala were anything like this. Chotol had mostly been ignored by both the government army and the

EGP. Normal harassment but nothing worse. She had done her best to make sure of it.

"They have always wanted us to disappear. No more *indigenas*. No more inconvenience about who owns the land. No more trouble about the majority of the people getting representation in the government. No more awkwardness about evicting people from their homes and moving them into 'model villages' by force. No more interference by outsiders concerned about native people's life expectancy of only forty-five years. So nice, so *tranquilo*. Best of all, the tourists and their dollars would still come to see the ruins of the past."

Suzanne stared at Umán, not just because he had spoken in English but at the black bitterness in his words that ran deeper than she could imagine. The Daykeeper was no naive, untutored peasant who lived in a past he only dimly remembered. Only those who saw him and his people as expendable could see him like that.

"Now you know why we're running so fast and so hard. I hate to admit it, but we could use your help." McCoy looked back down the trail as if he could see their pursuers. "If we can get to Belize, I know I can get these pictures into the world press. This is just a touch dramatic, but the lives of thousands of jokers depend on getting this film out. Not to mention what the proof of the army's genocidal practices could do for the native cause. Come with us. We've got to cross the Petén. Neither of us knows anything about the Lowlands. We need a guide, and your talents would come in very useful."

"I already have a cause: Chotol. I'll get you out of the mountains but that's it. Once we hit the Petén, you're on your own." She slung her pack across her unencumbered shoulder and waited until the taltuza climbed on before shaking it into place.

Two more days and nights of travel with little rest brought them down out of the mountains and into the lower hills. At least twice each day, the helicopters had been overhead searching for them. Suzanne had to keep them out of clearings in the thickest navigable brush she could. They had kept moving around the clock, with only a few hours of sleep when the terrain allowed it. She used the eyes of the nocturnal animals to guide them. The flashlight was a giveaway for any searchers. She never mentioned it. The two men followed as best they could, stumbling over rocks and drop-offs they couldn't see when the moon was hidden. Umán continued to surprise her. When she watched him, he appeared to move slowly and awkwardly, but he was always there, never lagging behind. His main complaint was that she never allowed him enough time to read their possible futures with his *tz'ite* seeds or his crystals. She kept telling him they would have much more of a future if they kept moving. He didn't argue long.

McCoy cursed softly and continuously when she took them off one path to cross the jungle to another. Still, he was careful not to break branches or leave other evidence of their passage if he could help it. In its way, it was frustrating. They gave her no excuses to abandon them. While they were in the Highlands, the days were warm, but the nights were bone-chillingly cold. Now, as they descended to the Lowlands, both days and nights were hot. The humidity made it difficult to draw a breath.

She wished for Balam more than once. The food from the village was long exhausted. She and Umán collected fruit when it was possible. They took water from streams as they passed. McCoy was popping Lomotil as if it was candy to ward off any bugs he was picking up, although she was using water purification tablets in the canteens. Suzanne made sure they stayed away from any habitations. Spies could be anywhere. And even if a village held no spies, their presence was too dangerous.

On the fourth day out, she got her wish. Balam suddenly appeared at the edge of her range. By the time she had made her way in to join Suzanne, the woman knew what had taken place in Chotol and how close the army was behind them, taking it from the jaguar's memories.

The first soldiers she had seen were only members of

a routine patrol. But Umán and McCoy had been tracked to Chotol within a few hours of their departure. Both Balam and the human sentries of the village gave advance warning so that there was no one in Chotol when the Kaibiles arrived. They searched every house for traces of their prey, destroying their contents as they went. The English-language books in her house excited them. That was enough to proclaim the village a haven for *subversivos*.

When they found no one to take captive, they poisoned the well and burned all the houses. After that, they tried to find the villagers in the jungle but had no success— with one exception. Young Luis Ek had wanted to be a warrior, just as his ancestors had been. He had taken his ancient rifle and picked off two Kaibiles before they had taken him. He had been tortured to death. Balam's memories of his mangled body were so vivid that she had to shut Balam out of her mind. He was, had been, only twelve.

Balam had killed two Kaibiles as well, and the traps had taken three more. But the destruction of their homes and their corn and bean fields would cripple their efforts to avoid work on the coastal *fincas*, the coffee and cotton plantations they had finally managed to escape. For at least a while, they would have to move elsewhere. The Kaibiles would not soon forget the death of their fellows.

Suzanne was now a permanent exile. Her presence would mean the death of anyone with whom she was associated. With Balam at her side, she walked into the jungle. It was only there, with no humans near, that she allowed herself tears of grief at the loss of her home. She tried to blame it all on the two men she was helping, but she could not convince herself. The guilt was hers alone, despite her knowledge that the blame lay with the army, not with her.

She returned in silence and refused to speak for the hours of a forced march down into the Petén. Only when neither McCoy nor Umán could walk further did she stop. She considered the options she had left. The most attractive was entering into a personal guerrilla war against the Kaibiles. Joined by Balam and others, she could cause a respectable amount of damage. She was willing to bet her life that she could escape detection. The problem was that she knew Umán and McCoy would never make it across the Petén alone. She was not even convinced that she could get them across the Lowlands.

"Chotol?" Umán had the courage to ask the question after he caught his breath.

"Gone. Burned to the ground." Suzanne glared at them, still wanting to make it their fault. "But the people survived. Only one casualty—unless you count the Kaibiles."

When she gazed out into the forest after Balam, their eyes followed.

"She is quite territorial."

"So, what are you going to do now?" McCoy's hands were trembling as he eased the cameras off his shoulders. Suzanne tried to feel regret at how hard she had run them. She felt nothing. For the last few years, she had put the Bagabond persona behind her. Bagabond felt little emotion because it was not a survival characteristic. Bagabond could kill anyone she found a threat without hesitation. Not even Jack Robicheaux, the were-alligator who had joined her in the shelter under the streets of New York, knew what she had done before they met. Suzanne did not want to become that person, that feral creature, again. Guatemala had begun to heal her, but the damage was too deep for her old personality to have been entirely erased. Bagabond had just been buried. And the Kaibiles had dug up the body.

"I thought I might undertake a rearguard action. Balam and I could do a lot of good." Her head twitched as Balam took down her kill, a deer. After feeding herself, Balam would bring what was left back to them. A small fire was safe here under the thick leaves of the trees. The smoke would not show if they put it out quickly. She picked up the driest wood she could find.

"You could do more by getting us to Belize." Umán helped her gather fuel for the fire.

"This is my home. Shouldn't I defend it?"

"If this is your home, then your people are my people." Umán spoke patiently. "I think that the saints have chosen this way to ask for your help in saving our people."

"Which 'our people'? Jokers and aces, or Indians?"

"Why do you think it matters?"

Suzanne was furious. She was being guilt-tripped by an Indian shaman. She hated being wrong. Nothing more was said until after the deer had been cooked over the open flames. The fire brought up images from her past, from New York and from the sanitarium. Few of them were good memories. To clear her mind, she sent it out around the jungle among the monkeys and the birds. They had no past to haunt them. At the very edge of the area she could read, she caught indications of the army. They were setting up camp for the night.

"I got involved before. People got killed; some of *them* were 'my' people. Are you sure you want my help?" She leaned back against Balam's warm fur, trying to look bestial. She suspected it worked from the look in McCoy's eyes.

"We all have our *nahuals*, the animal spirits who accompany us in life. You just seem to have more of them, and the power to speak to them directly. A great gift." Umán was not at all discomfited by her display.

"Okay." Suzanne sighed. Maybe she had become too human. Leaving the two men to their own devices was something she could not accept. "McCoy, they used to call me Bagabond, a particularly horrible nickname I always thought. If you use it, I'll hurt you."

"*Nooo* problem." He dug into his camera bag. "You should have a couple of these, too."

She snatched the two plastic film canisters from the air.

"If only one of us makes it, something will get through." McCoy looked back at her without drama.

"Four hours of sleep, then we move on." McCoy was already out. When she looked at Umán, she saw that he also knew how close their pursuers were. In the flat Petén, with the trees alternating with broad savannahs, it would be much easier for the helicopter gunships to spot them. Up until now, they had had a relatively easy time, moving east through terrain that could shelter them. Now they would be moving through country where the smoke from a fire could be seen for kilometers. Before, they could use trails that had existed for centuries, sometimes millennia, and avoid leaving signs of their passage. The land they were entering was sparsely inhabited. They would be cutting their own paths through thick undergrowth. The border with Belize seemed even farther away.

Before Umán slept, she asked him why he had not gone to earth in the Highlands, where it would have been safer for him. He took his time in answering. As the fire died, the hieroglyphics that marked his body seemed to brighten and dim as they shifted. The priest brought his right hand down his left arm, fingers moving rapidly across the words as if he were a blind man reading braille, but without showing any sign of knowing what they meant.

"That one had become my friend," he said, nodding at the sleeping McCoy. "He would have been killed if I had left him. And I, alone of my town, survived. I do not believe that this could have happened by some chance. The saints are protecting me. I must honor their desires. I could not honor them by hiding for the rest of my life."

Saints had become a Maya codeword for the old gods, fit one way or another into the Catholic pantheon. As a lapsed Catholic, she was fascinated by the way it had been done over the centuries, with the gift of Mayan gods' attributes to the various saints. In her part of the country the fundamentalist protestants had made little progress in converting the people to their new Christianity.

"But, if you don't reach Belize, your knowledge as a *Chuchkajawib*, a mother-father of the people, could be lost forever."

"No. Those I have taught who then returned to their own villages will continue the rituals and follow the old calendar." Umán smiled across the tiny clearing, lit now only by the waxing moon high overhead. It was a sad smile, Suzanne thought, but not hopeless, only resigned. "I am told by my blood and my readings of the seeds that I am destined for a long journey. Perhaps it is the longest one, perhaps not. I can only hope that the ending of that journey will benefit my people. I will have no other memorial. My family and friends have vanished as surely as our ancestors a thousand years ago, according to the archaeologists. Myself, I think they are still here in each of us. I will not see our people vanish. Our stories of creation tell us of world upon world, coming into being and then destroyed. It may be that it is time for ours to return."

"I heard about the Hero Twins. They fought back to regain the ancient Maya lands and rights. Do you believe they could do everything it was said they could?" Suzanne had heard word-of-mouth, third- and fourth-hand tales of magic abilities and blood sacrifices. She had found it hard to credit.

"Yeah." McCoy coughed and sat up groaning. "I never saw them personally, but I saw some very impressive footage of what they could do. I know the people who covered the Maya uprising. They believe. Me, I think maybe they were aces. Or maybe they really were the reincarnation of the heroes of the *Popol Vuh*. They came close. A lot of U.S. money went into defeating them. Some of that money was probably from the Card Sharks, but most of it was because Washington and a number of other countries in and out of this hemisphere couldn't let them win. Their success would have meant revolutions by native populations from the Arctic to Tierra del Fuego. Nobody wanted the American Indian Movement getting any ideas. Is there any venison left? I'm still starving."

Suzanne cut some meat from the haunch she had wrapped and put beside her pack.

"Thanks, babe." McCoy waved the meat at her before biting off a chunk. The taltuza hissed and the jaguar growled. Suzanne confined herself to a baleful glare. McCoy smiled broadly back at her.

"Time for all good revolutionaries to shut up and get some sleep."

Twenty kilometers behind them, in an army camp of thirty Kaibiles, three helicopters landed. Two were gunships to be used in aerial reconnaisance. The other, larger, chopper brought two passengers. Even the fearless Kaibiles turned aside as they got off and made their way to the commander's tent. The stench was overwhelming, that of a long-dead animal left in the sun to rot. Forewarned by a downwind breeze, the colonel, sliding on his reflective Raybans, stepped out to meet his new allies. The smaller man introduced himself as Dr. Peter Marcus Alvarado, a New York associate of Dr. Faneuil. The effect of his perfectly tailored jungle fatigues was marred slightly by the two white smears of menthol beneath his nostrils. The second thing he did was proffer the colonel a small blue jar of Vicks VapoRub.

The other man was the source of the vile smell. Crypt Kicker. Despite the heat, he was dressed entirely in black, including a mask and cowl. The mask was designed to cover one side of his face. At six feet, two inches, he towered over the others in the camp, but his body was misshapen. One shoulder rose above the other, and he dragged his left foot when he pulled himself across the ground of the encampment. What most caught the eyes of the Kaibiles was the flaming red cross on his chest. Speculation ran the range between an agreement between militant Protestants and the government, the return of General Efrain Ríos Montt's regime to power, or perhaps a radical right Catholic movement, as to who had supplied him. Answers were not forthcoming.

"Our troubles can be contained as soon as they start across the Petén Lowlands." The Kaibile colonel spoke with great confidence. "The helicopters will spot them. We know they aren't far ahead anyway. The Indian and that *gringa* he picked up will be slowing him down. Our only real threat would come from any *subversivos* he might contact in the area. Of course, they are as likely to kill them as not, anyway. Animals."

The short *norteamericano* nodded without as much enthusiasm.

"What do we know about the *gringa*?"

"Ah, another aging hippie out to save the world. We get them all the time. They like the climate, I think. Disgusting. This one hasn't tried to convert anyone or make any 'improvements.' She has not even endeavored to turn anyone to communism. That's why she was allowed to stay. Harmless, but potentially useful as an information source—under the proper stimulus—or a hostage." He ran thumb and forefinger over a perfectly-groomed mustache, now striped with the white VapoRub. Behind his sunglasses, his eyes moved to the gangling walking corpse who stood before him silently. The grass turned brown beneath his feet, and marked his trail through the camp. "I'm sure my Kaibiles, my tigers, will be able to eliminate this problem, but perhaps you will find it educational."

"Ah heah one a those fugitives is a devil-worshipper." Crypt Kicker spoke, although it was difficult to understand more than every other word with the Texas accent and what sounded like a cleft palate birth defect. "Witches can't be suffahed to live. Bible says so."

The other two men were silent. Neither could think of a reply.

"Get a few hours of sleep. We'll be after them at dawn. My aide will show you to your tent. Tents. Food is available in the mess."

"That would be for me. The gentleman accompanying me requires neither rest nor food. But thank you, Colonel. Your hospitality is appreciated."

Suzanne took a break from cutting a path through the underbrush to wipe away the sweat pouring down her face. It was beginning to occur to her that a woman who would be forty on her next birthday had no business in the middle of a rain forest. Avoiding a fer-de-lance was not normally recommended as an aerobic exercise. Her hair was pulled up into a knot on the top of her head. She and Umán were taking turns at the machete. McCoy had given it a try once, but he could not manage the rhythm that put enough strength behind the swings to make any real headway. Despite Umán's "handicap," once more he turned out to be as able as she. With one hand braced against the bark of the ceiba, she used the other to wave away flies.

"Trouble will overtake us soon." Umán came up behind her and grasped the handle of the machete to pull it from its resting place in the trunk of a lightning-felled mahogany. "From the sky, I think."

As fatigue took its toll on everyone, language skills seemed to evaporate. No one used more words than he or she had to, regardless of the language being spoken. Last night's four hours of sleep had done little to refresh any of them.

"Helicopter gunships." McCoy came up to join them. He was drenched with sweat.

"One, maybe two. Lots of ground to cover." The taltuza waddled over and she extended an arm for it to climb.

"North." From Umán, it was both statement and question.

"We're about to hit a logging road." She rolled her shoulders as she looked back at the trail they had hacked through the jungle. It might as well have been outlined in neon. It was probably safe from the air because of the jungle canopy, but if anyone spotted it from the ground, they were dead. "We've got to stop making it easy. It's a trade-off. We'll make more time and they may well lose our trail if we can hide where we turn south and east again. But we'll be much easier to spot from the air. My ears will protect us there."

"Great. Well, we'll have the advantage of being able to hide quickly." McCoy was trying to convince himself. "What do the *tz'ite* seeds say, Umán?"

"Danger lies ahead of us as well as behind." Umán looked to the east.

"No offense, but I could have guessed that one."

"Closer. There's a rebel encampment southwest of here. EGP, maybe, or I've heard there are some off-shoots of the Shining Path operating up here now. That could be bad. They don't care for non-Maoists much. Small, though, just five or ten men." Suzanne closed her eyes for an instant, and the image of the camp as seen by a band of howler monkeys flashed into her mind. "Lots of guns. In fact, they could be drug dealers or running guns to the guerrillas."

"And just how do you know that? Been reading Umán's crystals? Or are they friends of yours?" McCoy's voice held sudden suspicion. Suzanne realized that she had been keeping most of her knowledge of their surroundings to herself, and most particularly how she was getting it. Having both herself and Umán as oracles must have been irritating the hell out of McCoy. McCoy had been thinking of her as simply the Doctor Doolittle of Guatemala.

"I'm no guerrilla. We'd have guns and protection if that were true. Sorry." Suzanne and Bagabond warred for a moment inside her head. This time, Suzanne won. "I, uhh, see through their eyes and use their ears to listen. The other senses as well."

"Say what?" McCoy was obviously wondering if he was following a madwoman around Guatemala.

"Now, remember what you said about learning to believe in wild card powers. I have a . . . connection to wild creatures. I can share their perceptions." Bagabond made her stop short of discussing how much influence she could wield over their behavior.

"What the hell. My girlfriend has wings." He sighed with feeling. "But I'm not sure I'll ever get used to all this."

"How far is this logging road?" Umán was impatient. Suzanne suspected that he had figured this out many kilometers back.

"Another half hour of hacking." Suzanne reached for the machete, but Umán had already turned and begun swinging. Instead, she and McCoy followed the older man, pulling out the vegetation as he cut a path through it and arranging it behind them as naturally as possible. McCoy began humming "Talk to the Animals," and she threw a nice, thorny branch at him. He went back to cursing.

Stepping onto the lumber road was like stepping into heaven. They were re-energized by the instantaneous ease of passage, compared to what they had just endured. Balam had kept pace with them in the undergrowth, but now she bounded ahead and out of sight. Suzanne knelt and the taltuza marched down her arm and onto the soft earth.

"Walk on the crown. You'll leave less noticeable tracks in the gravel and rocks there." Suzanne put them in a single file.

Moving east toward Belize once more, the three fugitives walked as quickly as possible down the rough road. It was obvious it had not been used in some time, so there was little worry about drivers seeing them. Every hundred yards or so they skirted or clambered over a fallen tree blocking the track. But after the claustrophobic jungle, Suzanne felt terribly exposed. Seeing the deep blue sky overhead only made her more nervous. Now Umán was at a disadvantage. The speed at which he could struggle along set their pace. More than once, Suzanne and McCoy traded glances at the set of his face and agreed not to help him unless asked or the situation became critical.

After three hours and a good six kilometers, Suzanne— listening with sharper ears than her own—heard the heart-stopping rhythm of helicopter blades. They took immediate shelter in the dense growth beside the track. Umán was most appreciative of the forced rest stop. The helicopter prowled low, following the lumber road's turns only a few feet above the treetops. They froze as it passed directly overhead, pressing themselves into the shadow of a fallen mahogany ignored by the loggers. When not even Bagabond's borrowed ears heard the gunship's rotors, they got up and brushed themselves off.

"They'll be back." McCoy shook his cameras back into place. "This country's too damn small."

"Be happy. If it were any larger, we'd have no chance of walking across it, would we? Maybe they're just looking for that rebel encampment back a few kilometers." She pushed stray hair back off her face with both hands and wiped the sweat off her forehead with the back of her arm. She opened her eyes to return the dubious gaze of the journalist. "Just a thought . . ."

Umán had propped himself against the trunk of a ceiba. He was gray and could barely hold himself up, even after their nerve-wracking rest. McCoy offered him a hand, which he shook away.

"We've got to stop for rest. We haven't eaten in hours or gotten any sleep. Nobody can keep up this pace. Even you have to get tired sometime, don't you?" McCoy never looked at Umán, but Suzanne saw and felt the problem. She was surprised that the front she was trying to keep up was still working, but she felt like Umán looked right now. She was not happy about it. This part of the Petén was about to turn into savannah. Crossing that grassland of little or no cover would be the most dangerous part of their trek. After that, it was only a few more kilometers of rain forest to the border. Just a little matter of ten or twenty.

"Okay, but let's move back from the road." She frowned as she examined their immediate options. Viewed through the animals' eyes, the terrain held no completely sheltered spots. It was a measure of her exhaustion that she almost forgot to call Balam back in.

"There is a place nearby. It should be safe." Umán pushed himself fully upright while trying to hide the pain he was suffering.

McCoy followed the shaman across the road and into the bush on the north side. Suzanne hesitated, switching her vision among the animals without seeing their possible destination. She shook her head, but after a pause to gather up the taltuza, she made her way into the wall of jungle after them.

After half an hour of climbing over and picking their way around the huge trees and the tangled underbrush, Umán led them into a partially cleared area that opened up one side of the ruins of a pair of Mayan temples. They were small, as befitted their location in an outlying town under Tikal's influence. Their platforms rose about fifteen feet above the floor of the forest. Other mounds could be discerned as dark shadows in the rain forest behind them. The temple on the right was a pile of tumbled stones, torn apart by the roots of the chicle trees growing on top of it. But the left temple was partially intact, its entry framed by a combination of hieroglyphs and plaster god-masks. From what little research she had done, Suzanne believed that she recognized the face of the mythological character known as God K by his forehead mirror. The ridiculous nature of the name given him by archaeologists had stuck with her. A trench a meter or more deep ran up to and under the temple. Thieves had been here, but the ditch was old and crumbling in on itself. She was amazed the masks had survived. Maybe they had forgotten their chainsaws.

Umán was transfixed by the inscriptions carved into the stones of the ancient building. Suzanne compared them with his own scarifications. The words carved into his flesh were different, although it was more a feeling of style rather than direct comparison that made her believe it. Another dialect or perhaps just the hand of the artist. She was still curious to know if he could read any of them, but was loathe to interrupt him.

McCoy was hauling himself up the side of the platform before she made the connection that her weariness had almost hidden.

"Stop! McCoy." Still mindful of their surroundings, she kept her voice imperative but low. He halted, one hand poised to grab the next upturned step.

"Now what's the problem? I'm getting out of this heat." McCoy glared down at her.

"Don't move." Suzanne glared right back, but still refused to raise her voice.

The first contact was always the most difficult, especially with animals of higher intelligence. After frequent contact, such as hers with Balam, it seemed that neural pathways formed that led her into the areas she needed to access. Her mind penetrated that of the temple-dweller, twining around his fight or flight instinct that had begun to trigger when he heard them blunder into his home ground. Balam had scented their invasion of another's territory and stayed at a respectful distance, but Suzanne had missed it. Probing gently, she pushed gently at flight, not making his choice but influencing it.

When the puma burst out of the temple and onto the overgrown platform, McCoy did not have to be reminded to remain still. He froze, staring at what should have been the agent of his death. The puma's head swung toward him, but Suzanne again redirected his attention, this time to herself. She walked to the base of the platform as the puma delicately picked his way to the ground. Their eyes met and held, recognition of a kinship beyond that of fur and skin or claws and nails in both. Suzanne withdrew part of her influence and the cat, with a strange mixture of a whine and a growl, leapt across the clearing to disappear into the forest.

Suzanne looked up at McCoy, who had turned and was sitting on a displaced block from the staircase. He stared down at her as if he had never seen her before.

"You really do talk to them, don't you?" McCoy watched Balam enter the clearing and pace to Suzanne's side before turning her gaze after the puma. She dropped the body of a peccary on the ground.

"In my way." Suzanne turned to look for Umán. In the time it had taken her to ask the puma to leave, he had opened his cotton sack and begun removing what she took to be religious objects. He looked up when he felt her eyes on him.

"We should ask permission and blessings before we encroach on the place of gods." He was using the lowest intact step as his altar, carefully placing the copal incense on the ancient stones.

"It's clear." Suzanne smiled maliciously at McCoy, who was coming backward down the side of the platform. "Not so much as a fer-de-lance."

He hesitated for just an instant before taking his next handhold.

"We can use all the help we can get. Let him go for it." Once down on solid ground, McCoy bared his teeth back at her. She shrugged.

"Just make sure there's no smoke." She rocked her head back and looked up through the small break in the trees above them. Fighting back exhaustion, she skipped through the senses of the arboreal creatures in a search for another helicopter. She heard nothing through the ears of the howler monkeys, but she caught herself swaying when she came back. She knew her range was not nearly as wide as it should have been. Suzanne put her hand to her forehead as if that could stop the pounding and collapsed slowly to the ground. "No smoke."

Bracing her head on her hand, Suzanne sat in the dirt and watched Umán light the incense and begin a soft chant. Suzanne tried to concentrate on Umán's ritual. In her village—former village—the people practiced traditions that were obviously pre-Columbian, rituals for childbirth, planting, harvesting and the other major events of life. But they had not had an *ajk'ij* or any kind of religious leader. Whatever couple served as the village leaders took on that role as well. Despite the mix of traditions, they all thought of themselves as good Catholics.

Umán continued his prayer as he offered tobacco leaf and a splash of *aquardiente* to his gods or saints. How much difference was there between Umán's words and gifts and those presented here thirteen hundred years ago? Of course, this time there was no human blood. Umán bowed before the ruined temple, apparently asking permission for them to enter.

Despite herself, she found herself disarmed by McCoy's respect for the ceremony. The reporter crouched to Umán's left. His ever-present cameras sat on the ground out of reach. Looking intently into Umán's face, he occasionally held out objects from the priest's bag to the Daykeeper as the ceremony progressed. Finally, the Maya placed his seeds on the altar and waved some of the incense over them in what she took to be a last blessing. He bowed once more and began disassembling his altar, removing the traces of worship.

When Umán turned to look at her, a calm had come into his face that she hadn't seen in days of travel with the quiet man. It impressed her, but she was envious of his peace. Hers was disintegrating with every passing minute.

Balam was up the temple's tumbled steps in four leaps. Suzanne took rather more time and effort to gain the top. She surveyed their surroundings once more before turning and entering the small chamber, with her flashlight in hand. McCoy swore at her again when he saw it.

The chamber was in remarkably good shape. It looked safe in the small circle of light that she shone around the roof. The center arch high above them was intact. As she played the light across the walls, all three were startled by the murals. Incomplete, but still holding much of their original bright color, scenes of battles and the courts of the gods were divided by bands of inscriptions. The musky scent of puma only added to the alien feel of the site. Alien to McCoy and herself. Umán could have been one of the men pictured here. What she noticed most were the recreations of the royal courts presided over by gods, but containing rabbit scribes and other animal advisors. That part was familiar to her.

"You know, Menotti, when you smile, you actually look part human." McCoy dumped his belongings on the bench running across the back wall of the room. He was careful to avoid scuffing the art.

"Being around you, McCoy, doesn't give anyone much reason to smile." It was a half-hearted slam. Suzanne sat cross-legged in the middle of the floor. "Jose, can you read any of the hieroglyphs?

"Some are familiar. Others are too different." He rubbed his left arm unconsciously. "A different time, another world."

His words, shaded by a millennium and a half of pain and loss, echoed in the room. Suzanne clicked off the flashlight.

"Let's get some rest."

*   *   *

Balam's cry woke her, shattering her sleep from inside
and outside her skull. It had to be about four AM. Dark
outside. The moon was setting. Moving as little as possible, she prodded Umán awake with her foot and hissed
at McCoy, sleeping on the ledge. Suzanne watched the
guerrillas approach the temple from all sides. They were
surrounded. Balam had scaled a tree to escape. The soldiers were ignoring her. It was the only positive aspect
of the situation. The guerrillas had come from upwind,
alerting few of the animals. Suzanne had simply missed
the other warnings.

In her mind, she retraced their steps, searching for
any trail they might have left. If the guerrillas were
on routine patrol—and no one thought to check the
temple—they might come out of this alive. Then she
remembered Umán's ceremony. The odds got much
longer. He had cleared away the main debris, but the
burn marks were left on the stones to be washed off in
the morning. Another stupid mistake. She put her head
down and hoped Umán's gods had paid attention the
night before.

Now that she was fully awake, she used the eyes of
some howler monkeys to watch the rebels. To her
disgust, the point man surveyed the temple steps and
immediately spotted the remnants of the tiny sacrifice.
He motioned to his captain. The captain looked up at
the temple and waved five of the dozen men up the
broken stones to the top of the platform. Their guns, a
mix of Uzis and M-16's, were aimed squarely at the doorway. Before they could rush in, Suzanne stood up and
walked out into their midst. The weapons snapped up to
point at her.

"I am alone," she told them in her worst Spanish. "An
archaeology student."

"*Buenos noches.*" The captain was female, much to
Suzanne's amazement. She had not known the guerrillas
were quite so gender-blind. Suzanne winced as the captain ordered four of the men to search the temple. Without an altercation, Umán and McCoy were escorted out

of the temple. The remaining moonlight was reflected from the limestone of the ruins as the captain looked back at Suzanne, who shrugged, the barrel of an Uzi four inches from her head.

The rebel who acted as the point man drew the captain aside. She thought that they had to be discussing Umán, given the looks in his direction. When they came closer to inspect the hieroglyphs on his body, they were more respectful than she would have expected. She and McCoy were well-guarded but otherwise ignored. Suzanne took the opportunity to examine the guerrilla team. The mix of uniforms included traditional clothing. Usually, she understood, the Marxists and Maoists tried to break down tribal identity as being counter-revolutionary. But there were two *ladinos* among the other ten *indigenas*. The captain herself was four feet, eight inches of solidly-built Maya, a woman she could have imagined seeing in Chotol. Without the Uzi. She was dressed in standard military fatigues that were a couple of sizes too big for her. But the turban and a thin band of embroidery across her shirt seemed to indicate she still followed some traditional ways. Suzanne couldn't see the embroidery sufficiently well to even guess at a people, but she guessed Kekchi from her face.

Her attention moved on to the point man. At first, she thought he had painted his face with spots like an ancient Jaguar warrior. When he came over to search her, she saw instead that he was a joker. His body was covered in short fur, marked like the jungle cat's. When she moved too abruptly during his pat-down body search, retractable claws sprang from between his fingers to stop her. She was jealous.

While Suzanne and McCoy had been body-searched, Umán was simply asked if he carried weapons. When he indicated his machete, the captain removed it from his belt, but did not search him further. Nor did she check the bag he carried. Her pack, and McCoy's bag and cameras had been confiscated. What kind of rebels were these?

Balam tracked them as they were led away to the north

down the hidden trail the guerrillas had used to enter the small temple compound. Not fifteen words had been exchanged during their capture. Even McCoy kept his mouth shut. Suzanne and McCoy had their arms bound in front of them. Umán was unrestrained. The captain deferred to him in setting the pace. Watching them, Suzanne felt sure that the two guerrillas who walked beside him were more bodyguards than captors. Curiouser and curiouser.

What was the affiliation of these rebels? They shouldn't have been in the Petén. With so few people down here, there were neither potential converts nor army patrols to fight. It was too far from the war zones of the Highlands to be a staging area. On the other hand, it was much safer than being guerrillas in the mountains. But these people were not playing at it. They were serious, well-trained and well-disciplined. If they were involved with smuggling, they would have killed them immediately. Thinking about the Kaibile unit following them, she wondered if they were about to get all the trouble they could ever have imagined.

After four hours of jungle trekking, the prisoners marched into a broad clearing in the midst of the forest. The trees here were huge, fifty feet high. Their crowns nearly joined overhead. Where gaps might have revealed the camp below, camouflage netting had been stretched. Half a dozen shafts of sunlight still penetrated the foliage to add an almost unnatural golden glow to the scene stretched out before them. Fifty or more tents stood below the giant trees. A more traditional thatched roof, supported by six columns, stood at the far end in front of what looked like a temple mound. That was their destination.

Children walked between the tents, carrying water and firewood. They were as serious as their elders, but they looked well-fed and happy, making games of their work until they saw the strangers. Older people left their tents to watch them. Umán occasioned many comments, but she caught only a few dissociated words in Quiché as they walked past. Women cooked tortillas on their *comales* throughout the camp, and the pat-pat of their hands against the dough made Suzanne think of Chotol. A crowd fell in behind them as they passed among the tents.

One of the two men beneath the shelter stood up as they approached. Although Maya, his fatigues bore no indication of the people from which he came. The other man sat cross-legged with his back to one of the center posts. There was no mistaking the fact he was Lacandon Maya. No one else would have worn a pure white cotton shift like that. He smoked a huge cigar, staring at the rising smoke as if it was revealing the future to him. She recognized them with a sense of disorientation. Hunapu, the Lacandon, and Xbalanque, his "brother," the Hero Twins. They were dead, murdered a year ago. Perhaps they had all been killed as they slept and this was some kind of Maya purgatory. But why was she still so tired if she was dead? She shook off the unreality of it. Although no one believed much of what the government said, no one had seen these two since Nebaj. But who looked in the Petén? Glancing sidelong at McCoy, she could tell he felt the same shock of recognition as she. She could not tell if Umán knew who he faced. There had been a lot of talk of human sacrifice around these guys. She had dismissed it at the time as the government's attempt to scare people away, but the rumors sprang into her head anyway. Suzanne forced her attention back to their present problems. Xbalanque had interpreted her stare correctly and spoke in English.

"We're hard to kill. The gods failed." He laughed easily. "Why did you think the Guatemalan Army would succeed?"

Hunapu gestured for Umán to join him on the reed mats covering the dirt floor. The Lacandon was obviously as fascinated by the Cakchiquel's joker manifestation as the others had been. Whatever it took to keep them alive. The two traditional men spoke in Quiché, but it was far too fast and too soft for Suzanne to follow. Hunapu offered him the cigar. Umán turned his back to the onlookers and opened his shirt to show Hunapu the hieroglyphs covering his body. Xbalanque had begun searching her pack and McCoy's camera bag.

She began mentally searching the surrounding jungle for any possible allies. Balam was out there at the perimeter, but she was always aware of her presence. A margay, the small arboreal cat, had nasty claws if it came down to that. There was a tribe of spider monkeys that could wreak havoc within the camp. Otherwise, there were no creatures to come to their aid beyond the brilliant tropical birds like the toucans, who were primarily good for confusion. She felt sure that she could escape, but the chances of getting Umán and McCoy out were not good. Suzanne began considering whether getting those two canisters of film out outweighed all else. Bagabond had returned. When she drew her mind back and began to look for escape routes, she turned her head to meet the jaguar warrior's eyes. His stare was fixed on her.

Hunapu conferred with Xbalanque, drawing Umán into the conversation at times, apparently to emphasize some point he was making. Xbalanque kept shaking his head, but Hunapu's persistence wore him down. Suzanne fervently hoped they were not discussing the finer points of blood sacrifice. More old rumors ran through her head.

Xbalanque helped Umán up as his brother rose. Hunapu gave commands to their guards, but not in the Quiché she might have understood. When the jaguar warrior drew his machete, she was ready to bring all her potential allies into play. But when the machete dropped, her hands were free. It was only when everyone looked up to hear all the normal sounds of the jungle resume at once, that she realized that she must have taken over almost every non-human creature within half a kilometer without conscious thought. Behind the impassive mask of his face, the jaguar warrior had made the connection to her. He tilted his head to one side as she had often seen Balam do in listening to the forest. To her amazement, she caught sudden laughter in his eyes. He turned away to free McCoy. Xbalanque was speaking to them.

"My brother believes that you are innocent travelers, fleeing the army, our mutual enemies." Xbalanque was not as sure. "This film you're carrying could be important to our cause as well. It will be returned to you."

There was another exchange between the two resistance leaders. Xbalanque protested, Hunapu demanded. During their discussion, members of the patrol handed back their confiscated belongings. McCoy knelt and began checking his cameras and equipment bags to make certain that the contents were intact. Suzanne had decided that his cameras were his links back to a normal life, rather than one being spent on the run in the Guatemalan jungle. She just hefted hers. The weight was right. She slid into it, strapping her machete back around her waist.

Things were suddenly looking good, but she wanted out before they changed again. By now they had lost ten or twelve hours, counting the walk back to their camp at the ruins. She had no idea where the Twins' camp was, but she knew it couldn't be far from Flores. The only passage through the Maya Mountains was either to the south or beyond Tikal to the north. The south was less populated and therefore they had fewer chances of meeting an army border patrol. It was their best chance. The only good part of this was that the Kaibiles had to be almost due south of them, wondering where the hell they were. But the border patrols must have been alerted by now. It would surely no longer be a Kaibile-only operation.

Xbalanque had evidently lost again. She had a sneaking sympathy for him. She knew exactly what he was going through. This time Hunapu spoke to them directly and the captain of the patrol that had captured them translated.

"Tecún Umán has told me of your plight. He assures me that the gods have protected you on your journey. I believe that the prophecies written on his body tell of the importance of his mission. I am honored to aid Tecún Umán in escaping the Spanish this time." He spoke to the captain directly while Suzanne tried to sort out what he meant. Tecún Umán was a Quiché hero who died fighting the conquistador Pedro de Alvarado. He had become a symbol of the five hundred years of Maya resistance. She was captivated by the thought that Hunapu could actually read Umán's hieroglyphs. Could he teach Umán? She had come to the conclusion that they could well be meaningless gibberish, a joker manifestation.

The captain began to outline the plan to get them across the southern Petén to Belize. One of the *ladinos* would drive a truck from one of the rare Petén *fincas* with a load of Maya "farm workers." They would be hidden in the back. New papers would be provided to get them across the border without a battle.

Bagabond considered leaving Umán and McCoy in the hands of the resistance. Let militants take care of militants. But as she looked out over the quiet camp, she remembered once more that she had nowhere else to go. Chotol was gone and her presence was deadly to anyone she met. Exile seemed to be the only choice.

While the others slept, she sat up and sent part of mind wandering the jungle, touching the minds of the animals she had come to know. These creatures had given her peace and a home as much as the people of Chotol. Balam's mind and hers had become so intertwined that sometimes she could not find their division or know who the huntress in the jungle was. When she had said goodbye, she lay down for her last night in Guatemala.

This time the helicopter buzzed them, coming in low and staying directly overhead. Without changing speed or acknowledging its presence, the forty-year-old International truck lumbered along the rutted road. This chopper, or one that sounded just like it, had followed them for a few minutes earlier in the morning. In the tarp-covered back of the truck, Suzanne felt both slightly nauseated and claustrophobic. Lying across her feet, Balam panted, trying to draw a clean breath. She, McCoy and

Umán sat all the way inside, just behind the cab. The rest of the rear compartment held Maya resistance fighters masquerading as workers heading for Guatemala's major ports. They were armed. Guns had been offered to the three of them as well, but each had refused.

They had been on the road since six that morning. Now, seven hours later, they were only five kilometers from the border. It had occurred to her, each time the truck tilted its way over some obstruction and smashed her head back against the roof support, that walking might not have been such a horrible prospect. Within the passenger compartment, the air stank of too many people in too small a space. Since the sun had moved directly overhead, the temperature must have risen to well over a hundred extremely humid degrees. But anything less would not have looked realistic.

Umán was off in his own world, praying, she hoped, for their deliverance. Last night, Umán had vanished with the Hero Twins to perform rituals to protect both the Maya resistance and themselves. She had no idea what they had done, but in the morning they looked as if they had wrestled the gods personally. McCoy was asleep again, although she could not imagine how he managed it. They crashed into and up out of another pothole and she leaned forward and back in rhythm; she had finally learned to protect her head. Looking to the far end of the truck, she caught the eyes of Maria K'anil, the woman who had led the patrol that had captured them, and looked up. Maria nodded. She had already passed the word through her people to get ready for trouble.

The helicopter didn't move away after another two kilometers. The southern crossing into Belize was the least-used entrance since it was the farthest from Belmopan. While it was the least heavily guarded, this fact also meant that any travelers on this road stood out. The Kaibiles would not give up until they were dead. She had ignored these Card Sharks of McCoy's until last night, preferring to worry about a danger she knew. Now she wondered what allies the Kaibiles might have. It was time to marshal her own allies.

This close to the Maya Mountains she had good choices. But choosing who might live or die was not something she could do dispassionately. The Bagabond who was could have called in any and all creatures to defend herself and those she wished to protect. Suzanne had to find a middle ground, create a new Bagabond with the old strength and a new compassion. She sent her mind spinning out to identify all the possibilities, drawing them to her.

She saw the roadblock coming through the eyes of a brilliant orange and black toucan. She warned Maria before the coded banging on the back of the cab began. Guatemalan Army. The Kaibiles. She reached over and shook McCoy awake. Umán drew himself up. Their truck gathered speed and swayed with enough force to throw McCoy onto the truck bed. Abruptly, the driver hit the brakes, skidding the aged International sideways toward the army trucks blocking their way.

The Maya guerrillas were leaping from the back of the truck before it had come to rest, firing as they landed. Bagabond had drawn her machete to slice through the tarp and cut a path for them to get out on the far side from the battle. She jumped out first, followed by Balam. McCoy helped hand Umán down to the ground and then joined them.

A flock of neon-bright green parrots shot across the road from the jungle, camouflaging their dash to cover. McCoy's bootheel slid down the side of the road's crown. He barely caught himself before falling. Bagabond grabbed him by a flailing arm and hauled him into the brush. Balam had been joined by two spotted jaguars. She sent them ahead to clear out any hidden Kaibiles. Her plan was to get around the roadblock by end-running it through the jungle while the guerrillas kept the Kaibiles busy. The border was four hundred yards ahead. Bagabond sent more avian waves at the soldiers. More effective than pigeons, they were larger and their bright plumage was far more distracting. But she could do little more to help. Her attention had to be focused on her own problems.

To their right, an ocelot and a soldier cried out simultaneously and fell from the tree where the soldier had perched. He landed first, in a heap; the ocelot leaped away. They slid forward, avoiding the body. Bagabond was only half present on their dash for freedom. Most of her conscious mind was dedicated to throwing the unexpected at the army and watching ahead for danger.

The guerrillas pinned the soldiers down from the front. The predations of jaguars, pumas and ocelots both demoralized and eliminated the enemy. There was a pleasant irony in their destruction by the very animals they had chosen as their namesakes. They had been trained to fight rebels; no one told them they would be slaughtered by demonically-driven beasts. Still, they held ranks. But their shots became wild. Trying to hit a puma, two of the soldiers shot each other. Half a dozen men were down, writhing in pain from being mauled. Maria's sharpshooters had killed another four.

Bagabond shepherded Umán and McCoy back out to the lighter vegetation by the side of the road. More parrots swirled around them in a red, green and orange tornado. They were halfway to the border station, which had been left with only four regular army men to defend it. The Belize contingent was long gone. She organized a troop of howler monkeys to drive them off by throwing stones and branches. Faced with the jaguars coming at them and the monkeys' terrorism behind, they grabbed their guns and ran for Belize themselves, even leaving their Jeep.

She felt a quick, savage joy at their success, which lasted only until she spotted the helicopter gunship landing between her charges and the border. A limping cadaver dressed in black with a red cross emblazoned across his chest dropped to the ground followed by a man dressed in *GQ* fatigues. The chopper pulled up and its wash sent a stench like nothing she had ever smelled before, even in the sewers of New York City. It was enough to stop them on its own.

"Just give us the film, McCoy." The dapper commando smiled at them benevolently.

"Fuck off." McCoy stood his ground as the wild jaguars stalked the two newcomers. "You're Faneuil's pets."

"Bobby Joe, take care of the kittycats, will you, please?"

Bagabond watched the plants wither and die where the cowled man stood. She tried to stop the cats, but they were already in mid-spring. The ... thing in front of her spread its arms and gave off a fine spray she could barely see. It gathered the cats to its chest. Their screams of pain echoed in her brain as well as her ears. The feedback of anguish was nearly unbearable.

"Heathens. Idolaters. The Bible says you have to die." It spoke, but the words were barely intelligible. It dragged itself toward them slowly and inexorably. She pulled Balam away and sent her running into the jungle as far as she could. Behind them, the Kaibile colonel was forcing what was left of his men into a rear guard. The man McCoy had called Faneuil's pet slid a clip into his Uzi and took his time in aiming it at them, smiling all the while.

"Get behind me and get ready to run like hell." Bagabond's urgency came out in tones as hard as steel. "I can slow them down. *Get over that border.*"

Every creature within her reach was readied to throw themselves alongside her at the automaton marching toward them.

"No. That is *mine.*"

Umán evaded her and walked out to meet it. Bagabond shoved McCoy hard into the forest, herding him with the howlers. When she turned back, the fundamentalist zombie struck at Umán. The Daykeeper spun and took the blow on his left side. The killer's arm *melted* into the stone of his flesh, but Umán's body reformed behind its passage. It was trapped, if only for the few moments it would take to understand what had happened.

The Maya raised his left arm and plunged his hand through the center of the cross, down into the thing's chest, withdrawing his fist holding its acid-dripping heart. The zombie stared at its own heart with disbelieving eyes before crumpling to the ground with the release of an even more noxious stench. As it fell, its own arm was pulled out of the Daykeeper's side. Finally, Umán acknowledged his agony with a wail.

The zombie's companion was stopped by what he had just seen. He let his sights dip, but not long enough for Bagabond to act. He backed up and waved the gunship back down as he brought up the Uzi.

"Kill anyone left standing," Bagabond heard him shout into his radio headset. She was looking down the barrel of his gun even as she was flying with hundreds of birds that simultaneously attacked the helicopter. It exploded, raining burning debris down onto the border guards' office and setting it ablaze. She was the puma that appeared from the forest and sliced away the assassin's abdomen, spilling his intestines onto the Guatemalan dirt. Then she was none of those creatures. She was helping Umán limp toward the flames marking the border. McCoy appeared, to take his other arm.

The Kaibile colonel, knowing he had been betrayed by his allies and defeated by the people he considered beneath contempt, raised his own Uzi to kill them. Suzanne saw it, but she had used all the strength she had in the last two minutes. She tried to concentrate, but there was nothing there. No contacts.

Balam left the jungle in midair and crossed the dirt in two bounds. Before he could react, she knocked aside the gun and, with a single swipe of her claws, she tore out his throat. Standing over him she threw back her head and howled.

Suzanne was crying, uncontrollable tears of pain and exhaustion running down her face, cutting paths through the dirt.

"She remembered Chotol."

The Color of His Skin

Part 4

"You were wonderful again on Peri's show last night," Jo Ann told Gregg as he entered the office. Her skin was more emerald than usual, as if flushed. "My God, the pictures Mr. McCoy took, that awful Faneuil ..." She shook her head, and a warty finger impaled the morning paper. "The response has been good—if you ignore the minor riot near J-Town afterward."

"I heard about it on the way in. How bad was it?"

"Mostly just taunting and some bottle and rock-throwing back and forth between jokers and nats. No one killed, anyway."

"That's good," Gregg said. "So what are they saying?"

"Well, let's see ..." Jo Ann fluffed out the pages, scanning. "'The Davis-Hartmann revelations, coupled with the *60 Minutes* exposé and other reports, and now Josh McCoy's startling photographs from Guatemala, make a compelling portrait of ugliness in action,'" she quoted. "I like that one. But Pan probably doesn't like this: '... The knot of reporters around Rudo and Herzenhagen abruptly doubled in size late last night....' Ummm ... a little further down: '... Sources within WHO say that the board is pressuring Rudo to either answer the increasing accusations or to resign. . . .' Pretty interesting. How about this, from the editorial page: '. . . President Barnett's request that the Senate reconsider a mandatory virus testing bill has set off a vitriolic exchange of words between the opposing conservative and liberal camps. This observer wonders whether we are not seeing a reflection of the increasingly violent polarity of the public. . . .' "

Jo Ann dropped the paper back down. "You get the drift, boss. Every magazine from *Time* to the *Sun* has had an article about the Sharks, pro or con. Some are blaming the conspiracy for everything from the Dodgers' loss in the World Series to the last recession, at least those who aren't saying that it's all hogwash and the only way to eradicate the disease is to sterilize the carriers. I'll give you one thing—no one is sitting on the fence with this. You sure have an impact when you try."

See, Greggie? I told you. Use the Gift wisely and you'll be rewarded. . . .

Gregg chuckled. "I guess. And you're still smiling. What else is up?"

"Good news," Jo Ann said. "Got a FedEx letter from Marilyn Monroe's lawyers this morning. They're dropping the defamation of character suit they filed. And Hannah's in your office."

"You have a really idiotic smile, Jo Ann. Did you know that?"

"Hey, *I'm* not the Cheshire Cat around here." Jo Ann turned dramatically away and flicked on her computer. "I'll be busy writing letters. I won't hear a thing."

"Jo Ann—"

"Your visitor's waiting. Get in there."

Shaking his head, Gregg went into his office as Jo Ann began rattling the Macintosh's keys. He shut the door behind him. "I have to get a new secretary," he said. "This one treats me like a younger brother—when she's not bugging my office at a client's request. I should have fired her when I had the excuse."

Hannah smiled. "Jo Ann believes in you," she replied.

"Uh-huh," Gregg said, going around his desk and sitting. Hannah's blue-green eyes followed him. He found that disconcerting, and pretended to study his appointment book. "And how about you?"

"I'm beginning to get there."

Gregg looked up. Neither of them said anything. Gregg felt inside himself for the Gift, the power, and he reached out with that newfound sense to see within her a surprising multi-hued swell. He let the Gift touch her, wonderingly.

Greggie! Stop it! The voice came suddenly, wrenching his gaze away from Hannah's. He fell out of the Gift with a grimace.

"Gregg?"

This isn't what it's for. Leave her alone.

I haven't DONE anything.

You can't. You mustn't.

It's MY Gift. MY power. I can use it as I choose.

No, you can't. Don't you see? You can't even THINK that. . . .

"Gregg?"

"Sorry. Just a twinge—I . . . I pulled a muscle yesterday."

You can't . . .

Gregg glanced at his watch. "We're supposed to meet the WABC people this afternoon, right? Why don't we hit lunch and decide what we're going to say? McCoy's pictures are going to stir the pot even more, and we should be ready for that."

. . . can't . . .

Gregg rose and went to the door. He opened it, watching her as she nodded to Jo Ann and took her jacket from the rack.

He smiled.

But I can. Once again, I can. . . .

In the time since the War for the Rox, and especially in the last few months, Jokertown and the district surrounding it had increasingly become polarized, armed enclaves. During the daytime, there was little trouble as

long as you kept to main streets and avoided alleys and
other lonely places. During the day, jokers and nats mingled on the sidewalks, and if they avoided one another
or if there were stares, words, or an occasional more
intense incident, well, that was the chance you took.

But at night . . .

Walking in or out of Jokertown was like passing
through a border. A nat violating the unmarked bound-
aries risked being harassed by vigilante bands of jokers.
A nat in J-Town was well-advised to wear a mask. Nor
was it any less dangerous for a joker walking out of the
district, for a block or so away, youthful nat gangs bullied
hapless jokers.

At night, there was violence. There were fists, knives,
clubs, and guns. There was blood and even the occasional
death. At night, if you wanted to move in or out of J-Town,
you drove. Even then you stayed to well-lit streets, you
kept the doors locked and the windows up, and unless
there were other cars, you didn't stop for lights or signs.

In the erratic, block-wide no-man's-land girdling Jokertown, the order of society had broken down entirely.
In that space, a joker moved: a limping, assymetrical travesty like two different bodies bisected down the middle
and glued together. In the shadows of the boarded-up
buildings, other shapes moved with it.

"Hold up a second, John!" Gregg tapped the minivan
driver on the shoulder. "Can you pull over?"

The driver, a bearded nat, glanced over at the woman
sitting in the passenger seat. "Debra?" The woman
shrugged back at John, and he looked at Gregg in the
rearview mirror. "Here? You two call the shots, but
you're out of your minds if you want to take a stroll in
this place." John turned the wheel of the minivan over
until they bumped the curb.

"Gregg?" Hannah said. She was sitting next to Gregg
in the rear seat. Behind them, a videocamera sat on top
of boxes of equipment and coils of cable: John's equipment. "What's going on?"

"Just give me a moment." Gregg was already opening
the side door to the van and getting out.

The four of them were on their way to Jokertown. Debra Rashid was a reporter for WABC; John was her videographer. Gregg and Hannah had just taped the interview in the station when Gregg suggested that they continue the interview while walking the streets of Jokertown. Debra had agreed quickly: added color would enhance her chances of getting feature play with the story.

Gregg hadn't quite known what he'd planned to do, but it seemed that fate had handed him a plum. The emotions here nearly knocked him down with their intensity.

Across the street, the pathetic joker glanced at them once and then continued his hobbling progress toward Jokertown. This block was one that had seen far more than its share of trouble in the last few years. Most of the buildings—three story tenements, for the most part—were vacant, blinking down at them with windows of broken glass. Only a few lights betrayed the presence of those too poor or too stubborn to move away. Trash littered the gutters, the streetlamp poles were rooted in the broken glass of their shattered lights. At eight o'clock, the street traffic was already zero.

Greggie, this is grandstanding. You don't need this.

Just shut up. I know what I'm doing.

Behind him, Gregg could hear John grunt as he lifted his videocam to his shoulder. Hannah was a warm presence at his shoulder, and he could feel Debra's unease, like a taint of blood in water. And there were other emotions out there, ones that only Gregg could sense. "Hey!" Gregg called to the joker. "Let us give you a ride."

The joker looked at them. Gregg caught a glimpse of the face: half-feminine, half-male, and totally mismatched. Two entirely different faces. S/he didn't speak, but stared at them for a moment before shaking the head. The joker lurched forward, almost falling before the much shorter left leg touched the pavement. "Look, my friend, get in so we can all get the hell out of here. It's not safe," Gregg called after him.

"You got that right, mister."

The voice was an adolescent snarl. Four teenagers strolled confidently out from between two buildings; another trio appeared at the mouth of an alley across the street. They were street punks—all leather and chains, their hair spiked and multi-colored, and they were nats. The leader, a kid with electric-blue hair and a dragon tattoo snarling down his left arm, smiled at them evilly, flipping a long knife in one hand. The blade sparkled in the minivan's headlights. "Newspeople," he said. "Hey, Debra Rashid—I recognize you. Great tits, even on the tube. You out to catch some nasty footage?"

The rest of the gang had casually blocked the joker's path, spreading themselves out in a wide circle around him/her. They were laughing, taunting the joker and joking between themselves.

"Hey, maybe we cut it down the middle and get *two* jokers, y'know."

"Hey, Skunk, you like boys—you take the right half."

"Fuck you, asshole."

The joker still hadn't spoken. S/he whirled around frantically, clumsily, its eyes wide in terror. Knives and chains had appeared in the kids' hands; the intensity of the emotions upped a notch in Gregg's head. Two of them had handguns, and Gregg felt a quick fear. There were more of them than he'd thought, and the guns scared him. His confidence did a nosedive.

He heard the whir as John thumbed on his camera. Dragon-tattoo's gaze went to John, saw the camera, and he took three quick steps, placing his hand over the lens. "You turn that fucker off, man," he snarled.

At the same time, Gregg felt a change in the emotions of the kid. Where before there had been only scarlet rage, there was now a faint tracing of cool blue coming from him. *He's not entirely sure about this,* Gregg realized. *He hates the camera.* That decided Gregg.

"Get the hell out of here," the kid was saying. His knife was pointing at John's abdomen, and another kid—with a semiautomatic pistol leering from his fist—came over to back up Dragon-tattoo. "This ain't none of your business. Give me the damn tape and then get the hell out, or you get the same treatment as freak meat over there. Your choice, tourists. We don't gotta be nice."

John was glaring at the kid, but Gregg could sense that it was only bravado. Debra touched Gregg on the prosthetic. "I think we'd better go," she said, her voice shaky. "Please. Hannah, get back in the van. John, give him the tape. Mr. Hartmann—"

It won't work, Greggie. The power's not strong enough. Fuck you. It's MY Gift. I know what I can do with it.

Gregg stepped forward, interposing himself between the kid and John. John's lens followed him, still taping.

"Don't do this," Gregg told Dragon-tattoo, and let the Gift loose. With the words, the trace of azure uncertainty in the young man shivered as if struck.

The kid snorted, then wiped at his nose with the back of a leather-clad hand. "Wassa matter, you don't like seeing violence, dude? You must not watch much TV." The youth looked at Gregg with suddenly narrowed eyes. "Hey, I know you, too," he said. "You're goddamn Gregg Hartmann, ain't you? And the blond chick's the Davis woman. Shit, guys, we got a fucking celebrity audience tonight. Genuine joker lovers."

The rest of the gang laughed. "Don't let him give you no shit, Blades," one of them called out, and at the same time suddenly swung his chain; the steel links slashed air and caught the joker on the side of the head. S/he screamed and went down, blood gushing as the side of the face opened with a jagged cut. The joker fell, and they kicked the helpless body as they stepped over it, coming across the street to Gregg and the others. The joker moaned, unconscious.

"See, the meat'll keep for a few minutes," Blades said. He smiled toward Hannah. "You want a swing at freak meat, lady? Feels good. It really does. Almost as good as sex."

"You're sick," Hannah scowled. She started toward the injured joker, and Blades reached out for her with his free hand at the same time. Gregg intercepted the hand. For a second, the tableau held: Gregg staring at Blades, his good left hand clenched around the teenager's wrist while the emotional matrix swirled around them, strong and vivid. He could sense the muzzles of their weapons trained on him.

Careful, Greggie . . .

"Hey," Gregg said. The word flared with the Gift. "Let's call this a draw. You guys go your way, we'll go ours. Violence isn't going to solve anything. It isn't going to make the virus go away."

"It is if we kill every one of the fuckers." Blades wrenched his hand out of Gregg's grasp. "And right now you ain't in much position to bargain, are you, old man? I look around and I see we got all the big cards. High caliber ones. Sharp ones." He grinned, twirling the knife edge in front of Gregg's eyes. He still grinned, but underneath Gregg could still sense that unease. He let the Gift wrap around it, slowly, carefully coaxing it forward. *So slow, so clumsy, this power . . .*

But it's all you got, Greggie. I told you, but you wouldn't listen. Now you'd better be right.

"That's what they want you to believe," Gregg told him. The Gift made his voice powerful, but only Blades was responding to it. The others were lost in a bloodlust, their emotions too powerful and opposed to alter. The realization made his strategy at once simple and difficult: unless he turned the leader, he could not control what might happen. Fear lent desperation to his words. "That's the lie they want you to buy into, but it isn't true. And guns and knives aren't power. Not really." Each word chipped away some of the confining anger and isolated the young man's underlying unease at what he was doing.

He's the key. Turn him and the others follow. . . .

Gregg continued, hurrying the words. "You don't want to make a mistake here. Think about it. We're not some poor lone joker who wandered onto the wrong block. Touch us, and there's going to be a big response. People know who we are and where we are. They know when to expect us, and they're probably already looking. You're going to have cops all over this place. *Your* place. Call tonight a draw, my man, and no one loses face. C'mon." Gregg gestured toward the fallen joker. "You've made your point. There's no reason to hurt him anymore, or us."

"You're scared, Hartmann."

"You're damned right I'm scared. No one wants to die. No one wants to be hurt. Not jokers, not nats. Not you." The kid's uneasiness flared into more saturated fright. The Gift strengthened inside Gregg, arcing outward like an acetelyne flame.

The kid scoffed. "I ain't scared, Mister Suit. Ain't none of us scared of protecting our turf." The rest of the gang scowled and muttered behind Blades, and there was nothing in them but hate. Nothing Gregg could use. Their emotions threatened to shatter the uncertainty contained in their leader's own rage, and Gregg hurried to shield Blades with the Gift.

"But you *are* scared," he said. "Just like me. You wouldn't be out here if you weren't scared—scared of the wild card, scared because you know that there's always a chance for the virus to infect you, and you might turn out to be just like *that*." Gregg pointed to the fallen joker across the street. Inside Blades, there was a surge of pale white against the red, dampening it. "Think about it, Blades. He isn't any different than you. Not really. It's a goddamn *virus*. You don't choose to become a joker."

"Man, you talk too much. You know that?"

"You're right, I do. So why don't you use that? You want the jokers to stay out of your territory, right?"

"You got it, old man."

"Then let *me* tell them for you. You know who I am; you know the jokers listen to me. I'll tell them for you; I'll tell them all to stay away. That's what you want, right?" Repeating. Reinforcing. Shoring up the emotions.

Blades sniffed. He shrugged. Gregg said nothing, watching instead the intricate play of emotions within the boy. Suddenly, the kid shoved his knife into the scabbard stuck in his boot. "You better tell 'em good, old man. You tell 'em good, 'cause the next ones we find, we kill. You got that?"

"I got it, Blades . . . thanks."

The kid turned without another word, stalking off. One by one, the others followed. In a few seconds, the four of them were alone in the street once more.

"Fucking *great* footage," John whispered behind Gregg.

Hannah and Gregg went to the joker as John continued to film, as Debra began to lay a commentary in the background. Together, they helped the bleeding person to his feet. Hannah smiled once at Gregg as they walked slowly across the street toward the van.

"You were incredible," she said. "God, I was petrified, but *you* . . ." She shook her head. "You got us out without any more violence."

He had no answer for that. He shrugged, suddenly almost shy, and he marveled at the azure admiration for him that he sensed inside Hannah.

I did it! Gregg exulted as he and Hannah placed the joker on the floor of the van. *You see? It's more powerful than I thought. I can make them do ANYTHING!*

Greggie . . . Softly. Sadly.

Hannah began to clean the joker's head wound with sterile bandages from a medical kit Debra handed her. She paused a moment, looking up at Gregg as she brushed her hair back from her face.

She smiled again.

Her smile was far, far more compelling than the voice in his head.

The following night, Gregg took Hannah to dinner at Aces High, with Oddity along for protection. Aces High was a shadow of its old self—nearly deserted, the service mediocre, the food good but not exceptional. Hiram wasn't in, and Gregg recognized only one or two of the few patrons. Despite that, the three of them enjoyed themselves. Hannah especially seemed to shed the shadows the last year had wrapped around her, laughing and talking in an animated voice. She touched Gregg's hand often, sitting very near, and there were times when he imagined he could feel the heat of her leg close to his under the table. They stayed for two hours, lingering through appetizers, dinner, and dessert.

Oddity left them after they returned safely to Jokertown. As they walked up to the door of Father Squid's parsonage, Gregg could feel Hannah's admiration for him. The woman genuinely liked Gregg. She considered him a friend and an ally. Like the glow from a banked fire, her feelings promised heat beneath.

As he had all evening, Gregg blew again on the embers with the breath of his Gift.

Stop it, the voice cautioned him. *I tell you—this isn't why the Gift was given to you. You abuse the power and you betray yourself!*

Gregg just smiled as he held the door open for Hannah and they went inside. *It's mine. I'll abuse it any damn way I want,* he answered. "Here," he said to Hannah, "let me take your jacket. Where's Father Squid?"

As he slipped it from her shoulders, he let his fingers graze the skin of her arms. So soft . . .

"He's staying overnight with a sick parishioner." Hannah flicked on the lights, moving around the small living room before going to the chair where Quasiman sat staring into the night with unseeing eyes, lost in his own world. Hannah looked out to where the stark framework of the new steeple rose in the yellow glow of security lamps, then tenderly hugged Quasiman.

"Quasi, we're back, okay? We're here if you want us."

There was no answer. Hannah smiled at him and kissed the top of the joker's head. "Poor man," she said. "I owe him so much . . ." Tears suddenly brimmed in Hannah's eyes and she stopped. She sniffed and shrugged to Gregg, smiling sadly. "Sorry," she said.

"Don't you dare apologize," Gregg said, his voice low and deep, letting the power course through them. "Never ever apologize for compassion and love, Hannah."

The words flashed inside her, igniting against the flame of her friendship. She smiled again at him, brushing her long hair back from her face with what was almost a shy gesture, looking at him sidewise. "I was so paranoid about you at first, Gregg" she said to him. "I was so

afraid that I was making a mistake going to you. Now . . ."
She stopped. Smiled once more. "You're a very good
man, Gregg," she told him.

"You flatter me, Hannah. I'm just an old man trying
to do the best I can. I'm not a saint. I'm as flawed as
anyone else. More." His voice was laden with the power
inside him, stroking her emotions, slowly brightening
their colors, deepening their hues. *So much slower than
Puppetman, so clumsy in comparison, but . . .* And the
other voice yammered its constant warning: *Stop it! You
taint all that you have!*

"I don't believe you," Hannah answered. "You have
courage." She smiled up at him, taking a step closer to
him. "You have compassion and you have—" She paused
a heartbeat. "—love."

Her hand stroked his shoulder and remained. Gregg
could feel her touch, as if her finger were molten. She
felt it too, for she suddenly looked down, breaking the
eye contact with him as she gasped. Gregg reached out
with his left hand and cupped the side of her face, her
hair silken through his fingers. She glanced up into his
eyes once more, her face questioning. Almost in defiance,
she moved her head quickly to the side and kissed his
palm. When she looked back, her gaze dared him.

He found that he truly did not know what to say. In
that moment, the linkage between them was no longer
in his control. He felt dizzy and disoriented. The emotional matrix sparked and throbbed, wrapping about
them both, impossible to hold or guide. The feedback
screamed in his head, and he knew he must either let it
go or surrender to it.

But to let go meant that he would lose her, lose the
sudden promise in her eyes. Gregg held on.

The interior voice howled at him: *Stop this! This isn't
right, and this isn't real. It's a middle-aged man's fantasy
with no substance. Greggie, this is rape. You're forcing
her reactions. Stop before you ruin this like you ruined
all the rest of your relationships. . . .*

"I . . ." he began. Stopped. The power crackled in his
head; the voice screamed. For a moment, guilt threat-

ened to make him let go. "Hannah, I should be leaving. It's late."

She held his gaze. "You don't need to."

"I was in my twenties when you were born."

"And now I'm in my thirties and all grown up, Gregg. I'm a big girl. I can make my own decisions. Unless it's not what you want—"

"No!" he said quickly. The power was blinding. It pounded, it surged, it filled him with heat and light and burned away the guilt. *So you've learned nothing from all the pain you've inflicted, Greggie. It's still Greggie and his power and fuck everyone else. You've been given your chance and a Gift and you're proving only that you're no different now than you were. What happened to all the shame, the nightmares, the prayers for release?*

"Gregg, you look so sad. If I've embarrassed you or if I'm presuming too much . . ."

"No," he said again, and shut his mind to the voice, the nagging voice, the lecturing voice. "Oh God, no."

Hannah reached up with both hands and pulled Gregg's head slowly down to her, her gaze always on his until the last moment. As her eyes closed, their lips touched, hers impossibly warm and soft and yielding. The power was a storm around them, its thunder drowning out everything else. He opened his mouth, tasting her sweetness; his hand cupped her breast, feeling the nipple rise and harden beneath the cloth of her thin blouse and bra. He could feel her body pressing against his, her arms around him, and he responded, growling under his breath. *You see! And she's not a joker . . .* He started to bear her down to the floor, but her mouth came away from his, gasping.

"Not here," she said huskily, glancing back at the silent form of Quasiman. "I can't . . ." She pulled away from Gregg and took his hand. "My room," she said.

Hannah led him away into darkness as the voice yammered at him: *No! This is the old pattern, don't you see! You're sick and you'll be punished, Greggie. I guarantee it.*

He didn't listen.

As he moved on top of Hannah, as he entered her, Gregg thought of Sarah Morgenstern, of Ellen, of Succubus, of Andrea, of all his lovers' ruined lives.

He groaned in delight.

Feeding Frenzy
by Walter Jon Williams

1

Puppetman.

The word sang through Shad's mind as he paced his cell, a rhythmic accompaniment to the old Dexter Gordon tune that floated somewhere in his backbrain. In George Divivier's thudding bass he heard the refrain: *Puppetman.*

Gregg Hartmann's secret ace, the one that had driven Shad into a frenzy, made him kill. That had led him, eventually, to this place, to this cold concrete cavern carved out of Governor's Island.

Puppetman.

Shad was planning to meet Puppetman some day. And then, after him, some other people. George Battle, for one—who lied to him about the promise of a pardon, then let him get slammed away on Governor's Island.

He didn't feel anything any more. No compassion, no fear, no love. His own personality seemed very far away, buried somewhere, latent. None of that could help him survive.

Thoughts of Puppetman filled his mind. They were the kind of thoughts that would keep him alive.

It was good, in a place like this, to have a reason to live. Because someday he'd figure a way out of here, past the concrete-and-rebar walls, past the titanium bars and bulletproof glass, past the armed sentries of the Governor's Island Maximum Security Psychiatric Unit, the Coast Guard sentries on the rest of the island, the cold waters of New York Harbor and back to the city itself, to its mirrored fortresses of glass where his enemies danced their dance of power, and then it would be Shad up on the bandstand, voice a low whisper telling everyone, *Hey, motherfuckers, last waltz* . . .

Philip Baron von Herzenhagen adjusted his pearl-gray fedora and walked expressionlessly through the media vermin swarming on the stoop of his townhouse. He opened the door of his Jaguar sedan and stooped to enter.

"What about the latest revelations of the Card Sharks?" A booming baritone voice, chiseled features, razor-cut hair. Some local television news personality, tired of covering back-alley murders and city council elections, here trying to make the big time.

Herzenhagen rose from his crouch and put on his world-weary face. "Really," he said, "what evidence exists for these 'Card Sharks'?" Putting the quotes in his voice. "As I understand it, the chief witness against me is a talking hat." He pulled off his own hat and held it up for the camera. "Shall I call my own hat as a rebuttal witness?"

This got a laugh. Herzenhagen figured he'd made the news.

He gave them a brittle grin. "Again for the record, the last time I drew a government paycheck was 1945." He looked at the reporter again. "You can look it up, if you're so inclined."

He got in his car and headed for his club.

What he was really afraid of was that one of those media lice actually *would* start to do his own research, instead of just parroting the Hartmann allegations or each other. Because, though it was true he hadn't drawn a government paycheck since 1945, that was only because in the CIA, founded in large part by gentlemen with independent incomes, one could still check off a box on the application form whereby one could return one's salary to the government. And if the little media weasels got really lucky, they'd discover that, though Herzenhagen had left the Agency in the fifties, he'd been a member of one covert organization or another ever since.

Biological Research Unit. Unit Omega. Special Control Group. The Vice-President's Special Executive Task Unit.

The Sharks. All the Sharks.

Herzenhagen took off his hat, smoothed the brim, and was heartily glad it couldn't talk.

The allegations had to end, he thought.

Something had to happen to Gregg Hartmann. Something *bad*.

And soon.

Herzenhagen rather thought he knew what it was going to be.

Shad wondered why Chalktalk hadn't walked through the walls and helped him escape. Maybe she hadn't heard he was in trouble. Maybe she didn't like him any more.

Names went through his head like a mantra. *Puppetman. George Gordon Battle. Crypt Kicker. Pan Rudo.*

He hoped they would all live long enough for Shad to catch up with them.

Your-mentality defines Pan Rudo=enemy?

The question rang in Shad's mind with a voice of thunder. Shad's heart thundered.

"Who the fuck . . . ?" And before he could stop himself he was looking around, head jumping on his shoulders like a thing out of a jack-in-the box.

This-unit is known to you as Croyd Crenson.

Croyd? Shad had been scoped by telepaths before and hadn't liked it one little bit. Cautiously he beamed out little thought-particles. *That really you, man?*

This-unit is known to you as Croyd Crenson.

Your-mentality is defined=Home/Black Shadow/Neil Carton Langford=ally. You define Pan Rudo=enemy?

He's the shrink who put me in here. A two-hour interview, man, and me full of anaesthetic: next thing I know, I'm declared insane and slammed in the jug.

Pan Rudo-mentality defined=enemy. Defined=Shark. This-unit's purpose=termination Pan Rudo-mentality.

Shad couldn't help but be impressed. *I can get behind that, man. Only thing—why are you talking like that?*

This-unit flew to United States to attempt assassination of Pan Rudo. This-unit fell asleep on aircraft, awakened incarcerated. This-unit capable of advanced multi-path calculation, telepathy. This unit incapable of termination Pan Rudo-mentality without allies. Your-mentality defined=ally.

"Uhhh, thanks."

This-unit will arrange escape. Arrangements must conclude within 28 hours before this-unit sleeps again, before arranged pandemic occurs Governor's Island. Your-mentality stand by. Affirmative?

Shad straightened, alarm tingling in his nerves. *Hold on. What's this about a pandemic?*

Card Sharks/Governor Raney/Pan Rudo/Phillip Baron von Herzenhagen/CO Ramirez/CO Shannon plan release toxic virus chosen targets Governor's Island. Objective: termination Black Shadow, Croyd Crenson, Tea-Daddy, Glop/Boris Scherbansky, Fade . . .

The alarm was wailing now. *They're gonna kill us?*

Termination is Sharks' objective. Medical care will be onsite but deliberately ineffective or lethal. Autopsies will be performed by Shark pathologist brought in for purpose. Diagnosis will be death by Legionnaires' disease.

You're telling me the Sharks are real?

Escape will be arranged. Your-mentality stand by. Affirmative?

Stunned. *Got nothing else to do.*

Shad's mouth was dry. He licked his lips and his frame shuddered to a useless adrenaline charge. *Run!* the adrenaline said. *Fight! Something!*

Stand by. You bet.

He hadn't known whether to believe in the Sharks or not. Whatever it was, he knew, Hartmann was scamming somehow, using his television tease to Puppetman's advantage.

That Correction Officers Ramirez and Shannon were Sharks, Shad could believe—they'd always been bastards. But the governor of the facility? Planning on dumping a virus in the air-conditioning?

Shad could feel gunsights on the back of his neck.

He hoped Croyd knew what he was doing.

George Gordon Battle blinked myopic eyes. "Jesus, Phil, it's bad enough being joker. Now you want me to be a *liberal*?"

"Only for a few days," Herzenhagen said. "And then the liberal can have an accident. Or perhaps kill himself in despair at being duped." He reached in his pocket for his cigarette case. "I'm leaning toward the latter, myself."

"I feel so useless in this damn place," Battle said.

The dinner table was covered with dirty dishes and a half-finished game of solitaire. Dismembered guns sat on every horizontal surface. A flak jacket hung on the coat rack.

The field agent at home.

Since his transformation, Battle had been hiding in a safe house—safe apartment, really—in the East Fifties. He'd had to be smuggled in, since jokers weren't permitted in such places anymore, and he'd had to stay in here with nothing but the cable TV for company.

"As soon as we can get Mademoiselle Gérard up from Washington, we'll do it," Herzenhagen assured.

He lit his cigarette and watched Battle with some interest. He had never been repelled by jokers, was in fact mildly fascinated by them. His desire to eliminate the wild card wasn't a result of any personal repulsion, only science—only clean, objective facts.

History was a progression, Herzenhagen thought, an endless, inevitable progression to better things, perhaps to racial greatness. All his life he had considered himself a servant of history, a servant of that progression—

smoothing things here, advancing them there. Fighting the irrationality of fascism, then Stalinism.

It was Einstein who proved how the wild card could spread, had shown Herzenhagen and Hughes and the others the math. The wild card was a random factor of incredible dimensions. The progression of history stumbled, lurched, leaped ahead, stepped cautiously back. The numbers wouldn't add up anymore.

Einstein—brilliant, compassionate, yet tormented by the numbers. Einstein, Our Founder. The first, after being called in by Truman, to see the chilling facts clearly.

The plague had to end in order for history to become orderly again. In order for Herzenhagen and people like him to be able to control things again, to move them along in their proper order, proper perspective. And it was Albert Einstein who'd shown him the way.

Einstein, the first Card Shark, the one who had recruited all the others. Who had finally been driven mad by the truth, gone all wiggy and sentimental and soft, and who had finally had to be disposed of. Herzenhagen still regretted it, the fact of it, the necessity. The restraints, the gag applied gently, the loaded syringe put to the old man's arm, the stonefish toxin that stopped his heart . . .

Herzenhagen had no personal animus. He had nothing against wild cards. He had nothing against rabid dogs either, only knew they had to be put away, with rigorous efficiency and as little sentimentality as possible.

"I can still do it!" Battle said. He was a little joker now, bright yellow, less than four feet long, with six limbs. He could walk precariously on the last pair, or run on four legs. He had a perfectly ridiculous face, with what looked like a red putty nose right in the middle and more red putty noses where the ears should be. Little tufts of bristly hair stood out on his body like rebellious cowlicks, and his voice piped like that of Mickey Mouse.

"I can overcome this body!" Battle ranted on. "It's all a matter of will. Give me that lighter."

Dutifully Herzenhagen passed his silver Dunhill

Rollagas to Battle. There was no point in trying to stop Battle now: he was determined to prove himself in front of his chief.

Battle flicked on the lighter with one of his middle limbs, held it to the yellow flesh hanging under one of his upper arms. His eyes went wide. Then suddenly the mutant body was in motion, zooming over the floor, up the walls, across the ceiling, moving too fast for Herzenhagen's eyes to follow. Battle kept it up for twenty or thirty seconds, cursing a blue streak the entire time. Paint flaked off the ceiling as he crossed it. Finally he stopped in the middle of the living room. Herzenhagen stood and collected his lighter.

"Jesus, Phil," Battle panted. "I didn't mean to do that."

"So I gathered," Herzenhagen said. He patted the little joker on the head. "But don't be overanxious. We'll get you a new body, tomorrow or the next day."

Your-mentality prepared/jailbreak?

Shad practically bounded out of his cot at the touch of Croyd's unearthly mind.

What the fuck else do I have to do?

It was two hours past shift change, and Ramirez was on duty in the corridor, a fact Shad gleaned from the observation that his TV and heater had been shut off.

Take position upper northwest corner of cell.

Shad looked at the featureless concrete ceiling of his cell. *Which corner's the northwest?* He'd never seen the sun, never been out of this concrete cage, and he didn't know.

Upper right, your-mentality's perspective.

Shad climbed the wall, planted one foot on the ceiling, waited.

Reach out with your power. Above and to west.

Which way's west again?

Instructions followed. He reached out to the extreme limits of his power, found a thin trickle of electrical energy, sucked just the faintest bit of it.

Your-mentality stand by. Take all power on my signal.

Would you mind telling me why?

Croyd's answer was instant. *All cells monitored by hidden fiberoptic lens. Essential/escape plan to blank monitor in Dervish's cell . . .*

Mind explaining the rest of the plan?

Shad swayed as a mental picture invaded his mind. Croyd wasn't telling him the plan, just broadcasting the action as it happened, slices transmitted from other people's heads.

At the moment he was looking down at a pair of elderly black hands that held a cup of tea. Tea leaves swirled in the bottom of the cup.

I say this moment be's auspicious. An old voice, speaking with an antedeluvian rural accent Shad couldn't place.

Shad was outraged. *You're having your tea leaves read?*

Croyd didn't reply, but the mental channel switched. Suddenly Shad felt himself in a small body that didn't feel right at all—center of gravity all wrong, weight distribution strange. His mind was heavily concentrated, straining a power that wasn't quite clear to him.

Click, click, click. He realized the body was female—that's why the center of gravity was wrong—and that she was trying to push buttons. Buttons that weren't actually in sight. Croyd had to tell her where they were, in what order to push them.

The buttons, Shad figured, that opened the electric cell doors.

Splitscreen. Suddenly he was in two heads at once. The other had to be a guard, because he was wearing a brown uniform shirt and sitting at a console filled with television monitors with views of prisoners, all except for the one turned to Jay Leno.

Lots of prisoners, though. Jokers, mostly, but he recognized himself hanging upside-down in the corner of his cell. There were other natlike prisoners who presumably had a hidden ace or two.

And one old black man, shrunken in his prison coveralls, staring into a cup of tea. What the hell had he ever done to get here?

Now.

Croyd's command rolled into Shad's head. He strained his power and ate the electricity from the distant source. And he watched, through the guard's eyes, as one of the little monitors went black. But the guard barely paid attention, he was watching Leno.

And then Shad was in another head. The walls loomed in toward him, as if they were seen through a distorting lens. Everything looked terrifying. Little creatures, half-seen things with scaly glistening bodies and silver fangs, slithered in and out of vision. Sometimes they offered advice; Shad could see their lips move. But he wasn't receiving audio and didn't know what they said, and for that he was grateful.

This was a maximum security sanitorium, after all. Some of the inmates had to be genuinely crazy.

Dervish. Croyd had given Shad the madman's name.

Titanium bars slid, and then the point of view spun into the corridor. Walls and cell doors swam past. Shad realized that Dervish wasn't walking straight, probably couldn't: he spun as he walked, turning circles.

But he moved fast. Out of the corner of the guard's eye, Shad saw Dervish coming—a massive long-armed torso above tiny crooked legs, knuckles almost dragging, evil red eyes and a shaggy mane that covered head, shoulders, upper arms. The guard half-rose from his seat, held out a hand, *stop,* and then Dervish swarmed onto him, and the guard's point of view thankfully went blank.

Apparently Dervish wasn't up to pressing the buttons that opened the cells, because the woman's point of view returned again, and she strained once more to the limits of her power.

Shad's door whirred open, the one time that had happened since he'd been here. He was out in a shot.

He ran to the console and stopped short, his heart crying, when he saw Dervish crouched over Ramirez's body. The huge joker had pulled off an arm and was eating it like a turkey leg. He looked up at Shad and growled. Blood matted the hair on his giant chest. Shad called the photons to him, shrouded himself in night, and then cautiously moved to the console and began pressing the numbers Croyd gave him.

On the monitors he could see people wandering out. A big joker in the lead, with claws and a set of wolf's fangs set in a pointed snout. She would have looked like the Wolfman if she'd had any hair, but she was bald, and bright orange to boot. The woman whose telekinesis had opened the doors came next: her Caucasian body was shaped like that of a nat, but she had a nose that drooped past her chin, and earlobes that fell past her shoulders. Shad wondered why she hadn't had cosmetic surgery. She was followed by the old black man, still holding his cup of tea.

Then came a muscular white man, hard-eyed, wearing a muscle shirt and prison tattoos—and hatred warred with wariness in Shad's mind as he recognized the man. He called himself the Racist in the same way that John Wayne was the Shootist—he was fast, supposedly capable of two hundred miles per hour on the straights—but he was a racist in the other sense of the word, too, a member of the Aryan Brotherhood. Some of his tattoos were swastikas. He'd been an ordinary stick-up man until he'd volunteered in prison for an experiment with the wild card virus, and to everyone's surprise he'd drawn an ace and escaped prison. Not that he'd stayed out of the slams for long—Straight Arrow had caught up with him and held him in a cage of fire.

Shad wondered idly if he should drain the Racist of all his photons and leave him here on the prison floor.

No/forbidden. Racist/Mark Wagner is necessary to plan.

Just thinking. That's all.

Shad watched, and pressed more buttons. A dark-haired white woman came out, attractive and anonymous in prison coveralls. A long-haired, long-bearded man in his forties whose brain had literally exploded out of his head, running down over his ears like oatmeal boiling out of a saucepan. Shad knew of him—he was an old hippie who'd become a projecting telepath, able to make others experience his psychedelic visions. Not surprisingly, they called him the Head. He sold his talent to young acid-head wannabees—it was illegal to deal drugs, but not to get others stoned by telepathy. There'd been some interesting court cases, and the Head had won them all.

Until, apparently, the case that put him here.

Next came a joker who puddled into the room, looking like fifty gallons of lime Jell-O—no skeleton, no visible organs, nothing but shimmering translucent green. He was followed by a chitinous creature in black armor, with a vast, swollen head and side-mounted eyes. This turned out to be Croyd.

There were more levels to the complex, more electric locks, more guards—but no more master control rooms full of cameras, no reason for Shad to use his power. Witchy picked the locks, seeing through Croyd's mind and reaching out with her TK; Racist and Dervish took care of the guards, always messily—and the last door, the door to the outside, opened with a simple push.

Cold sea-air blew in. Shad filled his lungs with it, let it slide over his tongue. Felt it fill his heart.

The smell of freedom. Nothing was going to stop him now.

Everyone held hands. Shad called photons and covered the whole group in darkness.

Holding hands, they shuffled out of the building. Governor's Island was a curious mixture: there was the Coast Guard establishment, frame buildings filled with high-ranking guardsmen and their families, serviced by their own ferry that ran back and forth to Manhattan. Green lawns ran down to the water's edge. The snug family dwellings of the Coast Guard shared uneasy quarters with the wild card psychiatric facility and its dangerous collection of aces and jokers, all confined in the concrete monolith on the south side facing the rubbish of the Rox across the bay. And then there was the old stone bulk of Fort Jay, with its display of rusting cannons dating to the War of 1812, ready to contest the passage of King George's frigates.

Shad's heart lifted as he saw the lights of Manhattan

rising above the sensible frame buildings of the Coast
Guard facility. Freedom was *that close* . . .

Shad saw two figures take to the air—one a man who
flew silently into the sky like Modular Man, another who
flapped on mantalike wings.

Where are they going?

*Will assassinate Governor Raney and CO Shannon.
Death of Sharks not necessary to plan, but may sow confusion and cover our retreat.*

Shad thought about it. *Solid,* he decided.

The Governor's Island Ferry was docked, closed for
the night but brightly lit. Keeping to the shadow of Fort
Jay's rough stone walls, Shad slipped his people past, to
a motor launch in another slip.

All-mentalities inside Commander's gig.

Shad dropped his cloak of darkness so the others could
find their footing on the dock. Racist was first in the
boat, heading for the ignition.

Then there were shots. Three distinct shots, bang-
bang-bang, and as Shad's nerves leaped in reaction he
heard an alarm, a furious urgent buzzer, endlessly
repeated. Floodlights came on automatically, and suddenly the dock was lit brighter than day; a hot white
glow that pinpointed the refugees, caught frozen in their
tracks by the sudden onset of light.

Apparently one of the assassinations hadn't gone well.

Shad turned to where Racist was still bent over the
gig's controls. "You doing all right there, speedy?"

"Shut the fuck up."

Shad turned at the sound of running feet and saw
guards with guns, assault rifles held at port arms as they
ran from the complex, heads swivelling as they looked
for escapees.

Shad called more darkness to him, dropped to a
crouch. He was going to have to stop those people before
they started unloading automatic weapons at the packed
escapees in the boat.

"Wait!" It was the dark-haired white woman, jumping
to the dock. She threw out her arm in the direction of
the pursuers, her fingers crooked slightly—and then a

giant bloom of white light encompassed the guards. Shad, eyes dazzled, thought for a moment that there had been an explosion—but no, it was silent, and when it faded the guards were unharmed, just fallen, hands over their dazzled eyes.

The gig's engine caught, boomed loud in the night. Shad threw off moorings fore and aft, then followed the white woman into the boat. She held out a hand.

"Lady Light," she said. Her voice was small and feminine.

"Black Shadow." Taking the hand. "Pleased to meet you."

They lurched as the boat took off toward the towering lights of Manhattan, dead ahead.

"Lights are on," Herzenhagen reported as he peered into his telescope.

"About fucking time," piped Battle.

They and Mademoiselle Gérard—Herzenhagen couldn't quite bring himself to call her Mam'zell, as everyone else did—stood on the roof of a building across from Gregg Hartmann's apartment. They'd been there for hours, since Battle's joker form had scaled the building, opened the roof door, and let them all in.

"Is he alone?" Battle asked. With his poor eyesight he couldn't see for himself.

"Apparently." Herzenhagen peered into the scope once more, saw Hartmann clearly as the former senator stood by his window, staring moodily at the night while he took off his jacket and loosened his tie. Herzenhagen turned to Gérard.

"Viens ici, s'il vous plaît."

"Bien."

She was a tough-looking French girl, maybe sixteen, in jeans and a leather jacket. Brainy, too, because she'd trusted the government amnesty and left the Rox before it was destroyed.

Now she worked for Herzenhagen. Maybe she believed the Shark allegations, maybe not. It didn't seem to matter to her. She had the life she wanted—she was jumping, and living well, and had all the protection the government could give her.

Jumpers. Herzenhagen had the only three jumpers still active under his control, and his only conclusion was that it made him remarkably like God. He could decide who lived, who died, and more importantly, who got to be who. Who got scrambled. Who got a new chance at life in a new body. Who was condemned to old age and death.

Who got to be Gregg Hartmann.

Lux fiat, he thought.

Roofing gravel crunched under Mademoiselle Gérard's boots as she approached the telescope and put one dark eye to the eyepiece. Herzenhagen reached into his pocket for his Browning Hi-Power, ready for what would come later. Gérard concentrated for a brief moment . . . and then her body came unstrung, fell to the roof like a puppet with its strings slashed.

Battle reared himself up on his hindmost pair of legs, and thumbed on a large flashlight to illuminate his absurd face from below so that Mademoiselle, in Gregg Hartmann's body, could see him from the window. Then there was another shock—Battle dropped the flashlight and fell to all six limbs—and then Mademoiselle's body gave a start, and she sat up with a little cry of satisfaction.

Triple jump. Leaving Battle in Hartmann's body, Hartmann in the ridiculous yellow joker, and Mademoiselle back where she started.

Now all that remained was to finish off Hartmann. Since people were normally paralyzed after being jumped, Herzenhagen planned simply to shove the spastic six-limbed body off the roof—though he did carry the Browning Hi-Power just in case things didn't go according to plan.

But what he didn't expect was that the joker would give a whoop and run like a mad six-legged racehorse, kicking up gravel as it scuttled to the roof parapet, yellow rump flashing as it went up and over, all before a stunned Herzenhagen could raise his gun to the firing position. . . .

Just as the joker had done when Battle had tried to

do his stunt with the lighter. Apparently it was some kind of automatic defense mechanism.

Herzenhagen moved quickly to the parapet, looked down, and saw the joker body already on street level, zigzagging madly along the street, screaming all the while. Herzenhagen raised his gun, then decided against it. He'd probably miss, and shots would only call attention to what had just happened.

He'd have to move faster, he thought. Get the Hartmann business over with, accelerate the viral test on Governor's Island, head to Washington to try to move the Quarantine Bill through Congress. . . .

Herzenhagen turned to leave. Mademoiselle Gérard was watching him, hands in her jacket pockets, a quizzical expression on her face.

Herzenhagen shrugged. *"Quelle affaire,"* he said, and offered her his arm.

Above, the shattered span of the Brooklyn Bridge stretched across the night sky. Underneath, in the shadows of the great arches beneath the bridge approaches, Shad paced along, followed by figures in prison coveralls who scuttled from darkness to darkness.

The jokers were making their way deeper into Jokertown. Most were following Witchy, who had promised them that the Twisted Fists would help smuggle them to one of the Jokertown havens, Jerusalem or Guatemala or Saigon . . .

That, Shad realized, was why she hadn't had cosmetic surgery. She was an ideological joker as well as a physical one, and accepted her deformity as part of her joker identity.

The aces were left on their own. Racist had chosen to keep the Coast Guard boat and take it over to the Brooklyn side, where he had friends. Shad hoped that would confuse and divide any pursuit.

You still there, Croyd?

This-unit is monitoring.

Can we talk? We might have business to discuss—you want Rudo, and I want certain other people.

Your-mentality may accompany me.

Good. You wait here, I'll get us transportation.

Shad stole an old Pontiac on Pearl Street and brought it back under the bridge approaches. Croyd waited there. Shad leaned across the front seats and opened the passenger door.

This-unit knows of safe house uptown.

Sounds good.

The Pontiac pulled away from the curb. Shad headed north out of Jokertown on Fifth Avenue. At one point he had to swerve wildly to avoid a bright yellow six-legged joker that screamed as it raced across the street.

Shad thought seriously about his own safe houses and whether he could trust any of them. The places he trusted most were in Jokertown, and he wanted to avoid Jokertown for the moment. That's where the search for the escapees would be at its most intense.

Still, he could probably trust the Diamond house and the Gravemold house. Not but that his skin didn't crawl at the thought of disappearing into the Gravemold identity with its hideous chemical stench. . . .

There was a horrible mental scream from Croyd, a cry so intense as to jangle pain through Shad's mind.

Your-mentality=Black Shadow=Neil Carton Langford= Mr. Gravemold!

Oh hell. Gravemold had once captured Croyd when he was in one of his psychotic fits. Shad had almost forgotten about it, but Croyd had just plucked the thought from his mind and wasn't about to forget.

Croyd lunged over Shad's shoulder for the wheel. Shad fought for control, felt wheels rebound from the curb . . .

Your-mentality=Gravemold! Your-mentality redefined=enemy!

"You were crazy, Croyd!" Shad shouted. "You were killing people left and right and—"

Die, enemy! Croyd's hands fumbled for Shad's throat.

The Pontiac crashed into a parked Thunderbird. Croyd's head drove into Shad's from behind, slamming into the mastoid. Shad blinked stars from his eyes.

"Dammit, Croyd!"

He turned around, blood boiling, ready to backhand Croyd out of the way, but the joker had crumpled into the back seat, limp as a ragdoll.

"Croyd?"

Shad could see Croyd's chest moving up and down. Maybe he'd been knocked unconscious when they banged heads.

Shad checked Croyd carefully and saw he wasn't bleeding or damaged in any obvious way. It looked as if he'd just gone to sleep—gone to sleep right in the middle of a fight, which had to be something new even for him—and if that was the case, Croyd could be gone anywhere from days to weeks.

Shad slid out of the car. He would just leave, eat photons and walk up a building and get away.

But that would leave Croyd in the hands of the authorities.

Your-mentality redefined=enemy!

Shad hesitated. He couldn't leave Croyd to the tender mercies of the Sharks.

He went back into the car, worked Croyd out, and carried the joker into the night.

He had a horrid feeling he was going to pay for this sooner or later.

Herzenhagen smoked a cigarette and pondered the news as he watched Peggy Durand draw on her clothes. All the wild cards on Governor's Island, gone. None as yet recaptured. All the Sharks killed—though at least Shannon seemed to have wounded his attacker before his head was ripped off.

For a moment he was distracted by the vision of Peggy drawing on her Spandex bicycle shorts. Amazing, he thought, the things available for young people these days. He'd been raised on Long Island with wealth and privilege—his morphine-addicted Danish grandfather had married American money—and he'd thought himself lucky. But the eighteen-year-old Philip von Herzenhagen, he suspected, would have thrown it all away for a chance to live in the Nineties and chase girls who wore Spandex.

He dragged his mind back to business. It couldn't be a coincidence, he thought, that of the five men killed during the escape, three were Sharks, and that two of these had been killed, not in the escape, but executed quite deliberately in their beds.

None of the Sharks killed were those named in the Hartmann accusations. Which meant that the killers had other sources of information.

A leak? Possibly. Perhaps one of the other guards had helped the escapees. Possibly the escape had been arranged from on high. The prison break bespoke *organization*. Someone in the facility, familiar with its procedures.

Perhaps there were counter-Sharks out there. Shark Hunters.

"Be careful," he said.

Peggy cocked an eyebrow at him as she arranged the feathers of dark hair that fell down her forehead. "What was that?"

"Something's going on, and I don't know what. But I don't think I want to trust the phones. If you need to call me, I'll be at the club every day from noon till two, and again at dinnertime."

She smiled at him, her eyes glowing with an intelligence beyond her apparent years. Peggy Durand had been Herzenhagen's mistress in Germany after the war. He had found her in the shambles of the Runstedt Offensive, a naive little girl from Idaho who sold Red Cross doughnuts to angry GI's at ten cents apiece and other favors—exclusively to officers—on a mattress in the back of her truck. He had shown her a better life. Peggy had been attentive and learned her business well, and when the CIA had been formed, Herzenhagen had recruited her as a courier. And, after the CIA, she'd followed him into the Sharks. The last few decades she'd been living with Faneuil, but now things had changed.

After the fiasco in Guatemala, she'd been jumped into the luscious body of an eighteen-year-old runaway named Dolores Chacón, and it was thought too dangerous for her to associate directly with Faneuil, even though he was in another body as well. She was employed as den mother at Latchkey, the organization's jumper facility in Maryland, but Herzenhagen kept finding reasons to call her to New York. He found the combination irresistable—the juicy young breasts and flat belly, the round buttocks and smooth long legs, all inhabited by a sophisticated woman with a lifetime of experience. Better than any real teenager could ever be.

Peggy sat on his bed, took his cigarette from his fingers, drew on it.

"When you get back to Washington, you'll have to warn Rudo," Herzenhagen said. "That Croyd creature, for one, was swearing vengeance on him."

"Warn which Rudo?"

Herzenhagen looked up at her. "Both of them, of course."

Mr. Diamond peered owlishly through gold-rimmed spectacles and hefted a metal briefcase full of hundred-dollar bills. He searched in his pocket for keys, remembered he didn't have any, and uttered a mild reproach to himself.

Then he climbed up the wall and went in a window.

The ineffectual pleadings of his criminal attorney had drained Shad's cash supply, and he needed to increase his liquidity. A small packet of diamonds, retrieved from a safety deposit box in Brooklyn, then transported into Manhattan's diamond district, would do for a start.

Mr. Gregory Diamond was one of Shad's aliases. He lived atop a building in Jokertown owned by the Diamond Company, Ltd., a division of Diamond Transport, a company held by Diamante N.V., incorporated in Aruba. Diamond's apartment had its own entrance, a huge steel door with massive locks, and its own stair leading to the apartment door.

For both of which Shad had lost the keys.

The apartment itself was fairly modest—neat, inexpensive furniture, some throw rugs, and a steel-lined safe concealed behind sliding panels. Shad put the suitcase of cash in the safe, then put Coltrane's *Black Pearls* on the sound system, jacked up the volume, and took a long shower with the sound of the music wailing over the hissing water.

It was his first shower in three years. He made it last till the album ended, tried to wash Governor's Island out of his soul. Then he toweled himself off, put on clean clothes, and decided to catch up on the news.

He snapped on CNN.

Gregg Hartmann looked ill-at-ease, and had put on fifteen or twenty pounds since Shad had last seen him. Usually a fine off-the-cuff speaker, he now read from notes. His voice was either inaudible or a booming fortissimo.

It was the content that was riveting. Shad found himself leaning forward, elbows on knees, as he warred in spirit with what the voice was saying.

"I call this conference in a spirit of sorrow," Hartmann began. "I regret to inform you that I have been deceived. Although I believe that my informants were well-meaning, my own investigations have shown to my satisfaction that they were wrong. The so-called Card Sharks, I now believe, do not exist. They never existed, except in the minds of a small number of deluded people, among whose numbers I until recently counted myself. From the escape and existence of Etienne Faneuil, we unhappily created a fantasy conspiracy. . . ."

Puppetman, Shad thought. *What game are you playing now?*

Maybe he'd better find out.

"Mr. von Herzenhagen? The telephone. Mr. Gregg Hartmann, sir."

Herzenhagen stubbed out his cigarette, and followed his club's balding concierge from the smoking room to where a telephone waited in a small office. He thanked the man, held onto his polite face while the man left, and closed the door before he picked up the receiver.

"Yes?"

"Hi. It's me."

Herzenhagen pursed his lips. "Where are you calling me from?"

"From the apartment. I haven't been out all day."

"That's not a secure phone."

"Hell, nobody has any reason to tap it but us."

Herzenhagen found it eerily disturbing to listen to Battle's words and cadences in Gregg Hartmann's voice.

"Only this once," he said. "But after this, use a public phone."

"I can't. That Hannah woman is staking me out. She's been calling all day, and she finally showed up on the doorstep, but I told the doorman not to admit her."

"That was good."

"I think she needs taking care of."

Herzenhagen gave it some thought. "All in good time," he said.

"I mean it, Phil. She went batshit after she heard the press conference. Jesus—do you know that she and Hartmann were fucking?"

Herzenhagen laughed. "So give her a good screw, George! Maybe that'll shut her up!"

"Listen, this is *serious*. She knows too much. She's got to be taken care of."

"It will happen," soothingly, "I promise you. But first she must be thoroughly discredited—after that, no one will care what happens to her."

"Listen, I want out of here!"

Out of his body.

Perhaps, Herzenhagen thought, Battle could be jumped into Hannah, and then Hartmann's body, with Hannah inside, could take a walk off a pier, after leaving a poignant, disillusioned note behind, lamenting chances lost. Kill two birds with one stone.

Herzenhagen smiled as he anticipated Battle's aggrieved complaints at being jumped into a woman's body.

"Don't worry," he said, "I think I have a way of neatly wrapping up the whole adventure."

* * *

The words rang in Shad's head. *I call this conference in a spirit of sorrow.*

He forced the window open and slid silently into Hartmann's immaculate kitchen—apparently Hartmann didn't cook much. From another room, Hartmann ranted on the phone in a grating voice that Shad had never heard before.

The voice of Puppetman.

Shad's gloved hands opened drawers until he found a kitchen knife—always useful—and a couple of extension cords.

Shad heard the phone hang up. Anger bubbled in his veins. He left the kitchen and walked past a dining room and living room to Hartmann's office. Hartmann, in slacks and a striped shirt, stood behind his desk and stared moodily at the phone. Shad walked into the room, and as Hartmann's eyes tracked up Shad stole just a bit of heat, enough to cause an involuntary shudder to run through Hartmann's frame.

"*You!*" The line, and the dropped jaw, was straight out of a melodrama.

"You expecting someone else, Gregg?" Shad walked forward, leaned on the desk, tried to smile, but hatred kept turning the expression into a snarl.

Hartmann recovered, composed his face. He brushed at his graying hair with his prosthetic hand and, as if he wasn't used to it yet, bumped his forehead in the process.

"Sorry," he said. "You caught me at a bad moment." He frowned. "I suppose you think I can help you."

"All I want is to meet a friend of yours."

"Yeah? Who?"

Shad smiled. "Puppetman."

Shad had hoped for a start of surprise, a guilty catch in the voice. Instead, Hartmann seemed genuinely puzzled.

"Who? Could you, uh, refresh my memory?"

A good actor. Shad had to hand it to him. He leaned closer to Hartmann and bared his teeth.

"You know who, all right. An old friend. We first met—when was it, '76? When I was just a kid, and I was working for you. And the next thing you know, I strung some guy up from a lamppost and ran him through with a needle." He gave a cold laugh. "I didn't know I had that kind of anger in me. I thought I was a good guy, you know? Just trying to help people. I didn't know that kind of rage existed. Did you?"

Hartmann edged away from him, eyes wary. Keeping the desk between them. "What are you talking about?"

"I figure I met Puppetman again later that day, when I joined the rioters. And later, when I strung up a couple of muggers on the Deuce. And then when I busted up the Los Bozos clubhouse. And—"

"What do you want?" Hartmann said. "If it's help, I can arrange it. I've got friends who can hide you."

"What do I want?" Shad repeated. The rage boiled in him, exploded in a shriek. *I want the man who wrecked my life! I want Puppetman!*"

Alarm and confusion warred in Hartmann's face. "Calm down, okay? I'll get you what you want. But you have to tell me who to call. What's Puppetman's name?"

Shad laughed as he came around the desk. "You don't know?"

Hartmann looked blank. "No. I don't."

"Perhaps you can call up—oh, I don't know—George Gordon Battle? Was he the one who paid you off?"

Shock drained Hartmann's face of color. Shad grabbed him by the throat. Hartmann reacted quickly—for a nat, anyway—by trying to kick him in the knee, and by driving his linked hands up as a wedge between Shad's forearms, breaking the stranglehold. But Shad was faster than a nat, and stronger, and he avoided the kick and doubled Hartmann over with a mid-knuckle punch to the solar plexus. He grabbed Hartmann again, slammed him down in his chair. Hartmann tried to smash him in the head with his prosthesis, but Shad rapped him in the face with a fist, hearing the nasal cartilage crunch, and then stunned him with an open-hand slap to the side of the head.

Hartmann put up a surprisingly good fight, all things considered. Maybe he remembered his old Army training.

Shad tied him to the chair with extension cords.

Hartmann coughed on the blood running from his broken nose, spat, looked up with incredulous eyes. "Wait!" he said, "I'm not who you think I am."

"Yeah, Gregg baby," Shad said. He wadded a piece of paper and stuffed it in Hartmann's mouth. "I know that."

He took out the knife and showed it to the bound man.

"This is going to be unnecessarily brutal," he said. "But hey, it's only what you taught me." He smiled. "And if you've got any fancy mental powers, better use 'em now."

Shad found he hardly had to think at all. He'd had it done to him once, he knew how it went. It was a thing he'd already thought about, already visualized so completely during his years in stir that no mental effort was required—no thought, no feeling, nothing that stirred or repelled. Nothing but business.

Hartmann babbled a lot when Shad took the gag out to ask questions. He talked about will and the flames of cigarette lighters. He kept trying to pretend he was someone else, presumably someone this wasn't happening to.

Shad could have told him that didn't work. He'd tried all his life to be someone else, and it wasn't something a person could do.

Eventually Hartmann told him things. He wasn't very coherent by that point, but it was a place to start.

None of this was going to make Shad any happier. It wasn't going to release or bury his demons. It was just something that had to be got out of the way so that, in some future moment, he could become more himself. Free from Puppetman. Free from the ice that prison had injected into his veins.

Free to be, in some distant future time, horrified by everything he was doing.

In Hartmann's blood Shad wrote *Race Traitor* and *George Battle Lives!* and *Sharks Revenge* on the wall. Then he changed his blood-spattered clothes and called the police. He told them that he lived across the street from that nice Senator Hartmann and that he'd seen several men in masks break into the apartment. Then he called every television station in the city and told them the same thing.

When he went back to the apartment in Jokertown, he went to the shower and stayed under the hot spray for a long time. He ate the heat as it rained on him, and the water fell to the porcelain floor cold as ice.

The Color of His Skin

Part 5

Gregg had a vague memory of his soul being wrenched away from his body, and then of running screaming through the night, followed by a period of darkness. He wondered how long he'd been out.

Gregg wasn't quite sure what he felt like. That told him that he was still in shock, because he knew damned well that he should be screaming.

He'd been jumped.

He seemed to have come to rest in a midtown alley in a nest of discarded rags. They smelled of ... well, a dozen varieties of piss, a trio of motor oils, a trace of lingering perspiration from six or seven people, ancient semen and vaginal secretions from a few encounters, at least thirty old food stains, and a hundred things that he'd never smelled before—it seemed his new body had a wonderful sense of smell; hardly an asset at the moment.

He squinted toward the light at the end of the alley, realizing that anything more than a few yards away looked blurry, and the street beyond the alley's mouth was just a wash of color. He might have a great nose, but the eyes sucked. Wonderful. He was going to need glasses.

Gregg lifted his right arm: the stubby caterpillar limb that came into his myopic view sent his mind reeling again. He shut his eyes, shivering like a frightened baby. He tried the experiment once more—and once more what he saw wasn't even vaguely human. There were three short fingers at the end; he could wiggle them.

Taking a deep breath strongly spiced with the varied aromas around him, Gregg bent his head to look at his body. He looked like a four foot long *weinerwurst* dipped in fluorescent yellow paint. Six legs/arms. Spiky tufts of hair protruding from the cylindrical rolls in the skin. He couldn't wait to see what his face looked like.

"Fucking shit, I'm a *joker*!" he squealed, and heard a voice that sounded like Alvin the Chipmunk.

Gregg waited for the mocking, taunting voice inside. He knew what it would say: *Whassa matter, Greggie? You finally got what you've always deserved, that's all. . . .* But the voice didn't come. Inside his head was only silence.

It seemed a very small compensation.

He crawled out of the rag pile. He had to find someone. He had to get help and find a way to get his body back.

He couldn't hail a cab—they wouldn't stop for a fire hydrant with legs. Besides, he couldn't even see them until they were nearly on him.

He walked to the nearest bus stop. The nats who were there when he scuttled up gave him sour looks of disgust and moved on, refusing to stand near him—which was fine by Gregg, as he found that they all reeked. Three buses went by in an incredible wash of fumes before Gregg decided that none of them was going to stop.

He went around the corner, waited until a group of nats had assembled and the next bus had stopped, then scurried quickly toward the open door. The driver looked down at him as he humped his way up the stairs, and the glare was plain even with Gregg's poor vision.

"Get off my bus, Mac."

With Puppetman, it wouldn't have been a problem. Even with the weaker new "Gift," he might have been able to blunt the antagonism. But this body had no such powers. He couldn't feel the man's emotions at all—all he could do was smell the stench of his body. He suspected that the driver was on the second or third day in this pair of underwear. "Look, buddy," Gregg answered, "this is an emergency. I'm Gregg Hartmann. I've been jumped."

"Yeah. And I'm Elvis, and my wife's Amelia Earhart. Get the fuck outa here."

Gregg narrowed his eyes and drew up on his hind legs. He suspected that the gesture hardly looked intimidating. "This is public transportation. I have as much right to use it as anyone."

"Yeah? I don't see no fare, and I don't see no tokens, and I don't see no pockets where you could hide 'em, either. Now, you gonna back outa here or am I gonna have to toss you out, worm?"

Gregg glanced at the faces of the passengers. Most were pointedly ignoring the confrontation, staring fixedly through the windows. Those that were watching wore matching scowls.

"Fuck you," Gregg said. "Fuck you all." Even to his ears he sounded like a two-year old. Laughter followed him down the steps.

Okay, he thought. *I'm midtown in nat country. Who'd help me here?*

"Erin, I have to see Peregrine."

The nat receptionist peered over the edge of her desk as if she'd just discovered a hairball on her rug. Gregg could distinctly smell her shampoo, her deodorant, her perfume, the dry cleaning fluid on her dress, the coffee in the mug on her desk, the bagel she'd eaten that morning, and the toothpaste she'd used afterward. "I'm sorry, but that's not possible," Erin told him.

"Look, Erin, I know this is damn near impossible to believe, but I'm Gregg Hartmann. You and I just talked last week, remember? You were trying to set up an interview with Pan Rudo. I was jumped into this damn body, and I need help, and I need to talk to *Peri!*" The last word was a soprano squeal. Erin's face had gone stiff and red, but at least she picked up the phone. "Thank you, Erin," Gregg said.

Half a minute later, the office doors swung open and the lobby guard—another nat—was giving Gregg the hard stare. "This the one?" he asked Erin. She nodded. "Come on, bub. Let's go."

"I'm not leaving until I see Peri."

The guard almost smiled. He smelled of aftershave and last night's beer. And gun oil. "You can come quietly or you can make it tough for yourself, short stuff," he told Gregg. "I don't care either way."

"Erin—" Gregg began.

"I don't find your sick little joke funny at all," the receptionist said. "Especially not from a joker."

"Hey, I was *jumped!*"

"I had a lot of respect for Gregg Hartmann—he was a good man. Now please leave."

Gregg looked from Erin to the guard. They had the same look the bus driver had. He dropped to all sixes, sighing, and padded through the door the guard held open. "But I was *jumped*. I really was," he told the guard as the man escorted Gregg to the rear entrance of the studio. "I *am* Gregg Hartmann."

The guard opened the door for Gregg, let him out and shook a finger at Gregg like a parent scolding a child. "Listen, buster, I see all kinds here. I don't normally mind. But you're sick. Anyone who would make a joke like this after Hartmann was murdered like that . . ." The guard stopped. He let the door swing shut and walked away.

"Wait!" Gregg shouted through the glass, his voice piping. "What do you mean, *murdered*?!"

He found out some twenty blocks later, near Jokertown.

A half dozen television sets tossed blue light from an

appliance store window. The evening news was on. Standing with his front legs up against the glass, squinting, Gregg watched the body bag being brought out of his apartment building. There was tape of the interior— blood was splattered everywhere, and slogans had been written on the wall in blood. The camera focused on one: SHARKS REVENGE, it declared, written in shaky, smeared block letters. The reporter on the scene was talking about ". . . one of the most brutal, vicious, and sadistic murders the city has seen. Back to you, Peter."

Behind Peter Jennings, one of Gregg's old publicity photos smiled blandly back at him. "Ex-Senator Hartmann had created an uproar with his press conference only yesterday, in which he denounced the conspiracy he himself had publicized on *Peregrine's Perch*, the so-called 'Card Sharks' group . . ."

A short clip of the press conference was shown. In a quick sound bite, Gregg watched "himself" state haltingly that the Card Sharks ". . . never existed, except in the minds of a small number of deluded people."

The report cut back to Jennings. "Reports that several masked persons were seen going into the Senator's apartment have not been verified. Given that Mr. Hartmann refuted his own part in the Card Shark speculation, it would seem counter-productive for a true Sharks organization to assassinate him. There is speculation that jokers angry with Hartmann's reversal of stance may instead be responsible, but we stress that, right now, *nothing* is certain beyond the fact that our country has lost one of its more colorful and controversial political figures."

Gregg felt sick. He reeled away from the display, nearly falling off the curb. His body heaved, a rippling spasm. Something sour and huge choked him; Gregg coughed and spat. A hard spheroid of brown, crusty *stuff* rolled off the curb and into the gutter.

He had no idea what it was.

He had no idea who *he* was.

"Oddity!"

Gregg had caught a glimpse of the figure in the

Jokertown alleyway, a darker shadow against the night.
Gregg hurried across the street toward Oddity, who had
stopped. Gregg could smell the three distinct odors
under the ankle-length cloak, but the eyes behind the
mesh of the fencing mask were lost in his fuzzy sight. "I
have to see Father Squid and Hannah," he said. "They
jumped me. I don't know who was in my body when it
was killed, but it wasn't me. I'm Gregg. Gregg
Hartmann!"

"I know who you are. I also know that the jumpers
are dead, Battle," Oddity said. John's voice—that was
hardly comforting; John had been Puppetman's favorite,
but he was the least pleasant of the trio. "Bloat's dead.
Hartmann's dead. Too many damn people are dead. Keep
bothering me, and you might be, too. I don't know what
kind of shit you're trying to pull with this, but it isn't
going to work."

"Please!" Gregg lifted up on his hind legs like a beg-
ging dog, clutching at Oddity's cloak with his clumsy fingers. "I can prove who I am if you'll give me a chance.
I have to see Hannah!"

"Get *off* me!" Oddity kicked Gregg away. The joker's
powerful muscles tossed Gregg halfway across the alley.
He hit the ground hard. He felt the unbidden reflexes
kick in once more—a roar in his head as adrenaline
flooded the body, as the world seemed to go into slow
motion around him. Suddenly he was tearing around at
full throttle like the Roadrunner with Wile E. Coyote
right behind him: across the street and back, darting
between the jokers on the sidewalks, back into the alley
at top speed, up the side walls, leaping a dozen feet in
the air, caroming off garbage cans and fire escapes.
"Jesus, the little sucker can sure *move*," he heard Oddity
say, and then Gregg was streaking off again, back out
into the Jokertown streets.

When the buzz wore off and Gregg was able to control
the body once more, he was six blocks away. When he
finally got back to the alley, Oddity was gone.

Gregg was hungry, too. Considering the cranked-up
metabolism this body possessed in stress situations,

Gregg wasn't surprised. In fact, something in the alley
smelled . . . *good*. Gregg sniffed, unbelieving. Yes, the
garbage can there by the wall—not the noisome contents,
but the can itself. His joker body was salivating, and an
odd pressure was building up somewhere in his gut.
Gregg opened his mouth as if to belch—he was surprised
when a liquid glob the size of a softball jetted out. The
odd stuff clung to the side of the garbage can like trans-
parent jelly.

And the aluminum can melted around it like can-
dlewax. The resulting metallic pabulum smelled delicious, and the ache of hunger surged. Gregg glanced
around to make sure no one was watching, and dipped
his head to lap the steaming goo tentatively.

Hiram Worchester had never made a better meal.

Great, he thought. I eat my own vomit. And I *like* it.

His apartment was a lost cause; Gregg didn't even
consider going there. He tried his office and couldn't get
into the building. The doors were locked, and probably
would have been too heavy for him to budge even if
they'd been open. He couldn't reach the public tele-
phones to call anyone, not that it mattered since he didn't
have a quarter and no one would have recognized his
voice anyway. The constant police patrols around J-Town
were looking at him strangely.

"Hey, Battle!" one of the cops called once, leaning out
of the car. The face under the NYPD visor looked like
crumpled parchment paper. "What the hell you doing in
J-Town?" Gregg didn't answer, and the cop finally
shrugged and gunned the cruiser on past.

Hannah and Father Squid had gone into hiding again
in the wake of "his" murder—a priest he didn't recognize
answered the door and would tell Gregg only that Father
Squid had gone to a "conference" until the weekend. He
couldn't find Oddity again or Jube or anyone else who
might be of help.

He wanted to shout to whatever god would listen that
he was very, very sorry for everything he'd ever done
and while this was wonderfully appropriate penance he'd

learned his lesson and could he please, please be just a normal person again. He'd never misuse the Gift again. Never ever.

No one seemed to be listening.

Gregg decided that he had no choice. After all, Hannah, Father Squid, Peregrine—none of them could really help him. He'd been jumped out of his body. His own body was dead, but there was a way to get a new one. He needed a jumper. The *Sharks* had a jumper.

So Gregg needed to go to the Sharks.

Feeding Frenzy

2

Shad's wiretap of Herzenhagen's phone got him precisely nowhere, so he got on the motorbike he'd bought that morning and followed Herzenhagen's Jaguar to his club. He returned to his apartment long enough to pick up another wiretap kit and his phone company uniform. Then he stole a phone company van he found double-parked, drove it to Herzenhagen's club, and tapped the phone. He abandoned the van, changed, and went up the building across the street.

Most of what he heard was junk. He had to keep switching from one line to another in order to monitor all the calls. But finally he heard the one he was waiting for.

"Philip von Herzenhagen, please."

"The Quarantine Bill is stuck in conference committee," Senator Flynn said. "President Barnett could resolve the whole thing with a few phone calls, but he's not making them."

Herzenhagen adjusted the receiver to his ear. "What's giving him cold feet?"

217

Flynn was Gregg Hartmann's successor as chairman of SCARE, the Senate Committee for Ace Resources and Endeavors. It had taken the Sharks years to get him in place. "He's getting information from somewhere else. My guess is that it's the Vice President's office."

"Zappa."

"Yeah, Zappa." The Oklahoma accent dripped with scorn.

Inchoate anger flailed in Herzenhagen's head. He'd *made* General Frank Zappa, Jr. Recommended him for the job of destroying the Rox, introduced him to the old political hands who promoted his memoirs and built him into a candidate.

Damn it. Zappa's *father* had died of the wild card. Zappa had fought with the Joker Brigade in Vietnam—he had to have known what a menace they were. And he'd made his reputation fighting jokers on the Rox.

Who'd have thought he'd turn soft now?

"Zappa's got his own connections. He spends a lot of time with Barnett. Barnett always wanted to be in the military—he ran off to join the Marines at sixteen, remember—and Barnett really looks up to Zappa. So they get together a couple times a week, and sometimes Zappa brings along his stepfather, the Marine, and they all smoke cigars and tell war stories and Barnett just laps it up. And what Zappa is saying is that the Quarantine Bill isn't necessary, that if what we really want is to find a cure for the wild card and help the jokers, all we need to do is use the clinics and systems already in place, and just fund them better."

"Damn it."

The hell of it was, Zappa was perfectly right. The existing system *was* more efficient than quarantining all the wild cards in "Hospital Centers" on Federal reserves in the western US.

The only reason—the *real* reason—for moving the wild cards into the camps was so that, at the right time, they could be dealt with all at once.

Faneuil had demonstrated how, back in Africa, then again in Central America.

"I think I should come to Washington," Herzenhagen said. "We need to meet in person."

"Who with?"

"The General and Rudo are in Europe. I should see Peggy, so that she can liaise with Rudo. Is Hughes still in town?"

"Yeah. He's doing some discreet lobbying for us while he's supposed to be concerned over the transportation bill."

"Where will you be staying?"

"The Statler. As usual. Tell Peggy I'll be in tomorrow."

Shad stood outside Mr. Gravemold's Jokertown apartment and hesitated. The scent wafting from under the apartment door was tomato sauce and cheese.

Already? Shad thought.

He looked over his shoulder, made certain no one was looking, then covered himself in darkness and used his key.

A brown-haired white man in his thirties was in the kitchen eating store-bought lasagna from its white microwave tray. Two frozen pizzas, visible through the glass door of the oven, were beginning to bubble. A half-eaten gallon of ice cream, the spoon still stuck in it, sat on the counter.

The man looked up and saw Shad's cloud of darkness.

"Oh, hi," he said casually. "Thanks for leaving all the food."

Shad had put Croyd in the Gravemold apartment on the assumption that it wouldn't tell Croyd any more than he didn't know already.

"I knew you'd be hungry when you woke up," Shad said. "You are who I think you are, right?"

"I'm Croyd Crenson, if that's what you mean. Join me in some pizza?"

"It's a little early for me." No point in reminding Croyd that he hardly ate anyway.

"Yeah? What time is it? And what day and month while you're at it?"

Shad told him. Croyd seemed impressed. "I usually

sleep longer. But it varies, you know." Croyd's eyes narrowed again as he tried to peer at Shad. "Uh, is there a reason you're clouded up like that?"

"Do you recall the last moments of our previous meeting?"

"Oh." Croyd seemed a bit shamefaced. "Well, yes, I do. But I wasn't quite myself at the time."

"The point is, am I still redefined as enemy?"

"No. I'm in my right mind now, and I don't hold that business on the docks against you." He seemed amused. "So you're Gravemold, huh? How do you stand the *smell*?"

"Various methods. Usually I snort a whole bunch of cocaine."

"Yeah?" He screwed up his face. "I used to use that stuff, but I gave it up. You sure it's safe?"

"You're a speed freak, and you're giving me advice about drugs?"

Croyd shrugged. "Each to his own, I guess. Which reminds me—about this Gravemold business. If you're around me when I've been speeding—well, I get paranoid and irrational, and you should probably avoid me if I'm crazed. *I* don't hold a grudge, but when I'm speeding I see things differently." He shook his head. "Boy, that last joker body was a wrench. No feelings, no real thoughts even, just priorities and calculations. It must be what Mr. Spock feels like *all the time*."

"Figured out what your power is this time around?"

"Well, I don't fly or levitate, I don't make things move with the power of my mind, I don't walk up walls, I can't cook the frozen pizzas with my heat vision, and I can't read minds or control people with my thoughts."

"How do you know about that last one?"

Croyd smiled thinly. "I just tried."

"How about strength?"

"I don't know. I didn't want to wreck your nice furniture."

Shad let his darkness drain away. "The question is," he asked, "have you retained your prime directive from your last body?" Croyd looked quizzical. "Rudo," Shad said.

"Oh, *that* kraut-eating bastard. Absolutely. I should have killed him forty years ago." Croyd took a few bites of lasagna. "How about *your* little nemesis? Gregg Hartmann?"

"Taken care of."

"Already? You sure work fast. What was it he did to you, anyway?"

Shad told him. By the end of the story Croyd had finished the lasagna and gotten halfway through the first pizza. Croyd shook his head.

"Boy," he said. "I coulda sworn Hartmann was a nice guy. Not that I ever knew him particularly well." He turned melancholy. "Not, for that matter, that I ever really get to know *anyone* particularly well."

"Hartmann was working with the Sharks. I found that much out. My guess is that he was threatening to expose them just so they'd pay him off somehow. Or maybe it was something more complicated than that, some elaborate game the Sharks were playing."

Croyd's eyes turned cold. "The Sharks."

"Rudo's a Shark. Hartmann was working with them, even if he wasn't a Shark himself. It's all part of a package. And you know what I'm thinking about the package?"

"You're thinking it's time to bury it."

"Six feet under."

Croyd smiled. "Might as well start with Rudo. You know where he is?"

"I called his office at the UN. He's inspecting sanitary conditions in—I think it was Kirghizia. But he works right here in New York, so he'll be back sooner or later."

"There are other Sharks," Croyd said. He took a thoughtful bite of pizza.

"You know how the Sharks work, right?"

"Know how they work? Shit, man, I was inside their heads! Raney and Shannon—what a *cold* couple of bastards. They were gonna kill us with some bug, just like that Faneuil did in Guatemala ..."

"The point is, nobody knows who they are. There's no visible connection between the Sharks and their victims. There's no apparent motive for what they do. And they set up others to take the fall. There's no way any of this could go through the courts—everything's too deniable."

"My guess," Croyd said with a mouth full of pizza, "is that you're not planning on taking it through the courts."

"You know we can't."

"You're going to do it to them."

"Their own medicine. Their own style. Yes."

"You'd like my help."

"Help, yes. If you're willing. But I'd also like your advice."

Croyd blinked. "Sure."

"I mean *moral* advice."

Croyd began coughing on his pizza. Shad pounded him on the back. "I'm not exactly Fulton J. Sheen, you know," Croyd said finally.

"Listen. We're going to be hurting people. Messing them up bad."

"I thought that was the *point*. I thought that's what you were good at."

"I *am* good at it." Shad reached for words, found some that would do. "But that man was Puppetman's doing—he's responsible for a lot of it. And ... this is kind of funny—I really don't know who I am anymore. I refuse to be Puppetman's creation. But what does that leave?"

Croyd was thoughtful. "I can see this being something you wouldn't want to go to Dear Abby about."

"Well, yeah."

"I'll give you what advice I can. But—like I said . . ."

How pathetic was it, Shad wondered, that he was asking moral comfort and suasion from a onetime professional criminal who had slept away nine-tenths of his life since 1946, and who spent most of his waking hours out of his mind on crank?

"That's okay," Shad said. "Whatever you can do."

"Where do we start?" Croyd asked.

"Hartmann gave me a list—it's pretty much the same one he gave on television. I was going to leave it here

for you, for when you woke up . . ." Shad's voice trailed
away as he looked up to see a man staring back at him,
a black man with a cold, intent expression and scars that
creased the uniformity of his short prison hair, a man
straining on the very edge of violence. With humming
nerves Shad recognized the man.

Himself. Suddenly Croyd looked just like the escaped
homicidal maniac Neil Carton Langford, aka Black
Shadow.

"Croyd," Shad said, "I think I found out what your
power is."

"Yeah? What?"

"Take a look at yourself in the bathroom mirror."

Croyd munched pizza as he ambled to the bathroom
and stared into the mirror. A brown-haired white man
stared back.

"So?" he said.

Shad flailed for an explanation. "To me you look like
someone else. You look like *me*."

"Say again?"

"It's got to be a kind of projection telepathy. You make
people *think* you look like someone else, but your
appearance really doesn't change."

"Huh." He scowled at the mirror, drew his brows
together, and puffed out his cheeks. Then he looked at
Shad. "Who do I look like now?"

"Still me."

"I was trying to do Richard Nixon. No joy, huh?"

"No."

Croyd ambled back into the kitchen for pizza. "I'll
work with it a bit and see what happens. Meantime, you
tell me about the Sharks."

"Well, for starters, it looks like there's gonna be a
convention of them in a few days in Washington."

Herzenhagen propped himself up in bed and watched
as Peggy Durand pulled her tight jeans up over her hips,
her butt wriggling back and forth as she tugged them on.
Watching Peggy dress was becoming his second-favorite
afternoon activity.

She saw him watching—she *always* saw him watching—and gave him a flirtatious glance over her shoulder. "Are you horny *again?*"

"Flatterer."

She sat next to him, patted his round, ruddy tummy. "And they say old men can't cut the mustard anymore."

"They just need the right inspiration."

"Just think what you'll be able to do when you finally get a young body. You're going to wear me out."

He laughed. "Goodbye, Peggy." Herzenhagen gave her a serious look. "Take care, now."

"No one will follow me to Latchkey. No problem."

"And how are our jumper friends?"

Peggy looked amused. "Mam'zell's restless. Life on a little Maryland farm isn't really to her taste. The others—" She shrugged. "They're happy with their toys."

"Let's remember to keep them happy."

They're the things that make us as gods.

Peggy Durand used multiple evasion procedures on her way to the Maryland farm. But she hadn't checked her car for bugs; and Shad and Croyd were able to follow the two transmitters in her car, and arrived at the farm called Latchkey without having to keep her vehicle in sight.

You didn't want to be in sight of the target, Shad knew. Not if there were jumpers involved.

Croyd and Shad had emptied their various hiding places and come south with a smoky-windowed van filled with enough weapons to outfit a SEAL team, and sufficient surveillance gear to supply a Central American intelligence agency. There was even room for Shad's motorbike in the back.

Shad drove slowly past the farm once, then found an elm tree by the road and went up with a pair of binoculars. He scanned Latchkey slowly, saw the electronic gate, the two guards ambling around the buildings, and a young girl in a leather jacket kicking around the back half-section like she was bored and looking for something to do.

"Ahem." Croyd's voice.

Shad looked down and saw him standing at the foot of the tree. He looked like the waiter who'd brought them their room service breakfast at the Statler that morning, a tall, thin Somali in a white uniform.

"I can't climb like you can," the waiter said in Croyd's voice.

"Right."

Shad dropped down the tree, picked up Croyd, and with a certain amount of effort carried him to a convenient limb. By the time he arrived, Croyd looked like the little old lady who'd served them the crabcakes they'd eaten for lunch the day before.

Croyd was still honing his power. As Shad had guessed, he used a form of projection telepathy to convince other people that he looked like someone else. But he couldn't look like just anyone—he had to be around a person for a while in order to "absorb" his looks. He couldn't look like Richard Nixon unless he'd spent at least a few minutes hanging around the real thing.

Mirrors would give him away. So would his voice—he never sounded like anyone but Croyd. This was going to demand a certain amount of caution in using his power.

Shad handed Croyd his binoculars.

"So far as I can tell, the security isn't much," he said. "But there are probably alarms out there, and I'd have to get a closer look at them tonight. After we get back from the meet at Hughes' place."

He thought about the last time he'd met with jumpers, and old bullet wounds—ribs and leg—began to ache. He realized he was having a hard time breathing, that his heart was racing. He remembered lying in his own blood as he leaned against a brick wall in Jokertown, remembered the warmth of Chalktalk's breath as she kissed him.

No, he thought. It wasn't going to be like that.

This time it was going without a hitch.

Croyd yawned vastly. Shad looked at him in surprise. "You just yawned."

"I must have."

"You're not getting sleepy, are you?"

Croyd lowered the binoculars and looked surprised. "Maybe I am. And since I didn't sleep very long, either, maybe I'm doing everything faster this time around."

Shad just looked at him. Without a hitch, he thought, right.

Herzenhagen waited for Senator Flynn and watched Howard Hughes do bench presses. The old man grunted as he did his reps. Fourteen, fifteen . . .

The heavy iron free weights clanged as Hughes dropped them onto the weight bench supports. He sat up, mopped his little goatee with a towel, and then moved toward the curling machine.

There was a buzz from the wall speakerphone. "Senator Flynn is here, sir. I'm sending him up."

Hughes looked at Herzenhagen. "Open the door, will you, Philip?"

The machine clanked as Hughes began to do arm curls. Herzenhagen rose and opened the door for Flynn. While he waited for the senator to leave the elevator he turned to gaze out the clear glass wall of Hughes' penthouse. The Washington Monument, some miles distant, thrust out of a murky haze of ozone and auto exhaust.

Hughes was a fanatic about his health. He was so terrified of the wild card virus that he filtered the air in every one of his residences so as to weed out any random spores. He worked out daily in a gym that he dragged with him from place to place on his own aircraft. His diet was supervised by a full-time employee—a gorgeous redhead—who, Hughes maintained, also fucked like a weasel.

At least it was better than in the old days. Herzenhagen remembered the insomniac Hughes who kept a dozen starlets stashed in apartments throughout Los Angeles, and who ate trash, hot dogs and corned beef hash right out of the can, as his driver shuttled him, all night long, from one girl to the next. . . . The current lifestyle seemed a lot healthier.

And it worked. Hughes was in amazing shape for

someone his age. Perhaps he could star in a TV show
about it, Herzenhagen thought, *Eightysomething*.

Flynn entered. He wore a western suit and a string
tie and bore the dark skin and high cheekbones of his
Shawnee ancestors. Herzenhagen shook his hand.

Hughes grinned with effort. "Would you like a drink,
Henry?"

Flynn looked around the room. "Carrot juice?"

"We can find you the hard stuff if we look."

"I don't really have time. I've got a meeting with field
investigators at three."

Prosecuting wild cards, of course, for violations of the
registration and public health acts.

"To business, then," Herzenhagen said. He started to
light a cigarette, saw Hughes' look, then sighed and put
it away. "A triple jump, I think, with one of the holdouts
on the conference committee."

"Congressman Phipps," Flynn said. "He's been waf-
fling for weeks on this—won't say yes, won't say no."

"I'll head to Latchkey to tell Gyro to get ready. Henry,
if you can get hold of Phipps' schedule . . . ? Let's see if
we can get Phipps in the body of some fat old tourist
lady from Philadelphia."

And if *that* didn't nudge Barnett, Herzenhagen
thought, he would unleash a barrage of jumping incidents
throughout Washington society, not forgetting to include
his little friends in the press. Stick Ted Koppel in the
body of a foreign tourist named Indira, and see how long
the press was willing to editorialize about civil liberties.

And if *that* didn't work, Herzenhagen had a little plan
of his own.

The Lord, he thought, moves in mysterious ways his
wonders to perform.

Hughes dropped the weights and mopped his face.
"You're ruthless, you know that?" His tone was admiring.
He turned to the senator.

"Now, what about the logistical support you were saying you need?"

Herzenhagen stood. "This really isn't any of my

business. I should head out to Latchkey and let Gyro
know about his assignment."

And maybe, he thought hopefully, squeeze in an hour
or two with Peggy.

Shad had heard every word. To anyone with a para-
bolic mike, the glass wall of Hughes' penthouse formed
an exemplary diaphragm to amplify the sound of anything
inside.

As soon as Shad heard the door close behind Herzenhagen he left the roof of the building opposite, moved
quickly down the outside of the building, crossed the
alley between them, waved to Croyd in the van, then
went up Hughes' building. He ate enough photons to
keep himself from having a human silhouette, and it
looked as if no one was paying attention anyway. People
simply didn't *look* for people to walk up the side of a
building as if it were a sidewalk.

Strains of *Scrapple from the Apple* floated through his
mind, an odd little instrumental accompaniment to his
thoughts.

Shad vaulted over the railing of the balcony and tested
the glass door. It was open—who expected an enemy
from this direction?

Eyes turned toward him as the door slid open. He
sucked every photon from the room and went for Hughes
first. Shad knocked the old man down, drew a Smith &
Wesson, and emptied it, six shots, into the chest of Senator Henry Flynn.

Hey man, some inner voice said, *you just killed a US
Senator! Is this some kind of great or what?*

His old wounds ached as he saw Flynn fall. Then pain
crackled up his leg as Hughes sank teeth into his calf.
He grabbed Hughes's ear and yanked—he didn't want
to bruise the man—and Hughes let go. Shad slipped a
forearm around his throat and put a sleeper hold on him.
Hughes struggled—he was strong for an old guy, and a
nat—but he was elderly and hadn't even so much as
Hartmann's combat training, and he passed out quickly.

There was a sound outside. Shad dragged Hughes to

the door and locked it from the inside. "Howie?" The voice of the bewildered dietician. "Is there something wrong? Shall I call security?"

Shad smeared Hughes' fingerprints all over the Smith & Wesson, tossed the gun next to Flynn's corpse, then hoisted Hughes into a fireman's carry, and started walking down the building with him.

"Howie!" he heard. "You're scaring me!"

Croyd had the rear door of the van open. He looked like the little old crabcake lady. Shad tossed the old man inside, slammed the doors, walked to the driver's door. As he drove away he heard the rip of duct tape being torn off the roll, heard one of Hughes' awakening moans being snuffed out by tape placed across his mouth.

Shad made some random turns, found a pay phone at a corner. "Got the list?" he asked.

More tape ripped. Croyd dug the phone list out of his jacket pocket, spilling gel caps in the process, then made a series of phone calls alerting the media and police to the fact that there had been a shooting in Howard Hughes' apartment.

Shad always liked to use the cops as his allies when he could. It was harder to cover up stuff when the police were actually wandering around taking pictures.

Croyd got back in the van and Shad took off. Hughes was puffing and blowing and trying to fight his arms out of the duct tape. "You know," Croyd said, "I thought you were going to be asking my moral advice from time to time."

His voice sounded pretty strange coming out of an elderly waitress.

Shad shook his head. "They were planning on jumping a congressman so that they could pass a law to put us all in camps."

"Oh. Okay. But I was going to advise you to snuff the bastards anyway."

Shad looked over his shoulder, saw Croyd's little-old-lady eyes gleaming bright. "We're not out of control, are we?" he asked.

Croyd picked one of the gel caps off the floor of the

van and popped it in his mouth. "No," he said. "Why do you ask?"

"Would you like a date with Katherine Hepburn?" Hughes asked. "I can get you one. Mr. Connections, that's me."

They'd slapped him around some with a towel, trying to get answers out of him, and Shad had drained a bit of body heat; but Hughes, simply in being kidnapped, seemed to have regressed into some strange, alternate personality. His mind floated around the Forties without ever quite landing anywhere.

"General MacArthur Johnson," Shad said, giving it another try. "Who's he?" He was on Hartmann's list, but Shad had done some checking and found out there was no MacArthur Johnson in the US Army, Marines, or Air Force, or on the retired list, either.

Maybe the fucker was Canadian.

"How about Jane Russell?" Hughes grinned. "Some hooters, huh?"

Shad considered again the possibility of the Hartmann solution, fun with a kitchen knife, but found his heart wasn't really in the idea anyway. He didn't have quite the same grudge against Hughes that he'd had against Gregg Hartmann.

Besides, he was afraid Croyd would enjoy it too much.

"The hell with this," Shad said, and picked up his Skorpion. "Let's do it."

"You betchum, Red Ryder." Croyd's face twitched as he taped Hughes' mouth shut and left the van. The cool night Maryland countryside opened up around them. They began walking down the lane toward the lights of Latchkey, a quarter-mile away.

Croyd rotated the yoke on his High-Standard semiautomatic shotgun so that he could fire it from the crook of his arm, just by pointing. His current appearance was that of a three-piece suit executive standing next to him at the McDonald's counter that afternoon, an image that contrasted somewhat with the weapon.

"I suppose Red Ryder was before your time," he said. He was having a hard time *not* talking, Shad noticed.

"I suppose he was."

"Who'd you listen to when you were growing up?"

"Watch, not listen to. Scooby-Doo, I guess."

Shad traced the phone line from the house, went up a power pole, cut the line. "Never heard of Scooby-Doo, the bastard," Croyd snarled from below. "I'm getting disconnected from my culture, you know that?"

That's not all you're getting disconnected from, Shad thought.

"It's like mathematics. I always wished I learned algebra."

"Quiet for a second, okay?"

Shad covered himself in darkness, glided forward, checked out the detectors on Latchkey's fence. Infrared, he saw. Piece of cake. He swallowed enough photons to conceal body heat and waved Croyd forward over the fence.

There would probably be motion detectors on the farm itself, he thought, but by that point it would be too late for the defenders. He put a dark cloud just in front of himself and Croyd as they walked to the farm, to conceal them from anyone with a night vision scope.

"You learned algebra?" Croyd asked.

"I almost got my doctorate in physics."

"No shit!" Croyd was impressed. "I never knew that, homeboy! Why didn't you finish?"

"I sorta got into the vigilante business."

"Yeah. The bastards. They always screw you out of everything."

Shad wasn't too clear on the antecedents of this remark, but he let it pass. "There's a lot of suffering out there," he said, "and most of the time you really can't help. The situation is just too complicated. But sometimes you know exactly what the problem is, and exactly who's causing it; and sometimes that person is invulnerable. I mean, who's going to go up against Howard Hughes?"

Croyd giggled. "We are, homeboy."

"Well, yeah, but that's my point. Who the hell else? The Sharks are part of the government. They're part of industry. They're part of show biz. They bought *Gregg Hartmann,* for chrissake!"

Croyd looked at him. "Do you always have to talk yourself into it this way?"

Shad took a breath. "Sometimes. When I realize I'm going to kill a bunch of people I've never met, and that some of them are kids."

"Well, do whatcha gotta do to get yourself up for it. But they're jumpers, you know, and even when I was on the Rox they gave me the creeps."

"You were on the Rox?"

"Yeah, but I fell asleep, and the next thing I knew I was waking up on the Jersey shore, and the Rox wasn't there anymore."

"Huh."

"Just remember who put us in the slams, bro." Shad looked at Croyd and his nerves started to wail—Croyd had shifted his appearance to look just like Shad again. Croyd gave a twitchy grin. "This way we don't get confused and shoot each other by accident. Right?"

Shad tried to calm his shrieking nerves. "Fine, man. Whatever."

"Jesus. What's that *smell?*"

"Something died, I expect." The odor seemed to be coming from one of the farm's small outbuildings. Shad scanned it, found no sources of body heat. His heart sank. "They've probably killed someone and stuck him in there," Shad said.

"We'll check later, if there's time."

Shad looked at Croyd's automatic shotgun. "Sing out if you want to shoot that thing," he said. "And I'll hit the deck."

Shad stepped closer to the farmhouse, and suddenly lights switched on.

"Showtime," he said.

Try to remember who put us in the slams. That thought helped a lot.

Shad felt oddly disconnected from the whole business as he walked through the back door and killed two people in the kitchen with his silenced Czech submachinegun—one of the guards and an Asian kid, presumably a jumper. He realized he'd fallen back in prison mode again, not feeling anything. He kept a cloud of darkness in front of him and around him and no one could see where the danger was coming from. He advanced into the house and shot another guard, a man who fired a few blind rounds into the walls before he fell. And then there was a huge booming crash that set his nerves shuddering, and a stunning blast of odor that felt like the shock wave from the first blast. Shad flung himself on the floor. There was another crash, then another, then the sound of a body falling. Waves of a hideous stench flew through the air like echoes of each shot.

Shad whipped around, saw Croyd standing with his shotgun smoking. A man was sprawled in the doorway from the kitchen, a big man in a black fighting uniform with a one-eyed black hood over his head. The man began to move again.

"*No!*" Shad shouted, just as Croyd fired for a fourth time. The man shuddered and lay still.

"Shit!" Croyd said. "He just kept coming!"

Shad jumped to his feet. "That's Crypt Kicker," he said. "He's a friend of Battle. If we'd taken him, he might have told us where Battle is." He must have been living in the small house outside, where his smell wouldn't offend people.

"Too late now." Disgust at the odor twitched across Croyd's face. "Too late for some weeks, smells like."

There was a hissing sound from the body. The acid that ran in Crypt Kicker's veins was melting a patch on the linoleum.

This had taken too long already.

"Let's get moving," Shad said. "You guard the stairs. I'll go up and out."

He threw open a window and went up the outside of

the building. The top floor was dark. Once he found who he was looking for, it was over in seconds.

No one else was in the house, though there were two bedrooms—one filled with the foul odor of French tobacco—that there were no bodies to match with.

Croyd opened file cabinets in search of documents while Shad went out onto the grounds. He found an empty space in the garage where a car had been parked, Crypt Kicker's cozily furnished little outbuilding, complete with Hank Williams poster and a well-thumbed Bible, and nothing else.

"Lots of documents," Croyd said as he returned.

"We missed two of our targets," Shad said. "Peggy Durand and that girl in the leather jacket."

"Stick around and wait for them to come back?" Croyd offered.

"No. Leave enough of the documents to show something incriminating, then go get Hughes. We can find Durand again just by following Baron von Whatsisname."

Shad guarded the gate when Croyd went back for Hughes. The night was so quiet that he could hear Hughes offering Croyd a date with Rita Hayworth as Croyd marched him back across the field.

I'm not feeling anything, he told himself. But still a part of him cringed as he heard the shot, and Hughes' voice ceased.

Herzenhagen's heart hammered in answer to the banging on the door of his suite. He gasped for breath, reached for the drawer with the pistol in it, took the weapon in his hand.

He looked at the clock. Not quite four in the morning.

He chambered a round in his Hi-Power, put on his dressing gown and stepped to the door. He looked through the peephole, saw Peggy standing anxiously in his fish-eye view. He put the pistol in his pocket and opened the door. Peggy stormed in.

"We've just come from Latchkey," Peggy said. "Something's happening. The place is swarming with cops and press."

"Have you heard about Flynn and Hughes?"

"No. What?"

Herzenhagen took a firmer grip on his pistol.

"Let's talk," he said.

News filtered through from people Herzenhagen knew, and he tried to put it all together in his mind. The jumpers—dead. How does someone with a gun kill a jumper at short range without being jumped? Let alone jumpers that had four of the General's best men guarding them? It didn't make sense.

Gérard could have died with them, if Peggy hadn't decided to take pity on her and drive her to DC for an evening's pub-crawl.

Gérard, whom Peggy had stashed at a Baltimore hotel before coming here.

Only one jumper left. He was going to have to use her very carefully.

A terrible thought entered his mind. What if the jumpers weren't in their bodies when they'd died? What if they were elsewhere now and . . . working for someone else?

Dawn leaked past drawn blinds. The coffee and pastries he'd ordered from room service had been consumed.

"Let me think here," he said. "All the jokers from Governor's Island escaped, and all of *our* people dead. Hartmann dead just when he was becoming useful. Flynn dead just when the Quarantine Bill is stuck in committee. Hughes missing, and being blamed for Flynn's death. The jumpers dead."

"Someone's got it in for us," Peggy said.

"But look at the style," Herzenhagen said. "No witnesses. No suspects except for those *intended* to be suspects. No apparent connection between the crimes. No apparent motive . . ."

"They're good," Peggy said.

"It's *us*," Herzenhagen said. "It's *our* style. That's how *we* operate."

Peggy stared at him. "What are you saying?"

" This may not be a battle. This may be a coup."

Peggy considered this. "Who?" she said.

"Brandon. The General. Casaday. Who knows? But we've both had narrow escapes today."

"And all the ID connected with *this* body," Peggy said, "was left at Latchkey. Which makes *this* body a suspect."

Time for the backup plan, Herzenhagen thought. He couldn't know who was doing this, but things had grown too dangerous, and he still had his *deus ex* jumper. Time for a new lease on life.

"I've got to get the Quarantine Bill out of committee," he said.

Peggy seemed dubious. "How? Flynn's dead."

"We've got one jumper left. And one President. Sounds like a fair trade to me."

Disbelief entered Peggy's eyes. "Who have we got that ballsy? And who could pull off an impersonation of Barnett?"

Herzenhagen smiled. "Ever want to make it in the White House?"

Peggy looked shocked. Then she smiled.

"Who knows?" she said. " They say power is an aphrodisiac."

"Just long enough to sign the Quarantine Bill. And then Barnett and Zappa can have an accident, one with enough freaks and jumpers to turn the public against wild cards for all time."

And then there was a crashing at the door, and Herzenhagen and Peggy turned to stare down the bores of police shotguns.

Just long enough to sign the Quarantine Bill. The words sent cold fingers up Shad's spine.

"Ever want to make it in the White House?" Croyd mocked. " These old Sharks sure talk about fucking a lot."

Shad laughed, but a train of thought had been set in motion. Herzenhagen and Faneuil and Durand, Hughes with his redhead ... older men, most of them, with younger women. Shad wondered if there was some pervasive potency metaphor at work here in Sharkland, if the whole organization was based on a bunch of fading, hollow old men trying to recapture the power and splendor of youth, reviving a time where they were in charge, unchallenged by the wild card.

They watched as DC cops drove Herzenhagen and Durand away. Media lights burned bright on the two stolid faces.

"Do you think we stopped it?" Shad said.

"Stopped what? The Sharks?" Croyd laughed.

"No. Jumping the President."

Croyd laughed again. "Who cares? If Leo Barnett ends up in some French bitch's head, that's copacetic with me. What's that cracker ever done for *me* except stick me on Governor's Island and wave bye-bye?" He laughed again.

Shad shook his head. "I don't want that Nazi cocksucker in the President's head, not for one second."

"Easy enough to put a stop to it, then." Croyd's brilliant eyes glittered.

"Yeah. We'll see."

We'll see how long those two stay in jail, he thought.

Early next morning, Crypt Kicker's body strolled out of the little Maryland medical examiner's office where it had been stashed pending an autopsy. People who saw him go were understandably disinclined to stop him leaving. Shad wished he'd known the man regenerated so quickly; he'd have taken the body and been waiting when the Kicker woke up.

Herzenhagen was released next morning, after questioning. No charges were filed, at least so far. Peggy Durand, whose body seemed to have been named Dolores Chacón, didn't quite have Herzenhagen's clout, and remained a guest in the DC women's facility.

It only cost Shad a few minor bribes to see her privately—Shad loved legal institutions in the East, where everyone was corrupt. Though he was dressed as a lawyer, in a blue blazer and tie, still the smell of a jail, the antiseptic mingled with foul body odor, sent a cold charge up his spine. And when the steel door of the interrogation room slammed behind him, Shad had to clench his hands in his pockets to keep them from trembling.

Make this short, he thought.

Peggy Durand seemed a lot less nervous than he was. She managed to make a shapeless prison jumpsuit seem elegant, and she'd gotten makeup from somewhere. A wisp of smoke rolled up from a cigarette in her hand.

And then her eyes leaped as she saw Howard Hughes.

"Hi, there," Hughes said.

Durand stared. Hughes gave her the thumbs-up pilot's sign and stayed by the steel door with a grin plastered to his face.

"What's going on?" Durand demanded.

"Housecleaning, Peggy," Shad said firmly. "A tad overdue, actually. Would you like some cigarettes?" He offered a pack of Marlboros.

"I smoke Dunhills." She flashed the cigarette in her hand.

"Keep them. You can use them for money in here."

Durand looked thoughtful for a moment, then took the pack of cigarettes and put them in her jumpsuit pocket.

Shad pushed Mr. Diamond's spectacles back up his nose, opened the briefcase, took out a tape player. "I assume you're a pragmatic woman, Miss Durand."

Durand's pupils dilated at the name. "You've got me confused with someone else," she said. "My name is Chacón."

"Goddam Gravemold," Hughes muttered to himself. "Motherfucker!"

Durand's eyes flicked to Hughes, then back to Shad. "Who *are* you exactly?"

"I'm an employee of an agency that is known to you."

She seemed amused. "An *American* agency?"

Shad feigned annoyance. "Of course. It is an organization that has been tasked with the ... Card Sharks matter."

" The what?"

" The Sharks," Shad began, "have been useful to friendly interests over the years. Because of their usefulness, they were granted a certain degree of ... unofficial latitude in regard to their, ah, viral obsession. A recent reevaluation of their status indicates that they have now become a liability, and even worse, an embarrassment. It has therefore been decided to bring the Sharks operation to an appropriate termination. As you are no doubt aware, certain Shark assets deemed too intransigent to be of further use have already been annulled. Whereas those who might continue to be of further use may be retained in another capacity."

Durand sat expressionlessly in her metal chair—lips clenched, eyes contracted to pinpricks. Thinking furiously. She jerked her head toward Howard Hughes.

"And Howard? Isn't he supposed to be dead?"

"Mr. Hughes has long-established links to the intelligence community," Shad said. "Those links will continue to be of service to this country."

"Fuck yes," Hughes mumbled. "But who'd have thought the smelly bastard would have screwed me on the docks?"

Durand drew on her cigarette, leaned forward. "And what precisely do you want from me?"

"You are, I believe, a practical woman. Your history demonstrates your resourcefulness and adaptability. I suggest that you acquire an attorney of your own—not the one the Sharks have found you—and turn yourself in to the federal witness protection program. You would know best which of the available prosecutors' offices would be immune from Shark penetration."

Durand peered at him. "Witness protection? You anticipate prosecutions? *Public* prosecutions?"

Shad smiled thinly. "That would be for the prosecutors to decide, wouldn't it? But the decision has been made that *something* has to go on the public record. Too many incidents have been without explanation for too long."

"Why don't you simply arrest me?"

Shad permitted his smile to broaden. "My agency does not have powers of arrest within the borders of the United States."

"Ah. Of course. You can't arrest, you can only ..."

" Terminate."

Durand stubbed out her cigarette, bit her lip nervously. "I'm not in every loop. I'm just—" She flashed a seductive smile. "I'm just a friend of some very powerful men. I only know what they tell me. They *use* me."

Shad looked contemptuous at the merest bit of heat from Durand's frame.

"You can rehearse your excuses later. It's not my job to believe one thing or another—that's for the prosecutor to decide."

"Goddam cracker president!" Hughes said.

Durand licked her lips. Maybe she was used to Howard Hughes being flaky. "I'll think about it," she said, "very seriously." And then she gave a sad little toss of her head. "Poor Etienne," she said. "Poor Philip."

In honor of the occasion, Herzenhagen wore a mourning band and the little red ribbon of the Legion of Honor, the decoration de Gaulle had awarded him back in '44. He could have worn all his medals, here at the veterans' cemetery, but most of them were too showy.

He didn't want to be vulgar, not here at his own inauguration.

Senator Flynn was being buried in a little dell surrounded by green hills and long rows of modest white tombstones, veterans anonymous in their ranks as during their service years. Around one side of the grave site were round green hills, currently crowned by Secret Service in black uniforms: the other side sloped down to a lovely autumn view of the Potomac Valley, with Washington and its white marble monuments glowing in the westering sun. An inspiring vista, truly. And absolutely perfect, because anyone on the sloping hills had a perfect view of Leo Barnett.

Barnett, an old preacher who couldn't resist a grave side service and a chance to give a homily to the cameras.

Well done, thou good and faithful servant. Barnett's words echoing Herzenhagen's thought.

For two days he'd been staying in a safe house with Gérard and a half-dozen of Johnson's strong-arm goons.

The press had been camped outside, but that wasn't what made the stay a nightmare. Gérard had jumped him repeatedly over the last few days, jumping him until the normal spastic reaction faded, until he could function in a strange body from the first instant.

So President Barnett might trip on a tombstone and fall down. Big deal. He'd get right up again, and go right to work on getting the Quarantine Bill passed.

And then all he needed to do was confirm a finding from the National Security Council, then sign an executive order, and every wild card in the country would be on his way to a nice new tent city on a federal reservation in some picturesque state like, say, Utah.

And President Barnett would be trapped in Herzenhagen's body, which would be hustled away to his limo by Herzenhagen's security, then loaded with stonefish toxin, the stuff the CIA stored by the gallon for any interfering defector, agent, or reporter, which would result in cardiac arrest and which wouldn't show up in an autopsy.

And all the media lice that had been following him around, and the surly cops who'd ordered him not to leave town—well, they'd be left with another body and no answers. And then strings could be pulled to get Peggy out of jail.

Out of reflex he glanced up at the Secret Service. Herzenhagen's own security, unarmed and inconspicuous, hovered at a discreet distance, until the moment of the jump when they'd arrange for the President's heart attack.

Gérard—she'd been driven here in a separate car to avoid the press—drifted toward him. Herzenhagen didn't entirely like the way she moved—she moved jerkily, twitching, and there was a smirk on her face.

Oh well. He'd worked with less promising material in his time.

And in any case the whole thing was about to pay off. His life's work, reassembling into a perfect picture. The bits of history shattered by the wild card, nurturing it and caring for it and finally seeing it on its way like a good child—all about to be completed. As the President called for a moment of silence, Herzenhagen bowed his head and found himself thinking of the others, Einstein, Hughes, Hearst, Battle, and Flynn himself, the ones who had dedicated themselves to this triumph and who would not share in its consummation.

The President finished. Herzenhagen raised his head, found himself staring into the taunting eyes of Gérard. Annoyance flickered through him. He held her eyes, assumed his benevolent face, and nodded toward Barnett.

Gérard did nothing. Just smiled.

Barnett was moving down the line. He took the flag from the soldiers, handed it to the widow. Herzenhagen gave a more emphatic jerk of his head.

No response. Gérard stood on tiptoe, peered at the President. Herzenhagen moved closer, checked his six o'clock again, saw only a stout middle-aged woman in a K-Mart dress, a worried-looking black man with a beard and a blue blazer, a couple of small children separated from their parents. No one he had to concern himself with. The President was moving down the reception line, would soon disappear into the crowd. Herzenhagen leaned toward the jumper.

"*Vite!*" he urged. "*Allez-y!*"

Gérard gave him a scornful look. "Speak English." A disrespectful mumble.

Anxiety clutched at Herzenhagen's heart. "Jump him! Now!"

The President reached the end of the line. Gérard cupped her ear. "Whassat?"

"What game is this?" Herzenhagen demanded. "Do it! Jump him!"

He had spoken too loudly: the K-Mart lady was frowning at him through her bifocals. Gérard pointed at his red Legion of Honor ribbon.

"Your laundry tag is showing, Phil."

The President was disappearing. Herzenhagen lunged after Gérard, grabbed her lapel.

"Jump him!" Trying to keep his voice level.

And suddenly she wasn't Gérard at all, but a mocking

Howard Hughes, grinning through his little goatee. "Wanna date with Rita Hayworth?" Hughes said.

Herzenhagen realized who'd been behind it all. *"Howard!"* he screamed, and raised a fist, not really knowing what he was going to do with it. . . .

Something cannoned into him from behind. He stumbled and fell flat on a Navy man's grave, saw black hands close on his like steel bands, heard a voice screaming in his ear, *"He's got a gun!"* Screaming over and over. He tasted autumn leaves in his mouth. He tried to struggle, but was pinned. From somewhere came the scent of gunpowder and gun oil. Felt something underneath him, a solid iron lump, and more hands closed around him, white hands this time, and as he was lifted from the earth he saw something under him, a pistol, not *his* pistol but another; and he stared at it in shock and looked around him for Hughes and the black man, but he couldn't see either one, and rude hands were patting him down, demanding his name. His own security, unarmed and unable to intervene under the eyes of the Secret Service, had long since faded.

The President, down below, had already been hustled into his limo and was gone.

"Hughes," Herzenhagen said. A Secret Service man looked at him.

"Is that your name, sir?"

Herzenhagen straightened and realized he was in deep trouble. "I want my lawyer," he said.

Shad's nerves howled at him to stomp on the gas and get the hell away from Arlington, but the bridge across the Potomac was jammed. Instead he moved the rented limo into the queue, and waited.

"Did you see the way I fucked with his mind?" Croyd barked. He had his little-crabcake-lady appearance again. "Man, the look on his face when I turned into Hughes!"

"I wish you hadn't done that," Shad said. "If people were paying attention, they might figure wild cards were involved."

"Fuck that! You think I give a damn?" He snarled at

the stalled traffic ahead, leaned over Shad, hit the horn
button. He looked like Marjorie Main on a rampage.
"Move, you assholes!" he roared. Shad winced at the
volume.

"Let's try not to attract attention to ourselves, okay?"

"Who gives a damn, *Gravemold*? Isn't that your name,
asshole?" Croyd hit the horn button a few more times
for emphasis, then jerked back into his own seat. Shad
recalled how Croyd had attacked in the car on the night
of the Governor's Island escape. The vibes were turning
unpleasantly familiar.

"Oh, yeah," Shad said. He reached into a pocket and
pulled out a pill bottle. "I found these on the floor of
the car. They would seem to be yours."

"Thanks." Croyd popped the top on the bottle and
swallowed a mouthful of gel caps. "Wish I had Scotch
for a chaser. Nothing like a Scotch after you've killed a
bunch of people."

The last few days, Shad thought, didn't make him want
to do anything other than kill his own thoughts.

Shad had followed every detail of Herzenhagen's plot
through listening devices and phone taps. He and Croyd
had ample opportunity to evolve their plan.

Gérard and her driver would be found dead, in the
cemetery, in their limo, one rented by Herzenhagen. It
had been an easy enough hit, Shad filling the car with
darkness so that the jumper couldn't use her power.
Forensics would determine that the gun was the same
one that had been found under Herzenhagen when he
was arrested. And Shad made sure, when he grappled
with the old man on the ground, that he'd smeared the
gun oil and gunpowder residue from his own hands onto
those of the Shark, providing clear forensic evidence that
it was Herzenhagen who had despatched the jumper and
her driver.

"We get Rudo now, right?" Croyd said.

"As soon as he gets back to this country. In the meantime, maybe we can get some other names out of the
Latchkey documents."

Unfortunately, the documents would require careful

work. There was a lot of raw material; but all the money moved only in numbered accounts and the people were referred to only by code names. It was enough to keep a team of investigators busy for weeks.

Casaday. The General. Brandon. Names Herzenhagen had brought up on the tapes. If Shad could attach them to code names on the documents, maybe he'd have something.

And he really wanted to spend some time off the street anyway. Keep to himself, lose his prison self, find someone else to be.

Croyd's voice rapped out like shotgun pellets landing on a roof. "Hell with that, Gravemold. Hell with that. We fly to Kirghizia and scrag the bastard. Nothing easier." Croyd put a paternal hand on Shad's shoulder. "Stick with Croyd and his moral guidance, kid. I'll steer ya right." He laughed. "I called you Gravemold, didn't I? For some reason I can't get that name out of my mind."

Sit back, Shad thought, and let nature take its course.

Not everyone in the government was a Shark, and likewise the media. Shad hoped that enough furor had been created to generate any number of investigations. With luck Peggy Durand would turn state's witness. And if the investigations seemed to be dying down, Shad could start mailing the tapes he'd made, Herzenhagen and Durand and Hughes and the others. Or copies of the documents they'd taken from Latchkey.

Maybe Shad wouldn't have to do anything more except help Croyd take out Rudo. He owed Croyd that at least—and he owed Rudo, too, as far as that went.

"Kirghizia," Croyd said. "Lovely name." He opened his mouth as if to yawn, then shut it abruptly. "And you think we should look at *documents* when Rudo's on the loose?"

"Okay," Shad said. "Kirghizia it is."

"*Documents.* A lot you know about *documents.*" Croyd gave a grin. "I know something *you* don't know." He reached for the pill bottle again, popped the lid, swallowed another couple gel tabs. "Off-the-street crap," he muttered. "This shit's gotta be cut with something. The only speed you get on the street nowadays is smuggled up from Mexico or crystal meth people make in garbage cans. Not like when the pharmaceutical companies—"

"What is it, Croyd?" Shad asked.

Croyd smiled expansively, stretched, stopped another yawn. "I remember the good old days of speed. You could get anything—Black Beauties, desoxyn in all those pretty colors . . ."

"What is it you know," Shad spelled out, "about the documents that I don't know?"

Croyd chuckled. "Oh. Your old buddy Hartmann."

"What about him? Did you find something that said what he was up to?"

"See, there was this log of the jumps they were doing, and I kind of paged through it. Started with putting Mistral back into her body just after the Rox, and then going on to . . ."

He yawned.

"Going on to what?" Shad said. An ominous warning was sounding in his nerves.

"Going on to Hartmann. They jumped him." Croyd laughed lazily. "You got the wrong guy. It was your buddy Battle you killed."

"*You bastard!*" Shad pounded the steering wheel while Croyd laughed on. The horn went off again. Shad clamped his hands on the wheel and spoke through clenched teeth. "You didn't tell me?"

"I didn't want you running back up to New York when we were having such fun here in DC."

"So what happened to Hartmann? They killed him, right?"

"No. They jumped him into this puny little joker body, looked like a chrome yellow cartoon character, and he escaped." Croyd yawned and closed his eyes. "The Sharks are supposed to shoot him on sight. There's a description in the book." He tapped his jacket. "Got it right here. I'll show it to you," he yawned again, "once we get to Kirghizia."

"I don't think we're going to Kirghizia, Croyd."

"Oh yeah?" Croyd licked his lips and pillowed his head against the headrest. "Why's that?"

"Because of the drugs you've been taking."

"Heh. I'm a pro, man. Don't worry. My liver is safe."

"It isn't your liver I'm talking about. It's the fact that I emptied the crystal meth out of those capsules of yours and filled them with Dalmane."

Croyd dragged his eyes open. "That's a tranquilizer!"

"Yep."

"You . . ." he yawned again, *"bastard!"*

"Word, man."

Croyd was asleep. Shad dragged the documents out of Croyd's jacket, read furiously as the traffic inched its way toward Washington. Then he began to laugh.

Gregg Hartmann was stuck in the body of a three-foot-tall joker with bad eyesight and the voice of a ruptured countertenor. Puppetman's powers had to have died with Hartmann's original body. Every Shark in the world had orders to kill Hartmann on sight. And since Shad had just killed the last jumper on the planet, Hartmann was going to stay in the joker body for the rest of his life.

If you could call it living.

Shad tossed the documents on Croyd's lap and laughed. The Sharks had done Shad's job for him, had engineered a vengeance on Hartmann that was better than anything Shad could ever have done.

And if Hartmann the joker ever surfaced, maybe Shad could contrive a few additional disappointments for him. Just to remind him of who he was, and what he'd done, and what he'd deserved.

Yeah, he thought. Just like he'd said all along.

Let nature take its course.

Black Trump.

The word repeated itself in Herzenhagen's mind. Something to concentrate on as he sat on his bunk and watched the shadows of the bars form patterns on his cell wall.

Black Trump.

Herzenhagen wasn't talking, even to his own lawyer,

would let the man fight the accusations without his help. Because sooner or later the Shark mission would be fulfilled, and then it didn't matter what happened to Herzenhagen.

Black Trump.

Only a matter of time.

> Between the idea
> And the reality
> Between the motion
> And the Act
> Falls the Shadow.
>
> —T. S. Eliot, *The Hollow Men*

The Color of His Skin

Part 6

Gregg waited a week. That wasn't really his intention: it was his body's fault.

He had to molt.

Only a few hours after he'd decided to call Rudo, he had a sudden, instinctive urge to find a private, dark place. Not long after he'd pulled aside a loose grating and slithered down into the New York sewer system, pieces of skin had begun the long, slow process of peeling away. Molting felt like having the worst sunburn in the world. Every moment of it was agony: scraping against the rough stone walls to help the skin loosen, the raw new layers burning for hours until they hardened, more layers sloughing off in long streamers.

Afterward, he didn't look or feel any different except that his vision was a little better and he was ravenously hungry.

He ate a manhole cover for breakfast.

It wasn't fair, Gregg decided. It wasn't fair at all.

It took a while to dig up the necessary humility to beg for change, but it got easier each time he tried. When he had a few quarters clutched in his front legs, Gregg went looking for a phone he could reach. It took half an hour or more to find one of the old-fashioned booths with a seat he could use as a perch. He dropped a quarter in and held the receiver up to the clown nose that served as one of his ears. That left the other end dangling several inches from his mouth. He dialed Pan Rudo's private extension at WHO. Pan had a habit of working late—he hoped tonight wouldn't be an exception.

When he heard the receiver click and Rudo's cautious "Hello?", Gregg moved the phone to his mouth.

"Don't say anything," he said. "This is Gregg Hartmann. That's right. By now your goons must have told you that I got away after you jumped me out of my body." Gregg heard a faint tinny squawking and quickly moved the phone back to his ear.

". . . are you talking about? How did you get this number? You—"

Back to his mouth. "No need to get so *shrill*, Pan. That's not like you. You gave me the number back in January at the van Renssaeler New Years party—on the embossed private card you use for your personal contacts. I *am* Hartmann. When you came over to my office the last time, you were wearing your double-breasted Italian suit—the blue one—and a floral tie. I told you I was sending you an invoice for the work I did on the Senate WHO funding—$35,900, it was. Your secretary's name is Dianne, mine is Jo Ann."

More squawking. Back to the ear.

". . . do you want?"

"I *want* a body. A nice normal one. And you'll get it for me. I still have the evidence, Pan, and now I have more. See you soon."

Gregg hung up on Rudo's protest.

Rudo's limousine pulled up in front of the UN plaza while the sun was still hidden behind the Manhattan skyscrapers. The driver got out and opened the door for Rudo while a tall, muscular black man got out of the other side: Rudo's security chief, General MacArthur Johnson. Gregg moved from where he'd been pretending to look at the landscaping by the street and hurried toward them on his six legs. Johnson spotted him before he was halfway there. Johnson's right hand disappeared beneath his jacket, and Gregg called out loudly in his cartoon character voice: "Pan! Sorry I'm late for our appointment, but it's hell getting a cab when you look like this."

Rudo swiveled around awkwardly, nearly stumbling. "And you're usually so graceful," Gregg tsked softly. "Sorry I startled you, but I'm not exactly responsible for my appearance, remember?"

Rudo's pinched features contracted even more. "Just come with me and shut up," he said.

They entered the UN building. Rudo spoke with the guards and signed Gregg in for a visitor's pass before taking the elevators to the WHO floor. They didn't talk. Rudo left Johnson outside his office with his secretary, Dianne. He shut the door and turned to face Gregg. Rudo seemed uneasy and out of sorts. He sat in the chair behind his desk like a kid in his parent's office, uselessly straightening the calendar pad and toying with the Mont Blanc fountain pen on the leather-encased blotter. His eyes kept darting about nervously. He didn't seem comfortable at all, like a person in unfamiliar surroundings.

It hit Gregg suddenly. *He's* not Rudo. He's someone else. Rudo's been jumped, too. The implications staggered Gregg. The Sharks had a tame jumper—which meant that Rudo, Faneuil, Durand, Battle, Herzenhagen, *all* of them, could be safely ensconced in shiny new bodies. Safe.

"Oh my God," Gregg said.

"Not quite," said a voice. "But I did come for vengeance. A nice look, don't you think?"

Rudo was staring in fascinated horror at something behind Gregg. Gregg pivoted on his hindmost legs to see a shape coalesce out of air. Humanoid, it never seemed to quite reach solidity. Gregg could see the striped wallpaper of the office through it. "I'm Croyd, Pan," the ghostly apparition said in a cheery voice. "Just so you know."

"Croyd?" the false Pan managed to sputter.

"Yep. Amazing what a little nap will do for you, ain't it? Pan, I should have killed you long ago."

Gregg was never quite sure what happened then.

Croyd was whistling softly as he seemed to shape something in his hands, as if he were using the air in the room like clay. The outlines of the shape were suddenly visible: a long, tapering spear. "Crude, but effective," Croyd said.

And Croyd's arm flashed. The weapon flew unerringly toward Pan, who was rising from his seat. The spear tore through the man's chest as if Rudo were no more substantial than paper, and then seemed to explode. Gregg saw the man's back rip open. A gout of blood spattered the wall behind Rudo as if someone had thrown a bucket of red paint mixed with raw hamburger.

"Very effective, in fact," Croyd observed.

"But I'm *not* ..." Rudo screamed, but the scream quickly became a gurgle as blood frothed over his lips. "I'm not—" he said again, and keeled over on top of the desk, his mouth still open in the protest. The Mont Blanc went clattering to the floor.

"You're right. You're not anymore," the ghost of Croyd said, and chuckled. He waved to Gregg almost cheerily and disappeared in a roll of soft thunder.

It had taken perhaps fifteen seconds. The door burst open and Johnson rushed in, gun in hand. He looked at the carnage, at Rudo's body.

At Gregg. "You son of a bitch," Johnson said.

"No!" Gregg screeched. "I didn't do it!"

He moved at the same time, and Johnson's first shot grazed one of his legs. That was all that was needed. Gregg felt the sudden blinding panic, and Johnson dropped into slow motion. Gregg's joker body streaked for the door, turned left, and nearly left skid marks on the walls and ceiling as he half-ran, half bounced up and over Johnson. He landed on Rudo's body, legs pumping and skidding momentarily in the blood, then he was moving again. Johnson was trying to track Gregg for another shot, but he was hopelessly behind.

Out the damn DOOR! Gregg willed the body, and nearly ran down Dianne as he scurried from the room. The outer door was open now, with people running toward the commotion, but he couldn't make himself move in the right direction. He was all around Dianne's area: over the desk, tangling his multiple feet in the computer wires and taking the equipment over with him. The monitor shattered as he sped up and around the walls as if they were a racecourse specifically designed for him. Another shot tore great chunks of plaster from the wall in front of him and Gregg did an involuntary and impossible 90° turn as onlookers screamed and hit the floor. *The DOOR!* He felt like he was starting to get some control of this flight reflex, but it still took two circuits of the room before he managed to make the left turn out into the hallway. He heard Johnson shouting behind him and alarms going off.

He headed for the stairs.

And hit the door like a rushing bull. The door was harder than his head. He bounced. Johnson was pounding down the hall toward him, still bellowing and waving the gun. Office workers were scattering in his wake—under desks, behind chairs and filing cabinets. Gregg jumped for the handle and slipped off. Panicked now, he thought desperately of the garbage can he'd had for supper, remembered the saliva flowing and the pressure building and building—

He spewed onto the door panel, then could no longer hold his body still. He took off like a crazed gazelle toward Johnson, bouncing madly out of control from wall to wall and past the man as Johnson fired once more, missing. Johnson whirled around; the people who'd thought the trouble safely past them ducked for cover again.

Gregg reached the end of the hall, trying to gain control of this wild body and managing to spin around and came back the other way again, scurrying past Johnson one more time. This time when he hit the stair door it gave like hot caramel, and Gregg was spiralling down the stairwell with all six legs pumping.

At the bottom, he slammed into the crash bar with a grunt. The door gave enough for him to slide out, and now he was skittering across the slick marble floor like an out-of-control kiddie car. He slalomed into a crowd, one woman falling on top of him. The impact re-galvanized him and he heard himself screech while the world around him slowed down even more. The front door guards were pointing at him—*the DOOR, damn it, the DOOR!*—and Gregg tried to control his furious retreat. He hit the lobby fountain, spraying water as he slid in and out like a neon otter. He skidded halfway back to the elevators before he could get turned around again. The guards were scattering, trying to catch him, but they moved as if their feet were stuck in tar. Unfortunately, Gregg moved like a Formula One Lotus with no one behind the wheel.

Johnson had reached the lobby. Gregg smelled him, smelled the sharp terror of the gunpowder even though he couldn't see him. He managed to get himself moving toward the entrance: as Johnson shouted behind him, as the guards leaped belatedly for him, as a delegate entering the building gaped with wide-eyed confusion at a streaking yellow apparition slithering through his legs and out the door.

There was only one place Gregg could go now.

Jokertown. With the rest of the freaks.

A Breath of Life
by Sage Walker

Finally, standing on the cracked, stained sidewalk, after the appointments were set up with the defense attorney, after she'd figured out precisely how her best friend had framed her, Zoe Harris let herself whimper, once. No one noticed. This was Jokertown.

Zoe wanted to go home. Home to momma, and safety, and emotional shelters that would let her forget that she had been an up-and-coming CEO this morning, and had become a supsect in an embezzlement case by afternoon.

She was aware that her clothes were too good for Jokertown, that her Armani blazer, simple red silk, targeted her as a mark, but she hadn't been able to face getting to her townhouse in Chelsea and then back into Jokertown tonight.

Out of the acrid smog, kids appeared from an alley, five of them, taking up positions around her. Joker kids; the oldest couldn't have been more than sixteen. Their faces (but one of them didn't have a face, the kid had a head that looked like a soggy balloon, contours shifting as she moved) were greasepainted, divided down the center into black and white halves. They backed away from her on tiptoe, circling like stray cats. Hands in the pockets of their jackets, half black and half white vinyl, zippered on the diagonal.

"Bad. She's bad." The boy's square teeth were yellow against the dead white of the greasepaint. "She wants to stay bad, this richass bitch, she turns around and goes right back home."

Zoe started to walk through them, toward home, toward the smallest of them, thinking, Don't stop. Don't stop and they'll back off. They're *kids*. She could smell rotting garbage and trash fires. The street was a morass of discarded paper, broken glass, gray rubbish that even her New York eyes couldn't ignore.

"Nat! Nat! Go 'way. Go 'way. Not your part of town. You keep us here, but you don't come 'round our space. It's all we got, and we ain't sharin'."

She lowered her head and tried to keep walking. The street wasn't empty; jokers of all varieties went about their business and studiously ignored her.

Then there was no kid in front of her. There was a tearing sound, as of ripping silk; she thought she felt cooler air strike the sweaty place between her shoulders.

She spun around in time to see a flash of needle-sharp claws on the hand of the kid behind her. He tucked his hands in his pockets and smiled, gray-pink gums and translucent teeth like a baleen whale's beneath sad, sad eyes.

In a mincing falsetto, someone said, "Such *shoddy* workmanship these days. These *rags* just *hardly* hold together."

Three in front of her now, dancing backward, just out of arm's reach. She slipped her left hand behind her, fast, and felt the back of her blazer. It wasn't torn.

"Don't *be* this way!" Zoe said, very low. She kept on walking. Forward, another corner and then down half a block, she'd get home.

"Don't be *what*, bitch? Don't be jokers? Don't be hungry?"

The kid with the claws let them flash again, inches from her eyes. She knew that if she started to run, she'd go down, hurt, and they would vanish.

Black as night and as shiny as patent leather, an unlikely champion moved up through the crowd and took up a position beside her. She had never been so glad to see him. Jube wore his porkpie hat and he carried his papers, as if he'd stepped out of the past, unchanged.

"Chill out, Needles. She belongs here," Jube said.

She could see the stoop, with its wrought iron lace that she used to push her fingers through. Half a block and she'd be home.

"Looks like a nat," Needles said.

"She belongs here. Needles, Jellyhead, Jimmy, Jimmy, and Jan, allow me to present Ms. Zoe Harris."

The black and white retinue ducked their heads. Their hands stayed in their pockets.

"Ace, huh?"

Jube didn't say anything. Jube didn't know, did he? Zoe thought no one knew. . . .

"Okay, we'll mark her," Needles said.

Zoe wondered if he planned to "mark" her with his claws. She hoped not. He pulled a camcorder out of his jacket and focused its lens at her. She almost put on a smile for the camera.

"Safe conduct," the falsetto voice said. "Make it worth our time, bad lady. Our memories, they short, you know?"

Zoe felt someone touch her. The child called Jellyhead had grabbed a corner of her blazer. She rubbed it back and forth between her fingers, like some babies do with the satin bindings of their crib blankets. "Soft," the girl whispered. "So soft."

"Jellyhead! Mind your manners, please."

Zoe reached into her bra and pulled out her mugger's twenty. "It's all *right*, Jube. Here." She waved the twenty. "Needles? Jellyhead? Wait outside my mom's place. Then get me outa here safe. One of these every time I come around. Watch for me. You're my escorts, right?"

They hadn't stopped walking. The twenty disappeared, flicked out of her hand and into the pockets of the smallest one. One of the Jimmies, she guessed. Needles danced away and the kids widened their circle, but now it was defense.

"They *are* hungry. There's your mother, Zoe."

Anne waited on the stoop. Her eyes scanned the street, the silent, monstrous, wary array of jokers on their evening business. Zoe looked around at them, free to do so in the space people kept around Jube. No nat faces, and *no masks*. Zoe waved at Anne. Mrs. Pojorski, blue as a robin's egg, shouldered her way past Anne without a word.

"What's *happened* here, Jube?" Zoe asked. "Is Mrs. Pojorski mad at momma? They've been friends for years."

"You haven't been home in a while. The mandatory blood tests have flushed out the latents and the jokers who can pass as nats. And most of them have lost their jobs. Your mom hasn't. Some jokers hate her for that."

"Dad's still working," Zoe said.

Jube didn't say anything.

He handed her up the stairs to her mom's hug, the familiar soft warmth of Anne's six pairs of breasts under her loose caftan.

"Tell your kids how long you'll be. They'll come back. Evening, Anne."

"Jube! Come on up! Have some tea with us."

"Can't stay, lovely lady. Sorry." Jube turned to the black and white escort, who had ranged themselves at the bottom of the steps.

"Two hours," Zoe said.

"Got that?" Jube asked.

"Got it," Needles said. The kids vanished. Zoe couldn't see Jube anymore either; he'd fitted himself into some invisible space in the twilight.

The dingy stairs still creaked. The yellow fog put out by bare light bulbs still twisted the shadows into monstrous shapes. Home again, same as it ever was.

Bjorn sat in his disreputable leather recliner, his feet wrapped in hot towels and a heating pad, his thick legs covered in postman's blue twill. He still had his job, then. Jube had made her wonder.

"Hi, handsome," Zoe said. She kissed him, the bristle of his five o'clock shadow rough on her lips. Something was wrong, some pain had layered itself over his usual physical aches, had marked his face with deeper lines and reddened his eyes.

"Hi, skinny."

Zoe perched on the arm of the recliner.

Bjorn sat up and unwrapped his feet. Red-brown fur covered them, down to the vestigial claws on his splayed, short toes. He pulled on his ancient and disreputable slippers and leaned back again.

"Got news for us, do you?"

He knew it couldn't be just a duty visit. He knew her.

"Bad news. Very bad news."

He sighed and shifted his weight. "Seems to be the only kind there is these days."

And they waited, both of them, while she said, "Uh," a couple of times, while she tried to figure out the best way to begin. "I've been called to a grand jury hearing. About some theft that's been going on in the company."

"They want you to be a witness or something?" Anne asked.

"Worse than that. I'm likely to be indicted for embezzlement."

"You?" Anne said.

"Or *you*. The stolen funds are in an account with your name on it, momma."

"Oh, my," Anne said. She sank back into her corner of the couch and waited. Not panicked, though. Anne worked for a lawyer. Legalese wasn't likely to scare her.

"How much?" Bjorn asked.

"Half a million." And then the words came tumbling out, the neat, small transactions that Nosy had put together, the faked invoices for things that wouldn't have been noticed, now that the company had gotten bigger.

The mandatory wild card testing had started this. We can't have people like that working here, Nosy had said. Nonsense, Zoe had told him. Nosy, the disease is *not* contagious. But, he'd said. But nothing, Zoe had replied. This is a company that hires *chemists*. Jewish chemists, Japanese chemists, any old damned chemist who can do the work. And that includes wild card victims, Nosy.

She'd put her foot down, he'd looked abashed, she'd thought the matter settled.

"An order showed up for a tanker full of acetone for the plant in Jerusalem. Paid in full. We haven't *built* the plant in Jerusalem yet. Accounting spotted it and called for an audit. I got a subpoena today. And a lawyer. Mendlen."

"He's good. But you should have called me," Anne said. "No, you couldn't, I had a clinic appointment. I wasn't in this afternoon."

" The funds were diverted to a signature account. We'll get a handwriting expert on it, momma, and you'll be cleared of all this."

Mendlen hoped.

"So what do I do now?" Zoe had asked.

"Act as if nothing has changed," Mendlen told her.

Right.

Bjorn was staring at the mute TV set, and he was trying not to look worried.

"I *like* Mendlen," Zoe said. "I'm going to see him again tomorrow. Dad? What else is going on here? Jube seems to think you've lost your job."

"No. No, I still get to carry mail around. As long as I can walk, I guess." He reached his arm around her and patted her hip. " The job's fine."

"So what's wrong? Something is!"

"Zoe, it's nothing you need to worry about."

"Don't make me crazy. Tell me, daddy."

He sighed and shifted in the chair. "My pension's gone."

" That can't be! You're a federal employee, for God's sake. The government hasn't lost its pension funds!"

"I'm a wild carder. What they said, is that—oh, just a minute here." He rummaged along the edges of the chair cushion. "Here's the brochure. I got it today."

He held it at arm's length and began to read.

"See? It looks like real good stuff. Wild card victims get cared for in special 'Biological Research Units,' they say. No Medicare or Medicaid, not for us. We get 'special treatment,' and 'individual financial assistance.' Got that, honey? 'If medical problems arise from these tragic infections.' "

"Barnett," Zoe said.

"Yeah." Bjorn sounded resigned. Zoe took the brochure from Bjorn's hand and scanned through it. It was as opaque to read as an insurance policy, but a sickening concept came through. Sick jokers would be spirited away, isolated.

"They *can't* do this!"

"Well, they did. It's enough to make me believe the Card Sharks are real." Bjorn patted Zoe's hip as if she were the one who was hurt, not him. "Barnett's in the White House, and Hartmann's dead."

"I never trusted Gregg Hartmann," Anne said, *sotto voce.*

"I did. Let me finish, Anne."   •

From her nest of pillows on the couch, Anne winked at Zoe.

"We've got another election before I'm due to retire," Bjorn said. "I think the law can't stay on the books, Zoe. The ACLU and the JADL will get it revoked."

"Sure."

"So, daughter. This mess you're in. It's a business mess, it's a money mess, but you've got your health and your strength. You can't let it get to you, Zoe. I'd hate to think some nasty little nat could stress you so much that your card would turn. Don't let that happen, Zoe."

Denial was a wonderful mechanism. Bjorn and Anne *must* have known that their daughter was no latent. Her deceptions could not truly have fooled them, back when she was small and not so clever. She'd known, even as a tiny child, that they desperately wanted her to have escaped the wild card.

"There's pot roast and cranberries, Zoe," Anne said. "I can heat some for you, if you'd like."

Bjorn's dietary preferences ran to meat and fruit.

"Thanks, momma. But I had a sandwich at work." That was a fib. She just couldn't eat, not now. My family has always operated on a structure of polite lies, Zoe realized. Momma is facing a charge as an embezzler's accomplice, and she wants me to eat my dinner like a good girl.

Zoe got up from the arm of her dad's chair and went to sit on the couch by her mom. Muted by the thick insulated draperies Anne kept over the windows, a siren wailed, rap music blared, and the popcorn sound of automatic gunfire peppered the night, but it was far away.

As if tonight were an ordinary night, they watched while the TV ran its retinue of nightly news. The Great and Powerful Turtle was going to appear on *Peri's Perch*; tune in tomorrow.

"I've got to go home, momma," Zoe said. "No, don't get up." She paused with her hand on the doorknob. "*What* clinic appointment, ma?"

"Breast lumps. I'm waiting for some biopsy reports. I'll know tomorrow."

"Holy shit."

"Language, language, baby." Anne got up from the couch.

"I'll go to the clinic with you."

"You have an appointment with your attorney." Anne stretched on tiptoe and kissed Zoe's cheek. "You'd better keep it."

"Yes, momma."

"Your room's still here. There's *always* a place for you here, if you don't want to be alone."

"Thanks, sweetie."

Zoe kissed her and left.

She went down the stairs at speed. Her life felt unreal, the day's events impossible. Cancer. Poverty. Disgrace. She had to make these things not happen, and she didn't know how. Scenarios of a grim future kept popping into her mind; Anne dead, Bjorn locked in some walled enclave. She saw herself in gray cotton in a prison workroom, stitching useless things on old sewing machines. No.

Taking the first step outside always made her catch her breath, even though her fears of the stoop didn't seem quite real, even to her. Once, she'd seen an alligator under there. No fantasy, she'd *seen* it. A big one, too.

This time, she saw triangles of white that flitted away from the stoop when she came down, her "escorts" waiting for her. Jube was there, too, marked out of the gloom by the white rectangle of the newspapers he still carried.

"Hiya, people," Zoe said. "Hey, Jube."

Her escort fell in beside her, Jube at her left. There was something odd about the way he walked, as if his hip joints didn't connect in a standard fashion.

"Want a paper, Zoe?"

"No. Distract me. *Tell* me the news, Jube. I belong to a post-literate generation."

"Things aren't going well at home?"

Not exactly. "No."

The streets were nearly deserted, unusual for a citizenry who usually felt more comfortable in the dark.

"Where *is* everybody?" Zoe asked.

Three of the Escorts had placed themselves in a triangle ahead of Jube and Zoe. They rotated the point position, traded off by using some sort of hand-jive that Zoe couldn't follow, while the remaining two ducked in and out of shadows and alleyways, waited, and changed positions with the two kids who brought up the rear.

"Hiding, if they have a place to hide, Zoe. And some have moved away. Gone to Nam, or to Guatemala. Can't be that many with that much money, though. Makes you wonder."

Nam, Guatemala. And Jerusalem, where medical care was excellent and jokers were ghettoed, but relatively safe. Safer than Anne would be in Barnett's medical camps. How? Buy a ticket, that was easy. Convince Anne to go. Not so easy.

"I need to get my folks out of here," Zoe said. "How do I do it, Jube?"

Jube didn't speak for a while. She'd never known him to be reticent. The Escorts turned at the next corner.

"Where are we going, Jube?"

"Going to get you some news, Zoe. And maybe some help." His hand was firm on her upper arm, guiding her forward.

In the cluttered alley, a single forty watt bulb hung

over a rickety stoop. Needles knocked on a thick steel door, and a man in a hooded black cape opened it and ushered them inside with an exaggerated bow. Inside the cavernous, echoing space, the Turtle's battered shells hung motionless over a murmuring crowd of jokers.

Jellyhead slipped her hand into Zoe's. The hooded figure turned and Zoe saw his mask, a yellowed skull. He spoke to someone. No. Not a mask. Echoes richocheted from odd corners, sounds she couldn't recognize. She smelled burning Sterno.

"Who *is* that?" Zoe bent her head and whispered to the child beside her.

"Mr. Dutton," Jellyhead said.

Charles Dutton, the reclusive owner of the Famous Bowery Wild Card Dime Museum, a place as macabre as she had imagined. Even unlighted and motionless, the displays compelled the eye: Tachyon, with curls the color of cherry cough syrup; Jetboy, whose bloody wounds looked dusty and drab. Bloat, miniaturized, a blob with a boy's tortured face perched atop it, filled one corner.

"Jube, why did you bring me *here*?" Zoe asked.

Jube wasn't there. It was Needles who stood beside her. The boy put his finger to his lips and looked away from her, toward the bolted front entrance.

Blue Sterno flames flared out of what looked like a sturdy marble birdbath. A figure appeared from the shadows, scooped up some of the flames, and swallowed them. "It's time to begin," the fire swallower said.

"Can't see you, Hotair!" someone called out.

"Oh, sorry." The man hoisted himself up and sat crosslegged in the burning fountain. It didn't seem to bother him.

"Can we start with the report from Hester Street?" Hotair asked.

"Two beatings," someone said. "We didn't get there in time to film the attack."

"No way to identify the assailants?" Hotair asked.

"Description only. Shaveheads."

"Bowery?"

"We filmed a verbal assault," Needles said. "Shaveheads again. But we missed a knifing, damn it."

"They cut my dad. Someone did," Jellyhead called out. "He's dead." Her voice didn't even quaver. A joker woman moved close to her, and Jellyhead let herself be hugged, briefly, before she twisted away from the proffered comfort.

"Sorry, Jellyhead," Hotair said. "Any idea who did it?"

Jellyhead looked at the floor and said nothing.

"We'll move another team over to Bowery," Hotair said. "Johnson, can your team cover it?"

Johnson had pointed ears the size of dinner plates. "We'll have to leave our territory uncovered. But yeah, we can do it. We haven't had more than a couple muggings since yesterday."

"Ms. Harris?" The voice behind Zoe was well-modulated and low. "Jube said you might be of assistance to us, and asked me to speak to you."

Zoe heard the swish of a velvet robe.

"You're Dutton."

"Yes."

"But—" But I'm here to *get* help, not give it. A glint of reflected blue flame danced in the deep sockets of Dutton's eyes and then vanished.

"The patrols are trying to record episodes of violence against jokers, with the hope of forcing prosecutions. But it's difficult to stay funded. Camcorders cost."

"But—"

"Come with me. We can talk in my office."

Zoe followed him.

Dutton's office was loaded with computers, faxes, and modems. He ushered Zoe to a chair and settled himself behind his desk with a practiced flourish of his cape.

"I'm not a source of funds for joker streetfighters," Zoe said.

"Are you not? I am disappointed." Dutton's accent was Ivy League; his hands, folded on the desk, were normal and impeccably manicured. "Then what is your interest here?"

"My parents are jokers. They are not young. My mother is ill. I want to get her to Jerusalem."

"That is simple, Ms. Harris. One buys a ticket."

"She will need more than that. A place to live, introductions. Medical referrals. And some information I'm not likely to get from the Jerusalem officials, like how to buy protection for her. People get killed there, far too often."

"You seem to think I have access to such information."

"You seem to be providing a place where joker activists gather."

"Yes." Dutton steepled his fingers.

"I'll pay." How? The defense costs to keep me out of jail are going to take everything I have.

"Payment is not requested, Ms. Harris. I will make certain inquiries for you. I assume I can leave messages with Needles?"

Not at my company, please. Not at home, Anne will balk.

"With Needles. Yes."

"Give my regards to your father, Zoe." Dutton knew Bjorn? That wasn't surprising; rumor had it that the reclusive Dutton loved gossip. He got up and opened the door for her. The museum was emptying rapidly. Needles and one of the Jimmies fell into step beside Zoe and led her toward the back door. A fetid wind from the river enriched Jokertown's pervasive stench.

"Get me to the train, kids," Zoe said.

"Going uptown, right?" one of the Jimmies asked.

"Right."

At the station, one of the Jimmies ducked down the stairs. Zoe heard a whistle, and the tiny one—Jan, that was, a little girl who Zoe now realized was twelve or less, flashed her fingers at Needles, then stuck her hands back in her pocket.

"No trouble down there," Needles said. "You can go back home, Zoe. Where it's safe."

"Where do you . . . ?"

"Sleep? When it gets cold, we used to buy a bottle of

wine for Jellyhead's dad. He'd get drunk and we'd sleep
on his floor. But he's dead."

"There's *nothing* . . ."

"You can do."

Needles patted her hand, smiled, and turned away.

She walked down into the city's concrete guts. Wanting
to be able to tell him, to tell someone, even to tell Dutton, it's not my problem. I got *out*. I can't take in every
joker orphan in one *block* of this stinking place, much
less help them all. Don't ask me, Dutton. I have to take
care of my own, first. I have to take care of *me*.

Dank subterranean wind, rushing up the tunnel,
chilled her hands. She stuffed them in the pockets of
her silk blazer and climbed on the near-empty train.

Zoe dressed in an Anna Sui for work, floaty and fragile,
a perfect dress for injured innocence. She went into her
office and found Nosy sitting in her chair. Act as if nothing has changed, Mendlen had told her. Fine. Nosy
couldn't see her clenched fists, or the marks her nails
were leaving in her palms. "I'm going over to the Flat-
bush plant," Zoe said. Then she turned on her heel and
left.

She spent the day arranging to put the Chelsea place
on the market. Mendlen said that would be okay, if she
handled the transaction discreetly. She didn't tell him
she planned to use the money to send her mother to
Jerusalem. Zoe packed some clothes in Chelsea and went
back to Jokertown.

"It's cancer. In three of the breasts." Three of *the*
breasts, Zoe's mom said, not three of *my* breasts. "I'll
get to get rid of them, after all these years."

"When is the surgery?" Zoe asked.

"As soon as they can schedule the OR, Zoe. The Jokertown clinic is always so busy. Two or three days, Dr.
Finn said. They're going to take six off then, and later
another six. Too much trauma for one surgery, they said.
Then I'll be on chemotherapy."

"I'll start dinner," Zoe said.

"Nonsense. I don't feel any different than I ever did." Anne got up from the kitchen table and began to bustle, but Bjorn padded around and set out knives and forks and plates, not typical behavior for him at all, while Zoe chopped the vegetables Anne pulled out of the fridge. "How did your meeting with your lawyer go?" Anne asked.

"The grand jury hearing is scheduled in three weeks," Zoe said. "Nothing to worry about until then." Except you need to have your surgery in Jerusalem, momma, not in Jokertown. If the "Biological Research Units" start accepting "patients," you might be forced to go there, and that cannot happen. Zoe reached for an onion and sliced it. "Damned onion juice," she said, and Bjorn and Anne pretended to ignore her tears.

At four in the morning, she gave up on sleep. She tiptoed into the hall and stood at her parent's doorway, as if she were a three-year-old with a nightmare. She wasn't three years old anymore. She was thirty-four, and she couldn't climb in bed with them and say she was scared. They slept. Bjorn snored, with vigor and industry. Anne shifted and rolled over, but she sighed and didn't wake. Cancer. Biological Research Units. Rumors of a conspiracy determined to cleanse the world of the wild card. She remembered Hartmann's utter conviction, his intent, pleading gaze. She remembered old textbook photos, Jewish prisoners after the war, the ones still alive, who looked into the cameras with terrifying, terrible eyes.

Never again.

Not *here*. Not to those kids who live in the street, not to my *family*.

It's time to change things. It's time to do *something*, even if it's wrong.

Zoe tiptoed back to her room. She changed into jeans and scuffed high-tops and a nylon windbreaker. She pulled on a knit cap, stuffed her tawny curls underneath it, and went out into Jokertown, into the dark and the noise.

"Lookin' chill, Zoe lady. Think you fool us?"

Needles carried his camcorder in the front of his jacket as if it were an infant.

"Had to try, didn't I?" Zoe asked. "I thought you guys watched everything around here. Where were you when I came in this afternoon, Escorts?"

Jellyhead danced a quick end-zone dance and slipped her hand into Zoe's. "Sleepin'," Needles said. "Bad night last night. Can't take you home, though. You already there."

"I had to get loose for a while. Where's Jube?"

"Where's our twenty?" one of the Jimmies asked.

"Oh. I almost forgot." She handed it to him. He looked like a gangly nat adolescent, pretty much. His eyebrows were downy. So were his ears, she saw as he moved in to spirit away the twenty; faint peachfuzz feathers, still colorless, were just growing in. He was going to look very like an owl.

"No Jube. Can't touch that dude, for a time. Maybe you stay home. Best place. Best place in Jokertown tonight, you got a door to lock."

This Jimmy had stripes on his skin. Pale, but they looked like some sort of tropical fish. An angelfish.

"Oh." She'd been counting on Jube, his rotund stability. She wanted a buffer to guard her from the wall of deceit and decency at home. "I really wanted to talk to him."

" Talk to *us*." Jellyhead had nuzzled up close to Zoe's side.

"Ah, shut it, Jellyhead. We got the bucks, and I'm *hungry*." That was the tiniest one, Jan.

They hadn't stopped moving. They danced their circle around her, and she saw they had herded her down a street where a neon sign jittered and blinked out the word *Diner*.

"So am I," Zoe said. It was another fib.

The countertop was orange formica, the stools were covered in cracked yellow vinyl, the general effect was gloomy, and the man behind the counter looked like Humphrey Bogart.

"The usual?" he asked.

"Sack full," Needles said. "Extra catsup?"

"Don't got any." Moby's eyes were on Zoe.

"She's ours," Needles said. "She's ours."

"Looks like a fucking social worker," the man said, but he turned to his grill and laid out burgers.

"We don't sit down?" Zoe asked.

"Can't watch from in here," Needles said. "We got to cover our territory, you know?"

Zoe nodded. Needles and Jellyhead were beside her. The other three had vanished again. And Needles didn't have the camcorder; he must have passed it to one of the others on his way in. Damn, these kids were quick.

Needles took the grease-stained bag and the man gave back some change. And then the kids were herding her down the street again, twisting and zigzagging, until they turned into an alley. Concrete blocks stacked in triangles supported a lean-to of steel roofing. The interior space was a dark maze of nests of wadded clothing and smelled of old grease and sad child. The huddle was four feet high. Zoe crawled in beside the Escorts, sat down, and pulled up her knees to give Jellyhead, who shoved at her gently, room to get out again.

Jan sat down next to Zoe. Needles portioned out the burgers and fries. "No," Zoe said when he tried to hand her one. "No, I can't."

Jan gulped down half a burger at a bite.

"Hey, bitch. Too good for our food, are you? No way we shoulda brought you here. Maybe you best get out, now." Needles sliced at the air in front of her nose. "Go on! Get clear, fancy lady! We move this place, when we need to. You won't find it again, hear?"

"Needles! Don't, please. Not you, too."

This was too much. Even this pathetic refuge was closing to her. Zoe rested her forehead on her knees, utterly defeated.

"Got troubles, lady?" Jan asked.

"Not like yours," Zoe whispered.

"Whatsa matter?" Needles asked. "You lose your rich-bitch job or something?"

"Yeah." She snapped at him, too angry to hide the pain in her voice. She had no reason to hide pain from such as these. "An old buddy of mine decided he hated my wild card ass. And he's framed me with embezzlement."

"Whoa!" Needles said. "You like a fugitive or something?" His claws flashed in the air, moving around his face as if to guard it.

"The cops don't have a warrant, if that's what you mean."

"She *hurting*, Needles. You let her talk." Jan patted her knee. Jan looked like a normal, though thin, little sparrow of a girl, except for her eyes. Her irises rearranged themselves, constantly, like miniature kaleidoscopes.

"The job is nothing. My mom's got cancer. She's so *good*! Good people shouldn't get cancer."

The kids didn't say anything. Good people shouldn't get the wild card, either. "There's nothing I can do. There's nothing I can do about *any* of this shit! My God, this world is going crazy."

Not to mention that she was pouring out her troubles to joker kids who lived in an alley. "And I don't want to cry on my parents' shoulders and let them know I'm scared. My folks think I'm strong, and rich. They think I got out of Jokertown forever. But I didn't. I'm here. God damn it, I'm *here*!"

Needles bit through a french fry with his baleen teeth. "You got that note, Jan?" he asked.

"Got it." The child pulled a sheet of shiny fax out of her pocket.

"Dutton said give you this." Needles settled back with the rest of his french fries.

"It's dark in here," Zoe said.

"Oh." Jan reached for the sheet of fax and looked down at it. Her eyes sent out beams. Her eyes were bioluminescent flashlights; the light they produced had a chartreuse tint like that of a firefly.

The information you seek is available. Please contact me.
Charles Dutton.

Zoe folded the note and stuck it into the kangaroo pocket on her windbreaker.

See the man. See him. Get Anne out of here, and Bjorn too, if it were possible, and tell Mendlen you're going to do it. If he says Anne's leaving will break a law or several? Find out how to do it discreetly, then.

"You thinking," Needles said.

"I'm thinking." She felt the kids' sympathy, their support. Thinking about how to find the cracks in the walls of the world, how to step through them into safety. Thinking about how to be good in a time of evil.

"We like you," Jellyhead said.

"Thank you," Zoe said. What about these kids? She wouldn't be able to walk away and forget them, their survival, their odd sense of charity. They had offered bread and salt, in their own way.

Okay. Question. What could a female ex-CEO facing embezzlement charges do to change the opinions of a terrified, well-meaning population that was bent on quarantining a fearsome disease? A disease that killed nine out of ten and changed the tenth into an inhuman monster? She couldn't think of much, at the moment.

Angelfish Jimmy had replaced Needles near the door hole. "Up, Jan. We gotta go talk to Hotair. Time to make morning report."

"I should see Dutton. Will he be awake?" Zoe asked.

"Yeah," Angelfish Jimmy said.

Zoe crawled out of the lean-to and followed the Escorts toward the Dime Museum.

"Ms. Harris." Dutton did not seem surprised to see her. "I'm glad you're here."

He led her to his office, away from the crowd of tired-looking jokers. He offered coffee. Hot and fresh.

"Kona," Zoe said.

"Why, yes."

"You have information for me, or so the kids say."

Dutton tapped at a manila folder on his desk. "I have names for you. In Jerusalem. A flat that is ready for occupancy, if a deposit can be made in the next twenty-four hours. Several names of oncologists in Israel, but none in the city itself. However, the distances to the clinics are not large, and your mother should have no difficulty obtaining care."

"Oncology. How did you know Anne would need an oncologist?"

"Please, Ms. Harris." Dutton's protest was a mix of amusement and offended pride.

"Sorry," Zoe said.

"The Jerusalem information came from an organization you may not find—palatable. They are called the Twisted Fists."

"Terrorists."

"Dependable terrorists. Their organization has shown signs of maturity of late. It would be advisable, of course, for you to purchase round-trip tickets for your parents, ones that would indicate a relatively short stay in the Mideast. In light of your current—difficulties."

"You know about those, too?"

Dutton pushed the folder, gently, toward Zoe's side of the desk. "I grew up in Rhode Island. I went to Princeton. I was a successful stockbroker once, Zoe Harris. In spite of this face, this fate, I am 'successful' again. There is life after one's card is on the table. There *is* life. More coffee?"

Zoe shook her head, no.

"Please. Hotair is not going to be finished for a while. I enjoy your company, I must admit. It is not often that I have the honor of being of assistance to beautiful young women."

Zoe smiled and pushed her cup across the desk. "Thank you. And yes, another cup, please." She picked up the folder and held it tight to her chest.

"I am known to be a gossip, Zoe. But I am also a good listener, and my gossip is tempered with discretion."

She believed him. Stories of his charities, of his generosity, were part of the Jokertown mythos.

"I want to ask you something," Zoe said.

"Yes?"

"Do the Card Sharks exist?"

Dutton leaned back in his chair. "Conspiracy theories

are usually the product of the imaginations of the prose-
cuted. There are many internal consistencies in the stories I have heard. Too many. I *fear* that they exist. I
cannot prove it."

He spoke with great sorrow. Zoe sipped her coffee.
Tell him. Tell him what you've never told anyone before.

"There is so much hatred. I fear that my mother will
be locked away. My dad's pension has been commandeered. These things are *real*, whether or not the Card
Sharks are real. I've got to do something, Mr. Dutton,
even if it's wrong." She caught her breath. "I have—I
have a wild card power. It's not a great power, it's just
this little thing I can do, and I trained myself years ago
never to use it. There are other things, things like money
and political clout that might help the wild carders now,
but I don't have those things, not any more. I've lost a
lot of what I thought was *me*, since my partner framed
me for embezzlement. But that doesn't mean I want to
come out of the deck."

Through the closed door, she could hear murmurs of
sound, the jokers doing what they could to protect each
other.

"I'll send momma to Jerusalem. I'll talk to your
Twisted Fist people, because I might need them someday. I'll get my latents out of the country, the ones who
work for my company. There are thirteen of them, Mr.
Dutton. But maybe you knew that."

Dutton said nothing.

"That will take every cent I have, but that's okay. I'll
get momma out, and Bjorn. I'll start there. Then I'll deal
with this embezzlement mess. I haven't done anything
wrong. Things are bound to work out for me. The court
system is designed to protect the innocent, isn't it? This
thing with the company is just an awful nightmare *mistake*, that's all it is."

Dutton sighed. "More coffee, Zoe?"

"Yes. No. Yes, half a cup. It's not like I can use my
ace when I want to. I don't know *how* to use it! And I
don't want to. It's ugly, it's strange. Mr. Dutton, I hate
what I am underneath this, but *this* is me, too." She held

her hands palms up, her fingers stained, as always, with residues of the chemicals she still worked with, CEO or no, for she was *good* at finding the mixes, it was as if she shoved the molecules into place—and she moved her hands to indicate her flat belly, her long thighs, like a model on a runway pointing out design details. "But I've got to learn to use my ace. I've got to stop hiding from it. But I don't want to. I want to keep on hiding in the nat world. But I can't. I'd hate myself, every morning, if I did. Who can help me?"

"Turtle," Dutton said.

"Turtle? That man's a bag of neuroses! I mean, there's defense mechanisms, but his are made of armor plate!" And needless to say, *she* wasn't neurotic, or defensive, at all. No way.

"He's in town for a week." Dutton rummaged in a drawer, extracted a business card, and handed it to her.

Thomas Tudbury. A California address. There was a Manhattan number scrawled on it in ballpoint.

A knock sounded on Dutton's thick door.

"Zoe? Zoelady? You ready to go?"

"Yes," Zoe said. "Thank you, Mr. Dutton. I think."

Zoe tried to slip in quietly, but they were already awake. Anne, in her chenille bathrobe, sat in the kitchen drinking coffee. Bjorn, always warm in his fur, wore seersucker jogging pants. He paced back and forth, blowing on a cup of chamomile tea.

"Wups. You heard me leave, didn't you?" Zoe asked.

"No," Anne said. "But we worried, a little, when we found you were gone. I have to admit I'm—concerned—about this cancer thing, Zoe. That's why I woke up, I guess."

"Mother. The clinic. You can't go there." Zoe put Dutton's folder on the kitchen table. She shrugged out of her windbreaker and sat down. "Momma, you've got to go to Jerusalem instead."

"It's that bad, is it?" Anne asked.

"I fear for you."

"Bad times have come and gone," Bjorn said.

"This is different. Maybe the Sharks are real, maybe they aren't. But until this craziness is over, I want you safe."

Bjorn sat down. He looked mean and big. It was just his fur standing on end, but it *did* make him look scary. "You're right, daughter. I'm afraid that this time you are right. We'll go."

"Good. I want you to call a travel agency and book tickets to Jerusalem for you and Anne. And get me the price of tickets from New York to Saigon. I'm going to be buying quite a few."

"Quite a few?" Anne asked.

"I can't leave yet, not with this grand jury nonsense. But the latents who work for me—pardon me, that's who *worked* for me—they can get out. I've got to talk to them. Damn. What time is it?"

"Don't swear, darling. It's six."

"I can get to Maria's place before she goes to work. I need to talk to people face to face. Can I shower first, daddy?"

"Don't stay in all day, is all I ask. I've got to walk my route, you know."

"You're not going to the clinic with momma?" Zoe asked.

"Last time I was in the clinic, I ended up getting married," Bjorn said. "Anne says for me not to come."

True. He had come to the labor room and waited through Zoe's birth. "Must be mine," he'd said to the delivery room nurses. "Look at that red hair." Father Squid had married them while the nurse on duty had stitched up Anne's episiotomy. The doc had been attending a transformation crisis and hadn't made it into the room until later. It had been, Anne said, a typical night at the Jokertown clinic.

Zoe got her shower and came back to the kitchen. Bjorn, his bifocals perched far down his nose, turned over the last page of the morning *Times* and looked up at her. "Daughter? I don't want to use your money for these tickets."

"I can't desert these people! I know that most of them

don't have the cash to get out! I can't just watch them get slaughtered! Daddy—"

He stared at her with his "I won't take this nonsense from you, young lady" expression. "You need your money for your lawyers. Your mother and I have been talking. I have a savings account that isn't part of the pension. It just might cover the costs on this rescue of yours."

"It will leave you with no safety margin."

"I'm old. Your mother isn't so young. These workers of yours are young, and some of them have children. Let's get them out of here."

"You've always said not to run away from problems," Zoe said.

"Running away can be the only good choice, sometimes. This looks like one of those times."

"I can't let you do this," Zoe said.

"Since when, young lady, have you begun to decide what your parents can and cannot do?"

"Since never. Thank you, daddy." Zoe bent down and hugged him, hard. She hid her face against his chest, afraid that he would see her thoughts, and what she was thinking was—Daddy's contribution gives me a little more slack. Needles, Jellyhead, Jimmy, Jimmy and Jan, you're getting out, too.

He just wasn't what she'd expected. Maybe she wasn't what *he'd* expected; the short little man took a step backward, his hand still firmly on the hotel room's doorknob, and looked her up and down. This was the Great and Powerful Turtle? This graying, paunchy, blue-collar nerd? She knew he'd written *Shell Games*, the Turtle's story, himself, even if it had been published with an "as told to" name. She'd caught a glimpse of him on Arsenio once, but the cameras hadn't given her the leprechaun look of him. He wore chinos that were baggy in the butt, and a rust-colored shirt, some sort of brocade. But he *looked* like he'd be happier in a coverall, one with "Turtle" embroidered in red over the left pocket.

"Mr. Tudbury?"

"You're Zoe, right?"

"Yes."

"Come on in. Charles Dutton just called. Good thing he did, too. I was ready to call this off. Dutton made me change my mind." He waved her toward a table by the window, stacked with the remnants of a room service breakfast—for two. No bed, the room held a couch and end tables, and a desk with a laptop and modem.

"Want some coffee?" he asked. "Lemme get a clean cup, there's one on the dresser."

"Uh, I didn't mean to intrude . . ."

"You're not intruding." He ducked into the bedroom of the suite and came back with the promised cup. "Danny's in the shower." He poured coffee for her, indicated the sugarbowl and the cream pitcher, and sat down with a definitive thump, as if he planned to stay in his chair all day.

"I got another hate call this morning. The hotel usually screens the calls pretty well, but this was a real nut case. Gave the right names, you know, and then it turns out to be some fanatic who insists that the shell's forcefield, whatever that might be, made his roses die. He'll probably sue. They all do."

Turtle projected a sense of restless energy. He wasn't doing real well with eye contact. "It could have been worse," he said, as if he were talking to himself. "It could have been someone who lost someone on the Rox. To save people I loved, I killed people I loved. That's a bitch. That's such a bitch." He stared out at the bricks outside the window until Zoe thought he'd forgotten she was there. The shower kept running, and CNN's electronic ta-da-da-dat! came from the bedroom. "My old friend Charles says you want to be a hero. Do you?"

"No!"

"That's good. Only fools want to be heroes." When he smiled, he was a different person. "What *do* you want, then?"

"Mr. Dutton thinks you can help me learn to use my ace."

"Ace, huh. What makes you think you're an ace?"

"I've got a power. I can't use it when I want to. I tried

so hard to pass as a nat that I guess it just got . . . repressed or something."

"I'm not a shrink," Turtle said.

"No. You're an ace. How could I trust a shrink with this?"

"Good question. What's wrong with being a nat?" Turtle asked.

"*Nothing!*"

He was looking away again, and she feared she had lost him; he looked as if he were thinking about showing her to the door. "I've lost my company. My VP has framed me with an embezzlement charge. My father lost his pension because he's a joker. The feds are about to put jokers in fucking *concentration camps*! And maybe this shit about the Card Sharks is fake, or maybe it's real, but if it's real, it must be stopped. About the only asset I have left is a little wild card power that I can only use when I'm scared to death, and it's not any help because I *don't know how to use it*!"

His guarded look was replaced by one of wry amusement. "Embezzlement, huh? I've only been stuck with insurance fraud, myself. So far."

"But I didn't embezzle anything."

"You don't look the type."

"I'm *not* the type."

"You look like a total yuppie. I'm not *comfortable* around yuppies."

"I'm sorry."

"You're sorry. You've got money problems, is all I've heard so far. Money problems! Let me tell you about money problems. I've got the IRS on my ass, the City of New York wants *me* to fix the Brooklyn Bridge, the feds want the Statue of Liberty put back, on my tab, and that's only the money part! That doesn't even begin to get close to what I did to those jokers on the Rox!"

"My mother's got cancer, and I think the feds are going to lock her up in a Biological Research center! It's not just *money*, Mr. Tudbury."

He'd hunched his shoulders up as if he were trying to pull his head down beneath his collar.

"The tabloids said you didn't do anything but stir up some water. They say the kids went to never-never land. Some sort of alternate reality business. Jumpers, jokers, and all," Zoe said.

"You want me to believe the tabloids?"

"It would beat believing that you're a mass murderer."

"Yeah. It would. Some of the bodies were real, though. Kids in uniform, serving their country, or trying to. Jokers floating in with the tides, and the ambulance crews afraid to pick up the bodies, couldn't be convinced the wild card wasn't like AIDS. Sometimes I . . ."

He looked dazed, as if the world had slapped him, hard. Zoe pushed her chair back, leaned across the breakfast dishes, and reached for him. She held his face in her hands and kissed him, gently, half-convinced that she'd gone mad, and totally aware that a buttered muffin was squashed against the pocket of her Versace blouse.

"Hello?"

The shower had stopped running. The woman who had been in it stood in the bedroom doorway. She was drying her red, red hair with a towel, and she wore another draped like a sarong.

"Oh, sorry to interrupt. Tuds, you have more old friends than a politician."

Zoe disengaged from what was turning out to be a lingering and very satisfactory kiss, brushed crumbs away from her blazer, stood up straight, and offered her hand to the naked woman.

"Zoe Harris," she said. "You must be . . ."

"Danny Shepherd."

From his chair, Turtle yelped out in a voice that had suddenly gone about an octave higher, "She's not an old friend. I just met her!"

If Central Casting had a prototype for a perfect starlet's body, Danny Shepherd fit it. Periwinkle eyes, long legs, high firm breasts, a dancer's muscles, triple-cream skin, Danny had it all. And she had one of the most honest and infectious cheerleader's grins Zoe had ever seen.

"New friend, then."

"She's got a repressed ace. She wants some help, Danny."

"So help her. Jeez, Turtle, do what you can, okay? The way things are going, we're going to need all the ace powers there are. Right?"

"Thanks," Zoe said. "Thank you, Danny."

"He's shy, you know." Danny turned and bent to kiss Turtle's cheek. "Tuds, I forgot my razor. Can I borrow yours?"

"Sure."

Danny wandered back toward the bath. Turtle loved her. That showed in his eyes. She hurt him, sometimes. That showed, too. He braced his forearms on the table and motioned Zoe back toward her chair.

"She's beautiful," Zoe said.

"Yes. Yes, she is. Now about this power of yours."

"I ... animate things. I guess that's what you'd call it."

"What you do. Is it like teke?"

"It's not teke. I can't float a coffeecup in the air. But I could grow legs on it, and it would jump, or I could give it a big floppy ear where its handle is, and it could fly."

"Show me."

"Oh, no!"

"Why not?"

"I'm shy. Maybe that's part of it." So why had she kissed him? Well, because he'd needed it. So there.

"I'm shy myself. Show me."

"I can't do it while you're watching me."

"Fine. I'll go in the other room." He got up and left her there.

Can't work, won't work, nothing was ever this simple. Just do it? Zoe stared at the coffeecup, picked it up, breathed against it, tried to imagine the amorphous latticework of the fired clay flowing into new shapes, the metallic ions becoming gears and levers. Nothing. She heard Turtle say something, and Danny giggling. Zoe held the cup and tried again. Can't do it. Can't.

"Well?" Turtle reappeared at the doorway.

"I have to be scared. I have to be convinced I'm in danger. Sorry, Turtle. You're just not scary enough."

"That's what they all say," he said, very low. He looked disappointed, and wary, as if he still didn't believe she wasn't here on some sort of scam or the other.

"I hurt a mugger once. I think. He had a knife, or I thought he did. I grabbed my special twenty, you know, the one I carry in my bra, and made it turn into a little airplane. Like a paper airplane, but metal, with razor edges, and it went for his eyes. He ran."

"Weren't people watching you then?"

"On the street? No one looks. I'm trying to remember when I've used the power. Sometimes when I can't find my keys, I just open the locks anyway, if no one's watching. I try to forget when I do things like that."

"I'm not sure you can save the world if that's all you can do," Turtle said.

Danny came in and sat down on the couch. She had put on jeans and a bomber jacket, both in a deep butternut color. On her, the simple clothes were a designer's wet dream.

"If I didn't have to wait until I was scared, if I could plan things out in advance, I could think about how to use them better. I could set a watch to watch someone, or put a listener in someone's pocket."

"Electronic bugs have been around for a long time," Turtle said.

"I could make weapons out of things, vases, silverware, coffeepots. Design them to resume their original shapes once they'd been used."

"That has possibilities," Danny said.

"Yeah," the Turtle said.

"Small things," Zoe said. "I have to be able to pick them up. I can't do it with anything that's alive. The energies aren't right, they move around so much, anyway."

"Nothing alive. Nothing big. How big, Zoe?"

"The biggest thing so far was a . . ." She had just met these people. She couldn't tell them all her secrets. But if she didn't, she was running from possible help. And she *liked* them, both of them. ". . . a bedspread. It almost strangled a guy I was in bed with." There wasn't any way this was going to sound right. "No, no, he wasn't trying to rape me or anything. He just *scared* me."

"Your first time?" Danny asked.

"Yes. I just didn't realize . . ."

"How big they could get," Danny said. She began to laugh. Turtle didn't.

"Oh, the poor bastard," Danny said. "Did he recover? Enough to—"

"No. Not that night, anyway."

"But later?"

"Oh, yes." Zoe smiled, remembering his embarrassment, her confusion, the mutual reassurances which had blotted out, she hoped, his memories of the bedspread levitating above them, then twisting in the air to form a noose that snaked its way around the poor guy's neck. The relationship hadn't lasted long, though. A few weeks.

"But when you do the keyhole bit, you aren't scared then."

"No."

"How do you feel afterwards?" Danny asked.

"Uh . . . fatigued."

"For how long?"

"It depends. It depends on how much energy goes into the animation, I guess."

"Sleepy?" Danny asked.

"Yes." Zoe had never thought about it, but yes, sleepy.

"Uh, huh. Zoe, what's your schedule today?" Danny asked.

Time to go. They think I'm a total nut case, and Danny wants me out of here. "I'm due at the attorney's office." These were sweet people, but they couldn't help. Zoe had to meet with Mendlen again, and she dreaded the encounter, the questions, the mutual evaluations. "Soon. I really should be going."

"Let's do lunch," Danny said. "Tuds, you have an interview. Sell that book, honey."

"Where this time?" Turtle asked.

"It's a radio thing. Here's the address. I'll be back around midafternoon. Come *on*, Zoe."

"The attorney—"

"Can wait."

The waiter led them through a maze of tables and past stainless steel dim sum carts to a red leather booth where Danny sat, except Danny was beside Zoe and the Danny scarfing up phoenix-eye dumplings was a little more angular. Her absolutely perfect auburn hair was cut in a side-parted, chin-length wedge, the sort of cut that Zoe's waves would never let her wear.

"I can't blame you for feeling a little jittery," Danny said. "Lawyers can wreck your day. But you've got a couple of hours before you have to meet this shyster of yours. You'll feel stronger after a good lunch. Trust me."

And then, "Hi, Danny," Turtle's Danny said, and Zoe found herself seated between them, while the cart arrived and Turtle's Danny picked out an assortment of neat small fattening things.

Identical twins? Of course. But the thinner Danny stabbed a smoking hot pot-sticker and said, "Zoe, you made a hell of a first impression. The expression on Turtle's face when I came in from the shower!"

"Don't worry, Zoe," Turtle's Danny said. Their voices were identical. The effect was like listening to a stereo set for too much separation. "It's good for him to find that attractive women think he's kissable. He'll get used to it, someday."

"But *you*?" Zoe pointed to the thinner Danny.

"Oh, yes. I was there. I don't listen in all the time, but we're me."

"We are Legion," Turtle's Danny said.

"Uh, like clones?" Zoe asked.

"Better," they both said.

"I'm the Danny who lives with Rick," thinner Danny said.

"Rick?"

"Beautiful, black, Rick," Turtle's Danny said.

"How many of you are there?" Zoe asked.

"Only three," starlet Danny said. "Nobody wants to hide out and eat enough to bud another one right now."

"Turtle got a little freaked when we did that last time," Rick's Danny said. "Zoe, you didn't tell me everything about this talent of yours. A little more detail, please. Just eat your pot-sticker, there, and tell me how you get a lock to unlock. Like Turtle said, you won't get far if you have to be scared to death to do your thing. And you want to fix this in a hurry, it sounds like."

All right, fine. She was sitting in a Manhattan dim sum place with two women who were the same person, and the situation felt a little trippy, like the pot she'd tried only once, and then she'd gotten loose and floaty and not at all scared, so she'd had the napkins on the coffee table fold themselves into origami cranes and fly around the room. Fortunately, the three people around her had said nothing more than "Oh, wow," and passed off the experience as a contact hallucination. She'd never tried it again, and she didn't *ever* drink.

She felt drunk now. The world had gone tilt in a Chinese restaurant where reality duplicated itself and two selves could exist in one booth, but this was New York, after all, and no one seemed to notice. "It's not a verbal process," Zoe said. "But I'll try." She felt like a drab shadow between these two. Their porcelain skins made her olive coloring look darker, and to her eyes, muddy. "I think—I can't be sure, but it sort of feels like nano-engineering would feel, if anybody could really do that. I have to be close to things. Like this chopstick, say. It's not ivory, of course, it's plastic, so there's a way that the hydrogen links can bond and unbond fairly easily. It could have legs there, see, and little arms, and this chrysanthemum painted on the blunt end could be a mouth."

"Well?" starlet Danny asked. "Go ahead."

"Well, not *here*. But I would pick it up and hold it."

"That's all you need to do?"

"No. I would . . . breathe on it. What my breathing does is sort of *instruct* the molecular bonds. I think. When I was little, I sort of thought it was like giving CPR, or something. I guess."

But they were laughing, both of them.

"You *blow* on things to bring them to life?" starlet Danny asked.

"What's funny?" Zoe asked.

Starlet Danny grinned her cheerleader's grin again. "Zoe? I have to ask you something. How's your sex life?"

"What?"

"No, seriously."

"It's ... okay, I guess. No. It's not okay at all. I'm always afraid I'm going to get too involved and that whoever I'm with is going to find out about me. That I'll slip up and animate something. So I'm a little guarded."

"You fake it," Wall Street said.

"Well, yes." Faked sexual satisfaction, and then dealt with the frustration later, courtesy of a vibrator and a size C battery. And if she hadn't felt safe with these two, hadn't trusted them, she could never have admitted any of this.

"Zoe. Zoe, I think you've just told us what could replace getting scared to death, if you can handle it. No harm intended, now. This may be hard to accept," starlet Danny said.

"Think about it for a minute," Rick's Danny said. "What other activity, other than animating things or going to the john, would you rather have a little privacy for? What else makes you tired, a little sleepy, after? But relaxed, maybe? A little less tense?"

"Oh." The chopstick in Zoe's hand was warm, plastic, potentially malleable. She squeezed it harder. "Oh, that's ridiculous."

"Is it?"

"Oh, for gravy's sake."

"She's thinking about it," starlet Danny said.

"*That's* the equation? Animating things, for me, is a sexual activity?" Analytically, and she began to analyze, right then and there, it was possible. Profound changes in physiology, in neurochemistry, were part of sexual arousal and certainly occurred in orgasm. The whole chain of interactions, sex, violence, arousal, were so closely related in the architecture of the brain.

The chopstick broke with a snap. It wasn't animated in any way, it was just a plastic chopstick. She dropped the pieces on the table. But she knew, she knew to the level of her very cells, that what she'd keyed through terror, yes, could be keyed through desire. "I'll be damned." The Dannys were smiling at her. Their smiles were accepting, tolerant, and warm. "I think you're right."

"Will knowing it help?" Rick's Danny asked.

"I don't know," Zoe said. "I don't think so."

"Blowjob, honey, come back up to the hotel tomorrow night. Turtle and I are free then. We'll work on this, okay?" starlet Danny asked.

"Okay," Zoe said. "Blowjob?" Blowjob. Some of the more flamboyant aces wore costumes. She tried to imagine one for a woman called Blowjob.

"Why is this woman laughing?" Rick's Danny asked.

"I'll tell you later," Zoe said. "Maybe." She bit into a sweet dumpling covered with sesame seeds, and listened to the sisters talk. Thinking, at least talking with Turtle and Danny would delay, for a while, the prospect of another restless night and its fantasies of courts, jail, disgrace. And that she wouldn't have to think so much about Anne, about losing her, about how sick she was going to be in Jerusalem, with surgery and chemotherapy. Anne would need her there. As soon as the court thing got finished, she'd follow momma and Bjorn. Off to a country that she still thought of as a place with sand and camels, full of people who wore flowing robes, where all the men had big, thick beards, and all the women were beautiful, with eyes like roe deer, and their bellies were like heaps of wheat.

The kitchen at home was empty, the coffee cups washed and put away. Anne had gone back to work. Dr. Finn was displeased, she'd said, that Anne was delaying her surgery. Anne still seemed to think that things weren't all that bad, and she liked Finn a lot.

But she'd promised that she'd leave when the airline called. The flights were booked heavily for the next six months, El Al kept saying. The Israelis took political refugees, yes, but officially speaking, jokers weren't political refugees.

Zoe managed to talk to the first three latents on her list. She arranged lunches with them. Some of them didn't really want to talk to her. They hadn't known her that well; the rumor mill had told them she was in disgrace, even if she was still the official President of Subtle Scents. But Maria, this morning, had listened. "I'll do it. I'll leave. But Zoe, I'll pay you back," she kept saying. On her bottle-washer's salary, living in Jerusalem's inflated economy, Zoe didn't count on the money coming back real soon. But the thought was nice.

Danny wasn't in the hotel room. A soap producer, Turtle said, a meeting. He seemed uneasy without Danny, so Zoe suggested they get dinner. French, he wanted, which surprised her, and he drank white Bordeaux with it. She might have thought beer. But she got him talking about the *Shell Games* movie, and Richard Dreyfuss was going to play Turtle. Turtle liked that a lot. By the time the profiteroles arrived, he was almost, but not quite, expansive.

"I'm glad we came," Turtle said. "I was afraid someone would recognize me, but they haven't, so far. I hate it when that happens. Either it's someone who is delighted that I 'cleaned out the Rox,' or it's someone who thinks I'm a mass murderer and they want to kill me. Those guys, I can understand. They're the sane ones. The ones who make my skin crawl are the idiots who think it's neat that I killed a bunch of miserable jokers. They probably have my picture on the wall right between Hitler and Pol Pot."

"You've had death threats?" Zoe asked.

"Death threats, love letters from women I don't know, and three hundred lawsuits by people who claim they were 'telekinetically assaulted' by the Turtle. Most of those claims are bizarre as hell. A lot of crossover with UFO abductees, and all the kinky sex fantasies that go with it. Tom Tudbury and his big smooth round sex object shell." He polished off the last profiterole. "Are you still sure you want to be a hero?"

"I never said I *wanted* to be a hero. I said I was afraid not to."

"Danny told me her theories. What you talked about at lunch."

Tom seemed wistfully shy. Charming, Zoe thought. "Danny's sex theory on animation? She may be right, Tom."

"Well, she would never have a problem like that. You met Rick's Danny?"

"Yes. I like her, too."

"It bothers me. Rick's a nice guy. But when Danny makes out with him, Danny, my Danny, gets to make out with him, too. I mean, not there, but in Venice in the apartment, sometimes, she'll get this look, and I *know* what they're doing."

The check had come, had been examined; Tom's card had paid for it. He opened the heavy brass-fitted door that led them back out into Manhattan's night-time streets. They navigated back toward the hotel, dodging a mink-clad woman wearing tennis shoes, a crowd of shavehead wannabes in baggy pants and hightops, and a large poodle walking a small man.

"You're jealous, Tom."

"I guess. But it's more weird than jealousy. Sometimes I think about what Rick's Danny is feeling when my Danny and I are making out. I think about the fact that I'm in bed with two women at once, and one of them isn't there. It feels pretty strange."

The elevator took them back toward the hotel suite. Starlet Danny wasn't there.

"About this power of yours. You've been practicing?"

"No." There was a bar in the room, and one of those little refrigerators stocked with booze and chips and candy, with a card to check off what you'd taken out.

"Tom? What do I do if I learn to use it? Is there an organization I could work with?"

"There's the government, I guess. SCARE and the Justice department."

"No."

"Good. I'm glad you said that."

"But something else? There has to be something else."

"I really don't know. I'm out of the hero business, myself." He looked troubled.

"Tom? I'm in the mood for some cognac."

"Fine with me." He settled into the cushions on the couch.

Zoe poured cognac into tumblers, good stiff doses, and brought one to him. She *never* drank. She planned to play with her glass and sniff the fumes.

"Danny says she figures you don't drink," Tom said. "She make it sound really sad. You don't drink, you don't make love unless you're on guard about it. That's sad, Zoe."

"I'm not always on guard about it," she said. She sniffed at the cognac. It made her eyes water a little. She walked to the window, which had a view of a brick wall outside, and then back to the little bar. Pacing. She was tense, and didn't much care.

"What happens when you aren't? Do you animate, uh, modify, uh, do you—"

Poor man. No, I don't modify penises. "My talent doesn't work on anything living. The energies aren't right. I don't know how to explain it."

"But if you have an orgasm, things start jumping?"

"Well—yes."

"Should be interesting," Tom said.

Zoe wondered how it would be, to celebrate an orgasm with showers of confetti, with a round of applause from chiming crystal glasses on a bedside table, with chandeliers strobing themselves on and off. And someone else there to enjoy the show, not just her trusty vibrator.

The phone rang. Tom picked it up. He said yes a couple of times and hung up.

"Danny. She's going to stay with her sister."

"Oh. I wanted her to be here." She really did. Danny had this healthy, relaxed attitude about all sorts of things.

"Well. She won't be here. She'll be there. I hope Rick has a good time."

"Because you think they'll make out?"

"Because I know they will. Or Rick is a purblind fool who doesn't deserve a Danny in his life. Sit down, Zoe. You make me think I'm watching a tennis match."

She sat down.

"Now. You have to be scared to animate things. Or you have to be horny, Danny thinks. Or you have to be alone."

"That's right."

"No crazier than I am, when you come to think about it. Me, I have to have my shell to do really good teke. Little things, like this glass, I can lift without it, but that's about it."

Zoe put her glass down on the coffee table.

"Show me," she said.

"You're challenging your teacher."

"Yup."

"I'll try." Tom stared at the glass. He clenched his fists. Nothing happened. "This is harder than you might think," Tom said. He closed his eyes, opened them again. The room was very quiet. The glass lifted about an inch, the meniscus of cognac tilting as the glass swayed in the air. Then it thumped back down on the table. "Getting there," Tom said. "One more time." He tried again, and the glass sailed up, hovered in the air, and beelined for Zoe's face. It adjusted its angle as if waiting for her to sip. So she did.

"Oooh," she said. "Applause, applause. Clap, clap." She lifted the glass from the air, and sipped again. The cognac burned all the way down. It tasted of apples, late summer, and oak.

"Your turn," Tom said. He put his glass on the table. "Here. Maybe this will help." He reached up and clicked off the table lamp. The room was lighted only by a faint glow that came from the lamp in the bedroom. Tom got up and half-closed that door, too. "See? Nobody's watching."

"I'll try," Zoe said. She tried. Gossamer wings on the stem of the glass, that would be nice, and a program to flutter them to let the glass waft around the room. She really wanted this to work. She tried. "Nothing. Damn."

"My turn." Turtle lifted his glass for her. It seemed easier for him this time. "Drink up," he said.

"We're going to run out of cognac." Zoe spluttered on a too-large gulp.

"That's what room service is for," Turtle said.

It took them about a half-bottle to get from the couch into the bedroom.

"I guess," Turtle mentioned at one point, "that anything you can animate, I can move out of the way with my teke. Just keep it lightweight," he said.

"Sure." He didn't have a pelt, like Bjorn, but the curls on his chest were quite pleasant to stroke, all the same.

There wasn't any confetti to dance around the room. But, eventually, the glasses on the bedside table clapped their crystal hands against their bellies, and gave them a round of ringing applause.

"Damn," Tom said. One of the glasses leaped from the bedside table and hung in the air over their heads. "I think you did it, Zoe."

"Hell of a way to have to get things going," she said. "Tom, you may not always be there when I need you."

"You're right. It's going to be a problem, if this is what it takes to get your powers working."

"Maybe I jus' need a lil more practice," Zoe said.

"Good thought."

Good man, this Thomas Tudbury.

Sooner than anyone might have expected, the glasses again rang their chimes.

Turtle was gone, back to California with his Danny. Zoe had seen him again, but he'd seemed defensive, a little frightened, and she didn't want to get in his space and upset it. He'd said something about getting back in harness. He'd said he had to contact some people.

He left Zoe with memories, fine rich memories, and a wistful hope. Someday, someday, someone for me. If only.

The days lurched forward toward the grand jury hearing.

In her mind, she faced an inquisition, hooded figures cloaked in red who carried candles the size of walking sticks. They snuffed them out on the floor, and her breath died with the dying flames.

She became something she had never been, a drifter in Jokertown streets in the daytime, alone when the Escorts slept in the warm mornings. She heard tales of hunger and death and outrage. The tabloids kept up their barrage of joker hate stories. And in the *Times*, she read of the groundbreaking for the first of the Biological Research Centers.

Her bank balance sank daily. Some of her latents had asked for transfers to Jerusalem. Some wouldn't think of leaving. Zoe worked with Dutton and set the Escorts up as a student tour group, with Bjorn and Anne as adults-in-charge. The Escorts thought the idea sucked. She stuffed the tickets in their pockets anyway.

"You'll go when there's space for you on the damned plane. You'll check with my daddy every day to see if your flight is scheduled. You'll get the fuck out of here when he says go. These are round-trip tickets, kids. Think of it as cultural enrichment."

"Mess around with yuppies, and look what happens to us," Needles said. But in his streetwise eyes, there was something like hope.

Home base was her parents' flat, her childhood bedroom with its pink and white French Provincial canopy bed. Zoe rummaged through her closet, still crowded with mementoes of triumphs past, her prom dress, the first Calvin Klein she'd ever been able to afford, an Issey Miyake with its artful cutouts. She'd bought it the first year the company had gone public; still a lovely dress, but now hopelessly outdated. She had dressed for success, once. She had *been* a success, once.

She practiced. She thought about Turtle, and practiced. Alone in home's stuffy silence, trying to find a space in her mind where her power would work on demand. Yes, the dustcloth flew around the counters, her old Snoopy barked and chased the elusive rag, the little toy soldier raised his rifle. But now, she had him shoot bursts of laser light that left smoking holes in the playing cards she set up as targets.

Trying to convince herself that no one would notice, that no one would see her excitement when she animated something, that no one would recognize the sexual tension she felt while she worked. She had tried to animate things when the Escorts were around, trusting that they wouldn't pay much attention, or maybe even notice what had happened. She hadn't been able to do it.

And then she would pick up the phone, and try to convince another one of the latents to leave the country.

You'll be fine at the hearing tomorrow. Say this. Don't say that. Remain calm. Respond only to what is asked. Don't volunteer information. Mendlen's instructions echoed in Zoe's head. Furtive, watching the streets, she wanted to get home and she didn't want the Escorts to see her, but Needles danced up beside her. He was up early. It was barely past lunch.

"Dude sent this for you," he said. What he slipped into her hand was an El Al ticket.

"Who?" Zoe asked.

"Short little nerd. Kept wigglin' his nose, like it stinks round here or something."

Nosy? What the fuck did this mean?

"You told him where I lived?"

"Not exactly," Needles said. "We was just cruising, you know. So this stupidass nat shows up and we, like, in-terror-gated him a little."

"Uh-huh," Zoe said. First class, priority ticket, that identified her as an executive of Subtle Scents, Jerusalem. Maybe Nosy figured she would run, and look like a fool. Keep the damned thing? Would its use set off an alarm at the FBI or something?

But she didn't have the money to buy another. Mendlen's secretary had taken a big chunk today. Zoe Harris, CEO, was tapped out.

She stuffed the ticket in her purse. Bjorn waited on the stoop. Needles nodded at him and ducked away.

"Why are you home so early?" Zoe asked. He was out

of uniform, freshly shaved; he wore a polo shirt under his sport coat.

"I thought you could use a little company," Bjorn said. "A little distraction."

"Possibly I could." Zoe tried to smile at him.

"Your mom's on her way to Jerusalem. She fussed, but there was an open seat and she took it."

Brave momma. "Good," Zoe said.

"Let's see if I can say this like she would." Bjorn cleared his throat.

"Say what?"

"Dahling. Let's go shopping!"

"Perfect!"

"God knows I've heard it often enough."

"And groaned every time."

Bjorn had a great groan. He groaned it now, a subdued roar that seemed to vibrate the wrought iron on the stoop.

"Daddy. We can't spend any money. Are you nuts?"

"You'll feel better tomorrow in a good little suit," Bjorn said.

"I *won't* feel better in a good little suit."

"An expensive little suit?"

"Daddy, you're impossible."

"You're my daughter. You deserve to look wonderful."

Autumn in New York was the best of the city's seasons. The leaves were turning. A light breeze lifted most of the smog. Fifth Avenue's windows showed the fall collections, the furs, the silhouettes. Fuller skirts, smaller shoulders. Shorter fitted jackets with definite curves in their lines. The keynote color was green, which Zoe in no way could wear, but the season's stones were topaz and amber, big faux chunks of them. Topaz brought out cat colors in Zoe's hazel eyes. Very good.

Mary, Queen of Scots, wore a red silk petticoat to her beheading. Zoe would stick with a business suit, black, perhaps, with a closely fitted jacket. A Hermés scarf at the neckline, white and some bronze tones? Perhaps.

Bjorn limped along beside her on his ever-sore feet. Zoe pretended not to notice.

But she noticed, as always, the movement in the street around her, the moiling mix of shoppers and the aimless. A black mannequin in the Saks window wore a Donna Karan dinner dress, bias cut and loaded with long looped chains of gold and topaz, reminiscent of the thirties. It was a gorgeous ensemble.

Reflected in the Saks window, something changed in the street's motion. In a flicker of vision, Zoe saw a movement like the turning of a school of fish. Shaveheads in padded, pale denim, interchangeable faces with dead stupid eyes and one of them moved too fast. His hands snatched at the collar of Bjorn's shirt, jerking it open. Another shavehead circled behind Bjorn and pulled his sport coat down, trapping Bjorn's arms. The afternoon sun brought out gold highlights in Bjorn's thick auburn fur.

"Joker!" someone yelled.

The pack was on him. One of them shoved Zoe aside. She stumbled and caught her balance against the smooth glass of the Saks window. Bjorn went down, hidden under pounding fists and flailing arms. Zoe grabbed the shoulders of the thug in front of her, but her fists striking his back had no effect at all.

Yelling help, please, somebody help, but her voice didn't carry over the chorus of obscenities.

"Joker!"

"Mutant!"

"Fucking monster! Abomination!"

She ripped her fingernails across the throat of the thug in front of her. He jerked his elbow back, a hard punch that caught her in the stomach. The back of her head struck the glass. It boomed with the impact, but didn't break. Over the heads of the shaveheads, she saw the cyclops eye of a camcorder, a Japanese tourist filming the show.

She heard her voice yelling out "Stop it, stop it, you're killing him!" but it was as if someone had turned the volume down too low. Bjorn roared and growled. He kicked out and one of his shoes went flying. His naked foot, blunted claws and fur, connected with a thug's leg and the man yipped in pain. The shaveheads circled their prey like a dog pack, except for one, who humped away on top of Bjorn in a horrid parody of screwing. Zoe saw the flash of a knife in the thug's fist.

She drove her shoulder against the plate glass, again, again. Break, damn it, I need shard, sharp, weapon, silicon brittle edge, damn it, *break*! Bjorn kicked out hard and a shavehead slammed into the window next to Zoe, ass-first *through* the window, his arms and legs spread like a starfish. Above the crashing noise of the breaking window, Zoe heard a siren wail. She spun around and hoisted herself up onto the display shelf. The flesh of her palms parted on broken glass. She tackled the black mannequin and went down flat across its torso, her mouth pressed to the molded, elegant lips. One breath. Another. The total program, that's all you get. It's now or never, baby.

Zoe rolled away as the mannequin spun into motion. The animation leaped through the window, the gold and topaz necklace suddenly a garrote in inhuman, strong hands, looping around the shavehead's neck and twisting, twisting. The mannequin yanked back, hard, and the thug's head made a funny little jerk, as if he'd just heard someone say something really interesting.

Limp, the dead man and the mannequin sprawled over Bjorn's motionless body.

The Japanese tourist leaned forward and adjusted the focus on his camcorder.

In the ambulance, while terse EMT's said little and worked hard, pounding on Bjorn's chest, Zoe realized what the tourist had been doing. He wanted a closeup of Bjorn's face, of glassy eyes staring into nothing.

And if he took his little recording to the police? From embezzlement to murder in two short weeks. Turtle would be impressed.

Something in the attitudes of the paramedics told her Bjorn was dead. She watched while the gurney bumped across the concrete with its limp burden, and the doors of the ER hissed open.

"Daddy, what do I do now?" she whispered.

The door closed. She did not enter.

Stay and face charges. Act like a responsible citizen. Bjorn would want her to do that. Or would he?

Running away can be the only good choice, sometimes.

She had used her ace and killed a man. Yes, but the man who had killed her father would never kill again. It didn't feel right. It felt wrong. Being a killer felt wrong.

Stay. Let the process of law decide her guilt or innocence.

But what is innocence in a time of genocide? They *killed* my father in front of my eyes!

Never again.

The embezzlement mess could wait. The "stolen" funds were frozen, and Subtle Scents hadn't lost a dime. Let the lawyers sort it out.

Anne was in Jerusalem by now, the home of the Twisted Fists. They killed *five* for one, and managed to live with it. Perhaps they had some things to teach a fledgling, angry ace.

If the cabbie noticed her hands were bleeding, he didn't say anything. He took her to Kennedy.

Night flight to Jerusalem. Hassidim and their sober, beautiful children, a collection of Hadassah women chattering like magpies. Zoe followed the line through the corridor into the plane, heading for the Promised Land. She looked for her seat number, thinking, they haven't stopped me yet. The FBI isn't here. The cops haven't delayed the departure. So far, so good.

The lighting was dim. She sat across the aisle from a fairly handsome man, somewhat thin, with black hair, dark eyes, and a nose that would have been lovely if it hadn't had a marked bend toward the left.

"Hello," the man said. He yawned, reached into his jacket pocket, and pulled out what looked to be at least two pounds of chocolate-covered espresso beans. "Want one? They're Kona."

"Thank you, no," Zoe said.

The man began to munch on a handful. "Barely had

time to get these before we boarded. I woke up in a cab and found I was an escort for a tour group to Jerusalem. Odd. What about you, young lady? Care for a bean?" He offered the bag to the person in the seat next to Zoe, a small person who seemed absorbed in a book. *Useful Phrases in Hebrew.* The child read by the light cast by her own eyes.

"No thank you, Mr. Croyd."

Zoe looked across the aisle and saw black and white jackets in the gloom.

"Hi, Jan," Zoe said.

"Shalom." Jan wriggled in her seat and pressed against Zoe's side like a friendly puppy.

The Color Of His Skin

Part 7

There should have been a voice—Puppetman, or that
nagging Jiminy Cricket who had manifested after Puppetman had died. There should have been someone else
in here.

There was only himself.

And he despised the company.

He had run himself unconscious. He remembered
streaking into the city after the murder of Rudo, managing to get headed roughly north and east to where Jokertown offered some hope of refuge. Somewhere near
midtown, he'd blacked out, though he'd had the impression that the body continued running. At least it seemed
that his new form seemed to have the knack of finding
a safe haven while on automatic pilot. Gregg had no idea
where he was other than that it was dark and very . . .
fragrant. He also had no idea *when* it was, but he had
the feeling several days, at least, had passed. It seemed
there was a price to his hyperactivity, paid in lost time.

"Hey!" he said into the darkness. There was no
answer, inside or out, just a metallic echo of that piping,
high voice. He shivered. He sniffed, and took in a cornu-
copia of odors: the sewers. He was ravenous, too.

He tried walking, splashing through the black effluvium. He found that he could tell when he was about to hit something—a head sense that seemed to emanate from the silly clown-nose ears. "You'd have made a great cave fish, Greggie," he told himself.

No answer.

He was one. Only one.

A few hundred yards and two turns later, he saw sunlight streaming through the holes of a sewer lid. The finger-size shafts of light seemed like the glow from a dozen searchlights after the darkness. There were rungs set in the walls; he dissolved and ate the lowest one, just to take the edge off the hunger, then clambered up, discovering in the process that the body's multitude of legs seemed to have small, clinging suckers on the bottom pads.

Okay. Climbing wasn't a problem.

Gregg pushed at the sewer lid with his hands. It didn't budge. Gregg sighed, thought of his hunger, and ralphed up an enormous glob that splattered on the underside of the metal. He let himself fall; a few moments later, the lid sagged like heated plastic and clattered down beside him. He took a few quick nibbles of the feast and headed up.

He was in an alley, and it was either just after dawn or very near evening. From the odd collection of shapes and forms he saw walking along the street, he was also in J-Town.

What do I do now? Where do I go?

Silence. Unnerving, insistent silence.

Gregg padded out to the street, but discovered quickly that he wasn't going to find the anonymity he expected. He'd thought that he'd just be one of many there, another mishappen body in the midden of Jokertown; he'd thought that even those who might recognize his form as Battle's would ignore him. But . . .

Even with his myopic vision, Gregg could tell that he was attracting undue attention, even from those who looked stranger than he did. A four-armed woman just down the street jabbed a companion in his chitinous ribs and pointed in Gregg's direction. They were upwind; Gregg could smell an odd, sour scent to both of them that suddenly intensified. The couple quickly ducked into the nearest storefront. Puzzled, Gregg went to the window of the store, lifting the front end of his body up so that he could look in. He squinted. In soft focus through the smeared glass, he could see the four-armed woman at the public phone. Her companion was looking out; when he saw Gregg, he tapped the woman on the shoulder.

Gregg dropped down and hurried on, trying to convince himself that he was being paranoid. A block further down, an NYPD squad car passed him going the other way, obviously from Fort Freak since the patrolman driving had the face and hanging jowls of a bulldog. Gregg heard the car pull over behind him, smelled the exhaust and the sudden odor of stale cigarettes as the doors opened. He didn't look back, trying to convince himself that the cop wasn't stopping for him, but the jokers in front were suddenly moving aside, wide-eyed, and Gregg felt a prickling chill along his spine.

There was a scent of metal, of burnt gunpowder, of oil, of shoe leather, of tobacco.

"Battle!" a gruff voice like a talking St. Bernard growled. "You're under arrest. Stop right there."

Gregg thought about running, but he didn't know how to shift his body into hyperdrive without getting hit first. That didn't leave many good options, and Gregg suspected that if he was taken into Fort Freak he might end up being one of those suspects found accidentally dangling from the end of their belts in their cell.

At least he was still hungry. He turned around.

Bulldog-jowls had his gun out, standing just behind Gregg.

Gregg puked.

He had decent velocity and aim—in fact, he told himself, he was getting pretty damn good at this. The viscous globule splattered messily and noisily over Bulldog's gun hand. The officer recoiled involuntarily, staring in disbelief and disgust. The moment was enough. The short barrel of the official issue 9 mm. automatic drooped, the chamber sagged, and the vinyl grips were pressing against each other as the metal frame turned to taffy. The cop dropped the weapon as if it were molten, shaking his hand as what looked like cream of steel soup dripped from his unhurt fingers. Everyone watching was suddenly giving Gregg a wide, cautious berth.

Gregg didn't need a second invitation. He ran, nightmare-slow at first, but accelerating all the time. If Bulldog-jowls had had the inclination, he could have tackled Gregg before he moved five feet.

About three blocks down the street, the world finally shifted into slo-mo about him.

It was days before he dared to come out from the sewers again. He let himself run until exhaustion slowed him more, even though this time he didn't black out. He returned to the alley and the open sewer hole, and let himself climb down in a half-stupor. Gregg didn't fight the weariness.

You're defeated. Done. As far as the authorities are concerned, you are George G. Battle, the murderer of Pan Rudo, and you can add assaulting a police officer and flight to avoid prosecution to the charges.

So he slept, so that he wouldn't have to think.

Part of him hoped that he'd never wake again.

The weather finally drove him out. His new body didn't seem to mind the cold as much as his old one, but the temperature suddenly dipped drastically. He woke up shivering, with icicles hanging from the gratings above him and everything around him frozen solid.

"This is no way to live, Gregg," he said aloud, mostly to hear a voice, any voice. "You need a place to stay. You need money. You need to find Hannah and let her know what's going on."

It was snowing. The night air was luminous, and the sounds of the city were hushed and muffled. Gregg could smell the moisture and the cold like mint. He hesitated in the alley before going out onto the street.

Where to? Can't get to any of my funds—by now, my

estate's been settled. If I'm seen, someone's liable to call the cops. The Oddity's apartment isn't far away, but if John's in charge he's liable to kill me before I get a chance to explain, especially after the last time. Finn might know where they are, but the clinic's not going to be safe. Who . . . ?

He knew.

His secretary, Jo Ann, lived on the edge of Jokertown near his old office. The brownstones crowded shoulder-to-shoulder might have looked impressive a century ago, when trees had lined the street and gaslights had shed their warm glow on the dark fronts. Now they simply looked shabby and tired. Gregg eased his body up the worn steps to the front door. He had to climb the wall to get to the doorbell. As soon as he heard it ringing, he dropped back to the stoop.

The inner door opened. A man looked out through the screen door, then down. The skin showing around the sweatshirt proclaiming THE ROX LIVES! was beaded like a Gila monster with swirling patterns of glossy orange, black, and red—actually rather striking, Gregg thought. The eyes, startlingly human, squinted as the man peered down at Gregg through the mesh. Gregg could smell supper in the warmth that cascaded from the house into the chill air: baked potatoes, carrots, chicken: none of it smelled as appetizing as the cheap aluminum screen door frame.

"What do you want?" The breath was freighted with beer.

"I need to talk with Jo Ann. You're Sam, right? Her husband?"

"Yeah." Sam was making no move to invite him inside. "Wait here . . ." He turned and bellowed into the interior as he let the screen door close behind him. "Hey, Jo! Someone asking for you . . ." Sam's voice trailed off as he went further back into the house. He heard Jo Ann answer, and the two of them talking for a moment. Then Jo Ann came to the door. She stared down at him through the screen.

"I know who you are," she said without preamble. She

looked like she was ready to flee. Her hand stayed on the comforting thickness of the inside door.

"I know you think you do, but you're wrong," Gregg said quickly. "Please, I need to talk with you, Jo Ann."

"I don't think so."

"You hid a tape recorder in the office after Hannah came, that first time. You always kept the extra key to the office in the front of the file drawer, in the folder marked 'Receipts.' You and Sam met on Black Queen Night; Father Squid introduced the two of you. You two got married the day after the Rox disappeared—you said that something good had to happen that day or you couldn't stand it."

"How do you know all that?" Jo Ann asked. Her voice was shaky and she kept looking over her shoulder to where Sam's bulk loomed under the ceiling light in the hallway. "What do you want, Battle?"

"I need to see Hannah and Father Squid. It's very important. And I know all about you because I'm *not* Battle. I'm Gregg Hartmann." He saw her fairy-tale witch's face twist then, and the rest of the words tumbled out in a rush, falling over themselves. "They had a jumper, Jo Ann. They jumped Battle or somebody into my body before the press conference. It wasn't me who said the Sharks didn't exist, and it wasn't me who was killed—"

"Fuck you," Jo Ann interrupted. "You tortured Gregg before you killed him, Battle. He could have told you *anything*. For that matter, you could be reading my mind—the wild card's given that gift to a dozen people I can think of. I'm not talking to you and I'm not telling you anything."

The door slammed shut on his explanation. Gregg stood there on his six legs, his mouth open under the clown nose. A few seconds later, Sam opened the door again. He had a baseball bat in his meaty hands. "Get the fuck out of here," he said. "I won't have you or anyone upsetting her. I won't turn any damn joker over to the law, no matter how much I despise them, and you probably did a good thing killing Rudo, but if I see you

around here again, I *will* beat the shit out of your ugly
goddamn body. You understand me?"

"I'm not *Battle*, damn it—" Gregg began.

Sam kicked open the screen door. The corner of it
struck Gregg full in his cartoon-drawing face and sent
instantaneous adrenaline surging through his body. He
used the pain and the rush to catapult himself into a
double-speed retreat.

"Jube! Goddamn it, Jube . . . !"

Gregg's voice sounded like a two-year old with an ade-
noid problem; the cursing sounded almost laughable. He
had spent several nights lingering in the shadows of Jokertown, staying away from strangers and hoping to find
someone he knew, someone he felt halfway safe
approaching. There weren't too many on that list, but
seeing the walrus-shape of Jube lumbering by on an
otherwise-empty street was a relief. Jube knew everybody
and everything. Jube could help him.

The joker had turned at the sound of Gregg's voice,
his eyes trapped in the blue-black, rubbery skin peering
at the darkness where Gregg huddled between two
closed and boarded storefronts.

"If you're who I think you are," Jube said slowly, "I
don't understand why you're still hanging around
Jokertown."

"I'm not Battle."

Jube took a careful step away from him and stopped.
He moved his papers from one arm to the other and
pushed his porkpie hat back on his head. In the light of
the streetlamp, bright orange passionflowers wrestled on
the aching blue backdrop of his short-sleeved shirt. "I
doubt there are *two* yellow caterpillars around here,"
Jube said. He was backing away again, his voice sounding
falsely jovial. "Though I remember a joke along those
lines: What'd the doctor say to the joker woman after
she gave birth to triplets?"

"Jube, I'm not going to hurt you. I'm not Battle."

Jube looked like he was about to bolt, but he waited.
"I'm actually Gregg Hartmann," Gregg continued. "I was

jumped into this body. I need to get into contact with Hannah Davis and Father Squid. It's very important."

Jube blinked. He took another step away. "Please," Gregg said.

"I heard that was what you were telling people, a couple months ago, back before you killed Rudo," Jube said. "That's a pretty unbelievable tale, considering no one's been jumped in years, not since the Rox went down. Not that it matters. I was never much impressed by Gregg Hartmann. I wasn't surprised that he sold us out at the end."

"Damn it, he—I *didn't*!" The word came out as a screech and Jube jumped backward, a few papers scattering to the ground. "It wasn't *me*. I'd already been jumped."

Disbelief pulled at the thick skin of Jube's face. He was backing away again, and Gregg scuttled out from his hiding place before the joker decided to turn and run. "Jube, you have to believe me. What I have to tell them is urgent. I need—"

They both saw the squad car turn the corner and head down the street toward them at the same moment. Jube looked once at Gregg, then at the cruiser. His hand started to lift. "Jube, no," Gregg said, but the joker stepped out from the sidewalk, waving the cops down.

Gregg didn't wait to see any more. He fled.

"Ellen?"

"Who are you? This is an unlisted number—who gave it to you?"

"Ellen, please, just listen for a minute. When the Hartmann estate was settled, you were the prime beneficiary. There was also a safety-deposit box at First Manhattan Trust—about $20,000 worth of bonds in there. The will specifically mentioned an old grandfather clock that Gregg had kept as part of the divorce settlement, which was to go back to you. You and Gregg bought the clock in Germany during the WHO tour, just before Berlin— Sarah Morgenstern was along, too, remember? She was

the one who saw the clock first, sitting in the dusty rear
corner of that old antique shop."

"How do you know all this? Who *are* you?"

"Ellen, I'm telling you all this so you'll believe me. I
know what was in the will because I *wrote* it. I'm Gregg,
Ellen. Gregg. I need your help. I know I don't have any
right to ask you, but ... Ellen? Ellen? Hello ... ?"

Furs was a long-time companion. The lion-maned
joker had been on various of Gregg's staffs for years, had
been campaign manager for New York when Gregg had
run for president. Even though he'd drifted from politics
to general media consultation in the years since, he still
had worked with Gregg on various joker's rights commit-
tees and organizations, which was why Gregg had gone
to him for help with the Peregrine show.

Furs knew him. Furs had connections.

For Jokertown, Furs lived upscale. The apartment
building had a doorman, a burly joker with long, rubbery
arms and a decidedly suspicious demeanor. Gregg
decided not to risk the front door, not after his previous
experiences. He waited until night, scaling the side wall
of the building like a large yellow limpet, peering through
windows until he found Fur's fourth-story apartment. He
could see a television tossing light at the walls, but no
one was watching and the sound was off. The window to
the living room was unlocked; it opened when Gregg
pulled it up. He scrambled over the sill and into the dark
room with a thump, the curtains swirling. He looked
around the room—Furs was here; a beer, the head still
foaming, stood on the coffee table in front of the couch,
and Gregg could smell his presence somewhere close by.
Gregg moved into the room.

"Stop right there."

The voice came from the bedroom. Gregg turned to
see Furs standing in the open doorway, sighting down
the short barrel of a handgun gripped in both hands.

"Furs," Gregg said softly. "I'm not going to hurt you.
I need to talk." As Gregg took a step toward Furs, the
fingers tightened around the weapon.

"I know who you are. I also know what you can do to this." Furs waggled the gun. "Take another step, and I won't wait for you to get close enough. Now, back up into the corner over there. That's it—nice and slow."

As Gregg retreated, Furs moved into the room, going over the phone. His gaze still fixed on Gregg; he reached down for the receiver. "Furs, please listen."

"You're a Shark, Battle—"

"I'm *not*—" Gregg started to interrupt, but his tiny, high voice had no hope of carrying against Furs's booming bass. "Shut up. You're a murderer. You helped destroy the Rox. I have nothing to say to you." Gregg couldn't see well enough to tell what he was dialing, but Furs only hit three numbers: 911, then. He was calling in the cops.

Gregg wasn't going to wait for that. "Furs," he said desperately, and then words simply failed him. There was nothing to say. Furs wasn't going to believe him any more than the others he'd tried.

Furs let go of the gun with one hand to pick up the receiver. With the motion, Gregg leapt for the open window.

The sound of the gunshot was deafening. Something hot and powerful slashed across his rear body segment, the impact making Gregg's body tumble. There was no pain, only the sensation of heat and the horrible smell of gunpowder, and then the blinding surge as metahuman automatic reflexes kicked in. He heard himself screaming, and found himself tearing around the perimeter of the living room as a stunned Furs whirled hopelessly behind him.

Gregg saw the window on the second circuit. He turned in mid-air and half-fell, half-scrambled down the side of the building.

He ran through the streets of Jokertown like a demented banshee until he blacked out.

He came back to consciousness, as he expected, back in the sewers. His body had healed, though there was a long scar in the yellow skin. It was warmer, at least. He wondered how much time had gone by, and then realized that he didn't care. In the sewers, it was easy to feel despair.

"I can't live this way," he told the dripping walls. "I *won't* live this way."

The walls declined to answer.

"I don't want to be a joker," he said into the dripping, odoriferous darkness. Only the varied, pungent smells of the city's waste returned to him. He almost wished that the voice would sound in his head, scolding him and mocking him—at least it would be *something*.

But he sat in unyielding darkness and silence, and he knew there was no refuge for him—not with Hannah or anyone else. If he stayed in this body, he would spend the rest of his life running. The murder of Rudo would always be hanging over him: that was the lesson he'd painfully learned over the last weeks. He would spend the rest of his life in hiding, or he would find himself in the hands of the criminal justice system—for a murder he didn't commit, for the death of a man who wasn't Pan Rudo, but some stranger. In the maelstrom of his despair, Gregg could think of only one way to get out of the body in which he found himself trapped—a way he'd already tried unsuccessfully once before.

This time, though, he would use the one commodity that might purchase his freedom.

"I need to talk to Brandon van Renssaeler."

"Who is this calling, please?"

"Tell him. . . . Hell, tell him it's Sirhan Sirhan."

"Sirhan—? Who—?"

"Just *tell* him. Please."

Gregg drummed several of his feet on the telephone stand next to the couch. He kept his eye on the door, ready to bolt for the open window if he heard anything. Luckily for Gregg, it seemed that a whole slew of people in upper floor apartments didn't expect burglars to climb sheer walls.

"This is Brandon van Renssaeler," the phone

squawked tinnily on the table. Gregg leaned down toward it. "Who the hell is this?"

"Gregg Hartmann."

The retort came a breath too late. "Gregg Hartmann is dead, and you're a sick person, whoever you are."

"If you really believed that, you'd have already hung up, Brandon. Come on, my friend, we've known each other for years. You want details about you that only I could know? I can give them to you. But I'm sure your Shark friends have already given you my new description. After all, this was Battle's body first."

"Listen, I don't know who you are or what you're talking about, but I can't talk to you right now. If you'd like to come to the office . . ."

"Not a chance, Brandon. Remember, I'm wanted for Pan's murder—but it wasn't Pan, was it? The real Pan has a nice shiny new body, just like Durand and Faneuil. Well, I want one too."

"I don't know what you're talking about. Pan Rudo is dead."

"Just shut up and listen. We've both been involved in politics, so we know about compromises. Your little group's on the run, but you've managed a few victories lately; in fact, things are swinging your way again, and the last thing you want is to lose the momentum. The nat public's tired of the violence, and they're willing to make the jokers scapegoats if that means an end to it—I saw in the paper where Barnett has a new anti-joker bill on his desk for signing. Right now the person who's the main thorn in your side is Hannah Davis. The publicity Hannah and her group are getting is the only thing keeping Congress from passing the full-blown Quarantine Regulations. You took *me* out, but Hannah hasn't eased off the pressure on you, and I know the woman well enough to know that she's not ever *going* to do that."

Gregg paused, taking a breath and hating himself. Brandon didn't interrupt. Gregg could hear the man's breath, waiting. "She wouldn't, but *I* would," Gregg said at last.

"What do you mean?"

"You're interested now, aren't you? Look at it from my perspective. The truth is that I was never involved in this because of any moral conviction or idealism. This never was my fight. Right now I'm stuck in a joker's body and, frankly, I don't like it. I want to be *normal*. How's this for a proposition? Let's play your game once again: you jump me into Hannah's body and Hannah into this one; let her take the rap for Rudo. Maybe she'll even get killed resisting arrest, right? As Hannah, I can finish the job you people started with my old body—confess that poor murdered Gregg Hartmann was right, that the evidence was manufactured and the whole Shark conspiracy was a fraud. Once that's over, you can jump me into a new body of my choice and we'll call it even."

Silence.

"Brandon? Jesus Christ, Brandon, have some compassion. We're friends, remember? I don't care any more about the Sharks or Hannah or any of it. I just don't want to be a goddamn *freak*." Gregg could hear his voice break with the word, almost a sob. He took a deep breath.

"This . . . this isn't a decision I can make on my own."

"I didn't figure it was."

"How can I get in touch with you?"

"You can't." The feeling of hunger was washing over Gregg again. The metal table lamp smelled positively luscious. "Brandon—don't fuck this up. If I want, I can blow the Sharks entirely out of the water with everything I know. I've got absolutely nothing to lose. I'll turn myself in publicly and loudly, and eventually the truth will come out—*all* of it, Brandon, including stuff you'd rather no one knew. You don't want that—and *I* don't want to be a joker the rest of my life. Let's work together. I'll call you. Tomorrow at four."

"That's too soon. I . . . I need at least two weeks. There's people I need to get in touch with, and they're . . . hard to contact."

Gregg sighed. He had to *find* Hannah, somehow, in any case. That would take time. "Two weeks then," Gregg said. "You'll hear from me."

Gregg hung up before van Renssaeler could reply.

You're vile, Greggie. You're soiled beyond redemption.

Gregg waited for the voice, but the accusation never came. He told himself that he should be happy—he was free, free to do whatever he wanted or needed to do, free for the first time since he'd been infected with the virus. There was no Puppetman to foul him up with its demands, no Jiminy Cricket to nag at him from the other side. Gregg was on his own, he was whole. He could do whatever was needed and nothing, *nothing* inside him would disagree.

Gregg sat in the dark for an hour wondering why he felt so fucking miserable.

There was only one problem: finding Hannah.

At one time, Gregg would have known exactly where to start. There had been one person who knew everything that happened in Jokertown, and who would sell that information for the right price: Chrysalis. But Chrysalis was long dead, and the person who had inherited her mantle—Charles Dutton—wasn't someone Gregg felt comfortable approaching. He had no leverage with Dutton.

So there had to be another way to approach it.

Luckily, the sewers went everywhere. . . .

"Evan, so good to see you. It's been quite a while." Dutton's low tones echoed in the still hall of the Museum. From Gregg's refuge in one of the Turtle's old shells, hung high above the main gallery, the voice sounded sepulchral and ghostly—perfect for this place filled with the ghosts and shadows of Jokertown's past.

"Patti's been dominant for awhile. I've been . . . tired. I don't think I'll last that long, but I thought I'd get back to work on the church fire diorama while I could."

Gregg peered through one of the holes in the shell. In his fuzzy vision, he could see the Oddity's bulk, wrapped in its usual floor-length cape. Dutton's skull-like visage was just below.

It had taken more than two weeks. He'd found the

main sewer lines into the Dime Museum, wriggling up through the fragrant miasma into the basement of the building. The museum, with its ornate displays and labyrinthian rooms, had afforded as many hiding places as he needed. Each night, as Dutton was busy closing the halls above, Gregg would enter. He'd overheard dozens of Dutton's private phone calls in his office, late at night after the museum had closed, but none of them had revealed anything. He'd looked through the man's papers on the rare occasions that Dutton left the museum; none of them were more than routine. He supposed that he could have melted the locks on the desk or the office safe to see what was inside, but that would have revealed his presence, and the odds seemed against the careful Dutton having anything there, either. The man had visitors—some of the visitors and their concerns quite surprising to Gregg—but the snatches of conversation he'd heard from them had also afforded nothing useful. One night there was a meeting of local jokers headed by someone called Hotair, where there'd been extensive discussion about Jokertown affairs. While Hannah and Father Squid's names came up more than once, no one gave any clue as to where they might be hidden.

Gregg had already decided to give this up if he heard nothing by the weekend. But Dutton's next words caused Gregg to lean forward in the shell.

"How are our friends?" Dutton asked. "Holding up well, I hope."

"As well as can be expected. I think they're all going a little stir crazy. Father Squid's about ready to go back, at least. That's a small house, after all, and Father Squid says he's getting tired of the sirens at all hours. . . ."

"Hannah, you've got to get over this. Hartmann was a goddamn jerk. He betrayed you. Betrayed *all* of us. He always was a fuck-up, and he didn't deserve what you gave him."

The words hurt. Gregg felt a shiver run through him in the darkness.

He was hanging upside down, an overgrown caterpillar

hunched under the eaves of the tiny four-room house across the street from the Jokertown district fire station. It had taken him several days to find the place, checking smaller homes located near the Jokertown Clinic, St. Elizabeth Hospital, Fort Freak—the Jokertown police precinct, and—finally—the fire house. The Oddity was in the room with Hannah; the voice carrying through the screened window was John's, bitter and eternally angry. Gregg couldn't see much, but he could smell Hannah's perfume.

"John, I don't need to hear this again. Please." The familiar voice, touched with a tired huskiness and so close to the screen, almost caused Gregg to lose his grip on the slick painted wood of the eaves.

"You *do* need to hear it, Hannah. I'm sorry, but you don't realize how much of an effect you have on our fight. Without you, we're just a bunch of pitiful freaks howling about how oppressed we are. You're our *voice*, and it's been too damn silent since Hartmann sold us out, since he—" The Oddity's voice broke off.

"Since he was murdered," Hannah finished for him. "And without Gregg, my voice is being portrayed as that of a paranoid, silly woman, and things are getting worse every day. Death and violence are the only things I seem to be good at bringing out. I'm not effective, I'm not . . ." Gregg heard her exhale in disgust. He could imagine her arm swinging wide in frustration, her hair swirling with the motion. "Damn it. *Damn* it!"

"Hannah . . ."

Gregg heard the rustling of cloth as Oddity moved. The voice had changed timbre—John had given way to Patti. Even the scent of the triad joker had changed. "Hannah, I'm so sorry. John . . . John just *says* things. Sometimes he doesn't think about other people's feelings. I wish I could help you—I can see how much it hurts."

Hannah's voice was muffled through Oddity's cloak. "I fell in love with him, Patti. I probably shouldn't have, but I did. And Gregg returned my love—I know that. I'm sure of it. I just want to understand what happened. There had to be a reason, had to be *something*. He wouldn't talk to me, wouldn't see me—all of a sudden. Then that damn press conference, and the next night . . ."

Hannah was silent for a long time. Gregg wondered whether they'd left the room. He relaxed the fingers on his front two hands until the sucking pads released and let his head swing down a few inches. He could see the bulk of Oddity and the back of Hannah's head as she hugged the joker.

"Something *happened* to him," Hannah's voice said at last. "I can't . . . I *don't* believe Gregg would just turn like that. Not against us. Not against *me*." More quiet, then: "God, I *hate* it when I cry like this."

"It's okay, Hannah. It's okay. . . ."

This was perfect. Better than he'd hoped. Gregg's initial plan had been, well, *fuzzy*. When he'd called Brandon back to tell him he'd located Hannah, they had set up a tentative rendezvous and a time. Brandon had been insistent that only Gregg and Hannah were to meet him there. Somehow, Gregg needed to get Hannah alone and convince her to follow him.

He'd thought to sneak into Hannah's room and present himself as Battle. He'd tell her that since he'd become a joker himself, he'd had a change of heart. Somehow, he'd convince her that it was in her best interests to follow him—alone—and he'd lead her to the rendezvous.

The problem was that he knew Hannah wasn't that gullible. She'd suspect Battle would be leading her into exactly the kind of trap Gregg had set, and he no longer had the Gift to help persuade her. He figured he had at best a fifty-fifty chance of his plan actually working, but it had been the only ruse available to him.

But Hannah had unwittingly given him the edge he needed. *Now* he knew how to get to her.

All he had to do was tell her the *truth*.

He was Hartmann. He'd been jumped. It *hadn't* been him who betrayed them, but someone else—probably Battle himself. It had been someone else—probably *not* Battle, Gregg suspected, but some other poor dupe whose body Battle now inhabited—who had been killed. *Only you can help me, Hannah. . . .*

She'd be skeptical, but he could convince her. She *wanted* to believe, after all. She loved him.

It was all there for him.

Except . . .

He couldn't do it.

The sickness and self-disgust he'd been feeling since he talked with Brandon welled up in him at the thought, and Gregg knew that he'd never find peace again if he went through with this. He didn't need his inner voice to tell him that. He was *whole*—and there was suddenly no place to shovel the mental shit, no false personality construct to blame for his actions.

There was only himself in his head.

Gregg Hartmann, you've gone soft, he told himself wonderingly.

Glancing back once into the room, where Hannah clung to the comforting Oddity, Gregg let himself drop to the ground. He padded away, the sound of his passage no louder than the wind.

"Brandon?"

Gregg's piccolo voice awakened a few echoes in the warehouse near the East River. The rear doors had been open, just like Brandon had promised. Gregg could smell rat droppings, the papery scent of old packing cartons, the smeared oil on the concrete floor, the gritty residue of ancient machine tool shavings, all overlaid with the strong salty brine of the East River. But he couldn't see anything; all the details were lost in darkness and myopic blur.

"Brandon, it's Gregg Hartmann." Gregg sniffed again. Yes, there was *someone* here. He could smell perspiration, and a man's cologne. . . .

The rustle above warned him too late. The weighted net draped over him with a soft *thunk*. His body went into overdrive, but all that did was tangle him more tightly in the coarse strands. He threw up on the netting, but it didn't dissolve—he could melt metal, but it looked like other materials were impervious.

Gregg heard people shouting, saw the lights come on,

and when he managed to bring himself back into normal time again, someone he didn't recognize—young, strawberry blond, blue-eyed—was leaning over him, looking down at him with a strange mixture of curiosity and revulsion. Four other burly types were stationed around the net. One of them was familiar: General MacArthur Johnson.

"What's going on?" Gregg asked Johnson. "Where's Brandon?"

Johnson just grinned at him, the smile bright in the dark face. It was Mr. Aryan who answered. "He's not here," the man said. "You see, someone who sounded just like you called him about an hour ago and told him that the deal was off. Really, Gregg my old friend, when you kill someone, you should make sure that it's really the person you're after."

Something in the inflection, in the way the words were phrased, set off alarms in Gregg's mind. "Pan—" he breathed, and the man smiled.

"So you've guessed. You always were a clever man, Gregg. Where's the Davis woman?" Rudo was dressed in an expensive double-breasted silk suit—rather old-fashioned for his new body. Gregg wondered how joker vomit would look on the lapels—it wouldn't hurt Rudo, but it sure as hell wouldn't *smell* good.

"I didn't bring her," Gregg said. "I . . . I needed to make sure Brandon was going to keep his word first," he lied. "Let me out and I'll get her."

Rudo shrugged. "It doesn't matter," he said. "She isn't that large a problem. Not any more. It was *you* I wanted, Gregg. You're the dangerous one."

"You were never going to give me a new body. Did Brandon know that?"

Rudo smiled. "Brandon is an idealist, not a pragmatist. You were supposed to give him leverage over me. He doesn't like the project we're working on. Brandon wanted to negotiate with you and Hannah as collateral: everyone would compromise and everyone would get something they want. Brandon would get my work placed on a back burner, I'd get your little anti-Shark group scuttled, with your help. Even you would get something, Gregg. Too bad Brandon doesn't realize that his phone isn't secure. Too bad, too, that I never *could* give you a body, even if I'd wanted to do so. You see, all the jumpers really are dead now. Didn't you know that? A shame, really. But I still have some uses for you, Gregg. I probably should just kill you now, but I'd rather demonstrate to you just what we've been doing. What Brandon didn't want us to pursue."

Rudo gestured to his companions, and they lifted him, net and all, as Rudo brushed lint from his suit.

"I think you'll be impressed," Rudo told him. "I daresay it will take your breath away."

A Dose of Reality
by Laura J. Mixon
& Melinda M. Snodgrass

Clara van Renssaeler, Journal Entry, 31 Mar 94

A viable killer virus continues to elude me. I'm afraid I'll to have to abandon this random-insertion approach. As ever, none of the latest batch are showing any preference for attacking Takis A-infected cells over noninfected cells. The shotgun method for targeting the wild card initiation site is simply not working.

If only Battle hadn't bobbled the break-in.

Uncle Pan is outraged at Papa for not supporting the Black Trump effort. Papa just made some sort of conciliatory gesture in the last few days, I gather, so the tension has eased a little between them. A little. Still, Papa's resistance to the plan has made Pan impatient with my delays. As if I had any control over my father!

But I can understand Uncle Pan's concern. Hartmann's allegations have raised everyone's suspicions. The Feds are probably already digging; eventually they'll turn up a lead that will uncover our work here. We are running out of time, and I am out of ideas.

Uncle Pan is trying to pull the organization back together and stave off panic, and has insisted I make a

*presentation at one of his political meetings tomorrow.
("Uncle Pan." It seems odd to call him that. He's now a
good eight or ten years younger than I am. I miss the
old Uncle Pan, the elderly gentleman from my childhood
who let me crawl up into his lap and told me stories,
who helped me train my first horse and helped me with
my French lessons, and called me PC, his petite
cavaliere.)*

He's invited big wheels from all over the world. He
says the organization is in serious trouble and my virus
is perhaps our last chance to forestall wholesale defec-
tions—by forcing them all to focus on a single, common
goal: eradication of the wild card, once and for all.

I'm to give an overview of my research, to make it
clear why the Black Trump is necessary, and to "play
down the obstacles remaining, if you please, PC." To
leave the attendees with the impression only a few details
have to be ironed out.

I loathe this deceit.

Uncle Pan argues that desperate times call for desperate measures. That if we don't act as a unified entity
now, our cause is lost. What is a simple lie, he says, when
a world is at stake? He laughs indulgently at my protests
and tells me to trust him.

I suppose it's hypocritical of me to balk. Many things
have been done in our cause that I find personally
abhorrent.

If I could just get hold of Tachyon's files, I could trans-
mute the lie into truth! We know his Trump virus, Takis
B, is in essence a deletion virus that attaches at the Takis
A initiation site. Even if Tachyon hadn't known from his
work on Takis A—and the Takisians have clearly finished
mapping the human/Takisian genome—to engineer Takis
B, Tachyon had to know where that site is on the human
genome from the restriction map.

I've combed all the lab notes he donated to the World
Health Organization in the seventies. Notes on his Trump
virus work weren't included among them. They have to
be somewhere, though—and he developed Takis B in his
Jokertown lab. The information has to be there; QED.

I need that initiation site.

Clara entered the darkened conference room and waited for her eyes to adjust. The meeting was not yet underway, though most of the participants seemed present. No one seemed to notice her, other than the guard who'd opened the door. She chose a seat near the front end of the U at the U-shaped table, opened her satchel and pulled out her speaker's notes.

Muscular men with semiautomatics peeking out from inside their suit jackets stood at all the entrances. General MacArthur Johnson, Uncle Pan's security chief, stood near the shuttered windows, arms clasped behind his back and feet planted apart. If it weren't for his eyes, he might have been made of obsidian. Pan Rudo, graceful and catlike in his new, ectomorphic Aryan body, paced around the room behind the chairs, listening, exchanging a word here and there. He came over as she sat down, and squeezed her shoulder.

"Ready?"

"As I'll ever be."

"Good. We'll begin in a few moments."

In a counterpoint to the soft babble of interpreters' voices, the chandelier overhead tinkled in the air-conditioned breeze, glowing a dull amber. Glasses, coffee cups, and ash trays littered the polished mahogany table. The smells of smoke, of foreign perfumes and body odors, clogged Clara's nostrils and throat.

Perhaps thirty people or so, mostly men, sat at the table. Clara knew only a few of them. General Peter Horvath, an important British Shark for whom her father occasionally provided legal services, was there of course, and Eric Fleming, a multi-millionaire rancher from Australia who had been a close acquaintance of her father's since she was a girl. Most of the rest she knew only by name, if at all. They made up a hodgepodge of races—Caucasian, black, Oriental, Hispanic, Mediterranean—arrayed in a riot of costumes: business suits in a variety of styles, dress uniforms, fatigues, kitenges, robes, boots, loafers, sandals.

The fat Sikh to Clara's left wore an expensive gray business suit and white turban, for instance, and had a black beard rolled tightly up into the folds of fat at his chin. He chain-smoked, smiled at her in a way that made her uncomfortable, and completely ignored his interpreter, a strikingly beautiful woman in a ruby-red sari, who whispered in his other ear. Clara gave him her most intimidating owl-eyed stare, and eventually he coughed, stabbed out his cigarette butt, and looked away. On her right a tiny, stiff-faced man who might have been Central or South American wore a military uniform with lots of brass and ribbons on the chest. Two Orientals sat with O.K. Casaday—probably North Vietnamese representatives. And three members of the Meta-Greens—an extremist group from Germany, an odd marriage of the skinheads and the Greens—sat near Rudo's chair, looking young and insolent. One had his army boots up on the table.

Across the table from Clara sat Etienne Faneuil. His body may have been twenty years old, but the leer on his face belonged to a disgusting old man who should have died years ago. And now that he'd returned from his travels and gone into hiding, she had to share a lab—and the results of her research—with the psychotic son of a bitch. Clara shuddered.

She studied Pan.

Though it had been months, Clara had yet to feel at ease with this new Pan Rudo, this tall young man with the strawberry blond hair. Resemblances to whom he'd been remained—the fine bones, the violet-blue eyes, the mannerisms—but she couldn't help but feel as if she were dealing with a stranger who pretended to be Uncle Pan. And the way he'd used a wild card power for his own gain seemed wrong to her. More than her father ever had, Pan Rudo had had a vision.

First *Papa*, she thought, and now Uncle Pan. My icons are toppling off their pedestals all around.

Horvath slammed his hand on the table, apparently in response to something the man next to him said.

"Bugger that!"

Clara jumped, startled from her reverie.

"We have to do something about Durand. Now!" He turned to Uncle Pan, who was leaning over, whispering with Faneuil. "What will *you* do about it, Rudo?"

"And what about von Herzenhagen, for that matter?" Eric Fleming asked, from the other end of the table. "He's cozy with some of my connections—if he turns like Durand has, I'm finished. We have to do something. Assassinate him, if necessary."

"The hell you say," someone else said. "We should break him out. Pay someone off—whatever it takes. He's no traitor. And we need him."

Clara glanced at Faneuil at the mention of Durand, and the implied, possible assassination attempt. He didn't twitch an eyelid. No lingering feeling for his old flame. It figured.

Eric scoffed. "No one is indispensable. Not even you, Carruthers."

"Hartmann is the real threat," the Central American *generalissimo* said. "He knows far too much. Even as a joker he's dangerous."

Twenty arguments erupted at once. Clara buried her face in her hands. Sparks crawled behind her eyelids: incipient migraine. Not now, she thought.

She hated this. Why couldn't they leave her alone to do her research, and leave her out of these horrid wrangles?

Uncle Pan said, "Enough." It cut through the pandemonium like a scalpel through flesh. Voices died away and everyone turned to look at him—with a few nervous glances at Johnson, who had moved over to flank Pan, his semiautomatic visible beneath his arm.

"Stop this bickering. Listen to yourselves. You sound like frightened old women."

Embarrassed looks were exchanged as his words were translated. Even Horvath looked sheepish.

"Senator Hartmann has been neutralized," Pan went on. "As for the rest, the questions you've all raised need to be resolved, but now is not the time. I've summoned you here for a specific purpose." He paused. "This is a critical time for us. The forces that oppose us have struck some serious blows, and everything we have striven for so long to accomplish is in danger of coming to naught. We must combine our efforts now for a decisive strike, before they can stop us.

"I have summoned you here to reveal to you the existence of a secret weapon—one which promises to put success within our grasp."

That got their attention. Uncle Pan glanced briefly at Clara. She gave him a nod.

"To describe this weapon," he said, "which will wipe out the curse of the wild card, I give you the woman who has developed that weapon: the weapon that will trump the wild card once and for all, and put an end to the contamination of the human race. Ladies and gentlemen, one of the world's leading virologists, Clara van Renssaeler."

A delay while interpreters whispered. Then a murmur rose. The rumors about her father had spread, then. The color came up in Clara's cheeks. She gathered her notes and stood.

Eight pairs of eyes. All held in a net of wrinkles. *Why does power always come with age?* Normal human eyes. Widen the focus to include the faces. Seven men and one woman. An expanse of aged white skin wrapped tenderly in expensive fabric. Power also surrendered slowly to the fretful demands of equality.

Dr. Bradley Latour Finn shifted uncomfortably. He was standing, an unruly schoolboy called before the assembled faculty of an expensive boys' school, but of course that wasn't the case. He was standing because the tall leather chairs which surrounded the oval table had never been designed for centaurs, not even pony-sized ones.

The Board of Governors of the Blythe van Renssaeler Memorial Clinic shifted, too, and exchanged glances. The chairman rose, and extended a soft, manicured hand. Finn stepped forward to accept it. His own hand was equally well manicured, and, he noticed with some distress, as soft.

"Thank you for coming in today. It's clear some kind of permanent arrangement must be made. Although the requisite seven years hasn't passed to consider Doctor Tachyon deceased, the patients and staff of the Jokertown Clinic need a leader. In these troubled times the ad hoc administration which you cobbled together just won't do."

"Like I said, Mr. Wily, I'm a joker. I'm a doctor. And I'm your guy."

There were polite smiles around the table, and Finn felt a presentiment of danger. Dismissed it. Of course he would have preferred to have them leap up and anoint him on the spot, but it was only in movies (and not the kind his dad made) where that happened. Bradley nodded politely, reared slightly so he could execute a sharp spin on his hind feet, and exited.

Clara started out with a primer on *xenovirus Takis A*, the wild card. With a few graphics and two or three scanning electron microscope photographs, she described how the virus incorporated itself into the human genome and commandeered the cell, causing changes that led to the now-well-known outcomes: death, deformity, or, for a lucky few, a great psychic or physical benefit.

"I have developed a virus," she said, "that penetrates the human cell wall and seeks out the wild card initiator sequence in the DNA—the location where the wild card first insinuates itself into the human genome. If my virus finds the wild card, it will destroy the cell and spread to others, leading to the death of the person infected."

"What effect does the virus have on non-wild cards?" one man asked. It was Casaday. "Is there any risk?"

"Absolutely not. My virus will attack the DNA *only* if the wild card is present in the genome. People untouched by the wild card are safe. The virus will be carefully engineered so as not to harm anyone but the intended target." She sensed Uncle Pan's gaze on her and avoided a wince; the "will be" was a slip-up. Perhaps no one else would notice. "The scientific name for my virus is *necrovirus Takis*. In the lab, we've dubbed it the Black Trump."

Loud voices broke out, and Uncle Pan had to call twice for silence before she was able to continue.

"Now," she went on, "your next question might be, why is such a drastic solution necessary?" She looked around at the several dozen eyes focused on her, and wondered whether these people cared at all about the lives that would be lost.

Hartmann's allegations on *Peregrine's Perch* had shocked her. She'd known that things like that went on, but she couldn't believe all of what he'd said was true. For every Etienne Faneuil or George Battle in the organization, there were ten dedicated, principled people like her father and Pan Rudo and herself.

"Any humane researcher would seek to *cure* the wild card," she said. "Not kill those poor souls who are already suffering from its effects."

The young Meta-Green with his boots on the table made a scornful noise, which she ignored. She put her hands behind her back and gazed out at her audience, waiting for the interpreters to catch up. She thought of the stories she'd heard, the violence against those afflicted. Some of these people were responsible for it. How could they possibly understand?

"My years of research in the field—and let me set aside modesty long enough to state that I am considered the preeminent expert on the wild card virus today. Other than Tachyon, of course." A pause as her words were translated; laughter rippled through the room. "My twelve years of research have led me unavoidably to a terrible truth: the wild card cannot be cured.

"Tachyon is the only researcher who has even come close, in four decades of feverish efforts by thousands of researchers. With a wealth of advanced alien knowledge and technology at his disposal, he developed his *xenovirus Takis B*. The Trump virus. And look at the latest statistics on the Trump." She brought up a graph, and used her ruby laser arrow to point at the bars on the projector screen behind her.

"A cure is only successful in about twenty-four percent of attempts. Forty-seven percent of the time it doesn't work at all, and an appalling twenty-nine percent of the time, it outright kills the patient. In other words, it's more likely to kill than cure.

"In short," she said, "the wild card is such a complex virus, and modifies the genome in such an insidious variety of ways, that it not only defeats our science, it defeats the science of those who developed it, the Takisians. And meanwhile"—she flashed a chart onto the screen, showing the current rates of infection in the population—"as you can see, the wild card virus spreads ever more rapidly through the population. The numbers seem small now: barely seven hundred thousand jokers and aces, worldwide. But remember, they are only a small fraction of those infected. For every joker or ace you see, *nine others have died of this disease*.

"And complicating the picture are the latents. We estimate that the number of newly infected latents each year—the 'invisible' wild cards, if you will—is thirty percent of the total number infected. In other words, for every joker or ace, another four or five people have the disease lying in wait in their DNA, to someday go off like a timed charge."

She changed the slide, and pointed. "Last year we saw one-point-two million new infections. This was a sharp increase from the year before. Many of these were as a result of inhalation of the wild card spore, but the number of cases caused by genetic transmission is on the rise. Perhaps two million people now carry the wild card trait as a recessive in their chromosomes. They themselves won't become wild cards, unless they are infected by spores, and are counted separately in my totals. But they can pass it on to their children, if their partners are wild cards or carriers. In the same way that sickle cell anemia or hemophilia is passed on.

"Though the rate at which wild cards successfully bear or father full-fledged wild card children is comparatively low, they are responsible for the birth of a large number of carriers. And the average latent harbors the wild card gene for between five and fifteen years before it expresses itself—plenty of time to reproduce and pass the gene on.

"Thus, as you can see," she changed slides again, "we are on the heel of the wild card growth curve." She pointed with her laser arrow. "These three lines represent the projected cases of infection due to spores, due to genetic transmission, and the sum of the two. As this line shows, the rate of infection from spores will remain roughly flat for the next one hundred fifty years or so, at about six to eight hundred thousand new cases a year, and then begin to taper off, as the concentration of spores in the upper atmosphere is depleted. The rate of genetic transmission of the virus, on the other hand, will continue to accelerate. Dramatically.

"Using conservative assumptions, I estimate that by the year 2050, the number of people infected annually, worldwide, including latents and Black Queens, will surpass ten million. This means that in the year 2050 we will have"—she ticked them off on her fingers—"six hundred thirty thousand new jokers *a year*, most of whom will suffer gross deformities and greatly tax our nations' resources. Seventy thousand new aces, with their unpredictable and potentially threatening powers. Over three million new latents. And approximately twelve million new carriers born.

"And, of course, in that one year, six million three hundred thousand dead."

Several listeners gasped. She propped herself on the edge of the table. "A portion of those deaths will occur *in utero*, so in one sense the impact is not as great as it sounds. We estimate that roughly seventy percent of all wild card-infected fetuses spontaneously abort or undergo transformation at some point during pregnancy. However, many of those are second- and third-trimester miscarriages, or transformations during delivery, often threatening the mother's life. So this is not a trivial loss. And it also means decreasing fertility among our populations, as more and more carrier and infected couples mate.

"By 2100," she went on, "the annual number of infections climbs to forty million, and the number of carriers climbs to seventy million. By the end of the twenty-second century, one seventh of the world's population will either be infected, or a carrier."

She paused and faced the audience again.

"That translates to over two billion infected. *One-point-two billion* dead, every year. One hundred twenty million jokers, and twelve million superhuman aces. Six hundred million latents. And another fifth of the world's population, or almost three billion, will be carriers."

Shock hung thick in the silence. Even the Meta-Greens seemed taken by surprise; the young man had removed his feet from the table and sat upright.

"In short," she said, "the wild card threatens the human race. In a few hundred years our population will be reduced to a small, enormously powerful elite, a large pool of carriers, and another large population of those physically deformed, many of them barely able to function.

"Nearly every pregnancy, every birth will be a time of dread and suspense, as parents wonder whether their child will be one of the very few lucky ones, or one of those who must spend the rest of their lives suffering. Or one of the vast majority who must die. The human race as we know it will have ceased to exist."

She turned off the projector and perched on the table again, waiting for the murmurs to die down. Auras sparkled around the edges of her vision; nausea clutched at her stomach.

"I've heard enough." Eric Fleming stood. He spared a glance at Clara, and she thought she read disapproval in it. Then he faced Pan. "If this Black Trump virus of yours is such a wonderful thing, destined to save us from the wild card, how is it the girl's own father doesn't support it?"

And several heads nodded around the room, as the interpreters whispered.

"My father doesn't oppose me," Clara said, but the Meta-Green smirked and spoke over her. "There must be some reason—everyone knows he's always been Rudo's lap dog."

Loud voices broke out. Clara came to her feet, stiff with rage. Hallucinatory flashbulbs burst around the Meta-Green. Pan's warning stare—and a wave of nausea—were all that kept her from lashing out.

Pan came to his feet in a fluid movement. All gazes went to him as he moved to the front of the room.

"Van Renssaeler has been careful to take no official position on this effort. But it is true he has reservations." His voice, calm and thoughtful, settled over the room, and the murmurs stilled. "I believe that his reasons are personal. Clara is taking a great risk in developing this virus. Imagine what will happen to the creator to the Black Trump, if our efforts are uncovered prematurely."

She blinked, surprised. Perhaps that *was* it.

"Clara has made her peace with this," Pan was saying. "It is my belief that her father has not. So." He spread his hands. "If she chooses to offer this means to decisively solve our dilemma, will you, Mr. Fleming, refuse it?

"Consider. You've told me yourself that the wild card threatens your nation's stability even now. Think how much worse it will be in ten years. In twenty. We must act now."

Fleming shook his head, with a dense and stubborn look on his face, exactly that of a bull refusing to be herded. "Well, mate, it still smells wrong to me, and I'm not having any of it. Until I hear van Renssaeler's backing this plan, you can count me out."

He gestured, and his two aides stood. Clara saw a glance pass between Uncle Pan and Johnson; she thought for a moment they'd stop him, but the guards let them pass.

Uncle Pan surveyed the room. Clara shivered at the look on his face, and felt glad he was on her side.

"Anyone else?" he asked, softly.

After an uncomfortable silence, Daniel Mkonda, an

African political leader, addressed Clara. "How certain are you of those numbers?" He glanced at Pan. "These aces are a threat and a nuisance. My nation will be well rid of them. But for the rest ... you are talking many deaths on our heads. I have family who are jokers."

"Sentimental ass," someone murmured. Faneuil.

"Waziri Mkonda," Uncle Pan said, "it is a great tragedy what happened to your daughter last year—"

The African cut him off. "No, no, you don't understand. Many of my people suffer, and not just from the wild card. I have several wives and many daughters; if I must lose a child so that my children's children may be spared, then—" he paused as if words had been snatched from him, and looked around at the wall of silent faces. Clara wondered what he read there.

"Then so be it," he said finally, and his voice was like sandpaper. "But I would not pay such a terrible price unless I were certain that what she"—gesturing at Clara—"says about the future is true."

Clara nodded slowly. Taking a deep breath against the nausea, she gripped the table edge. It was almost as if she were alone in the room with him.

"I'm as sure as anyone can be. All my calculations have used very conservative assumptions. Believe me, sir, I understand your dilemma. It haunts me that history will remember me as the woman responsible for the deaths of over a million people. But I'm willing to pay that price. Because the alternative is unthinkable, and the Black Trump is the only means within my grasp to prevent it."

"But perhaps someone will discover a cure."

Clara shook her head. "We could gamble that sometime in the next two hundred years our science will advance that far. But it's a fool's bet. How can I explain this?" She paused, framing her thoughts. "Takisian biogenetics are several hundred years beyond ours. Maybe more. I've seen this with my own eyes. And I've studied Tachyon's work in depth. He was not merely a good researcher; he was brilliant.

"In other words, a brilliant researcher, after two

decades of effort, with the aid of a science half a millennium beyond ours, *couldn't find a cure.* That tells me it could be a millennium before our science is advanced enough to produce a cure. Or never. And I think you'll agree, that is far, far too late."

Uncle Pan, seated next to Faneuil, spoke. "And I think you'll also agree, Waziri Mkonda, that it is better we lose some kin—who are already suffering, most of them—than to sacrifice the future of the human race. The future depends on our courage. Our ability to stay the course and see this through to completion."

Clara spoke again, to the room at large. "The wild card must be stopped. At all costs. Now, before the population affected gets any larger. And the only means within our grasp is a simple killer virus that targets the wild card in the DNA.

"The loss of life will be minimal. Not much more than the number of people who will die of the wild card, this year alone." She broke off. Pain stabbed her behind the eyes; her hands trembled. She gave Pan a desperate look. He studied her, and comprehension dawned on his face. He stood.

"Dr. van Renssaeler has another commitment and must be going. If you have further questions, I'll be glad to relay them to her and get back to you. In the meantime, it'll be a few weeks before we're ready to mobilize efforts to disperse the virus, so I will keep you informed."

Lights exploding before her eyes, she found her way to the door and slipped out.

Back at the Clinic the other members of the triumvirate which had run the hospital since Tachyon's departure were waiting impatiently. Doctor Cody Havero, a tough, one-eyed cutter who had honed her skills in Vietnam, and traded that war zone for the "no man's land" of Jokertown. And Dr. Robert "call me Bob" Mengele, ("no relation to the *other* Dr. Mengele," as he was always quick to add). Dr. Bob had a reason for waiting. He too had applied for the position of Chief of Medicine at the Blythe van Renssaeler Memorial Clinic. Finn had kind of resented it, but in fairer moments realized that having one of their own—even if he was a nat—was better than some outsider.

A surprising addition to the mix was Howard Mueller, known affectionately to everyone as Troll: nine feet of horny overlapping plates, metahuman strength, and metahuman kindness. He was the Clinic's Security Chief, and his skills had been getting a workout in the past two years as acts of violence against jokers, and their Clinic, had increased. He usually didn't put himself forward in this way, but it dawned on Finn that every joker on the staff was anxious to *really* have one of their own running the hospital. Mrs. Chicken-Foot had followed Finn into the office, and Finn didn't have the heart to shove her out. She mothered him like the Jewish mother she was, and her position at the front desk was a thankless, and sometimes dangerous, job. She deserved to hear what news he had.

"So, how'd it go?" Bob Mengele asked.

Finn slid behind the desk, and began running quickly through his mail. None of it was important, and more to the point, none of it was money.

"Pretty well, I think. I kept my smart mouth zipped. I stayed professional, courteous—"

"Like a Boy Scout," Cody murmured around her cigarette.

Cody had smoked in Vietnam. She had begun again last year. Finn frowned; he hated doctors to smoke. On the other hand, the obvious parallel being drawn did not escape him.

"I presented my credentials, and I told them I thought a joker ought to run the Jokertown Clinic."

"You didn't!" gasped Mrs. Chicken-Foot.

"Oh yeah, real courteous," said Troll, his voice holding an echo of laughter like the rumbling of distant thunder.

"Hey, I was very polite."

Cody flicked the cigarette ash. "Now it can be told. The Board approached me last week. Wanted me to interview for the position." Three sets of joker eyes and one pair of nat eyes fastened on her. "I told them no.

Told them a joker ought to run the Jokertown Clinic."
She winked at Finn.

He felt a momentary regret. Wished Cody weren't
quite so much older than he was. Wished he was less
shallow. But he liked younger babes. And wanted a family
someday when he'd finally found that babe who could
love him for his mind, and not mind his joker flesh.

"Are you upset with *me* for applying?" Mengele asked.

Cody slid off the credenza where she had been resting
a hip. "No, Bob." She stubbed out her cigarette on the
sole of her boot, and tossed it into the trash. "Well, back
to work. Good job, kid. Now let's see if there's any justice
in this sorry old world."

"How is your headache this morning?"

Clara pressed the phone to her ear and a damp cloth
to her head. She lay on her back, staring at the lightning
worms that crawled across the high ceiling, and spoke
softly. "Better, Uncle Pan. A few lingering visual effects
is all."

"Excellent." His voice brimmed with energy. "I'm
about to leave the country on business, but before I left
I had to compliment you on your presentation. You made
quite an impact."

Clara licked her lips, which were cracked and sore, sat
up, and grabbed the jar of Carmex lip salve. "Not with
as many as I'd hoped."

"Mmm. Fleming. Yes. And we need him to effectively
cover the South Pacific." There was a pause. "Talk to
your father, Clara. We need his support."

She sighed, smearing menthol-tasting salve on her lips.
"He won't listen."

"We have no other way to reach him. You must try."

After a silence she said, "All right."

"And keep me updated on your progress at the lab."

"I always do."

Clara van Renssaeler, Journal Entry, 4 Apr 94
   Had to trash another batch of prototype viruses today.
   Uncle Pan says my talk on Friday went over well.

Some thoughts on the virus. I need to engineer an incubation period of at least two or three weeks, if possible, and make it transmissible via saliva and mucous membranes. It must be able to spread rapidly and easily. A deadly flu.

I called Papa this morning, and brought up the subject of my research. It was awkward; I just can't bring myself to pressure him, and I know he disapproves of what I'm doing. He asked how it was going and I told him the truth—it's not going well.

He said perhaps I was too close to my work and needed to step back from it for a bit. I needed a change of venue. That's not the problem. I know exactly what information I need. I simply don't know how to get it.

But perhaps in a sense I have been too close to my problem. I recently read an article in the Times about the Blythe van Rensselaer Memorial Clinic. The Jokertown Clinic. And it occurred to me a few minutes ago, the family still has connections with them; Grandmaman Blythe's trust fund has been donating money to the Clinic for years. Papa could get me a position on the staff, if I can persuade him to intervene on my behalf. If he won't do it, I'll get Uncle Henry to. And once there, I could certainly find a way to get access to Tachyon's lab notes.

I've got an urgent call into him. I'm pretty certain what I have in mind isn't quite what he meant by a change of venue. Oh, well.

There's the phone now. I'll bet that's him.

The unctuous voice was still rolling out its sonorous, lying periods even after Finn hung up the telephone. "*Such a difficult choice . . . The Board agonized for several days . . . Understood and appreciated your unique talents . . . Two thousand dollar a year raise . . .*"

The real message could be gleaned—"You're joker shit, boy, and you ain't gettin' this job."

Finn turned away from the desk, and leaned the length of his body against the wall. Closed his eyes, and felt the tears prick. He wanted to call his dad, but even dad couldn't fix this hurt. Also, he couldn't bear to tell his father, or Cody, or Troll, or any of the other nurses, doctors and staff at the Clinic that he had *lost, failed*. The humiliation lay like a sick, oily taste on the back of his tongue.

Stop thinking about yourself, your wounded pride. Figure out what this means for the Clinic, and her patients—the people who really matter.

Dr. Clara van Renssaeler. Who the fuck was Clara van Renssaeler? Aside from (presumably) some relative of the tragic and doomed woman for whom the Clinic had been named? Finn hurried to the AMA directory for the state of New York. There she was; MD Harvard, PhD bio-chem Rutgers, published papers—there was an impressive list, and Finn again felt inferior. He was a GP with some minor cutting skills.

There was the connection to Blythe—granddaughter. It was an irony really that the Clinic carried the name of van Renssaeler. The van Renssaelers had never done a damn thing for the Clinic. It was Blythe's family who had founded and supported the hospital even in the face of growing wild card bigotry. By all accounts Henry van Renssaeler, Blythe's husband, had been a wild card hater of monumental proportions. Enough bile to put him on this list of "Sharks" that Hartmann had been exposing before his death. So, it probably wasn't blatant nepotism. Maybe the Board of Governors thought the name would ease the pain when they appointed a nat to head the Jokertown Clinic.

For Dr. Clara van Rensaeller was undoubtedly a nat. Because if some kin to the namesake of the Clinic had been bitten by the wild card bug, and turned into a hideous joker, the Jokertown rags would have been full of the news.

A nat.

It was the unkindest blow of all.

He didn't know why, but it sort of helped that she wasn't very pretty. Looks, money, brains, and his job would have been just too much to take. Finn surreptitiously eyed the long (he sent up a mental apology)

horsey face, the big boned, almost awkward body. She
did have nice green eyes. Well, the color and size of
them was nice. The expression was that hard, flat stare
of the professional woman sizing up the playing field,
and deciding it would probably be a potholed bitch.
Cody, who was a woman who had long ago fought all
those battles of sexism and personal insecurity, stared
back at Dr. van Renssaeler with her usual warm, calm
air.

Finn had ducked behind the cafeteria counter for a
cup of coffee before Clara van Renssaeler had made her
entrance. It left him feeling at a decided disadvantage as
she nodded to the assembled staff. She said his name in
a questioning tone.

"I'm Finn."

Their eyes met, and that connection, which only a
young, straight, and horny man can make when he knows
a woman has just found him attractive, occurred. It was
a rare enough occurrence that Finn felt his heart lift.
Then he stepped out from behind the counter, and
watched the shutters slam down in her eyes.

Finn made the initial introductions, and he knew his
tone was icy; he couldn't help it. That teasing eye play,
followed by rejection, had deepened his fury. He
watched as van Renssaeler's eyes took desperate refuge
in the nice, normal features of Cody Havero and Bob
Mengele. Finn was a joker. He knew joker loathing when
he saw it, and Dr. Clara van Renssaeler embodied it.

Dr. Robert could always be counted on to play the
glad hand Charlie, and he didn't fail them now. He
stepped forward to chat up the new boss, and Finn
pulled Cody aside with a look, a grimace, and a jerk of
the chin.

In an undertone he said, "You take care of the tour."

"No."

The calm refusal took him aback. "Look, Cody, I can't
deal with this bi—"

"You better learn, or look for a new job. Like it or
not, she's here. She's in charge, and you're the person
who has run this clinic for the past three years. She

needs to be briefed by you, not by the Chief of Surgery. Quit bowling with your balls, and get on with your job."

They went from the top down. Moving silently from floor to floor. As a tour guide Finn left much to be desired, explaining each area with a terse single word; *lab, nursery, ICU, surgery, morgue.* Finn was at peace with his wild card, but as they viewed the suffering encompassed on each floor of the clinic, the presence of this horrified interloper suddenly reduced his tolerance for his own kind. *We really are disgusting,* he thought, and depression crashed over him like a wave.

The first spark of animation out of the silent Dr. van Renssaeler occurred when they reached the basement, and stood before the heavy vault-like door which barred access to Tachyon's private lab.

"Do you have a key?" she asked.

Her eagerness sent a shiver of unease down his spine. "Yeah. But there was an attempted break-in earlier in the year, and I'm even less inclined to let people in now. We spent ten thousand dollars upgrading the security on the lab. There's live wild card in there. *Muy* dangerous."

She stared flatly back at him. "Dr. Finn, my specialty is wild card. I'm fully aware of the dangers, and prepared to face them to continue my work. I want the key. It's my right."

"Yeah, it's your clinic now," Finn said. He made no effort to hide his bitterness. A new set of words were clamoring for release. He weighed, tasted, considered them. Decided to say them. "You ever actually *practiced* medicine?"

"No." Terse and to the point, and perhaps just a hint defensive.

Finn allowed that admission to hang in the silent air between them for several seconds, then he said, "The suffering and dying at this clinic surpass anything I've ever encountered—even when I was a Peace Corps volunteer in Africa. And unlike third world sufferers, the jokers in Manhattan are Americans—or at least until Leo Barnett succeeds in saying we're not—and they think they're entitled to an ease to their sufferings and a painless death. I think you'd better develop some bedside manner, Doctor. Well, shall we visit the wards now?" Finn concluded brightly.

The tour concluded on the fourth floor. Finn led his new boss down the hall, and pushed open the door to Tachyon's office.

"This is Tachyon's office. I've been using it. I presume you'll want it now."

Van Renssaeller walked past him, angling her body almost completely sideways as she passed to avoid touching him. It wasn't deliberate, he would have sworn it wasn't deliberate, but his tail suddenly flicked, the long white hairs whipped across her legs, tangling briefly in the strap of her purse. The woman shot into the room like she'd been launched. A couple of long strands, still caught in the purse, tore loose. She stared down at them in fascination. Untangled them from the strap, wrapped them around her index finger, suddenly brushed them off like a person afflicted by ants.

She was rattled. She stared around the room, and said stupidly, "There's no chair."

All the pent-up rage emerged in a spurt of angry, sarcastic words. "It may have escaped your notice, but I weigh four hundred pounds and have an ass a foot and a half wide. Chairs are not a big decorating item for me. Now, if you'll excuse me, I have patients to treat."

The days fell into a kind of tense rhythm. Nothing had really changed, and yet Finn couldn't shake this pressure band of rage and unhappiness which had settled about his temples.

He had laid eyes on the new boss once in the past week, when she had come to his office to demand the key and access code to Tachyon's private lab. Later he had bitched to Bob Mengele that van Renssaeler obviously liked germs better than people.

With a sigh that shook him from withers to flank, Finn gathered up his clipboard, and headed off for rounds. As he walked down the hall Finn gave the implacable face of the closed door a glance. When Tachyon had ruled the Clinic with his particular brand of noblesse, the door had always been open. Finn had continued that policy. Now the door, and the nat behind it, had become a metaphor for a joker's life in America of the mid-nineties.

A knock came around five in the evening, while she sat at Tachyon's desk sorting through the stacks of files she'd pulled from his office cabinets and laboratory file drawers. Her heart skipped into high gear at the sound. She had to restrain herself from hiding the contents of the folder she'd been translating.

Relax, PC—stop acting like a teenager they caught smoking in the girls' room. She removed her reading glasses, smoothed her wool jacket, adjusted the silk bow on her blouse, and arranged her features.

"Come in."

Cody Havero entered, a blue plastic file folder in hand, and surveyed the chaos Clara had made of the office.

"Dr. Havero," Clara said.

"Call me Cody." Her glance fell on the two Takisian-English references that lay open on Clara's desk—one a general usage dictionary; the other an unpublished, three-ring binder containing biomedical terms. Her eyebrows rose. "You speak Takisian?"

"Speak it? No. Merely read a little."

Cody glanced at the contents of the binder. "Someone's done some serious research, there."

Clara laid her hand on the binder, pleased. "I put this collection of terms together during my post-doc research at Harvard, to make use of the research notes Tachyon donated to the World Health Organization."

"Fascinating. You should consider publishing it."

Clara gave Cody a wry smile. "And enable other researchers to compete with me? Besides, I'm sure it's riddled with errors. I had to use a lot of guesswork."

Cody chuckled. Clara glanced at the folder she held. "You have something for me?"

"Tomorrow's surgery schedule." Cody handed her the blue folder. Clara slid her reading glasses back on.

"I'll look it over."

But Cody continued to stand there. Clara looked at the surgeon over the tops of her reading glasses.

"There's something else?"

Cody nodded. "Unfortunately, I'm here to dump a big problem in your lap."

Clara removed the glasses; they fell about her neck on their gold chain. She gestured. "Please, sit."

Cody dropped into the chair Clara offered—one of two old, taped-up, burgundy vinyl chairs Clara had appropriated from the staff lounge as a temporary measure. Propping her chin in her palm, Cody gazed at Clara with her good eye. Evaluating her, perhaps. "It looks like we'll have a severe shortage of nursing and radiology staff next Friday."

"I presume the heads of Nursing and Radiology can deal with these matters."

Cody shrugged. "They're trying. But frankly, it's close to unmanageable. With all this public hysteria, we're losing staff in droves."

Clara frowned. "What are you talking about?"

Cody gave her a rather surprised, *don't you watch the news?* look.

"The Clinic has been picketed by hostile nat groups five times in the last two months. The scuttlebutt on the street is we'll have another demonstration next Friday. A big one. That's why half the nursing staff called in sick. They get tired of the cow's blood and spoiled vegetable showers." A little shrug. "Can't say I blame them. We've arranged for escorts and human chains to protect the staff and patients, but . . ." Again, a shrug. "The demonstrators usually outnumber us."

Clara winced mentally. She didn't have time for this. She'd be up half the night doing research at her own lab as it was.

"I'll take care of it," she said.

Cody looked skeptical. "If you're thinking of calling the police, don't bother. We've tried that. They don't

show. We've already called on some of our own to protect us, though my fear is we'll end up with a riot, and
a lot of dead innocents, unless we're very, very careful."

The way she said "our own" bothered Clara. Cody was
a nat. Joker vigilantes weren't *her* people.

But Clara merely gave her a little smile. "I have an
idea or two that might help."

Cody appeared to be studying her again, with that
intent look.

"I hope you don't mind my directness, Dr. van
Renssaeler—"

"Clara."

An appreciative glance crossed her face. "Clara, then.
I have a confession. I'm a bit of an admirer. I've read a
number of your papers in virology and immunology.
You've done some impressive work on the wild card."

That caught Clara by surprise. "Thank you."

"And frankly, I'm surprised you accepted this position,
as you are so clearly a researcher. Not a physician, nor
an administrator."

Clara eyed the older surgeon for a long moment. Her
heart rate had picked up again.

"You want to know why I'm here, you mean. Why I
accepted this position."

Cody gave a shrug. "Forgive me if I'm being intrusive.
I'm merely surprised that you'd put aside your research
this way, when your career seems to be at its peak."

Clara sat back. She had better deal with this now.
Cody Havero was really doing her a favor—the questions
would be there, behind the polite faces, until she'd
addressed them. And, after a fashion, she could even tell
the truth.

"Research *is* my first love. You're right. My life's goal
is to eradicate the wild card. To find a way to purge it
from the human gene pool."

She said it flatly, but Cody's eyebrows went up. "You
feel strongly."

"You're damn right I do. The wild card is the most
heinous disease inflicted on the human race. Not as bad
as AIDS in its physical effects, perhaps—for most wild

card victims who die, death occurs quickly, and there *is* a ten percent chance of survival. Even a small chance of benefit. But because it can spread by both spores *and* inheritance, it's extremely difficult to eradicate. My great fear is that it may already be too late. And the way we were infected deliberately, that enrages me. I'll always despise the Takisians for that."

Clara broke off and unclenched her fists, disturbed by her own intensity. She fiddled with some papers on her desk.

Cody was watching her with that penetrating, speculative look again. Clara's outburst hung in the air between them like a bad smell.

"My mother died of the wild card when I was five," she explained. "It's given me strong feelings in the matter."

Cody's expression softened. "That stinks."

"So." It was Clara's turn to shrug. "I've dedicated my life to finding a way to loosen the wild card's grip on the human race."

Cody's gaze went again to the files and resource materials. "So you're here to expand your studies, then?"

Guilt made Clara's stomach muscles clench. "You might say. Obviously"—with a sweep of her hand encompassing the stacks of files—"I'm interested in Dr. Tachyon's work. But I'm also here to get a dose of reality. Make contact with the people the virus is affecting. Try to understand the disease on the human level."

The words tasted foul in her mouth. Nothing could be further from the truth; staying detached from the wild card's victims, keeping her perspective as clinical as possible, was critical. But the probing look on Cody's face had been replaced by one of compassion.

"I have some advice, if you'll hear it."

"Please."

Cody slouched in the chair and laced her fingers about her midsection. Her lab coat fell open. Beneath it she wore a cotton blouse, jeans, and short boots the same black as her eye patch. "With your background, I believe you have the potential to be a tremendous asset to this clinic. But you've already observed how nervous the staff is about you right now."

Clara thought of that joker physician, Finn. The centaur. A short laugh escaped her. "Bristling, more like."

"Granted. Some are angry. They wanted a joker administrator. It's nothing personal. Frankly, you must be aware of the sort of prejudice jokers are up against, and how defensive it can make them. So. My advice to you is, be the first to reach out. Let the staff know that you rely on them. Get involved. It's the only way you'll earn their trust. And it'll make your job a whole lot easier."

Clara looked the older woman over for a long moment. It would have been easy to feel condescended to, but something in Cody's easy manner penetrated Clara's reserve.

She nodded, thoughtfully. "I'll certainly consider your advice, Dr. Havero. Cody."

Once alone, she glanced at her watch. It was past midnight on the Continent. She'd probably wake him. With a wince, she picked up the phone and punched in an international number.

A series of clicks, as the call was relayed through several exchanges, then a man's voice said, *"Hier ist Rudo."*

The line hissed and crackled like water dropped on a hot skillet. Clara stuck a finger in her ear.

"Uncle Pan. I hope I didn't wake you."

"PC! Not at all. I am unfortunately all too busy these days; sleep is low on my list of priorities. I understand that you're official now. How has your first week been? How is your research proceeding?"

"Well." Clara cleared her throat. "That's why I'm calling. I have a bit of a problem. Apparently some anti-wild carders have been picketing the Jokertown Clinic, and it's interfering with my research. A demonstration is planned for next week. I wonder if there's anything you could do to stop it?"

"Hmm. That's too soon for me to be able to do much."

"I was afraid of that."

"As you know, it could be viewed as rather counter-productive to interfere with the demonstrations."

So. The demonstrations were being orchestrated by someone in the organization.

"I think I understand your difficulty," she said slowly. "My problem is, the Clinic's trustees are divided over my appointment—I was appointed over the head of a popular joker physician, and a couple of the Board members are looking for any excuse to get rid of me. So I can't afford to look like I'm not doing my job. And the more hassles I have to deal with here, the less time I'll have for my own research back at the UN lab."

"I see. So perhaps, strategically, it would be wise to take the heat off the Clinic for a while."

"Exactly. If you could at least pull some strings so that we can get the local police out to keep things under control—"

"I'll make some calls."

"Thanks."

An awkward pause ensued. "Have you spoken to your father yet?"

"No." It came out a bit too sharply.

"I'm not trying to pressure you."

The hell you're not, Clara thought, and then felt ashamed.

"I know how much you adore your father, and how confused his attitude must make you feel."

Clara wiped away a truant tear. "I'm a grown woman, Pan, and a scientist. My father's choices have done nothing to confuse my own. I'd appreciate it if you'd keep that in mind."

It felt better, not calling him uncle.

She thought she could hear him breathing on the other end of the line, amid the pops and hisses.

"I'm glad to hear it," he said finally. Another pause. "Talk to him, Clara. You're the only one who can reach him now, and we need him."

The woman's hand resting on his was moist and puffy—compared to the grip of most jokers it was a positive pleasure. What wasn't a pleasure was the state of her unborn baby, and the war which was being waged between her body, the baby, and the wild card. The mother's card wasn't that bad. Her eyes were set wide into her head, and three strange, antenna-like protrubances grew from each temple. She was also not a citizen of Jokertown. She was a happily married woman from Syracuse, but the hospitals and doctors in her home town had refused to afford her pre-natal care, or deliver the baby. She and her husband had come seeking help at Jokertown's Jokertown Clinic.

And we're falling down on the job, thought Finn. With each passing day it became less and less likely this baby would ever reach term. Her puffy hand tightened, giving his a quick squeeze.

"Doctor?" The unspoken question hung in the air.

Finn's bedside manner was not quite as brutal as his predecessor, Tachyon's, had been, but he didn't believe in lying to patients.

"The blood workup doesn't look good, Maggie. I've been talking to some specialists ..." The flow of words stuttered briefly as a new, novel, and annoying thought intruded. He resumed. "And while they've got some ideas, we're a long way from answers."

"Jimmy and I, we really want this baby. We can't adopt because ... because." The pain and humiliation showed in her face.

"Yeah, I know. We'll do something."

Out in the corridor he stood for several seconds; wrestled with his pride. It wasn't all that close a battle, his ego weighed against a baby's life ... no contest, but he dreaded the coming interview, and what if she refused?

Up two floors to that implacably closed door. Finn knocked, entered on her invitation. She wore reading glasses, and they looked good on her. Instead of making her look bookish they somehow softened the lines of that long face, and made her look cute. There was the usual brief struggle with her features, which she mostly won.

"Yes?"

"Thought I'd give you a chance to act like a doctor," said Finn.

"I *am* a doctor." The words were so icy they could have cut.

"Practicing is a usual component in that description." There was the briefest flare of pain in those green eyes, and Finn both exulted and felt guilty that he had scored a hit. The guilt won out, and he offered an olive branch. "I also really need your expertise on the genetic front."

Her interest was piqued, and Finn shook his head over the researcher's mind.

"What's the situation?" van Renssaeler asked, and Finn outlined it as best he could.

He concluded by saying, "She is a joker, but she doesn't look . . . well, real jokerish, so you—" He realized he was about to commit a real major social faux pas, and he cut off abruptly.

"So I what?" van Renssaeler asked softly.

They matched stares for what felt like several centuries.

"So you won't be too disgusted by her appearance," Finn finally said.

For an instant van Renssaeler kept her poker face, then the facade crumbled. "I try to hide it," she said softly.

"You don't succeed."

He held the door for her, and tried not to care when she used all available space to avoid contact.

They stopped at the nurses' station to pick up the woman's chart. Clara scanned it swiftly, with Finn standing by. She saw from the amino results that the fetus was a carrier, a girl. The joker mother was twenty-three weeks along—too early for the baby to have any real chance if they went in after her.

Clara studied the blood test results, and shook her head.

"Looks bad. Her T-cell count is way up. It looks as though the mother's immune system has identified the fetus as an invader, and is trying to destroy her."

"No shit."

She frowned and ignored the sarcasm in Finn's tone. "I see you've already tried Cyclosporin."

Her remark seemed to irritate him. "Yeah. Believe it or not, we have a few competent physicians on our staff."

She pinched her nose with a sigh. "I didn't say otherwise, Dr. Finn."

After scribbling a few notes on the woman's chart, Clara handed it to him. "I'd like to order some special tests. Have two hundred cc's of blood drawn and sent to the address I've written here. If you would," she added, to temper the edge on her tone.

"It's my own lab," she added at his raised eyebrows. "My other lab. They can run some highly specialized tests and find out exactly how the mother's immune system is attacking the fetus. Some experimental, genetically engineered immunosuppressants are currently under development in the leukemia and organ transplant fields. And I have contacts at Sloan-Kettering, where a big research project is underway. I expect I can get this woman access to one of their drug testing programs."

"I don't think so," Finn said. "Maggie has been denied insurance coverage. Her wild card was a 'pre-existing condition.' They can't afford a lot of expensive medical tests and medicines."

"Not a problem. I have a grant to study the wild card. I can justify the tests somehow as part of the lab's research. And the drugs will be experimental, so as a volunteer—if she agrees to try the drugs—she won't be charged."

A flicker of something less than hostile passed behind Finn's eyes. "You've got it."

Finn handed the chart to the nurse on duty, a severely deformed joker whose rubberized flesh was peeling off in long strips. Clara avoided looking at him too closely. He emanated so much heat that even four feet away it warmed her face and hands; and he smelled horrible, too, like burning rubber and bile.

It struck her that despite his jokerdom, at least Finn was pleasing to look at. He looked more like the fantastical creatures her mother read to her about when she was little, with his large brown eyes, prominent cheekbones and forehead, tawny hair and flanks. And he had a not-unpleasant smell—vaguely musky, like a horse, though not in any sense overpowering. Whether it was a nervous habit, or because he was angry with her, his tail kept twitching and flicking around his legs. Occasionally a hoof would lift and scrape a leg; his flanks quivered. The horsey mannerisms were familiar to her from her school days, not at all off-putting.

But even though he was by no means repulsive, being around him made her break into a cold sweat.

And Finn rescued her from thinking too well of him by saying, with a challenging gaze, "Perhaps you should examine the patient, while you're at it."

Cody Havero's words of the day before came back to her. *Earn their trust.*

Fear clutched at her. She clamped down hard on the feeling and gestured down the hall. "Lead the way, doctor."

The look of mild surprise on his face—he had so clearly expected her to refuse—almost made the coming ordeal worth it.

The woman's name was Maggie Felix. Finn had been right; she wasn't too bad to look at. Finn introduced Clara, explained that she was a leading immunologist, and then stepped back as Clara moved around him to the head of the bed.

Maggie answered Clara's questions eagerly, with mingled fear and hope in her exotic, insectoid eyes. Her antennae quivered and, as she spoke, her hands stroked the swell of her belly as if to protect the baby from her own immune system. Beside her, her husband gently stroked her hair. His eyes, too, were filled with expectations.

Clara tried to avoid looking too closely at the woman, focusing on the man's gaze instead. The walls seemed to lean inward, and Finn was blocking her way out the door.

"Why is this happening?" Maggie asked. "Why is my body trying to kill my baby?"

It was a question Clara could handle. She put on her best clinical manner.

"It's nothing you could possibly prevent. The wild card has given you a powerful immune system. It has identified the fetus inside you as foreign genetic material—which indeed it is—and the usual mechanisms that keep a mother's body from attacking the fetus aren't strong enough to contend with your charged-up immune system. So." Clara shrugged. "We'll find a way to trick it. Or disable it, temporarily. At least enough so that your body's natural mechanisms for protecting your baby have a fighting chance."

That made the woman cry. Clara stood there, embarrassed. She knew what it was to want a child; she herself planned to visit a sperm bank, if the right man didn't come along in the next couple of years. But this baby was a carrier. Mother and child would die when Clara's virus was released.

But what was wrong with giving them a chance at a little happiness in the meantime? More importantly, this would give her a chance to expand her knowledge of wild card immunology.

Finn left, pleading other responsibilities. Clara promised the couple she'd do what she could, and then went back to her office to call the lab and tell her people what tests she wanted them to run. This promised to be an interesting challenge. One she could really sink her teeth into.

What a difference a puzzle can make, thought Finn as he leaned on the front desk, and watched Clara go pelting past with this intent look on her long face. He also realized that he had used her first name. *Change on both fronts.*

A conversation going on between Mrs. Chicken-Foot and Puddle Man suddenly intruded.

"I think all these riots are being caused by these Sharks," the receptionist was saying.

"Chickie, that's like blaming the Sharks for bad weather. The Sharks are big. Much bigger than Jokertown. They're rich, powerful. They don't care about riots in Jokertown. That Durand hinted they were up to something *big* before they spirited her away."

"The government doesn't want people to know they've been manipulated," Chickie said.

"No," Finn heard himself say. "People don't have to be manipulated to hate. They just come by it naturally."

"Then you don't believe in the Sharks?" Puddle Man asked.

"Does it matter?" Finn shot back. "The results are the same. Coming through the doors of the emergency room." He remembered trying to save Bjorn, trying to inform Anne, Zoe, *someone* that he had died. Learning they were in Jerusalem, and remembered hating them for running.

His bleak memories were shattered by a faint, dry *hissing*, and Finn turned to greet all sixteen feet of Joan as she came slithering down the hall. Against the faded white of the linoleum tiles her scales had taken on rich gold and bronze tones.

"Hello, darlings." She didn't notice when she slithered right through Puddles. The joker noticed however. The water formed itself into a whirling dervish of liquid, and coiled and caressed Joan's length.

"Thanks, Joan, that's the closest I've come to an orgasm in twenty years."

Color like pale rubies glowed in the scales on her cheeks. The cobra's head closed briefly across her face like a veil. Muted, from behind the scaly skin, "Puds, you're awful!"

Puddles let out a watery chuckle, beaded and rolled away. Joan reared up three feet, opened her cobra's hood in greeting, and Finn bent his human torso, and kissed her on her scented, scaly cheek. She closed stumpy human arms around his neck, and hugged him tight. Thank God the strength in her arms couldn't match the massive crushing strength of her snake's body.

"How was Jamaica?" asked Chickie.

"Perfectly sybaritic, my dears. The scritch of sand on my scales, and all that lovely, lovely heat. I think Perry has finally reluctantly realized that if he wants the

354 Laura J. Mixon & Melinda M. Snodgrass

pleasure of my scintillating conversation we mustn't take
skiing vacations to Colorado. Having a reptile's metabolism plays merry hell with my sex life."

Listening to this cheerful, inconsequential burble
delivered in Joan's rich alto seemed to help ease the
tension knot which had settled at the base of Finn's neck.
Joan had that quality to make people feel that all was
well, and if you ever had a doubt, why, *"Darling, how
foolish, things can only get better."*

"So tell me all the news. Of course you got the job,"
Joan said, and the resulting stab of pain reminded Finn
that maybe he hadn't dealt with his anger and disappointment, merely buried it.

He couldn't speak, and after several uncomfortable
seconds of Mrs. Chicken-Foot clucking mournfully to
herself, the sounds resolved themselves into words, and
the secretary said, "No, they hired a nat."

"Oh, Bradley, darling."

Finn shrugged. "Feces occur."

"You should quit."

"And go where, Joan? In the current climate I can't
get a job in a nat hospital, and I'm damned if I'm going
to move to Vietnam or Guatemala or Jerusalem. I'm an
American, I'm not going to be driven out of my own
country."

"Who is this person?"

"Clara van Rensseaeler." Joan stiffened. "Yeah, nice bit
of irony, isn't it? Especially since she can't stand jokers."

"Is she ... around?"

"Just down the hall. Room 112."

"Bradley's finally got her working with patients. Well,
one patient," Chickie amended.

"Excuse me," Joan said, and slithered away down the
hall. As he watched, Finn saw her scales shift from metallic brilliance to a pale white. The only way you could see
her was as a blur against the floor.

"Oh dear, Joan can be very ... *sudden.* I hope she
doesn't bite Dr. van Rensseaeller," twittered Chicken-Foot.

"Or eat her," added Finn. He then considered for a

second. " 'Course, that would solve our problem. It's the perfect crime. No body."

Chickie was still making inarticulate clucking noises as Finn wandered away to begin the day's work.

Late that night, while preparing solutions to package a new batch of viruses in her tissue culture lab, Clara reflected on her reaction to joker deformities.

Tychophobia, clearly. Fear of the wild card. She had a bad case of it. Knowing her reaction was irrational didn't make it any less severe. Only brute will kept her from diving out the nearest window whenever one of them came near.

It was fortunate that the more attractive jokers, like Bradley Finn and Maggie Felix, affected her less violently than others—less, say, than most of the patients languishing in the wards. Otherwise this sojourn at the clinic would be unbearable.

She pinned her hair up, then donned a protective hood, goggles, overalls, two pairs of gloves, and a respirator, and picked up her jugs of plasmids and mix solutions. She opened the airlock to the Level III clean room and stepped inside; the outer door locked and the inner door opened with a hiss. Her ears popped. Clara set the solutions down on the bench, then removed a tray of tissue culture plates from the incubator and carried the tray past the blinking banks of lights to the hood.

A wild card is a wild card, she thought, perching herself on her lab stool to prepare her solutions. Any visual difference is illusory; at their core, they harbor the same genetic damage.

Knowing this didn't change the shape or texture of her feelings. So much for clinical objectivity.

Clara van Renssaeler, Journal Entry, 8 Apr 94
    At last! I've found the restriction map I need. Tachyon's work on Takis B progressed in exactly the direction I thought. He reports the wild card initiation site as being 70 base pairs downstream from Taq1 and 2kB upstream from Xcm1 on chromosome 14.

I'm repackaging several of my more promising viruses with the right initiation site receptors. To maximize recombinations and cell disruption, I've spliced into the packages a transposon element with terminal inverted repeats as well. We'll have to see.

But this feels right. I'm getting close—I can smell it.

A riot was fomenting in the street in front of the clinic. On the steps of the clinic stood the defenders. Troll, mountainous in his homemade body armor constructed out of pieces of old mattress and bumpers, was slapping a six foot long billy club against his palm. Despite the exhortations of the fundamentalist preacher, some members of the mob were eyeing the big joker nervously. Mengele, a few other doctors, and some random angry jokers completed the guardians. Finn was attired in more traditional kevlar. It still didn't make him feel safe. All he could think about was his exposed head, and the unprotected expanse of horse body.

"He's winding up," Troll said. "The rocks will be flying soon." Finn swallowed hard, nodded. "Herself said she was going to handle this?" Troll asked.

"I'll believe it when I see it," Finn grunted.

And then, miraculously, in the distance, they heard them—sirens. *And* they were coming closer. The mob was starting to exchange puzzled glances. Was it possible their fun was about to be spoiled?

A few seconds later, and police cars came wheeling around the corner. Nats scattered. Police erupted from cars, and ran off in pursuit.

"Look at that, will you. Police." Laughter tugged at Troll's voice.

"I wouldn't have known what they were if you hadn't told me," Bob Mengele added.

"She did it," Finn said simply, and was grateful.

The next Saturday Clara needed some of Tachyon's notes from the clinic. The taxi driver turned on the radio, and 1010 WINS reported a water main break on The Bowery at Canal Street, which explained why they got stuck in traffic all the way up at Spring Street. She paid the fare and got out of the cab to walk the rest of the way to the clinic. Through Soho and Chinatown, and into the heart of Jokertown.

The air had quite a bite. A hard rain the night before had washed the streets clean of their usual patina of litter and urine. It was before eight; closed, graffiti-sprayed gates barred the store fronts and few people were out on the streets. Clara stuffed her hands in the pockets of her big, woolly cardigan and set out at a good clip.

Jokertown. By all rights she should be terrified. But this morning her fear had an element of defiance, almost exhilaration. She could face anything.

It was easier than she'd expected. Jokertown's streets weren't crowded. The one or two jokers she encountered up close seemed as nervous around her as she was around them, and gave her a wide berth.

Just down the block from the clinic, in a large, fenced, asphalt lot, she heard shouting and laughing and the sound of wood smacking pavement. A small group of joker teenagers was playing polo.

Jokers playing polo? The idea seemed outlandish; the two didn't belong in the same universe.

Four of the teenagers had feet that could accommodate roller blades. Of the other two, one hopped on a sort of accordian leg and the other had the hindquarters of a pony, like Dr. Finn's. Then she realized it *was* Dr. Finn. Curious, she hung onto the fence and watched.

It was clear he way outclassed the kids and was holding back. Of course, his body was perfectly designed for polo. But she was struck by how well coordinated his movements were as he reared and turned, as he raced across the lot, as he bent low and swung his polo stick, and led the chase back across the length of the lot with his tail high and his hooves striking the pavement in a clattering beat: horse and rider in perfect synchrony.

It reminded her of her polo-playing years in prep school, and of the times her Uncle Henry used to take her along on outings with a local group of mentally handicapped kids.

The ball struck the fence near her and the ragged group raced over. They braked several yards away when they saw her, fear and suspicion on their bizarre and twisted faces. Clara averted her gaze. Finn trotted up, out of breath and flushed, looking surprised. He wore a sweatshirt with a University of California at San Diego logo, whose sleeves and neck had been cut out, and a sweat pad over his horse's haunches. Both were stained with sweat.

"Putting in some overtime?" he asked.

"Needed to pick up a few things. I didn't know you played polo. You play well."

"Um. Thanks." A hind leg stamped. He twisted a finger into the frayed neckline of his sweatshirt. There was something quite boyish and Californian about his embarrassment. At that instant it was as if she was seeing Bradley Finn, the man, for the first time.

A man atop a horse's haunches. The impossibility of it rattled her. She had a flashback to that first moment she'd seen him, before she'd known he was a joker. By God, but he was handsome. She'd had a horrible shock when he had come around the counter and she'd seen what the wild card had done to him. But she could see now how functional the combination was. Even attractive.

Her mother had read stories to her from Greek mythology when she was very young, and she'd taken quite a liking to centaurs. When she'd been in her "horses" phase, as a teen, she'd collected dozens of centaurs—paintings, posters, figurines of pewter and crystal.

Feeling awkward, she gave him a nod and moved on. She sensed his gaze on her back.

On her desk, along with the file she wanted, were piles of reports on various administrative hassles she'd have to deal with first thing Monday morning. She leafed through them and groaned.

Labor disputes. A discipline problem among the staff. Piles of funding requests, to replace dilapidated equipment that should have been replaced years before—requests that far outstripped the clinic's paltry budget. A snide letter from one of the Board members regarding a lawsuit by a former patient.

It struck her, heading down the steps from the clinic, that Bradley Finn knew how to deal with all these administrative problems; he'd been wrestling with them for years. He was one joker she couldn't afford to alienate. Not if she wanted things to function smoothly while she was there. She should be delegating a lot of this to him.

It did make things easier that he wasn't physically repulsive. She would imagine him as a centaur straight out of Greek legend. Not a joker, like those pitiful, deformed kids he was playing with. She would trick her phobia.

Starting Monday, she decided, I am going to make a real effort to make nice to him.

> . . . So, while I do apologize, I know you'll carry on splendidly without my tiny little volunteer efforts.
>
> Joan

The handwriting was lovely. Someone had had the benefit of a fine education. The fluttering, almost tittering tone of the letter made him crazy, and Finn forcibly separated his teeth. The hinge of his jaw felt immediately better.

At first he thought he'd imagined it, so light was the tap on the door. Then it came again, a bit more forcefully.

"Come in."

What entered he hadn't expected. Clara van Renssaeler. Finn started to scramble up out of his oversized beanbag chair, but she waved him down. She then stood, clasping and unclasping her hands, and staring silently at the floor between her feet.

"Would you like to sit down?" Finn asked, indicating one of the two chairs which served as a concession to more normal bodies. She shook her head. The silence continued.

"When did this laryngitis problem first manifest itself?"

Still nothing. "You know, it's amazing this effect I have on women. You're not the first woman I've struck dumb."

A dimple appeared in her left cheek. It never graduated to a smile, she had too much self-control for that. Witnessing that human emotion left Finn speechless. And a *dimple*? He would never have associated Clara van Renssaeler with dimples.

"The Independent Grocers Association came to visit me this morning," Clara said. "A new city ordinance has been passed banning joker owned and driven trucks from exiting Jokertown. And the Teamsters have hiked fees for deliveries into Jokertown."

"Sonofabitch!"

"Who do think would be the best person to negotiate with them?"

He considered, and tried not to focus on the warm little glow which had settled in his chest. *Probably heartburn*, Finn thought, *can't be a crush. Might be lust.* He had a feeling he was blushing when he finally looked back at her. It had been a long time for Finn, and even considering the hot'n heavy had him struggling to keep his dick in its sheath.

"I'd send Cody."

"Rather than me."

"Cody's real good in a locker room setting. You're too much of a lady."

"I'm not sure if we've both been complimented or both insulted," said Clara.

"Complimented. Cody comes across like a sexy comrade, someone you want to storm the barricades with."

"And me?" asked Clara. From the look on her face Finn suspected she hadn't meant to ask the question.

"You're the kind of woman men like to protect. Or fantasize about awakening." And now it was Finn's turn to regret his unruly mouth.

"What does that mean, awaken me?"

"Behind that scholarly nature, behind those tortoise shell glasses, beats the heart of a sexual volcano just waiting for the right man." Finn tried to keep it very light.

Another of the Finnmeister's meaningless, randy, flirting remarks.

"Oh."

It was the last response he had expected. For some reason the ridiculous remark seemed to have sent Clara into a deep blue funk. The woman scientist was standing before him. She had that inward, almost blank expression that researchers achieve when faced with some puzzling new germ, or bit of data which has upset their pet theorems. Finn wondered which worldview his sexual banter had undermined.

"I'll talk to Cody," Clara finally said in a small and distant voice.

She left, and Finn had a long talk with his unruly dick, and slapped his mouth around.

Clara van Renssaeler, Journal Entry, 16 Apr 94

Exciting news! I started the test cultures for my new prototype viruses today. Batch 94-15-04-24LQ is already showing evidence of virulence against the wild card cultures, and little to none against the control cultures.

Don't want to jump to conclusions. Must be patient. Give the culture another few days. But this looks like it!

It was late, after ten P.M., when Clara stepped out of Tachyon's office. The corridor lights were dim; joker nurses and orderlies carried their trays and rolled their carts and spoke in hushed tones: a freakish parade of horrors and oddities acting out a normal human routine.

Somehow, though, the scene felt like a clockwork: all components functioning smoothly. Perhaps a Salvador Dali clock.

Down in surgery, she stuck her head around the open door of the doctors' lounge. Cody had curled her legs up on the sofa with a stack of patients' charts in front of her, unopened. She was sipping a cup of black coffee. A dark smudge underscored her good eye, and her face looked haggard.

"Mind if I join you?" Clara asked.

"Have a seat." Cody patted the sofa cushion. "You're working late."

Clara dropped onto the couch. "So are you."

"Tough day. A serious trauma case, on top of the scheduled cases. I just got out of surgery." Cody stretched with a jaw-cracking yawn. "And I'm on call tonight." She gave Clara a curious glance. "So why are you still here?"

"I wanted to clear off my desk. A lot of little things had been piling up." And there was no hurry to get back to the UN lab; the test results on her virus wouldn't be ready until the following afternoon.

She folded her hands in her lap, and thought for a moment, while Cody browsed through her patients' charts.

"Cody?"

"Mmm?"

"What brought you here? To Jokertown?"

Cody set down the chart and slung her arm across the back of the sofa. "A chance to do something useful with my skills, I guess. And"—she shrugged—"there was a need. Why?"

"I'm not sure. Just curious. A surgeon like you could find a position anywhere."

"I'm not sure I like what that implies," Cody said, with a frown. "Jokertown Clinic has an excellent staff of competent, committed professionals. This is *not* a dumping ground for physicians who couldn't get placement elsewhere."

"No. It's not." Clara twirled a ring around her finger, thinking. "Jokertown Clinic—surprises me."

"Sounds like some cherished beliefs are going down in flames."

"I didn't realize the depths of my feelings." Clara paused. "I'm a tychophobe. A clinical case: panic attacks, the works. I've been having a lot of nightmares, and a hard time fighting off a migraine, lately. I feel as if something's buried down there, something horrible. This"— she gestured all around—"seems to be stirring it up. And it terrifies me."

Cody looked at her. "You say your mother died of the wild card?"

Clara nodded. A needle of fear passed through her chest.

"Perhaps that's the connection."

Clara raised her eyebrows at Cody. Then she sighed and sank into the couch cushions, pushed her hair back.

"I'm sure you're right." She was silent a long time. "I think it would have been terrible to see her suffer; it's better that she died quickly. But sometimes the selfish child in me wishes she hadn't.

"It might not have been so bad. Even if she hadn't become an ace, she might have been a joker like Maggie Felix. Or Bradley Finn. You know—not horribly debilitated or in pain."

Cody's eyebrows went up, but she said nothing. Clara felt a warm flush spread across her face.

"I mean, I'd never want her to suffer the way so many jokers seem to suffer. But . . ." she spread her hands. "Take Dr. Finn. He's so well-adjusted. I admire how he's overcome his—well, it's not even a disability, for him, is it? Nat furniture and attitudes aside, he seems to function extraordinarily well. He's been helping me a lot with some of the administrative functions lately, and—" Clara gestured again, paused. "Despite my phobia I find myself forgetting he's a wild card."

Cody lit up a cigarette, and shook the match out. "The wild card is not a simple disease, is it?"

Clara's laugh had an edge to it. "Not by a long shot."

Cody gave her a compassionate look, and inhaled some smoke. "How *is* Maggie Felix doing, by the way? She's in isolation, isn't she?"

"Yes." *Thank you, Cody,* Clara thought; *subject change deftly done.* "We have her on large doses of Aminosporin. No evidence that it's crossing the placenta or harming the fetus, though Maggie herself is suffering some side effects due to the high dosage. But the baby's T-cell count has dropped to a more normal level."

"That's good to hear."

"Yes. I want to give the fetus as many weeks as I can.

The situation is still pretty dicey, but—it's better than the alternative." Clara shook her head. "Her immune system is amazing. I doubt she's susceptible to opportunistic infections even now.

"Well." She slapped her thighs, and stood. "I'd best be going."

At the door she turned. "Oh, and Cody—"

Cody took a drag off her cigarette, blew a stream of smoke into the air. "Yeah?"

"Thanks."

Clara van Renssaeler, Journal Entry, 24 Apr 94

After a promising start, my 94-15-04-24LQ virus cultures don't thrive quite as energetically as I'd hoped. I need to do some tests to learn what the problem is.

Mustn't get discouraged. I'm still much closer than I've ever been.

Finally worked up the nerve to ask Papa out.

The restaurant was La Lucia, an expensive little Italian restaurant on the upper West Side, *Papa's* favorite. The tried-and-true, soften-him-up-digestively method. He had already been seated when she arrived.

Brandon van Renssaeler always looked good—trim, handsome, with silver at the temples and taut, Nautilus-trained muscles and an even, gold, tanning-room tan. But tonight he looked a little frayed around the edges. He stood and took her hand and kissed her on the cheek, and she realized he must be as worried about all the recent developments as Uncle Pan.

Clara removed her wrap and sat. Her nerves were twitching like little jumping beans. The waiter brought her a double gin and tonic.

"I took the liberty," he said. Clara nodded her thanks and downed half of it in a few swallows.

They chatted about inconsequentials for a few moments; she asked how Chloe was and how the practice was going, and he told her. The waiter took their order for appetizers. As the waiter walked away she pressed her fingers against her lip, mentally girding herself.

"We need to talk," she said.

His glance was sharp. He never missed much. "About your research."

"Exactly." She touched his hand. "*Papa*, why have you withdrawn your support? We need you."

He looked at her and said nothing, merely swirled his cognac and sniffed its aroma, wearing a thoughtful expression.

"Well?"

"You're your own woman," he said, and took a sip. "I can't stop you from pursuing the course you've chosen. God knows, I wish I could. But you're making a big mistake with this Black Trump project. And we're all going to pay."

"Damn it, I wish you would trust me. I know what I'm doing." She leaned forward. "The virus will work, *Papa*. I'm *that* close to perfecting it"—she held up thumb and forefinger. "We have the resources to disperse it. We have human immunology on our side. Once the virus is released there'll be no way to stop it. We'll be rid of the wild card forever.

"But Eric Fleming and his whole network won't cooperate unless you do, and if we don't have a series of vectors in the South Pacific, there'll still be large pockets of disease in the southern hemisphere. You must tell him to do what Uncle Pan says."

Brandon sighed, sipped at his brandy. The waiter brought *prosciutto*-stuffed wild mushrooms and gave them miniature forks. Brandon dug in right away, but Clara had no appetite. She sat with her hands in her lap, fighting the urge to lean across the table and shake him. Brandon asked the waiter to give them a few more minutes to select their entrees, and perused the menu. Clara seethed.

"Well?" she asked.

Brandon rubbed his forehead. "There's a word for what you're doing, and people are going to use it. Genocide. Mass murder."

Clara gasped, caught between outrage and irony. A laugh escaped her. "You don't mince words, do you?"

He sighed. "If you're going to go through with this, you'd better get used to that label, Clara. I've seen what the legal system, and the media, can do to people." She started to speak, but he lifted a finger. "Yes, I know your intentions are good. And I hate the wild card as much as you do. I'm not prepared to wage a frontal war against Rudo. But I simply can't support you in this."

"But why?" Clara's fists clenched. "*Why* won't you support me?"

Brandon shook his head. "It's going too far. I can't condone it. Your heart is in the right place, Clara, but this Black Trump scheme is deeply misguided. There are plenty of actions we can take against the wild card without spreading killer diseases."

"*Papa—*"

"As I've told Rudo, if he wanted to do this he should have used someone else. Left you out of it."

At her look of distress he took her hand, and his expression softened. "I'm very concerned about what will become of you."

She jerked her hand loose. "How can you say that? You lost your wife to the wild card—I lost my mother! How many more people have to suffer the way we have—the way she did—before something is done?"

"Your voice is carrying," he said.

She lowered her voice. "*Papa*, you have to help."

His look was piercing. "Who says so? Rudo? Has he been pressuring you to get to me?"

She felt her color rise. At her expression, his lips went thin. "Thought so. That's just his style. It's my own damned fault; I should have removed you from his influence years ago, before he got his hooks into you. They're in you so deep now I don't know if they can ever be extracted."

"You don't know what you're talking about."

"Oh, I'm afraid I do. Rudo has turned you into a tool of mass destruction . . . he's twisted your brilliance into something dreadful. . . . My God, look at you! Look at what you're doing! Look at your main collaborator—a man who spreads disease for the pleasure he gets from it. Doesn't that tell you anything?"

Clara dropped her napkin on the table.

"I didn't choose to work with Etienne Faneuil." She said it calmly, but she felt as if she were going to explode.

"No? Tell me, how is what you're doing different from what he's done?"

"I don't experiment on human subjects! I don't enjoy this the way he does. I'm putting an end to the suffering, and preventing the spread of a terrible disease. There's no other way!"

"Drop your work on the virus, Clara." He said it softly. "There are other ways to deal with the wild card, without resorting to genocide. Don't let Rudo manipulate you. You can walk away from it—there's still time. I'll protect you from any Shark fallout. Rudo doesn't dare attack me directly."

"*Papa* . . ." She struggled with tears, won the struggle, stood. "Your support would have meant a lot to me. But I'll go on without you if I must."

He merely stared at her with deep sadness. She stood there for a moment, speechless. Then she turned and walked out.

Clara van Renssaeler, Journal Entry, 27 Apr 94

Just got back from dinner with Papa. Still shaking. It was horrid. He all but accused me of being a carbon copy of Faneuil. How can he say that? How can he not understand? How dare he accuse me of genocide when it was he who inducted me into the organization to begin with? I'm furious.

I knew, I just knew it would end up this way. Damn him. Uncle Pan will have to find some other way to win Eric over. I've done all I can.

I wish things were like before. I want to talk to Papa about my research. And about Maman. With all this exposure to victims of the wild card, she's on my mind a lot. I want to ask him what she was like. I wish I'd known her. I barely remember her.

I saw two people draw the Black Queen at the clinic

*yesterday. When I think of how she must have suffered,
it's like a great hand squeezing my heart.*

*The Black Trump is the only way to stop the anguish
the wild card causes. If there were another way I'd take
it, but there's not. How can he wish what we've suffered—what she suffered—on the rest of the human race?*

*Damn you, Papa. I won't stop for you or for anyone.
I know I'm right in this.*

"I'm gonna ask her out."

Cody dropped onto a bench in the scrub room. Her
green surgical gown was splattered with yellow gore.
Finn stripped the scrubs off his torso, and bent double
trying to reach back to unwrap the horse body from its
sterile wrap. Cody gestured with a finger, and he allowed
her to catch the velcro edge, and strip him.

"Are you sure that's a good idea?"

"It's not a date date. She's hearing all the problems of
Jokertown, I thought it might be nice for her to see the
up side."

"Is there one?"

For the first time in all the years Finn had known the
surgeon she sounded old. And sad. And tired. He trotted
to her, the rubber booties on his four hooves making
squeaking sounds on the linoleum floor, put his arms
around her neck. They rested their foreheads against
each other.

"Yes, Cody, there is one. No, many. People still fall in
love, and children play, and old men squabble over their
chess boards in the park, and people trade books out of
the back of the Worm's station wagon."

Cody straightened, smiled, pushed back a lock of his
white-blond hair. "How old are you, Bradley?"

"Thirty-eight, why?"

"How did you keep cynicism at bay?"

He shook his head. "I don't know. Too dumb to be
depressed?"

She stood. "If an older, more experienced woman
might give you some advice. . . ."

"Any time."

"I would couch this request as if it *is* a date." She turned that single, all seeing, all knowing eye on him. "Because, of course, that's what you want. And if you phrase it like an educational tour she's going to turn you down, convinced that you're condescending to her again. And, of course, she'd be right."

"She'll turn me down faster if she thinks this is a date," Finn said glumly.

"I don't think so."

She started out of the scrub room. Finn made a leap after her, and ended up tangling three of his four feet. "What do you know?" he demanded when he finally regained his equilibrium.

"Everything . . . you know that, Bradley." She winked at him, and left.

Clara van Rensselaer, Journal Entry, 28 Apr 94

Well, the analytical results are back and I've had a chance to study them. I think I may have figured out the problem with virus 94-15-04-24LQ. The situation is not as bad as I'd feared; this is still a viable Black Trump virus. But it's not ideal.

To make sure the virus doesn't die out due to lack of disease vectors, I hid the Black Trump gene inside a more benign virus that affects both wild cards and nats—like a Trojan horse. The benign virus is a linear, single-stranded DNA virus, which contains a "negative" of my Black Trump as part of its gene sequence, and a locator for the wild card receptor. I packaged all this with a reverse transcriptase for the Black Trump gene and a transposon to encourage mutations.

When the viral package enters a cell and the benign carrier virus starts to reproduce, the reverse transcriptase is synthesized. The Black Trump m-RNA is split out and converted to a proper, double-stranded Black Trump DNA sequence by the reverse transcriptase. All as planned.

For the control cultures, in which the wild card initiator sequence isn't present in the DNA, the Black Trump has nowhere to attach on the genome, so it and the transposon remain as junk floating around in the cell. The carrier—a much less dangerous virus—proliferates instead.

In the wild card cell cultures, the Black Trump attaches at the initiator site on the DNA. The linked transposon element wildly recombines and reproduces the Black Trump, causing random genetic insertion and throwing the cell immediately into lytic phase. The cells burst, dispersing the Black Trump virus to other cells.

In theory this should be deadly. But the 94-15-04-24LQ virus got progressively weaker as it was transmitted from cell to cell.

According to my follow-up tests, it appears that— ironically—this virus is too virulent. Introducing the transposon has made it so wildly recombinant that it produces a host of missense mutations, weaker strains that are more successful than the original Black Trump gene at repackaging themselves before the cell bursts. So the more lethal strain gradually kills itself off. Progressively weaker strains result.

Given the rates of mutation in the tissue cultures, my calculations indicate that the first wild card who contracts the virus will die, and also the wild card who catches it from the first, for a total of about three to four generations of wild card transmission. The intervening nats who contract it don't alter the Black Trump portion of the virus, so they don't dilute the effect.

Given the length of the viral incubation period and the ease with which it's transmitted, three to four generations should be enough to kill most of the wild carders in any given population center, before it mutates to the nonfatal form. So this is a powerful virus, despite its limitations. But it means that we can't use the virus to effectively sweep the globe, without mounting a larger infection campaign than Uncle Pan intended. Its virulence will peter out within weeks of its release. Thus it might be stoppable with the use of quarantines, unless we hit all the major centers at once. It will also almost certainly miss isolated areas, and it will be useless against the inevitable new wild card infections that will occur. That in particular concerns me.

The other potential concern is that this virus is so recombinant it could mutate to a form harmful to non-wild cards, under the right circumstances. It's a small risk, but I'd be more comfortable with a rather less mutable version.

Overall, though, I'm fairly pleased with this virus. I've dubbed it necrovirus Takis I—Black Trump, strain I.

And I think a few modifications will make it truly unstoppable. I'm now trying the same viral package, but without the transposon. That should diminish the virus's mutability enough—I hope—that the lethal form has enough time to repackage itself before the cell destructs, and is able to compete against the weaker, daughter strains. It should also reduce the risk that the virus might somehow become harmful to non-wild cards.

I should have preliminary results on the new batch, 94-04-28-24LQ, Black Trump II, by Sunday.

I want to share this with someone—I'm so close to solving the puzzle! But there's only one person I can confide in, and I find myself reluctant to tell Uncle Pan about my progress.

Not that I could reach him right now in any event; he's off to Asia, trying to consolidate support for our plan. But he was back for a day or two, and Saturday night he came by the lab and asked me out to dinner. He took me to a lovely little restaurant in the Village and we talked for hours. As tense as things have been between us, I was relieved that our relationship was returning to normal.

He asked me about my meeting with my father. Of course I told him nothing of what was said, only that Papa was adamant. He urged me to continue my efforts. I told him it's pointless. Papa's mind is made up. I wish Pan would believe me.

And when he dropped me off he kissed me. I mean on the lips. A romantic kiss.

And—I don't know, I mean there's no doubt he's a very attractive man, especially now—but it feels vaguely

incestuous. Wrong. I've known him for too long as a sort
of second father to be comfortable switching roles this
way.

And I can't help but wonder, why now? And why me?

I feel terrible for harboring these thoughts against
Uncle Pan, but I feel there's something else behind all
this. I've overheard some of the angry remarks he's made
about my father in unguarded moments, and the other
day I heard him and Faneuil talking in Faneuil's office.
(I must confess to being a bit of a snoop; I listened at
the door when I heard my name.) Only caught a few
words, but he seemed to be saying that I wasn't to be
invited to some meeting or another. Faneuil mentioned
someone named "Nor" or "Ner." And Pan said that the
less I knew about any of Faneuil's work the better.

Faneuil's work is epidemiology—he has been working
on ways to disperse the Black Trump through the populace. I'm being shut out of a major portion of the Black
Trump effort. Because of my father, I'm certain.

And last night I dreamt about the dinner date, only
Uncle Pan really was Pan, the mythical goat. Grotesque
genitalia and all. He kept leering at me, and I was very
frightened of him, but kept laughing and laughing so he
wouldn't know. When we got to my apartment, Bradley
Finn rode up and shot Pan with an arrow. It didn't seem
to hurt Pan, but suddenly I was free of whatever spell
of fear he had cast over me. I jumped onto Finn's back
and he leapt out a window.

Then Finn turned into this Benji sort of dog, and a
big snake with the face, arms, and breasts of a woman
appeared and attacked him. I woke up shouting, in a
cold sweat, at four A.M. and I've been awake since.

I've dreamt of that snake before. She was a lamia. A
weeping lamia. More distorted Greek mythology.

Seeing auras and such, but no headache yet. I've taken
some medication to see if I can fend off the migraine.

I guess I'm just under too much stress.

It's odd that I should dream of Bradley Finn. Perhaps
it was because I've been thinking about him in terms of
Greek mythology, and that got linked to Pan's name.

Had a long talk with Cody Havero the other night. My feelings about the wild card are changing. My commitment to eradicating the virus hasn't changed; it must be destroyed and there is only one way. Even if Pan, or Papa—even, I hope, if I—contracted the virus, I would continue my work on the Black Trump, for the good of the human race.

But I do think that knowing the people—realizing these are human beings, not just statistics—is important for me to face. I don't want to become another Etienne Faneuil, whatever Papa says. And I have to respect people like Bradley Finn. I'm struck by the difference between his natural, enthusiastic charisma and Pan's, whose charm has the feel of artifice, of calculation.

It's a shame the world must lose people like Bradley Finn, when the disease is released. Damn Tachyon and his race, for inflicting this disease on us.

"Umm," Bradley Finn said, twining a finger in his lab coat buttonhole. His hind leg stamped and his tail swished. "Sunday is May Day."

Clara removed her reading glasses and eyed him. What on earth was he so nervous about? Was he afraid to ask for the day off?

"I know," she said, mildly.

"Well," he went on, "there's going to be a street festival, here in Jokertown."

"So I've heard."

"So." He cleared his throat. "You want to go with me?"

Clara gaped, flattening her hands on the desk. Her heart did a tap dance in her rib cage and her mouth went dry. "I beg your pardon?"

He stared back at her for a long moment. Then he tossed his head with a look of irritation. "Never mind. It was a dumb idea."

He wheeled in a clatter of hooves and headed for the door.

"Doctor—Bradley."

His hand was already on the door knob. He didn't

turn to look at her. She tried to catch her breath, which had gotten quite short.

"I'd be glad to." It came out quickly, before a more prudent voice could intervene.

He turned then, and the raw, open look on his face made her heart skip another couple of beats.

"So," she said, sliding her reading glasses back on and clearing her own throat. "Where shall I meet you?"

Afterwards, she wondered what the hell she thought she was doing.

They weren't just wandering randomly. There was order to this wander. They'd hit the May Day block party, eat great hotdogs, then the day would culminate at Joan's and Perry's apartment. Joan would invite them in, and give them tea on her beautiful bone china, and Perry would come in and snuggle with Joan. . . .

And Clara will run screaming, his baser, bigoted self said. *You're such a boob.*

Was it naive to think that seeing a joker/nat couple would make a big difference with Clara? And what was he after? To get laid? A permanent relationship with a joker-phobic nat?

He had asked her to meet him at P.S. 101—"Freak U," as it was known to the greater New York school district. He didn't want Clara to have to sit through his "use condoms, avoid dope and booze, and be *proud*" lecture. In the years when jokers made good human interest stories and the people of the United States hadn't decided to pretend they didn't exist, *People* magazine had done a feature on him. They had called him the joker Jesse Jackson, a happy, successful and well adjusted joker, busy telling joker youth that they, too, could make it. To some degree Finn agreed with this sentiment, but he didn't for a moment discount his father's money, his white, upper-middle class background. They had played their part in his success. But, liberal cynicism aside, Finn did feel that he could and should offer a positive role model to young jokers.

So each year he went to Freak U, and made a speech,

and this year when he looked up into the bleachers, he had seen Clara sitting there, and he realized that she had come early to hear him speak, and his heart had squeezed down tight, and he realized this was going to have to be one hell of a speech.

He risked a quick glance at her long profile as they went walking down the street. "You didn't have to sit through all that."

"It was interesting."

Hardly ringing praise, and the tense tone of voice made him decide not to pursue it further.

"Hungry?" he asked.

"I could eat."

He grinned at her. "I'm gonna take you to my favorite Jokertown restaurant.

They turned down Hester, but Arnie's cart wasn't in view. Jube was, however, sitting in his paperstand reading *Premiere* and eating peanuts in the shell. A couple of large, mangy and vocal crows were pacing up and down on the pavement in front of the stand calling in raucous voices. Periodically the black, rubbery-skinned joker would toss a couple of peanuts to his peanut gallery.

"Hey, Jube, how's it going?" Finn called out.

"Fucked."

The bitterness incorporated in that single word rocked Finn back onto his hindquarters. "Hey," he demurred. "At least we're not headed off to joker concentration camps any longer."

"No," Jube agreed. "These Sharks probably have something worse in store for us."

Clara changed colors, ending up a dull shade of red. In a slightly brittle tone she said, "You don't really believe in all . . . that."

Jube turned his close-set, piggy eyes on Clara and smiled, revealing another two inches of tusk. "Dr. van Renssaeler, I've never lost money overestimating the cruelty and paranoia of the human animal."

Clara looked to Finn. Her turmoil was evident. Quietly Finn said, "I didn't believe, didn't *want* to believe initially. Now I have to." It was hard to force out the words.

"I knew Peggy Durand ... in Kenya. Along with Faneuil. He made me an unwitting murderer. I believe everything now."

Clara turned and took a few hesitant steps away. The crows hopped away from her, crying raucously. Jube picked up the magazine, and flapped it at Finn. The crows reacted with sharp cries, and a half-hearted attempt at flight. "We're depressing the lady. Scoot."

"Coming to the block party?" Finn asked as he dug out money for an evening edition.

"I'll be along later. I gotta find my smile again. It's hard to watch everyone trying to have such a good time."

"Jube, they may be working at it, but the result is the same in the end. People have a good time." Finn touched a forefinger to his forehead in a little salute, and he and Clara moved on.

"Sorry about that, he's not usually so morose. Jube's been the jokester of Jokertown for all the years I've been here."

Clara gave an ill defined gesture. "It's all right, you don't have to ... The ... Sharks—"

Finn laid a finger across her lips. "Shhhh. No sad, bad thoughts today."

Clara nodded, determinedly changed the subject. "Shouldn't you be at that party before now? You're one of the organizers."

"Ah, let Dutton hog the limelight. It's his dough that bought the beer. All I did was harass people until they agreed to donate food, and stereo sets, and their classic Beatles collections. Besides, if I arrive before they're partying hearty I'll have to act dignified."

Clara choked on a little laugh, and without thinking Finn tucked her arm beneath his. He tensed for the flinch. It didn't come. He risked a glance at her. Her eyes were focused strictly to the front.

An hour later he was replete with three of Arnie's kraut dogs. The music of the Lizard King was throbbing down Hester Street, and colliding with Uncle Albert's Genuine Polka Band, and the entire musical smorgasbord was topped off with the fine sounds of Los Blues Guys. The shrieks of children, laughter, the grumble of conversation formed a counterpoint to the music, and overhead a few stars struggled to peep through the light haze of Manhattan.

"You ever been in the Dime Museum?" Finn asked, trying to find a safe topic.

"No." Clara underlined the word with a head shake.

"Want to?"

She pointed to a sign that said SEE HIDEOUS JOKER BABIES. "I don't really have to, do I?" she asked in a small voice.

"Naw, that's just hype. It's mostly wax figures and dioramas, and a couple of Turtle's old shells."

Clara nodded, stood up from her perch on the curb, and brushed off the seat of her jeans. It was very cute—the gesture and the ass. Finn sent stern orders to his dick. It stayed in the sheath. With a lurch and a heave he was on his feet. The sharp motion sent mustard, kraut and dog washing forward, and he belched. Apologized quickly.

"Can you vomit?" Clara asked suddenly as Finn held the door for her.

"Gee, that's an attractive after dinner conversation."

A little defensively she said, "Well, I know horses can't, and that's one of the reasons colic is so fatal. I just . . . hoped that wasn't the case for you."

"No, I can promise you I won't die from a belly ache."

"So you *can* vomit."

"I love researchers, they never let up until they have an answer. Yes, I can vomit, but it's very unpleasant because I have two stomachs. One here." He touched the front of his Hawaiian shirt, and for the first time really acknowledged the small paunch which was beginning to develop. He sucked it in, and reminded himself that forty was approaching, and jogging was a positive thing. "And one here." He reached back, and patted his horse gut with the flat of a hand.

"How interesting. I'd love to study it."

"Yeah, I'm planning on donating my body to science.

Assuming the family doesn't get a better offer from a dog food company."

Clara laughed, and swept into the museum. Finn shelled out the five bucks for tickets, and caught up with Clara. She was standing transfixed in front of the diorama of the Four Aces. Finn looked from the cool wax features of the grandmother to the face of the granddaughter, with its tiny sheen of perspiration on her upper lip and across the high forehead. There wasn't a lot of resemblance.

"She looks like Aunt Fleur," Clara said softly.

"No, Aunt Fleur looks like *her*. Blythe was Fleur's mother."

Clara walked a little farther into the museum. Stopped in front of the wax figure of Tachyon. Glanced back at Blythe. Back to Tachyon in his finery.

"Why did she do it?"

"I think because she loved him," Finn answered.

"And him?" The tendons in Clara's neck were etched cords beneath the skin. So much tension.

"I think she was the only woman he really ever loved."

"Easy for him to say. She's dead and gone forty years." The anger etched the words like acid.

"I knew Tachyon," Finn said gently. "Admired him, liked him, respected him, sometimes wanted to kill him, but that's another story. I watched him woo women, make love to women, use women. What always struck me about it was the desperation with which he pursued. I think he was looking for another Blythe, but was smart enough to know that couldn't happen."

"With the result being?" Clara asked.

"That every relationship was doomed from the outset."

"That doesn't make him very attractive."

"It wasn't meant to. It was meant to make him understandable." Finn felt anger prickling along his nerve endings. He fought the emotion. This was supposed to be a good day. *Their* day. He didn't need fucking Tachyon turning up like Jeramiah, and fucking everything up. He found something which he hoped would put the argument to rest. "And hey, Cody loved him. Loves him. Maybe you ought to talk to her about what made him ... him."

Clara walked away a few feet, and stood staring into the black glass eyes of her ancestor.

Finn took a tentative step forward, and laid fingertips against her sleeve. "Clara, she's ancient history. He's ancient history. Wild cards spend too much time agonizing about the past. It's not our past. It sure as hell isn't our future. Let's forget about it."

"Future." She turned the word over in her mouth. Caressing it with her tongue, biting at it with her teeth. "Do any of us really have an unburdened future? You wild cards are right—the future is ordained by the past. We're programmed by the hates and needs and attitudes of our parents and grandparents—"

"It doesn't have to be that way. We're not totally reflexive beings. We can learn, change."

"And what have you learned, Bradley Finn, independent of your joker nature?"

"That *this*," he slapped at his flank. "Doesn't define me. That this," he touched his head, "And this," as he touched his heart, "Are more powerful than a fluke of genetics."

"And I believe that genetics are everything."

"What about souls?"

"I've never seen one." Clara's expression was as bleak as ash.

"I'm sorry for you," was all Finn could think to say.

"I just want to stop and say hello. We won't stay long. Joan used to volunteer at the clinic, but her health. ..." Finn had hoped he was keeping it casual. Clara's expression was telling him he hadn't. Before she could demur he reached up and rang the bell. "Joan's like this incredible East Coast blue blood. Makes this surfer kid feel real inferior. The Finn's got money, but no couth. Guess I shouldn't tell you that. You're one of those blue bloods. You'll think you're slumming."

"Why are you so nervous?" Clara asked.

"Nervous?" Finn echoed. Fortunately Perry opened

the door before Finn's mouth could shovel out an even deeper hole. "Who's nervous? Hi, Perry."

Perry was slim, gray haired, and old-fashioned. The chain and fob of a watch hung from one pocket, and he was wearing a jacket even on a Sunday in May. He smiled in welcome. Clara visibly relaxed, and Finn began to breathe again. Maybe this was all going to turn out okay. "Bradley! How good to see you. Come in. Come in."

"Missed you at the block party, figured I'd see you and Joan boogalooing on the sidewalk," Finn said as he and Clara entered the vestibule of the apartment.

Perry lost some of his ebullience, and glanced toward the door to his right. "Joan's been a little stay-at-home lately." He offered his hand to Clara. "Perry Simon."

"Clara van Renssaeler." Perry's eyes widened. Clara (damn her perspicacious little self) didn't miss it.

"I'll fetch Joan." The fact that he left them standing in the hall was proof he was rattled.

Finn gave Clara an encouraging smile. And felt it curdle as raised voices came wafting into the hall. Perry had closed the door to the study, so no words could be distinguished, but the soprano member of the duet was clearly distressed, and from the hissing noises, Joan's snake nature was also getting into the act. Finn wondered bleakly what he had done to so antagonize this former friend.

Perry returned. His face was flushed, whether from anger or embarrassment or a combination of both Finn couldn't tell, but he was the urbane host, and invited them into the living room. Clara settled onto the sofa like a nervous cat, and Finn dropped awkwardly to the floor, folding his legs beneath him. Perry darted into the kitchen, and started filling the tea tray.

"I'm sorry you're stuck with just me. Joan's a little . . . er, indisposed, but she wanted me to make you both welcome."

He returned with the tray. Poured, offered Clara a cup. She stared down at the intricate Wedgewood pattern, and went white to the lips. Finn reared up, bracing

himself on his front legs, alarmed because she looked so
faint. Clara gave a tiny head shake, smiled, and took a
sip of tea.

"You're at the clinic now, aren't you?" Perry asked.

"Yes."

"Like it?"

Clara drew in a sharp breath. "Normal adjectives don't
really apply at the clinic. . . ."

"How so?" Perry asked.

"I feel like a traveler, a visitor in your world." She
stopped herself. "But you're an outsider, too."

"To a degree. I can't fully understand the joker experience. But I love a woman who happens to be a joker,
and after awhile you don't see the strangeness, you just
see the person." He laughed. "And you know something?
They say the same thing about me."

Clara laughed, and the knot of tension which had settled into Finn's chest dissolved. It wasn't as good as fantasy had imagined it. It would have been better if Joan
had been coiled on the couch, forming a nest for her
lover, but it was pretty damn good.

Clara's gaze roamed about the living room. Evaluating
the paintings, knickknacks, furnishings. All of it subdued.
All of it tasteful. All of it very much Joan. Her eyes slid
across the mantle, across the antique French clock, froze
on a silver framed photo of Perry and Joan. Her teeth
chattered on the gilt edge of the cup, and she sloshed
tea into the saucer as she struggled to place the cup and
saucer back on the coffee table.

"Bradley, I'm . . ." She couldn't seem to think of the
word. Her gaze was once again fixed on the photo.

Finn heaved to his feet. He got a hand under her
elbow, and helped Clara to her feet. "Thanks for the
hospitality, Perry, but I think I've run the stuffin's out
of this girl. Give Joan my love."

The frenzied words had carried them back into the
vestibule. Clara suddenly let out a mewling little gasp.
Finn whirled, saw Joan whip back from the study door
in a frenzy of glitter and scales.

Clara clutched at her head, and doubled over at the

waist. Finn grabbed her wrist. The skin was icy, clammy to his touch. Finn had diagnosed enough migraines over the years to recognize this one.

"Bradley, take me home. I want to go home."

Perry had the panicked look of a civilian faced with a medical crisis. "How did you get here?"

"Walked," Finn said tersely.

"Want me to get the car? I don't think she can make it—"

"No!" Clara's refusal was loud and emphatic. She then whimpered in pain, and clutched at her temples.

"Sweetheart," Finn said, and really didn't realize until much later he had used the endearment. "Put your arms around my waist. Now, just slide up on my back. Hang on tight now. I'll take you home."

The apartment was gorgeous. Upper East Side. Awnings. Doormen. Poodles. They had taken the subway. She was in too much pain for him to get his van out of the garage. During the ride uptown Finn had understood how Lady Godiva's horse must have felt. He had also understood what a happy horse he must have been. The flesh of Clara's thighs was warm and moist against his coat. Then Finn got embarrassed, and shut down that particular line of thought.

They trod in stately dignity up Park Avenue. Up the broad steps to the door. Clara's hair was falling down her back, there were patches of sweat on Finn's flanks, and beneath his armpits. The security guard at his horsehoe-shaped desk was giving them the eye. He was going to refuse to let them on the elevator. Finn could sense it. He grinned at the guy, leaned in close. The guard reared back in his chair.

"She always loved horses as a kid," Finn confided.

The guard gulped, put the filthy spin on it that Finn had hoped and assumed he would. Waved them into the mirror-lined elevator. Up to the top floor. Fishing the key out of Clara's handbag. Into the apartment. And a sterile environment. Elegant, expensive furniture, but not much of it. A couple of fine watercolors on the walls.

There was a big computer on the dining room table. Some heavy medical tomes lying on the coffee table and sofa. Empty diet Coke cans. And virtually nothing of Clara.

He was not a stupid guy. Seeing this cold box explained a lot about Clara van Renssaeler. She denied warmth, emotion, herself. And he wondered, why? Since he didn't have an answer, Finn decided not to waste time looking for one. He carried Clara into her bedroom, tilted so he could slide her onto the bed, and with perfect, clinical, doctorly, *saintly*, reserve, undressed her.

She wore pretty underwear. He didn't touch the lace briefs, but he did unsnap the lace and wire bra. She had lush breasts. Freed, they tumbled off to either side. Ivory white with dark rose nipples. Sainthood was vanishing. Finn prayed for forbearance. God heard. Clara groaned, rolled to the side of the bed, and vomited the contents of her stomach onto the pale lemon-colored carpet.

After this reminder that lustful thoughts carry their own penalty, Finn got serious. He snagged a steel mixing bowl from the kitchen, ice and Evian from the fridge, a wash cloth from the bathroom, and settled down for the long haul. The nausea lasted for hours. Finn bathed Clara's face after every bout of the heaves, slipped ice slivers between her lips, kept cool cloths across her aching eyes, wrapped her in blankets when she became chilled, and wiped away the sweat when she became feverish.

After a few hours she took to sleeping with his hand clasped in hers. He folded his horse body down next to the bed, and rested his head on the pillow next to hers. It wasn't comfortable, but it sure was sweet, and finally, around four A.M. the spasms stopped, and Finn and Clara drifted off to sleep.

The annoying beep of his wristwatch alarm awakened him at five-thirty. Groaning, Finn got all four feet beneath him, and heaved to his feet. Clara didn't stir. Finn rubbed a hand over his face, trying to wipe away tiredness, and felt the harsh rasp of stubble against his palm. He canvassed the bathroom, and ·found a used razor on the side of the tub. Remembering the last time he'd tried using a lady's razor on his face made him wince, and he decided he'd just go to the clinic looking like a bum. He washed his face, propped his front feet onto the back of the toilet, dropped and aimed, and relieved himself without mishap. Squeezing some toothpaste onto his index finger he tried to rub the fuzz off his teeth. His mouth tasted like the bottom of a parrot's cage.

"And when did you sample the bottom of a parrot's cage, Dr. Finn?" he asked his image in the mirror in a bad Groucho imitation.

There was a faint noise from the bedroom, and Finn backed rapidly out of the small bathroom to check on his patient. Clara had shifted onto her side, her cheek pillowed on a hand. It was really sweet. Finn noticed her hair was matted. Crossing to the dressing table he picked up her hairbrush, and returning to the bed, smoothed out the worst of the snarls. He then leaned down like a bowing circus horse, and softly kissed her on the cheek. It was taking advantage. He hoped God and his conscience wouldn't mind too much, but she just looked so sweet.

"Sleep tight, sweetheart. I'll check in on you later."

He left for early morning rounds at the clinic.

The ringing phone woke her. She kept the damp cloth pressed to her forehead and wished the sound would stop. Eventually it did.

Bradley Finn's voice floated in from the other room. A warm feeling she didn't want to examine too closely filled her; she waited for him to appear at the bedroom door. But a beep told her he wasn't there. He was leaving a message on her phone.

She remembered now: he'd stayed and cared for her all night.

Her headache was gone, though she still felt groggy. She stretched, sat up and yawned, scratching her head.

The LEDs of her bedside clock announced that it was past ten. With a groan, she threw off the covers and stumbled into the bathroom to take a hot shower. She was supposed to have checked the latest test cultures last night. And now she had to get downtown to the clinic. She was late.

The steam and soap cleared her senses, and she remembered what had triggered the migraine. The night before, that visit to see that couple: Perry, and the joker woman who had hidden from them.

Perry had reacted so oddly to Clara's name. The china was the same as *Grandmaman* Moresworth's heirloom design. And she'd seen the face of the snake woman in the photo on the mantle, and then caught a glimpse of the joker herself.

It was the lamia from her dreams. And the creature wore the face of her mother, who had died when Clara was five.

Only she hadn't died. At that instant in the hallway as they were leaving, the memory had surfaced from where she'd buried it when she was five.

Maman had turned into a snake. A joker. And then she'd gone away.

Clara recalled *Papa* holding her, Clara, and she was hitting him, screaming, trying to run after her transformed mother, who slithered away down the hall.

That's not your Maman. Maman *is dead.* Maman *is dead.*

He'd lied to her. Her mother had been alive all these years. A joker, living not five miles from her. All these years, he—and she, *Maman*—had conspired to keep the truth from her.

And who else knew? *Papa*'s long-time lover Chloe must know. And Pan? Her grandparents Moresworth? How many others were in on this lie?

She could understand why *Papa* would do such a thing. He hated the wild card, and a joker wife would have ruined his ambitions. He'd want to keep a joker wife as far from his life—and Clara's—as possible. But *Maman* . . . how could she have agreed to abandon her own child? To pretend she was dead, to hide—not to give her own child the knowledge of what had happened, and the right to make her own peace with it?

She pressed her forehead against the cool tiles. A tear fell. Another. The tears mingled with the heated water from the shower, drenching Clara in grief. She backed into a corner of the shower and clutched her sponge. Water sluiced over her, and sobs ripped their way out of her chest, and the water carried them away.

The grief left her exhausted. She wrapped herself in her huge terry cloth robe and called in sick to the clinic. Ignoring a number of other phone calls, including one from Pan, she rummaged through boxes she had in storage. She found one of her old dolls—the china doll her mother had given her—and her scrapbook, which held memorabilia from her early childhood: photographs of her and her parents when they were young, pressed leaves and flowers, a crayon drawing.

These, and the framed picture of her mother from before Clara was born, she took into the living room, where she curled up on the sofa with some tea, poached eggs, and whole wheat toast. The next few hours she spent reminiscing, touching old memories, crying some more. Then she slept for a while.

Clara didn't remember their address—and she didn't want to have to explain to Bradley—but she remembered what block the apartment was on, and wandered around till she saw a doorway she recognized.

"I'd like to speak to Joan van Renssaeler," she said into the intercom, when an unrecognizable voice answered. Her voice was steady and calm. She'd had a lifetime to learn to mask her feelings.

Silence greeted her. Her heart was beating so hard it filled her ears with a great roaring. She rang the bell again.

Perry came out to the front door. He opened it only a crack, blocking it with his body. "I'm sorry, I wish I could help you, but there's been some mistake."

But his eyes held sadness and knowledge.

She shook her head. "No. There's no mistake. I'm Clara van Renssaeler and I want to see my mother."

His pupils dilated. With a sigh and a nod, he let her in. Clara's heart felt packed in ice. She followed him down the hall to the apartment.

He made her wait outside. She heard voices rising and falling, as with the previous night, and then a long silence.

I'll stay here till you admit me, she thought. I won't go away. She folded her arms and leaned on the wall by the door.

Then the door opened a crack, and a face with scales like jewels appeared.

That was her mother's face; those were her mother's eyes.

All the way down from the upper East Side, in the taxi, she'd rehearsed what she would say. Rejection or denial was possible. She was prepared—armed with facts, clear memories, reasons.

But the suave, controlled professional wasn't with her; only the five-year-old child.

"*Maman*?" she said.

The joker woman covered her mouth with a gasp. "Oh, Clara. Can you ever forgive me?"

Inside the too-warm apartment, Joan showed Clara her own scrapbook—a more worn version of Clara's—and other memorabilia: photographs, figurines, trinkets. Many, many pictures of Clara as a little girl, in frilly dresses and ribbons. Some shots of her were more recent—a photo or two from her girlhood that Brandon must have given her; several candid shots: two from her years at Rutgers, one at a park a few years ago with a man she'd been dating. And she didn't remember them being taken.

Meanwhile, Joan talked. And Clara wandered around behind her, nodding, dabbing at the sweat that gathered on her upper lip, looking at this snake-woman who had—inconceivably—birthed and raised her, at all the familiar-strange objects. She felt as if her feet and hands were a mile away. Joan's voice flowed over her like water: she didn't hear a word of it.

Then Perry entered with a silver tray loaded with three or four kinds of tea, milk, lemon wedges, finger sandwiches, currant scones, jam and clotted cream. He set the tray on the coffee table with a sharp glance at Joan and Clara, and then left, closing the door. Clara felt relief, and gratitude. Sensitive man. She unbuttoned the top two buttons on her blouse and rolled up her sleeves.

Joan fussed over the tea in a manner so familiar and soothing to Clara that it alarmed her. Clara sat with her hands in her lap. She took the cup Joan pressed on her. Joan folded herself up onto the couch next to her, coil by coil, and reached for her own cup.

How beautiful she is, Clara thought, watching light reflect off her scales as she sipped her Earl Grey. What an exotic creature. Colors shifted along her coils, her torso and arms and breasts, her face. Like moonlight caught in a waterfall. A cameo pendent, her only garment, dangled between her scaled breasts.

Joker. What a wrong-headed name.

"Why did you leave me?"

The question came out without her even knowing she was thinking it.

Joan gave her a look of surprise and she realized she'd interrupted her in mid-sentence. With a sigh, Joan set her teacup down. She started to reply, but Clara couldn't hold the words in any longer. She sprang to her feet and the words tumbled out, fully formed.

"I thought you were dead, all these years, and you knew the whole time. Five miles away. Five miles! And never once did you even *try* to reach me."

Joan raised a hand. Her scales had gone a muddy gray, a dirty white. "Darling, I—"

Clara spoke over her. "Why, *why* didn't you stay? Or at least contact me? Let me know you were alive?" She grabbed a framed, recent picture of herself—it hadn't been on the mantle the night before—and shook it at Joan. "How dare you have pictures and knowledge of me, without my knowing of you? It's a cheat! Don't you know that it *killed* me when you left?"

She hurled the picture to the floor and ground her

boot heel into the glass, glaring at Joan. Then she bent
her face into her palms and cried.

Hands landed on her shoulders; she opened her eyes.
Her mother's altered face was only inches from hers;
those cat-green eyes Clara remembered studied her; all
the color had drained from her scales; they'd gone white
and clear as gypsum sand.

"How I've hurt you." Joan's voice was soft. "I can
never undo the harm I did, can I? Never give you back
those lost years."

"No," Clara said. She wiped at her eyes. "No, you
can't."

Joan enfolded her in a careful hug that included a
half-loop of snake flesh—and to her shock Clara didn't
feel the desire to recoil. "Dear Clara. You deserved so
much better than you got."

Can I forgive so easily? For all that pain?

No, she thought. I can't. She pulled back. Joan
released her and handed her a lace kerchief, with the
monogram *JvR*. She entreated Clara to sit.

"It's understandable that you should hold a lot of anger
toward me. You may never be able to forgive me. I simply want you to understand that my leaving had nothing
to do with you. It was me. All me."

Clara's voice was flat. "Does it matter any more?"

"Would you be here if it didn't?"

Clara stared at her and said nothing. Joan sighed and
took a sip of tea. Clara caught a glimpse of the fangs,
the altered tongue. More than anything else, that made
her realize just how physically altered her mother was.
How much of the woman she'd been remained?

"I wasn't a nice person, you know. Not at all. I spread
nasty rumors about my friends behind their backs; I
made a specialty of subtly mocking Brandon, tearing
down his self-esteem. What people wore was more
important to me than what was in their minds or hearts.
All I cared about was money and social position. I was
shallow, bigoted, and predatory." She gave Clara an owl-
ish look that reminded Clara of herself. " The only thing

390 Laura J. Mixon & Melinda M. Snodgrass

good about me was you. You were the only one in my life who mattered to me more than myself.

"When *this* happened to me"—she gestured at herself, at the loose coils of snake flesh draped all over the couch—"it was as if now the outside matched the inside. This change made me realize just how much of a predator I was." She hesitated. "I don't know how much you remember of what happened after I changed."

"Enough." Very little, in fact; Clara only remembered the scene in the hallway.

"Do you remember what happened to Frou Frou?"

"Frou Frou?"

"We had a Lhasa apso named Frou Frou. I'd had him since I was a girl. You adored him. He attacked me, that morning after the change, and I bit him. He died of the venom. Later, I—I ate him."

Clara grimaced. "You ate him?"

"I was starving from the change. And, well, my body is truly more a snake's than a human's now, dear. I eat live or freshly killed whole animals."

Clara frowned. "I remember—something, I think."

Joan nodded. "You didn't see me eat him, but you saw me bite him. And you were quite the little warrior; you gave me a punch or two in the nose."

"I did?" Clara tried to picture it—a tiny girl pitting herself against this huge snake creature. It didn't seem likely.

"Mmmm. And, Clara," tears filled the woman's eyes, "I came far too close to striking out at you as I had Frou Frou. It terrified me. To harm you, or through neglect let you come to harm, was my single worst nightmare."

"Are you trying to say you left to *protect* me?"

Joan winced at Clara's tone. "I know I failed you. You can't know how many times I've wished I had made a different choice. But you see, I'd had no experience with courage or self-restraint. And I didn't know then what I'd become. I didn't trust myself not to harm you. So—" she spread her arms in a helpless gesture. "I left Brandon to care for you. Much as we despised each other, I knew

he adored you, and would take care of you. But God,
how I've wished I had made another choice."

It was Joan's turn to break down and cry. Clara
extended her kerchief and Joan took it.

After a long moment, in which they both sat without
speaking or looking at each other, Clara said, " This is
an awful lot to absorb."

Joan laughed shakily, dabbing at her eyes. "Oh, my
dear, it most certainly is."

Clara stood and picked up her purse. She hesitated,
feeling awkward. "I appreciate your agreeing to see me."

Joan gave her a smile of great sadness. "I hope to see
you again. You are always welcome here. Always."

" Thank you."

"And, Clara—I want you to know that I love you. I'm
very proud of the woman you've become."

Clara gave her a little, bleak smile. "But you don't
know what I've become."

The flat nasal *blat* of an endlessly ringing phone. Five
rings, and the answering machine finally cut in again.
"Hello, you've reached 993-2323, leave a message." No
warmth, quick, level, professional. Like the first impression of Clara. Finn knew the nuances of the voice now.
How her eyes could warm, smile and sparkle. The
annoying bleat of the message signal.

"Hi, it's me. Either you're feeling better and you're
not home, or you've died. You better not have died. I'll
bring Chinese—no MSG—around six. Okay? If it's not
okay, call. Otherwise, I'm descending."

Finn hung up the phone. Felt giddy. Felt silly. Felt
sixteen again. *You're weird*, he thought, *most people don't
find vomit a turn on.* But it wasn't that. It was the fact
she had trusted him. Allowed him to see her at her most
vulnerable. Clung to him when sickness washed over her.
Then the cynical, armored side marched in, and wondered if he was overreacting to the night. Had he really
known it was him caring for her? If she hadn't been
quite so sick she would probably have preferred a different nurse. One of her own kind.

There was a knock. "Come in," Finn bellowed.

Cody entered, settled on the sofa, lit a cigarette. "You look like I feel."

"Well, you may be drawing an erroneous conclusion. 'Cause while I may look like shit, I feet great."

"Happy mind. Tired body."

"Yeah," Finn agreed.

"I didn't see you at the block party," Cody said.

"What time did you arrive?"

"Chris and I wandered over around seven."

"Clara and I had moved along by then."

Cody cocked an eyebrow at him. "And how 'far along' did you move?"

Finn felt himself blush. "Well, not that damn far. She got a headache."

Cody gave him one of her ironic looks, and he groaned with embarrassment. "Not that kind of a headache. I mean serious migraine. I took her home. I stayed."

"The things you men will do to get laid."

Finn swallowed his anger. It bothered him to have Cody reducing what he felt to mere sex. But his tone was light when he said, "Hey, in my case that's a lot. It don't happen enough for me to get blasé."

Cody stood, stretched, closed her eyes briefly. "Be careful, Bradley. I'm fond of you."

"Cody, what's wrong?"

She kept her back to him. Waved a hand helplessly in the air. "My kid wants to go to school at Harvard. Wants me to get a 'real' job. Something that won't embarrass him, hurt his chances to get into one of these Ivy League shit holes. When did my kid grow up and become a bigot?"

Finn came around behind her. Laid a hand on her shoulder. "He'll outgrow it. We always do."

"Not when the whole world makes it acceptable, preferable to tolerance." She turned back to face him. "So, when I see you falling for a nat, I worry."

"Thanks, Cody, but I'm not expecting anything."

She smiled sadly, brushed his cheek with the back of her hand. "Yes you are, that's why I love you. You never stop wanting and hoping and believing." She leaned in, kissed him softly on the lips, and left.

Left Finn confused and breathless and more than a little sad.

She got home at five twenty. Bradley had left another message on the machine, threatening to show up with Chinese food. But there was still enough time to call and tell him not to come. If she called right now. She orbited the phone, picked it up, put it back down.

She picked up her ancient, broken china doll, dropped onto the couch, tucked a leg under herself, and cradled it in her hands. The eyes opened and closed, click, click, as she rocked it back and forth. Bradley's face lingered in her mind like a touch.

He hardly knew her. She'd taken the position he'd so coveted—and then been barely this side of unpleasant with him for weeks. And yet, all last night, he'd stayed with her. Wiped her brow, cleaned up her messes, helped her to the restroom, held her hand. He'd been a perfect gentleman. And he hadn't abandoned her to her pain.

And he was a true philanthropist. He used his own power to buoy up those around him, not to trample them underfoot. She'd watched him with the patients and staff at the clinic: a word or look from him smoothed troubles like balm. And she'd seen the looks on those teenagers' faces when he'd spoken at the high school. He'd given them hope. At the spring festival, people's spirits were lifted by the celebration he'd organized, and by his presence.

And his face was such a transmitter of his moods—no secretiveness, no deception. If it was on his mind, it was on his face. With all the deceptions she was unearthing in her life, that seemed quite a comely characteristic.

Bradley Latour Finn. Wild card victim. No—wild card survivor. He'd made a lie of all her principles . . . because those lofty principles had been built on a huge, stinking pile of prejudices and fears.

Bradley Latour Finn. Clara had been involved with

any number of men, and she knew a good one when she found him.

She was falling in love with him. And that terrified her.

She was waiting when he arrived with a bag of Chinese food. The General Tso's chicken had started to leak, filling the room with its pungent scent, and making his palm sticky as he tried to keep the bottom from collapsing out of the sack.

Before he could maneuver for the kitchen, Clara shyly took his hand, and pressed it (sauce and all) against her cheek. She then kissed him on the cheek. Quickly, gently on the lips, then hid her face against his shoulder. General Tso's chicken slid with a plop onto the floor.

She mumbled something against his neck. Her voice was thick with unshed tears.

"Sweetie, what is it? What's happened?"

"My mother. My mother's alive."

Finn felt stupid, like a kid involved in a game where he didn't know the rules. He hadn't known her mother was dead. Or supposed to be dead.

"Hey, that's, that's swell."

"Papa told me she died. But I kept *remembering*, and then *you* gave her back to me."

Taking her gently by the shoulders he pushed her back until he could stare into her eyes. "Clara, I'll gladly take credit for anything, deserved or not, but can I know what the hell I'm supposed to have done?"

"Joan is my mother."

Joy exploded in his chest. He felt like he'd just chugged an Irish whiskey straight. "Joan!? She's a joker!"

"Yes, yes." She wiped the tears out of her eyes with trembling fingertips. "Why did you take me there?"

Embarrassment made him hesitate. She was too quick. She read it. "What?"

Finn took a nervous turn around the living room. "I wanted you to see her and Perry. To see a joker/nat couple. Loving each other."

Her silence was sudden and complete. He spun

around awkwardly, apologies tumbling from his lips. "I'm sorry, I shouldn't have made assumptions. I just . . ."

The assault was totally unexpected. Her fingers pressed into his cheeks as she grabbed his face, and kissed him hard. It took him by surprise, but Mama Finn hadn't raised no stupid children, and Finn took advantage of the miracle being offered to him. He clasped her close, opened his mouth, and her tongue shot between his teeth. They fenced lightly tongue to tongue, then he nipped softly at her lips as tears seeped from the corners of her eyes and ran down her cheeks.

"Am I making you unhappy?" Finn murmured against her mouth.

"No."

"I wish you ladies would provide us poor dumb males with a score card," he complained, trying to keep it light while his body felt like one large sexual lightning rod. "I can never tell if they're tears of joy, sorrow, or anger."

"Sometimes it's hard for us to tell," Clara said softly. "Especially when we haven't been allowed the luxury of emotion."

He pulled her head against his shoulder, stroked her hair. Her hand worked its way beneath the elastic base of his shirt, tickled his waist. Control departed. Finn let out a groan, and his penis dropped, sliding from its protective sheath.

"Oh, my," Clara said.

"I'm sorry," Finn gasped, and tried to pull it back. It wasn't working real well. The member was well and properly engorged, and it seemed to weigh twenty or thirty pounds.

"I treated you horribly," Clara said softly. "How can you want me?"

"Because you were scared. It took me awhile to understand that. I've watched you push past it. Taking an interest in me, the clinic, Jokertown. I haven't felt like you've been seeing *this*." He swept a hand back along his horse body. "For weeks. And now here I am sort of waving it in your face," he added miserably.

"Make love to me, Bradley."

It was that simple. And he felt himself freezing up. It wasn't all that easy to get a woman to this point. Then he had to get technical, and most of them went away. The few who went on usually did it because they were sensation junkies, thrill seekers. They weren't doing it for him, for the pleasure of his companionship.

"What's wrong?" The old hurt and vulnerability were back in her eyes. "I don't think I've misread the signals." A timid smile. "You do seem glad to see me."

It hadn't happened in years, but Finn felt himself blushing. "I am . . . I do . . . I want to make love with you very much, but it's kind of a major. . . . undertaking. . . . I don't want to disgust you—"

She laid a hand across his mouth. Slipped it aside, and muted the words with her mouth. Her tongue was back in his mouth, and there was nothing demure about the tonsil inspection. Eventually she stopped, stepped back and said, "I don't scare easily. Tell me what we have to do."

"We've got two locations, and three positions." His eyes flicked nervously over to the dining room table. "You on a high table. I brace my front feet on the table, and . . ." He made a vague gesture.

"Penetration," said Clara, teasing a little.

"Yes."

"Isn't that painful for you?"

"My hindquarters and back legs do tend to cramp."

"Let's try something more comfortable," Clara said.

"Okay, in that case we pull the mattress off the bed— so I won't break it—and you spoon in against me—"

She took his hand, and led him to the bedroom. It was a tight fit, but they managed to get the mattress situated between the foot of the bed and the dresser. On the dresser was a small Indian seed pot with a stick of half-burned incense in it, a scrap book, and a picture of a lovely young blond woman in a silver frame. Finn could see echoes of Clara's face in the photo, and a vestige of Joan's lovely, kind face in that spoiled and imperious visage.

Clara pulled him back from his reverie with an

imperious tug on his hair. Finn returned his attention to the daughter, and with a final thanks to the mother, he unbuttoned Clara's blouse, and pushed it off her shoulders. A quick flick, and the bra broke loose. Her breasts came spilling out. This time it was permitted for Finn to catch them in his hands, kiss each nipple. Clara sucked in a sharp little breath.

Hurried, clumsy fingers (it was probably a good thing she hadn't been a surgeon), and his shirt was unbuttoned, and tossed aside. She peered down his back, laughed delightedly.

"You've got a mane. How nice, I've got something to hang onto." She tangled her fingers in his curly hair, which followed the line of his spine, and tugged.

He got her pants open, and steadied her while she stepped out of them. Running a hand down her chest, he snagged her panties and swept them away. Awkwardly he dropped down onto the mattress, held out a hand to her. There was that tenth of a second of absolute terror when she glanced at his turgid penis. Her eyes widened, and Finn waited for her to say, "Nahhh," but it didn't happen, instead she knelt beside him.

"You have to do most of the moving," he whispered. "I'm not real flexible, and it's hard to heave this body around."

She smiled down at him, pushed his hair back off his forehead. "Do you know how attractive that sounds? Women never have a man at their mercy." Her voice was husky, warm.

Finn couldn't stand it, he heaved up, and locked his mouth on hers. He couldn't support it for long, but as he fell back she came with him, their breath mingling, tongues fencing. Her legs tangled in his four legs. Eventually they got the various limbs sorted out, and Finn turned her gently until her buttocks were tucked against his chest. Lifting her dark hair, he leaned in, and touched his lips to the nape of her neck.

"Clara, I . . . I love you."

It was an odd little sound. At first he thought she was trying to say something. Then he realized she was crying.

Frightened, he tried to pull back from her. She rolled over abruptly, and clutched at his shoulders.

"No, don't leave me." Tears blurred the words. "He took my mother from me. I'm not going to let anything take you from me." She rolled over, offered her buttocks.

Finn stroked down the line of her back, allowed his fingers to play in her moist, tangled mons. She gave a little cry of pleasure, and he slid his fingers into her. She rode him, and he brought her to a manual orgasm. The room was becoming musky with the scents of sweat and sex, and wet horse coat. Finn was trying to be patient, but it had been a while, and his penis was so turgid and erect that he felt like a touch would split it like an over-filled sausage.

Then Clara rolled over, and touched him. The shudder shook him from hindquarters to human torso, and yanked a groan from him. She weighed his member in the palm of her hand. Looked up with alarmed and dubious gray eyes.

"It's awfully . . . *big.*"

"I'm careful. I don't penetrate all the way," he gasped. She continued to stare at him. "Are you going to back out? If you're going to back out, could you tell me now? Could you maybe help me . . . ease the pressure before you back completely out." He was babbling.

She laid a hand across his mouth, transferred her mouth to the task of muzzling him. A few moments later she rolled over and slid down until her hair was tickling his belly button. Reaching behind her she took his penis, and guided it carefully between her legs.

Clara van Renssaeler, Journal Entry, 2 May 94
Just left Bradley sleeping at my place and came in to check my latest tissue cultures. The new virus obliterated the wild card cultures and left the uninfected cultures unharmed.

Batch 94-04-28-24LQ, necrovirus Takis II, is what I've been looking for. The Black Trump. The real thing. Unstoppable and utterly deadly. And I wish to God I'd never conceived of such a thing.

*Discovering my love for Bradley, and finding Maman
again, have opened my eyes. I've been so wrong. The
wild card is a horrible disease, yes. But its victims have
the right to make whatever they can of their lives. It's
not right for me to play God. I've been such an idiot.
How could I have been so blind?*

Chin in hand, she stared at the journal entry on her
computer screen for a long, long time. Then she closed
the file, leafed again through her write-up of the Black
Trump II test results, freshly printed, which lay on the
desk beside the computer, and brushed her hair back
with a sigh. She thought of the flasks of virus in the lab
refrigerator just down the hall, thought of her lamia
mother, thought of her centaur lover Bradley sprawled
across her mattress with his arm flung over his face.
Thought of what would happen if even a drop of this
stuff were to touch them.

Twelve years' work, she thought. Forty percent of my
life.

She exited the security software, and used the shred-
der function to destroy all her files on the virus. There
were few; she had been careful to avoid recording any
significant amount of technical detail on her research,
despite the expensive security system on her PC. After
a hesitation, she also shredded her personal journal.

Then she suited up in protective clothing, gathered
her notes, and went into the clean room. She got out all
fifteen flasks of Black Trump virus, both strains. The
microwave could hold ten flasks at a time, and fifteen
minutes at the highest setting would be more than long
enough. She got the first batch started, used a flint on
the Bunsen burner, and began crisping the analytical
results and notes. She dumped the ashes into the hazard-
ous medical waste bin.

A half hour later she was done. It amazed her, the
ease and dispatch with which she could wipe out a life's
work.

Afterward, she headed to the clinic. It was still early,

just after seven. The graveyard staff were still on duty and the halls quiet.

She had finished her resignation letter and was packing up her things when the phone rang.

"Dr. van Renssaeler. This is General MacArthur Johnson. I'm calling on Pan's behalf."

"Excellent. I'm glad you called; I wanted to give Uncle Pan an update. I'm just wrapping up here."

"Oh?"

"Mmmm. I'm afraid this gamble just hasn't paid off. I've decided to stop wasting my time at the Jokertown Clinic."

"On the contrary," he said. "We're all well aware of how successful your stay has been."

Clara closed her eyes, apprehensive. Calm, PC. Calm. "You have me confused."

"You've relied rather too heavily on the encryption software I had installed on your office computer, I'm afraid. Every time you saved your journal an invisible copy was made for me. I've been reporting your progress to Pan all along."

Clara gripped the desk's edge. Anger warred with terror, and, for a moment, won. "You've been spying on me, after all my years of devotion, all my hard work? That certainly tells me what kind of man you are."

"It's lucky I did." He paused. "This doesn't have to get ugly. All we want is for you to recreate your latest virus. What was it, batch 94-04-28-24LQ? *Necrovirus Takis II.* The Black Trump."

Clara pressed fingers to her lips. When she finally spoke, her words were calm. "I'm afraid I can't help you there. You'll have to get yourself another virologist."

"It's too late for that."

"No, I'd say it was just in the nick of time."

Another silence ensued. "I'm sorry you feel that way. I'll have to take other measures, then."

And he disconnected.

She dialed her father's home phone and got the answering machine. "*Papa.* It's urgent I speak to you right away. Pan and I have had a falling-out, and it's serious. I won't be reachable by phone, so I'll keep trying to reach you."

Then she tried his office. He was out and was unreachable.

"Tell him to check his messages at home," she told his secretary. "It's urgent."

And Bradley. If Johnson read her journal entry, he'd know Bradley was still at her place. He was in danger.

Clara dialed her phone number. But last night, for privacy, she'd set the answering machine to pick up right away, and had turned the volume all the way down.

Maybe, maybe he'd gotten up by now and by some fluke had turned the volume back up.

"Bradley, can you hear me? Pick up. Please pick up." Nothing. *"Shit."*

The super. He could take a message to Bradley. She called information, got his number, dialed it. No answer.

Clara bit her thumbnail, narrowed her eyes, and thought. She dialed 9-1-1.

"Operator, this is Clara van Renssaeler at 48 East 79th Street, apartment 6G. I have a medical emergency. A man has had a heart attack in my apartment. Send an ambulance right away."

She slammed the phone into the hook, scrawled a note to Bradley, to leave with the receptionist, that chicken woman. Then she grabbed her purse and ran.

She ran all the way to the City Hall stop and shoved her way onto a packed Lexington Avenue express train. They had several minutes' lead on her, maybe more. But Johnson's headquarters were located in Brooklyn, and at this hour all the streets, tunnels, and bridges would be congested with traffic. The subways would be faster. With luck, she'd beat them.

He woke suddenly and unpleasantly to the sound of a man's voice saying,

"Oh, God, how disgusting. She *fucked* him."

During his sleep Finn had managed to get himself cast against the bedroom wall. The only way up was to heave onto his back, and roll over on his other side. At times like this he was painfully aware of every ounce of his four hundred plus pounds. He heaved, and began the roll, and was stung by something hitting his belly. He managed to crane his human torso up enough to see the dart sticking up from his horse gut. Then the faces of the four men staring down at him got very fuzzy, and he slipped away into darkness. As unconsciousness took him he realized that he hadn't been imagining it. Clara wasn't with him.

The ambulance sat at the entrance to her building, lights flashing. Relief weakened Clara's legs. She yanked the outer door open, fumbled her keys out of her purse to open the inner door, and limped over to the elevators, half doubled over with a stitch in her side.

At that moment the doorman led four paramedics from the freight elevator. Bradley was laid out on a stretcher—head, limbs, and horse's buttocks hanging off all over. They'd already started an IV and oxygen.

Her heart leapt. Too late. She was too late. They'd gotten to him. She ignored the doorman's disgusted stare.

"Oh God—Bradley! What's going on?"

"We received a call," the head paramedic said. "It appears to be a poisoning."

She lifted Bradley's eyelids; the pupils responded to light and were equal in size, but were massively dilated. Breathing shallow and rapid, pulse weak.

They loaded Bradley in the back of the van, and she hovered over him, gave his hair and mane a worried stroke.

"Where are you taking him?"

"Lenox Hill. It's the closet."

"I'll meet you there," she told them, and ran for the garage to get her car.

The ambulance was pulling away, sirens screaming, when she reached street level. A string of cabs and passenger cars cut her off, not letting her creep in behind the ambulance. She swore and slapped the steering wheel—bullied her way into traffic as a second set of flashing lights appeared in the rear view mirror. Another ambulance pulled up to the curb at her apartment building and two paramedics got out.

A horrible suspicion began to form. Why did the other ambulance have *four* paramedics? She hadn't told them he was a four-hundred-pound joker. And why take him to Lenox Hill, which had a no-wild cards policy?

She abandoned her car in the middle of the street, ignoring the curses and horns of the drivers she'd trapped on the narrow, one-way street, and raced over to the paramedics getting out of the new ambulance.

"Whom are you here for?"

"We're here to pick up a heart attack victim," the woman said. "Apartment 6G."

The apartment showed no evidence of a break-in or struggle. She tried her father again. He was still out. She left a message for him to call her at home right away.

The phone rang. An international call. Pan.

His voice was saturated with disgust. "They tell me you *slept* with him. How could you have sunk so far? I'm sick over this. What would your father say?"

Her temper flared. "Frankly, it's none of your goddamned business what he'd say."

"I regret having to resort to this, but you leave me no choice. I've instructed Johnson to hold him at the UN lab. And your mother. You have half an hour to get there, or they die. If you tell your father, or anyone, what's happening, they die."

My mother? My mother, too?

"Half an hour? That's absurd! What if I get stuck in traffic? What if the train breaks down?"

"You're an intelligent woman. I'm sure you'll think of something."

She made them let her see them. Johnson had them locked up in one of the empty equipment storage rooms in the basement. Bradley lay in the corner on the concrete floor. Joan had made a cushion of her coils to lay his head on, and was stroking his temples. At first Clara missed her; her colors had faded to match the soft grays and greens that surrounded her till she was virtually invisible. The guard locked the door behind Clara, and Joan gradually appeared, turning an agitated blue, yellow, and orange pattern.

"*Maman.*" Clara swallowed a sob and came over to kneel beside Bradley. "I'm so sorry. Is he all right?"

"His vital signs are better. I think he's improving."

Clara checked him. Pulse stronger and more regular, breathing normal, pupils shrinking. She sat down cross-legged and lowered her face into her hands.

"Thank God. He'll be all right."

"Darling, what is going on? Who are these people?"

Clara heard a noise in the shadows, in a dark corner beyond the boiler.

"Who's there?"

It took her eyes a moment to adjust, but soon she saw the figure: a rather disgusting-looking, small, insectoid joker with a carapace the color of baby excrement. He—or she—stood, and Clara saw the joker was wearing some sort of collar, attached to about eight feet of high-visibility orange nylon rope, tied to a PVC pipe overhead. This gave the joker a range of about four feet. Both pairs of "hands" were also bound.

George Battle had been turned into a little yellow insect; she'd heard her father talking about it. And then he'd switched bodies with—

"Gregg Hartmann," she said.

Joan gasped. "Oh my! He was telling the truth!"

The insect nodded, a gesture at once comical and grave. "Dr. van Renssaeler," he piped. "And, I presume, Mrs. van Renssaeler."

"*Maman*—" Clara gestured, and Joan slithered after her. The last thing she wanted was for Gregg Hartmann to overhear what she had to say to her mother. He slumped back into the shadows.

"Clara, darling," Joan demanded, in a whisper, "what *is* going on here?"

Clara stared at her mother. She wanted to blame Joan. *If only you'd been there when I needed you—if you'd*

shown me what wild cards really *are. Instead you aban-doned me to the lies and bigotry of Papa and Uncle Pan.*
But that was absurd. Plenty of people lost their parents, lost loved ones to the wild card every day, without resorting to what Clara had.

So, keeping her voice low and making sure Hartmann couldn't hear, she told Joan everything. Without embel-lishment, without excuses. Joan listened calmly, merely nodding and asking occasionally for clarification.

"So they plan to use me and Bradley to force you to remake the virus."

"Exactly. *Maman*—" Clara's voice broke. "I just found you again. And I've just found the man I want to spend the rest of my life with. I can't let them hurt you. I don't know what to do."

Tears stood in Joan's eyes. She held out her arms. Clara laid her head on her mother's breast, and Joan held her close, stroked her hair.

"You must refuse," she said. "There is no alternative."

There has to be, Clara thought. There *has* to be.

"I'll be happy to marry her, sir." Finn came awake with the ridiculous words on his lips.

"You have my permission," came a familiar voice.

Finn forced open his gummy eyelids, and stared into Joan's delicately scaled face. She was laid out full length on the tile floor, so they were almost nose to nose.

Her tone had been light, but now that he could see her, Finn could see fear like a shadow in her strange eyes.

"Joan, where the fuck are we?"

"In a nest of Card Sharks. I guess Senator Hartmann was to be believed."

There was a flash of movement, and an incredibly silly looking joker scuttled into view, tied to a pipe. Finn felt a momentary flash of chagrin for being a bigot, but it *was* silly looking. Then in a piping, breathless, cartoon voice it announced:

"I'm Senator Hartmann."

Finn stopped feeling guilty—the guy was clearly a bozo.

"Could you, like, butt out? I'm trying to have a serious conversation here," Finn said. The joker puffed up, bounced up and down on his several legs.

"I tell you I'm Hartmann. I was jumped into this body."

Agitated, Finn tried to heave to his feet, discovered his back leg had gone to sleep, and that the tile was very slick, and went down in a welter of legs, hooves and flailing arms. The stupid looking joker raced backwards to avoid being hit.

"Shit." Joan slithered over, and massaged his leg until the bite of pins and needles signaled its return to life. He tried again, more carefully, and this time got to his feet.

"I *am* Hartmann," the joker insisted from across the room.

"Clara said he's telling the truth," Joan told him.

"Thank God," the joker senator piped, and sank down onto the floor as if overcome.

Finn turned back to face (he hoped) his future mother-in-law. "Joan, not to sound unduly humble, or totally stupid, but why would Card Sharks want to kidnap us? I know why they'd want Hartmann, but us?"

"Because of Clara," she answered softly.

Finn stared into her unblinking eyes. Forced his jaw closed so he didn't look stupid. "Joan, I'm gonna say this once, so pay close attention . . . Huh?"

"Bradley, what do you," she hesitated. "Feel for my daughter?"

"I love your daughter. I'm going to marry your daughter. Remember, you gave us your blessing."

"Remember that, Bradley, when you talk to her." And she slithered away to a far corner of the room, and coiled.

"Goddamn it. You're being inscrutable. What are you talking about?"

"You need to hear it from Clara."

Frustrated, Finn turned to Hartmann. "Do you know what she's talking about?"

The senator sat up on his hindquarters, and shrugged with his front limbs. "I'm new here too."

The first time he saw Clara he wasn't able to discuss jack shit with her. She was in the company of two young men. She was looking like a figure carved of ice, her deadpan scientist face in place, but there was a shadow of terror in her green eyes which Finn had a feeling he alone could see. The men were harassing her about something called the "Black Trump" (a title which did not fill him with confidence), and how she had to reproduce her earlier work. Clara refused, and then the two young men brought in two older, larger men who introduced Finn to their close personal friends, Pain and Suffering. At one point the goons took a break, and one of the young men walked up to Finn, grabbed him by the hair, and forced his head up.

"Recognize me, Bradley?"

He studied the sleek brown hair, deep-set black eyes, the taut, muscular body. Didn't ring any bells for him.

"You ruined my reputation. Turned me from saint to monster. I've never forgiven you for that, Bradley. It's a pleasure watching you hurt. It'll be a greater one watching you die."

There was a hint of a French accent, but it sounded strained, like the throat producing it was unaccustomed to the accent. Finn realized who this had to be, and felt bile forcing its way through both his stomachs. He choked it back.

"Faneuil," Finn forced through cut and swollen lips.

"The same." A predator's smile. Finn spat in Faneuil's face, spraying him with blood, spit and a lost tooth. Faneuil fell back with a cry of disgust, groping for a handkerchief to wipe his face.

The strawberry blond man who was keeping a grip on Clara made a moue of disgust. "You never had any balls, Etienne. Why don't you hit him?"

"I'm not a thug," said Faneuil in a prissy tone and left.

The blond guy sighed, looked down at Clara. Gestured to Joan.

"She's next."

In the corner Joan reared up out of her coils, and spread her hood. The two thugs who had worked Finn over exchanged dubious glances about their next subject. Hartmann was huddled behind her, his entire body quivering with tension. He didn't have to worry. No one was interested in him right at the moment. This party was being staged for Clara's benefit.

"What does it matter, Pan?" Clara suddenly blurted out. "If I do what you wish, they'll die anyway."

"We may be able to arrange something," the man said soothingly.

"That's horseshit and you know it. I designed this virus. There isn't a vaccine, there isn't a chance you'll only catch a mild case. This is my mother, and my lover. I can't do this." Her back was rigid, the tendons in her throat were stretched and taut, and a pulse was beating wildly. But nothing showed in her voice.

The man's soothing, unctuous tone grated. "You can watch them suffer, or you can give them a humane death."

Finn knew her face so well by now. Every nuance, every flicker of emotion. He could see her calculating, deliberating, reaching a decision, and whatsoever that decision entailed, it left death in her eyes. Clara stared at the men. The words emerged, low and grating.

"All right, I'll do it." And she turned and stalked out of the room.

And while the physical pain was horrible, it was less agonizing than the nagging terror of this mysterious "Black Trump."

Faneuil and his assistant, Michelle Poynter, both dressed as Clara was in protective clothing, shadowed her around the clean room. She first tried packaging a totally different virus, one of her early, failed ones. But Faneuil stopped her at the onset.

"Don't play games with me," he said, his voice muffled

by the respirator. He had Poynter line up the bottles of solution, the basic ingredients she should be using. The materials were specific to her latest work. They must have been spying on her all along.

"And we'd better see your wild card cell cultures die," he said. "If not, one of your joker friends is going to die instead."

She eyed Faneuil, thinking hard. Both Black Trump strains used virtually all the same ingredients. Faneuil wouldn't know the difference; even another virologist wouldn't, without being familiar with her methods.

Even Black Trump I was too dangerous a virus to give them. But it was far better than recreating Black Trump II. And it would buy her time.

She got to work.

She had tried to lose him in a blizzard of technobabble. *Virus sheaths, cell wall resistance, etc.* It confused, but couldn't obscure the bottom line—she, Clara, his lover, his lady, had created a virus which would kill wild cards. *All* wild cards. Aces, jokers, latents. Leaving a world cleansed of their polluting influence. That's why they had tortured him. Finn wished they'd killed him before he had to hear this confession. Before he knew what she had done to "save" him.

"So what was I?" he asked, and his voice emerged as an anguished groan. "Research? Did you fuck me so you could get some hot, fresh joker sperm?"

"Don't hate me, Bradley," she whispered through stiff, white lips. "I didn't know ... what you were like. I thought you were ... unhappy."

"Offering us the peace and contentment of the grave? Thank you very much, Clara. A little more van Rensselaer noblesse oblige."

"Bradley, please." He wanted tears, needed tears. He didn't get them. She was in clinical mode.

Instead, to his eternal embarrassment, the tears were his. The sob burst out of him. Tore at his chest and throat. The salt in the tears burned in the cuts on his face, and ate like acid at his soul and dreams.

Throughout all of this Joan and Hartmann were huddled presences in the corner of the cell. Finn plunged away from Clara. She didn't follow. That hurt too. Then Joan reared up, spread her hood, and *hissed* at him. Startled, Finn ran backwards, hooves skittering on the slick tile. Clara's hands were on his haunches. He bolted from her too. Irrational, he wanted her comfort, and couldn't bear her touch. He wanted the last few hours to be excised. He didn't want to know that while she had wooed him she had been killing him. He wanted to stop loving her.

Clara started for the door, but Joan shot across the floor, and blocked her daughter's escape.

"I want to live to be a grandmother," she said in her husky, humorous voice, that couldn't quite hide the fear and tension lurking beneath the surface. "I have a daughter again. I want a son. I want you both to stop fighting and grieving and guilt tripping each other, and *think* of something."

For the first time since Clara had begun her horrific confession, she and Finn actually looked at each other. Actually locked eyes. It surprised him a little—she was still Clara . . . and he discovered that he still loved her, even as he hated her.

"Joan, I'm not James Fucking Bond with four feet. I'm a middle-aged, out of shape joker."

"But you're both bright, so think of something," Joan insisted.

"Don't count on me," Hartmann offered. "This fucking body has a built in flight instinct. Danger rears its ugly head, and I'm gone. Nothing I can do to control it."

Clara ignored Hartmann. Stared thoughtfully at Finn. "You're stronger than a normal human?"

"A little. The extra weight helps. I got a lot of kick power in these legs . . . but no, I can't kick out that door. And I think they'd notice if I tried."

"We need to clear the lab," Clara mused.

"A diversion," Finn amplified.

"The virus," they both breathed together.

Hartmann stiffened in alarm. "Won't that . . . kill us?"

"We wouldn't really use it," Clara said. "But they watch me whenever I'm near anything toxic so I couldn't even— What?" she asked when she noticed Finn staring speculatively at Joan.

"I remember the day when you dropped that religious nut cold in twenty seconds. With no permanent effects."

Joan stretched her mouth open in a travesty of a smile. Snapped shut her teeth. Clara was staring at both of them like they'd gone insane.

"Mommy dearest's got venom," Joan said sweetly and simply.

Her timing couldn't have been better; the lunch line hadn't yet started to form when she got to the cafeteria. The neighborhood had a deficit of restaurants, and in half an hour the cafeteria would be packed.

Clara leaned over the counter and sniffed. "Hey ya, Peter. How's the lasagna?"

Peter, a gangly young black man with a lightning bolt-shaped bald patch over his left temple, a paper hat, apron, and numerous rings in his earlobes, shrugged.

"Hey, Doc. The usual grub—almost palatable. How come I haven't seen you around in a while?"

"I've been working nights. How were midterms?"

"A stone bitch. But I got through them. Even got a B on my microbiology test."

"Peter, that's terrific! And you thought you'd fail!"

He grinned. "Yeah, it's cool. Thanks for helping me prepare. Umm, do you think we could go over my microbiology exam together sometime?"

"Of course. Maybe later in the week. Say, Peter . . ."

She leaned on the counter, glancing at the guard who'd been assigned to follow her around. He was helping himself to a Coke at the soda fountain. That put him— briefly—with his back mostly to her. Clara gave Peter a wink and, pressing a finger to her lips, pulled a vial out of her pocket. She swiftly emptied the contents onto the lasagna, then pocketed the vial.

Peter gave her a strange look. "What gives?"

"A little special spice," she said in a low voice, and

jerked her glance toward the guard. "Serve it up as usual.
Nobody'll get hurt. I'll explain later."

Peter nodded slowly. "You got it."

"But between you and me, I'd avoid the lasagna."

An hour later, in the clean room, Poynter entered the
lab where Faneuil was overseeing Clara's work. Her hair
was coming out from under her hood and she looked
worried.

"A technician in the wet chemistry lab has collapsed,"
she said.

"The cause?"

"They don't know. It appears to be a severe flu. The
infirmary medic wants you there right away."

"Keep an eye on *her*," he said, jerking his chin toward
Clara. "Don't leave her alone."

Clara kept working, while Poynter sat on a lab stool
and glowered at her.

Ten minutes later the phone on the wall by the door
rang. Clara started for it, but Poynter snapped, "Leave
it!" and grabbed it herself.

"Uh huh? Yes, an RN degree. Shit! How many? I'll
be right there."

She hung up and turned to Clara. "You're to come
with me."

Clara followed her to the infirmary, and the guard
waiting outside followed them both. The medic, a cranky
old woman named Janice, was there with Faneuil. Clara
leaned against the wall while Poynter, Faneuil, and Janice
conferred in low, anxious tones. Inside the infirmary
were groans and the sounds of people throwing up.

As she stood there a young man staggered down the
hall toward them, and from another direction, a woman
helped another woman along. A crowd of concerned
friends and coworkers was gathering.

"Dr. van Renssaeler!" One of the technicians grabbed
her arm. "What's going on?"

Others turned to look. She said in soft, grave tones,
"Everyone should remain completely calm. We have no

definite proof that one of the experimental viruses has escaped containment and mutated."

There were gasps and whispers. "What did she say? What did she say?"

"An experimental virus is loose!"

Pandemonium broke. Everyone started running and shouting. Faneuil—who was starting to look a little sickly himself—raised his voice, trying to stem the panic, but Clara might as well have lit the fuse on a bomb.

She made her way through the ensuing chaos to the clean room. The guards had fled, including her own. She suited up swiftly and entered. The flasks of Black Trump virus she'd made so far were encased in coolers by the door, neatly labeled, awaiting verification of the test cultures.

Clara carried the coolers over to the microwave oven. All but three of the flasks fit. She'd have to do it in two batches. Fifteen minutes per batch would be too much time to gamble on, but ten minutes should be enough. She set the timer, and paced, watching the door.

When the alarm went off, she dragged the flasks of destroyed virus out, stuck the last three in, and reset the timer. Some sixth sense, or perhaps a faint noise, caused her to turn. A small compressed gas bottle was descending on her. Poynter's face was behind it.

Clara dodged and the metal bottle struck her shoulder. She buckled with a cry.

Poynter shoved her out of the way and grabbed the flasks out of the oven. She tried to run but Clara caught her by the leg and she stumbled, barely keeping hold of the flasks as she went down.

They wrestled for control of the flasks. Clara was larger but Poynter was younger and much stronger. She wormed free of Clara's grasp and scrambled to her feet, and hurled a two-gallon glass jug of plasmid solution at Clara, catching her in the gut. She sat down with a whoosh, all the air knocked out of her. The glass shattered on the floor between her legs, bathing her in sticky, acrid solution.

Poynter was gone by the time she'd recovered.

Clara stuffed the tissue cultures into the oven and

turned it on, then ran out to find and stop Poynter. She dodged into a room when she heard General MacArthur Johnson's voice; he and a squad of goons armed with semi-automatics ran past. They entered the clean room airlock behind Poynter. Clara waited till they were all inside, then hit the emergency button by the airlock.

Alarms started going off all over, signalling a contaminant release in the clean room. The airlock doors would now be sealed till they could get someone outside to activate the override.

But some of the virus still lived.

Clara ran for the basement, pausing only long enough to fan the flames of panic with a word here and there.

Hours passed. Finn imagined every possible catastrophe. Hartmann uttered them. Joan yelled at them.

Finn huddled against a wall, and imagined they had discovered her. Killed her. *Fuck that, nobody gets to throttle her but me,* he thought. He knew he was losing his mind. He never wanted to see Clara again, but the thought that he wouldn't was a sharp pain deep in the gut. Then, just when all hope was gone, the key grated in the lock and the door flew open. Clara stood revealed, her hair looking as if she'd combed it with an egg beater, a wild light in her green eyes.

For the first time Finn felt good enough to notice the environment beyond the door. It was really unexciting— stacked boxes, lab beakers lining shelves, sacks of bulk food supplies, in short . . . a basement storeroom. Clara noticed his abstraction, slapped him on his withers with an open palm.

"We have to hurry. Johnson's not stupid." She was almost stuttering as she tried to force the words out faster. "He'll figure out soon it's not the virus, and I don't know if I got them all. Guards I mean. He's got four. If some of them didn't eat . . ."

Finn shooed Joan out the door. She was a blur of camouflaging scales whipping across the floor. Finn leaped through the door. Clara grabbed him around the neck. Pressed a kiss on his mouth. He howled. She fell back, her hands pressed to her mouth, bumped into a stack of crates which went tumbling with a god-awful crash.

"Hurts," Finn muttered, wondering why he was reassuring her.

Hartmann skittered out of the room. "Want to give me a little nudge?" he asked. Finn stared at him in confuson. "Scare me," the senator amplified. He sounded irritated.

"I wouldn't think you'd need any help for that," Finn said.

"I need high gear. One of us has got to get out, give the warning. I'm probably the fastest of any of us. If you goose me."

Finn shrugged, and cow-kicked at Hartmann, clipping him lightly in the side. He levitated about a foot into the air. All of his myriad legs began churning, and he hit the ground running. Finn watched the senator go, swarming up the stairs and out of sight.

"Which floor?" Joan called from inside the elevator.

"Not the elevator," Finn yelled back. "If anybody's alert they'll shut them down. Trap us." Joan came out of the elevator at Mach two.

They crept up the stairs. Finn was having a hard time without his rubber booties. Finn, protecting the womenfolk and all that, emerged first from the stairwell and saw—a hall. It looked like any other hall in any other office building. Finn realized he was holding himself so tensely that his muscles were aching.

"Which way?" he whispered to Clara.

"Turn left at the end of the hall. That'll take us to reception. It's about twenty feet to the front doors."

From behind one of the closed doors which lined the hall Finn heard a low, hopeless, terrified sobbing. He didn't investigate. Joan headed out down the hall, Clara following. She looked back when she didn't hear the clop of his hooves on the linoleum floor.

Finn stepped to her, gripped her shoulders, turned her around, laid a hand between her shoulder blades, and pushed. "You and Joan go on. Call the cops. I gotta get Faneuil."

"*What?*"

"He killed thousands of people. He made *me* an unwitting killer. He's got to pay for that."

"We don't have the luxury," Clara said.

"This is a necessity. Does he have a lab? Where does he work?"

"You'll never reach him alone," Clara said. She turned to Joan. "Go on, Mother." Joan hesitated, regret and fear showing on her face. Then she went. Clara darted past Finn back into the stairwell. He followed.

They made it to the third floor without incident. Clara was right about him needing her help. Access to all the labs was through negative pressure clean rooms, and an access card and voice print were required. Clara's got them through. Faneuil wasn't in his office, or in the lab with its detailed maps of world cities. The only one Finn recognized in the brief seconds allowed to him was New York.

"He's not here. Come on! Let's go!" Tension thrummed in Clara's voice.

"How big is this building?" Finn asked as he pulled open another door. Closet. Faneuil wasn't in it.

"*Too* big for us to search. *Maman's* toxin will only last so long."

Finn pulled open a final door, and discovered a bathroom, and Faneuil seated on the shitter. His pants were down around his ankles, the bowl filled with his diarrhea. The paralysis induced by Joan's venom had finally hit, but it was too weak a dose to completely freeze him. He was struggling, moving like a man under water. Finn reached in, grabbed the man by the shoulders, and yanked him out of the john. With Clara's help they got him tossed over Finn's back.

Out of the lab. Back into the hall. Racing for the stairwell. People were starting to recover from the effects of the venom. Sensation returning to their limbs, rational thought to their brains. A couple of them clung to door jambs, and called garbled questions to Clara.

Through the door, and down the stairs. It was a bitch

going down. Finn's hooves kept slipping on the metal stair nosings, and Faneuil was an awkward weight on his back. The French doctor's struggles were becoming more violent.

"Punch him!" Finn ordered.

Clara pulled back her arm, and drove her fist into Faneuil's temple. He quieted down substantially.

Suddenly a voice from below called out. "You joker-fucking bitch."

Finn risked a glance over the railing. A burst of automatic weapons fire came back in reply. The sound was terrifying in the enclosed space, and bullets were whining and spanging off the metal banisters. One of the ricochets gouged a line of fire across the top of Finn's haunches. Clara hunkered down, her arms protectively covering her head. "It's Johnson Security. We're fucked."

The situation had clearly become desperate. Retreat was impossible. Walking down the stairs into that withering fire was equally impossible, and standing still was also impossible. There was only one thing to do—punt.

Finn reared slightly, sending Faneiul sliding off his back. He then gathered his hindquarters beneath him, tensed the muscles, and *leaped*. The man's mouth was a dark, stretched "O" as he watched four hundred pounds of palomino centaur descending from heaven on top of him. His gun was pointed straight into Finn's gut, but fortunately the sight of a flying joker made him hesitate, and in hesitating he was lost.

Finn came down on the man, heard bones cracking, a pathetic wheezing sound as the air went out of the guard. There was another gun-shot loud *crack*, and fire washed up Finn's right front leg. He went down in a welter of legs and arms. He craned up to see his foreleg. From the middle of the cannon bone it was flopping. He struggled onto three legs. Rambo was out cold on the stairs. Pieces of him were bent in funny directions, too. Finn looked up to see Clara, hands tangled in the lapels of Faneuil's coat, dragging him down the stairs. His head bumped on each step, and his trousers and shorts were pulled almost completely off his legs.

Thanking God they were at the first floor (Finn could not have done stairs on three legs), he hobbled to the door, pulled it open. Clara dragged Faneuil through. Down the hall. Finn wished he could help Clara with Faneuil, but knew he couldn't. With each limping step he could hear the bones in his leg grinding across each other.

"Do you know if they still shoot horses?" Finn asked hysterically. Clara grunted, kept pulling.

They reached reception, hobbled and lurched past the gaping secretary, a phone up to her ear, and into the street. In the distance were the sounds of approaching sirens. Joan slithered over to Clara, and rearing up, embraced her. Faneuil lay forgotten on the pavement. The first fire truck arrived.

Joan was a clever woman. Knowing a call of "jokers in distress" would arouse nothing but apathy, she had literally yelled *fire!*

Clara pulled free of her mother's embrace. Walked over to Finn. "I didn't get it all. They removed some of it." Finn just stared at her. "But it's a weaker strain. It falls dormant after three transmissions." The words emerged in a desperate rush.

"Yeah, that's great. I'm sure that'll really comfort the three deaders who get hit before dormancy is achieved."

An ambulance—a real one—took Bradley to the hospital. Meanwhile, a nearby cop loaded Clara and Joan into a patrol car. Hartmann was long gone.

Clara slouched against the door handle and looked out at the streets of Manhattan. It was twilight. Sodium, neon, and mercury fluorescents illuminated the many thousands of people spewing from the buildings and crowding the sidewalks of midtown. Traffic crept down Lexington. Horns blared and engines roared. The air smelled of ozone. Clara glanced over and saw Joan nervously eyeing the cop beyond the thick mesh. He was listening to the police radio, which spat police codes and static. At Clara's questioning glance, Joan leaned toward her and spoke in a low voice.

"Darling, do you still have your scrapbook—the one I gave you when you were little?"

"Yes. Why?"

Joan was wringing her hands—and her coils of snake flesh were wringing themselves. "This will seem rather an odd question, but—is there a picture of your father with a man of Mediterranean descent?"

Clara frowned at her. "What on earth is this about?"

"There is something I left out when I told you how I contracted the wild card," Joan said. "Something important."

"Oh?"

Joan nodded, looking miserable and flustered. "It's about your father, and, well, if I don't tell you now I may not have a chance later, and . . . I don't want you to think I deceived you in any way. . . ."

"Of course not."

"I would have told you when you came to see me, but that didn't seem to be the right time. But after all, I told that lovely young lady arson investigator, and I'm sure she told Senator Hartmann; I can't imagine why he didn't investigate further, but perhaps it's for the best, in a sense."

Clara frowned. Joan's flutterings were starting to grate. "Would you please just *tell* me, *Maman*?"

Joan looked at the cop again and lowered her voice to a whisper. "Back in 1968, Pan Rudo arranged to have Bobby Kennedy assassinated. And Brand paid off Sirhan Sirhan, the assassin. Brand was the—what do they call it?—the bag man."

Clara stared at her, a sinking feeling in her stomach. She wanted to say that *Papa* would never do such a thing, but she couldn't bring herself to say it.

"He was having an affair at the time," Joan went on. "With Marilyn Monroe. I hired a private investigator to follow him, and the investigator captured the exchange on film. The photo later disappeared, and I wondered if it might somehow have ended up in your scrapbook."

Clara thought about the very clear, close-up photo of her father handing an envelope to a dark-complected young man, whose identity Clara had occasionally wondered about. She merely shrugged and shook her head at her mother's gaze, and let Joan assume she meant no.

The first thing she did on reaching the police station was to request a phone call. She used a pay phone in the foyer and called her father at home. He came on the line immediately.

"Are you all right? Is the line clear?"

"I'm fine. The line's OK, I think. I'm on a pay phone at the police precinct. Pan was holding me—"

"—at the UN lab. I know. His man Johnson sealed off the UN lab to my people. I didn't even know he knew which ones they were, the bastard. We were about to stage an assault. And now they tell me the police have taken you in. What's going on?"

Clara took a deep breath. Here goes, she thought. "*Papa*, I'm about to turn State's evidence against Pan—"

"You're *what*?"

"—and the whole Card Shark organization. I'm calling you now to let you know you'd better get out of the country, because I'm not going to hold anything back."

Silence greeted her. After a minute Brandon found his voice. "What the hell are you talking about?"

"You never told me *Maman* was still alive."

"Oh. Oh, honey. I should have told you a long time ago—"

"Yes. You should have."

"—but that's no reason to go off half-cocked like this."

"It's not half-cocked. Pan has the Black Trump—or a version of it—and he has to be stopped. And I've had enough of the lies. You said it yourself. It's not worth it." Tears started rolling down her face. "I know that you've been wanting out. At least a little bit. I'm giving you your chance. Early retirement. Transfer all your funds to an international bank right now and get a plane ticket. Don't delay."

More silence.

"You're sentencing yourself to a lifetime of prison," he said. "Or at best, a lifetime of hiding. Don't do this."

"I don't think so. I think they'll let me cut a deal. I

can give them Pan Rudo, and they want him badly. So."
She cleared her throat. "Know a good lawyer?"

"Clara, don't do this."

"I love you, *Papa*."

She slid the phone into the cradle and turned. Several
police officers stood near the precinct captain's office,
where Joan was speaking to the officer in charge. She
drew a breath, squared her shoulders, and walked over.

She cut the photo of her father with Sirhan Sirhan out
of her scrapbook, cut it into tiny bits and burned it, and
flushed the ashes down the toilet. Then she went into
the bedroom.

The mattress was still on the floor. She buried her
face in the pillow, breathing his scent. She rolled onto
her side and sensations returned: the taste of his kiss;
the feel of his arms enfolding her, hand cupping a breast;
his horse's fur warm against her bare buttocks.

Clara rolled onto her back and covered her eyes with
the back of an arm, trying to summon the tender look
in his eyes when they'd made love, to recall his laughter
over shared, cold Chinese food. But all she saw was that
look on his face when they'd been torturing him, when
he'd realized what she'd done.

What the world thought of her meant nothing. Bradley's opinion meant everything, and there was no way to
make him understand. She'd lost him before she'd ever
really had him.

Maggie had started into labor. Finn had been checking
her progress, and emerged from her room intent on
ordering the incubation unit to the delivery room. Cody
was lying in wait.

"Oh, please," said Finn, and tried to dodge her. He
wasn't real successful with a cast on his leg and a cane
in his hand.

Cody caught him by the tail. He wasn't wearing his
rubber shoes, so his hooves were scrabbling for purchase
on the slick linoleum floor. He decided neither his

dignity nor his tail could survive much more of this, so
he craned around to look at her.

"Call her," Cody said. It was the sixth time she'd said
it in the past four hours.

"No."

"Stop thinking about yourself, and start thinking about
your patient ... patients. That baby needs Clara's
attention."

"She left notes," Finn caviled.

"Not the same. Clara knows this case better than
either of us."

"I can't face her."

"Finn, I know how hard this is—"

"No, you don't! You can't! You're not one of us. As
much as you care, as much as you've given, you're not a
wild card, and you're not living under a death sentence."
His voice was rising. A couple of passing patients gave
him an odd look. Finn dropped to a whisper. "I'm a
doctor. I see death all the time. And I'm scared. I don't
want to die."

She laid a hand on his hindquarters. Stroked softly.
"You've given the warning. It's in the hands of others
now. All we can do is live, work, and not give in to
despair." She paused, walked around to face Finn,
grabbed him by the front of his Hawaiian shirt, and
pulled him in close. "And save this baby."

He took the elevator up to Tachyon's old office, his
old office, now his office again with Clara's departure.
Picked up the phone. Dialed her number. She answered
on the first ring.

"Hello, hello. . . . Oh, it is you."

"Maggie's in labor. We need you."

He hung up the phone before he could hear any more
of the pain or the joy in her voice.

At three and a half pounds, Mary Louise was frighten-
ingly small. And she looked so helpless with her eyes
squeezed shut, with green tubes in her nose, electrodes
on her chest and back, an IV taped to her leg. The heart

monitor next to her incubator showed a strong, steady little beat, though. And the transfusions had stabilized her condition. She had an excellent chance.

Clara lifted the incubator's lid, took the infant in her hands, and—careful not to dislodge electrodes, oxygen, or IV—lowered herself into the rocker by the incubator. She unbuttoned the top buttons of her blouse, laid Mary Louise on her bare skin, and rocked her. She was so small Clara could hold her in one hand.

Mary Louise whimpered. Clara moved Mary Louise's head into the crook of her neck, and planted a gentle kiss on her forehead.

"Poor little thing," she whispered. "You've had a rough beginning, haven't you?"

Joan was at the door, watching her.

"*Maman*."

"Hi."

Both kept their voices low. Joan slithered over and reared next to the rocker. Clara laid a hand on her mother's arm.

"I remember the first time I held you," Joan said. "I've never known such complete joy."

Clara gave her a smile.

"Have you heard anything about your case?"

"Mitchell says negotiations are going well." Clara shrugged. "We'll have to see."

After a pause Joan asked, "Have you spoken to Bradley?"

Clara shook her head. "He's avoiding me. He doesn't want to see me." She glanced over; Joan was looking at her. She shook her head again.

"I can't face him, *Maman*. I couldn't bear the look on his face. I couldn't bear his rejection."

Joan sighed. "Clara, darling, for twenty-five years I suffered, for not going to you, for not braving the look on your face."

Clara nuzzled the baby-soft hair and skin of Mary Louise's head and said nothing.

"Don't make the same mistake I did."

Still Clara said nothing.

"Do you love him?" Joan demanded.

Clara gasped. "Of course!"

Joan squeezed her hand. "Then go to him. He's in his office. Go now. I'll take over with the baby.

"Just try. This once," Joan said, and gave her a smile. "You can handle it. All he can say is no, right?"

Clara gazed at her mother, nodded with a sigh.

"You're right."

She handed the infant over and kissed her mother on the cool, dry, glittering scales of her cheek.

"*Maman*, I am so glad I found you."

Gazing out over the skyline of Manhattan, the dirt, despair and poverty veiled by a spectacular smog-generated sunset, Finn felt again the weight of that newborn child resting in his hands. He had delivered plenty of babies. The birth of this one, however, raised a visceral reaction—fierce joy that she had survived, and despair that he would never hold one of his own.

He didn't want to think about Clara, but she was an insidious presence in any thought pertaining to babies. She had lost weight in the past days. Since Finn hadn't seen her, the gauntness seemed all the more severe, the shadow of sadness all the darker in her gray eyes. Until she had accepted young Mary Louise from his hands, and her eyes had shone with the same fire of achievement he had felt. Clara had vanished with the baby, carrying her away to the neo-natal unit to begin blood replacement treatments. Finn was avoiding the neo-natal unit. He checked his watch. He'd give it another twenty minutes. By then Clara should be safely gone. Because if he saw her he wasn't sure what he'd do—kiss her or kill her. Probably kiss her.

"Bradley?"

He whirled too fast, got tangled in his own legs, the cane and the cast, and went down on his hindquarters. Clara reached out, took a step toward him, then folded back in on herself like a frightened touch-me-not. Finn got his feet under him, and limped behind the desk, placing it like a buffer between him and her disturbing presence.

"Hi," Finn finally said.

"Hi."

Long pause. Finn had to fill the silence. "How's the baby?"

"Doing wonderfully."

"We did it," Finn heard himself say, and then he smiled at her.

Tears clouded Clara's eyes. "You looked at me. This is the first time since ... since ... that you've really *looked* at me." Finn couldn't think of anything to say. "What do you see, Bradley, when you look at me? Monstrous killer? The woman you made love with? Which?"

"I don't know, Clara. You tell me which one you are. Explain to me how you could plan genocide when you'd been trained as a healer."

She half turned, gave him her profile. In a soft voice she began. "For years I'd had nightmares about my mother's death. The wild card had killed her. There was something monstrous about the way it killed her. That's what they told me. *Papa* hated wild cards. Pan hated them, but with a scientist's objectivity—they would destroy the human race. I was a motherless child being raised by men whose strongest emotion was hate. For years as I studied and worked I lied to myself, told myself I was doing this for the sake of humanity, freeing those poor souls from terrible suffering." She paused, drew a shaky breath.

"It was a lie. I was doing it as a way to take vengeance against the disease that had stolen my mother." She turned to him. "And then you, a wild card, a joker, destroyed my beliefs. You weren't suffering, horrifying, praying for death. You were living and loving, and you showed me I was the one with no life, no joy. And then you gave me back my mother."

"Yeah, I'm swell, but that doesn't tell me what you want from me, Clara. Forgiveness? Okay, I forgive you. I don't think it matters a damn because you have to decide if you can forgive yourself—"

"No."

The single word interrupted his diatribe. Finn gaped at her. "No? No, what?"

"I don't want your forgiveness."

"Then what the hell do you want?"

"I want to know if you still love me."

They had both lost that stiff, on their dignity pose, had stopped talking like characters in a soap.

"Don't the two sort of go hand in hand?" Finn asked.

"I don't know, do they?" She paused for an instant. "Do you love me?"

Finn hesitated, hedged. "Do you love *me*?"

That dimple was starting to appear. "You have to go first."

"That's not fair. I have more to lose."

"How do you figure that?" she demanded.

"I get rejected more," Finn said.

"You can't know that. I was terribly unpopular in school."

"Goddamn it, Clara, if I can survive you driving me crazy I'll probably love you 'til I'm old and gray."

And then she was in his arms, laughing and crying. Her tears dampened his shoulder, her cheek warm to his touch as he stroked back her hair. They kissed, and it took a few moments for evil reality to intrude.

Gently he took her by the shoulders, held her at arms length. "Clara, I don't know how long we've got together. . . . His voice failed for an instant. He coughed to clear the sudden tightness. "The virus . . . But however long I've got, I want to spend it with you."

"I'm working on a vaccine," she said, her voice a thin thread of sound.

"And you keep working on it, but you can't work too late at night, and you gotta work here because I want to be with you," Finn said.

Clara sighed, and snuggled in close. "What else can we do, Bradley?" she asked after a few moments of silent communion.

"Live and hope."

And he found reasons for both in the taste of her lips.

The Color Of His Skin

Part 8

"The Sharks got away with three vials before van Renssaeler could destroy them," Hannah was telling them. "Pan Rudo escaped too, with this General MacArthur Johnson."

Father Squid's voice was calm and soothing. "The police have assured us that every possible step is being taken to find and apprehend them. Dr. van Renssaeler has come forward and is willing to testify. The authorities—"

"—will do *nothing*," Gregg interrupted. "Every last person infected by the wild card virus is now under a sentence of death."

The voice, coming from high above them, caused everyone gathered in the room to peer up into the shadowed, distant ceiling, where the hulks of the Turtle's old shells loomed, dark ghosts of a painful past. Gregg could see the fuzzy image of the people in the room below: Dutton's skeletal face, Hotair in the midst of his flames, Oddity standing silently against the wall, Father Squid, Troll, Jo Ann and her husband, maybe a dozen or more others.

And Hannah. She peered up to where Gregg was hiding, but his myopic sight could tell nothing about her expression. Still, seeing her again sent the air rushing out of his lungs. For a moment he couldn't breathe, making eye contact with her in the darkness. Somewhere down below, Gregg heard the click of an automatic weapon being taken off safety. The scent of the crowd was bitter and fragile.

"Oh, Leo Barnett will say he's very concerned," Gregg went on from his perch on the shell. "He may even put together a task force to study the problem, but nothing will happen until it's too late. When you're all dead, maybe they'll build you a nice wall with all your names on it."

"Who *are* you?" Hannah called.

"You won't believe me. No one believes me."

" Try us."

Gregg wriggled out the blackened, ruined interior of the Turtle's shell, which still smelled faintly of smoke, sweat, beer, and old food. Someone hit a switch, and Gregg blinked as the tracklights around the ceiling illuminated him. "It's Battle . . ." he heard someone say as he made the short leap from the shell to the wall alongside. The pads on his multiple legs gripped the wall; headfirst, he wriggled down to the ground. He could smell the stench of Hotair's Sterno flames, the sharp tang of oil from the weapon he knew was tracking him, and the floral scent of Hannah's hair.

He started toward her, but as he passed Troll, the joker grabbed a handful of loose skin just behind his head and lifted him like a kitten in the grasp of a mother cat. Gregg's legs began to pump in an automatic frenzy, but the grip was tight and unbreakable and his limbs pumped uselessly in the air. Troll turned him, and Gregg saw the man's grim face.

"Battle, you son of a bitch," Troll said. " This is for all the jokers who died on the Rox. This is for all of us the Sharks killed." His other huge hand drew back, fisted. Hotair chuckled in the background.

"No!" Gregg shrilled, his voice piercing. "I'm not Battle, damn it."

"Like hell," Troll said. "Which is where we're sending you right now."

"It's *true*. Please. You have to listen to me." Gregg wriggled at the end of Troll's grasp like a hook-speared worm.

"Troll!" Hannah said. "Let's hear him out."

"He's *Battle*, Hannah. We all know what he's been saying, but—"

"Troll . . ."

"If I put him down, he'll be gone," Troll persisted. "He's fast, remember? Look at how quick those little feet are going."

"I can stop . . ." Gregg muttered. He forced himself to cease running; it took several seconds, but at last he hung still in Troll's grasp. Troll lowered him carefully to the ground, and Gregg went over to Hannah, rising up with his first two segments as he looked at her.

"Hannah . . ." he began. His body shuddered from the effort of standing up after all the running in place he'd just done; he dropped back to all sixes, peering up at her. "Hannah," he said when he could speak again. "Do *you* believe me?"

Grief and hope mingled on Hannah's face, but she pressed her lips together. She glanced at Father Squid and Dutton. "Give me a few minutes with him, Okay?"

"Hannah," Father Squid began, "I know what Dr. Finn said, but . . ."

"I'm the one who'd know best, aren't I? Just . . ." She blinked hard. "A few minutes, that's all." She looked down at Gregg, and he could see nothing in the blur of her face. "Come on," she said, and walked from the gallery into the next room.

On one side, Jetboy struggled with Dr. Tod in the gondola of the careening dirigible while in the background the bright red pieces of the JB-1 began their long fall to the city below. On the other wall, a frozen, tragic scene from the WHO Aces tour: Kahina stood over a bleeding Nur; Hiram Worchester fisted his hand as Sayyid crumpled in agony; Jack Braun gleamed golden while bullets ricocheted from his chest; Tachyon lay crumpled and unconscious. Gregg was there too, his shoulder bloody as Sarah Morgenstern tended to him and Peregrine flew overhead to attack the Nur's guards.

"Not one of my favorite moments," Gregg said softly.

"What?"

"Nothing." Gregg sighed—it sounded like a tea kettle boiling over. She was staring at him, but when their gazes met, she quickly looked away. "Hannah . . . I don't know where to start. My God, I've missed you—"

"Shut UP!" The words were torn from her throat, harsh and shrill. Hannah closed her eyes for a second, biting her upper lip. "Just shut up," she said more calmly, her eyes still closed. When they opened again, she was looking at Gregg's waxen image in the Syrian diorama. He could see her reflection in the glass. "I . . . I've never finished grieving for Gregg. The last few days of his life were so *strange*. He wouldn't see me, wouldn't talk to me or Father Squid. The press conference almost killed me; I felt betrayed and violated and used, and then . . ." She stopped. She leaned her forehead against the glass, her hands pressed against it. "When he was murdered, the pain was worse than I thought anything could be. I've never stopped grieving. Not yet."

She looked at him, and her eyes were as cold and sharp as blue ice. "And then you came around. People told me that you were saying you were Gregg, but . . ." Hannah stopped. She looked again at the Syrian exhibit before turning back to him. "Finn said you were there, in the lab. Is that what you came to tell us?"

"Yes, but it seems you already know it," Gregg said. "But you can't just wait for Barnett to save you. You can't count on the police or the feds or anyone else taking care of the Black Trump. *You* have to do it."

"Not me," Hannah said. She was staring at him.

"What do you mean?"

Hannah crouched in front of him, close enough that he could see her face clearly. Her breath was mint touched with a lingering trace of coffee. "Let me ask you again. Who are you?"

"I'm *Gregg*," he said, and saw her visibly wince with the words. Her smell changed at the same time, subtly. "Hannah, no one wants to believe it, but I was *jumped*—before that damn press conference, before my body was killed. The Sharks did it: in fact, that was probably Battle who was in my body during that last meeting. Hannah—" His body wriggled; he guessed it was his new equivalent of a shrug. "I remember the first time we made love—in your room at Father Squid's parsonage, after we'd gone to Aces High. Father was gone, Quasiman was sitting downstairs in one of his fugues. . . . Would Battle know that?"

Hannah breathed, a hoarse exhalation. Still crouching, she let her head drop. Her long hair hid her face. "I don't believe you. This is a trick."

Gregg took a breath, cursing his new body and the puny voice it gave him. There was no power to it, no Puppetman, no Gift: it was only a voice and the words had to convince by themselves. It wasn't fair. "The second time we spent the night at my apartment. You said you hadn't figured me for a reader. You asked me if I'd actually read all of the books in my office."

"No . . ."

"You'd forgotten your toothbrush. I gave you one from the closet in the bathroom: red, I think. We made love again that morning and that—" Gregg stopped and took a breath. "That was the first time you said that you loved me," he finished.

"Gregg." A whisper. Her head came up. She was staring at him, her hands clenched into tight fists on her knees. Light from the diorama painted harsh shadows under her eyes. "It's really you." It was no longer a question.

"Yes. I'm Gregg," he said, and the knowledge that she believed him set blood pounding in his temples. Relief flooded through him, its depth surprising him. He hadn't known how important it was that someone—anyone—believe him.

Hannah sobbed once, a choking gasp that she muffled with her hands. Her eyes were wide and frightened. "I wanted to think it was real," she said. "When I heard from Oddity, Jube, and Jo Ann, I wanted so badly to believe you were still alive. Then when Dr. Finn said it might be true ... Oh God, Gregg ..."

Her hands came toward him, trembling. They smelled of soap. The first touch was feather light, but it burned deliciously on his skin. Her fingers caressed him, withdrew, then returned, until she cupped his head in her hands.

He realized that it was the first time anyone had touched him in some way other than violence in months.

"I'm so sorry," she told him. Tears drew glistening trails down her cheeks. "Gregg ..." On her knees, she pulled him to her. She hugged his joker body to herself, and Gregg marveled. Her warmth was an aching fire, her smell jasmine.

She still cares—without the Gift, without anything. Yet if it had been Hannah instead of me, if she had been twisted into this mockery, I couldn't ... "How can you?" he husked, wonderingly, and a deeper guilt ran through him like a blade.

Her arms tightened around him. Her voice sounded deep, resonating through him. "How could I not?" she asked him. "I loved what you were, what your are: your mind, your compassion, your leadership. The body ..." She pulled away from him. Her eyes searched his face, unashamed of the tears. "I wasn't your friend for that, Gregg. Please don't hate yourself, because *I* don't. You're alive—that's what matters. Nothing else."

If you knew ... Some of that self-loathing spilled out. "That's goddamn easy for *you* to say," he retorted, the words out before he could stop them, but she only nodded into his rage.

"I know," she said, and there was no anger in her voice at all, only sympathy. "I still believe it's true."

"Hannah, they took away *everything*. Everything I was and everything I had. And I can't ... I can't get it back."

His body spasmed. "I hate them," he said, and the truth of it rang like cold iron.

"Then use your hate," she told him. "You say we don't know what we face or how important it is. Then you have to *tell* them." She nodded her head toward the other room.

He was suddenly frightened. "No. I've already told you. I—"

"You don't understand, Gregg. That's what I was starting to say before. I can't lead these people, not any more. I'm a *nat*, and no matter how much they know that I care, no matter how much I've done, I'm still a nat and the bottom line is that this Black Trump virus doesn't threaten *me*. I'll do everything I can to help them, but they need a symbol, a focus. That can't be me, not any more; besides, you'd already taken over that spot, ever since I gave you my information. The truth is that it couldn't have been *you*, either, not as a nat. Father Squid and the others have danced around it politely and they'll deny that anything's changed, but the truth is that this is a joker problem; it demands a joker leader." She paused. He knew what her next word would be.

"You," she said.

Gregg shook his head, half-waiting for the voice inside him to return. *This is justice, Greggie*, it might have crowed. *This is fate*. He wanted to run, but Hannah's eyes had snared him. "Anyone can do what needs to be done. Father Squid—let him speak for the jokers," Gregg said.

"Father Squid will help, but he'd be the first to tell you that he's not the one to head the opposition. Gregg, we need someone who knows people, someone with a knowledge of government, with international contacts, someone used to organizing."

"No," Gregg responded. "What you have to do is destroy the vials. You have to find them before Rudo digs in somewhere where he can't be pulled out, before they culture enough of the virus to start a global infection."

"Gregg—" Hannah's hand stroked his head and fell away again. "Why did you come here?"

"To—" Gregg stopped. "I didn't have a plan," he said. "No agenda. I felt I needed to tell you all that I knew. I . . . I wanted to see you again. I wanted you to know I was alive before—"

"Before you left."

"Yes," he admitted.

"Where were you going to run, Gregg? Where could you go that would change what you are now? What other place could you find where you belonged, where you were more needed?"

She smiled at him, softly. She bent down, and her lips brushed against his skin. Sparks of delicious heat radiated out from the kiss as she rose, brushing her hair aside as she looked down at him. "I'm going back in now," she said. "Come with me."

Hannah turned and left the room without looking to see if he followed. Gregg stared at the Syrian diorama, at the image of his old self. The focus of his weak eyes shifted involuntarily, and for a moment he saw instead the faint reflection of the yellow creature looking in the glass.

He turned away. He walked back toward the gallery where the Turtle's shells hung. As he entered, they were all watching him: faces and bodies that had once—before the virus—been as normal as his had been. Faces now forever altered. Lives forever changed.

"I'm Gregg Hartmann," he told them. "I'm one of you."

GRAND ADVENTURE
IN GAME-BASED UNIVERSES

With these exciting novels set
in bestselling game universes,
Baen brings you synchronicity at its
best. We believe that familiarity with
either the novel or the game will
intensify enjoyment of the other.
All novels are the only authorized
fiction based on these games and
are published by permission.

THE BARD'S TALE™

Join the Dark Elf Naitachal and his apprentices in
bardic magic as they explore the mysteries of the
world of The Bard's Tale.

WING COMMANDER™

The computer game which supplies the background world for these novels is a current all-time bestseller. Fly with the best the Confederation of Earth has to offer against the ferocious catlike alien Kilrathi!

Freedom Flight by Mercedes Lackey & Ellen Guon
72145-3 * 304 pages * $4.99 _____

End Run
by Christopher Stasheff & William R. Forstchen
72200-X * 320 pages * $4.99 _____

Fleet Action by William R. Forstchen
72211-5 * 368 pages * $4.99 _____

STARFIRE™

See this strategy game come to explosive life in these grand space adventures!

Insurrection by David Weber & Steve White
72024-4 * 416 pages * $4.99 _____

Crusade by David Weber & Steve White
72111-9 * 432 pages * $4.99 _____

FOR COMPLETISTS: COMPLETE IN ONE VOLUME

Some concepts are too grand, too special to be confined to one book. The volumes listed below are examples of such, stories initially published in two or more volumes, collected together by Baen Books to form one unitary work.

The Fall of Atlantis
by Marion Zimmer Bradley
65615-5 • 512 pages • $5.99

The saga of an Atlantean prince. Combines *Web of Darkness* and *Web of Light.*

The Complete Compleat Enchanter
by L. Sprague de Camp & Fletcher Pratt
69809-5 • 544 pages • $5.99

Includes *all* the de Camp & Pratt Harold Shea *Unknown*-style stories of the Incompleat Enchanter and his intrepid adventures in lands of fable and story.

The Starchild Trilogy
by Frederik Pohl & Jack Williamson
65558-2 • 448 pages • $4.99

Epic, galaxy-spanning adventure, beginning with an Earth enslaved by the rigorously logical Plan of Man, and ending with the creation of a newborn intelligent star. . . .

The Compleat Bolo
by Keith Laumer
69879-6 • 320 pages • $4.99

Combines all the Laumer stories dealing with Bolos,

the ultimate weapon and the ultimate warrior in one. Includes the Retief Bolo story.

The Devil's Day
by James Blish   69860-5 • 320 pages • $3.95
A bored multi-billionaire hires a master of black magic to summon up *all* the demons in Hell and release them upon the world for a night—but once released the infernal legions have no intention of returning to Hell . . . Combines *Black Easter* and *The Day After Judgment* in one of the scariest apocalypse stories ever written.

Wizard World
by Roger Zelazny   72057-0 • 416 pages • $4.95
Banished as a child from his universe of sorcery, Pol Detson must return from Earth to defeat a master of technology who is conquering his lost homeworld—but will he return as a liberator or a new conqueror . . . ? Combines *Changeling* and *Madwand.*

Falkenberg's Legion
by Jerry Pournelle   72018-X • 448 pages • $4.99
The governments of East and West have created a tyrannical world order that will not rule the stars— because of John Christian Falkenberg, a military genius who will not permit mankind to be cast into eternal bondage. . . . Combines *The Mercenary* and *West of Honor,* two of the cornerstones of Pournelle's future history.

The Deed of Paksenarrion
by Elizabeth Moon   72104-6 • 1,040 pages • $15.00
The brilliant saga of grittily realistic fantasy. Combines *Sheepfarmer's Daughter, Divided Allegiance,* and *Oath of Gold* into one BIG trade paperback.

Across Realtime
by Vernor Vinge   72098-8 • 560 pages • $5.99

The ultimate defense against *all* weapons leads to the ultimate tyranny—but also leads to a way to escape into the future, where the Earth is inexplicably deserted. . . . Combines *The Peace War*, *Marooned in Realtime* and "The Ungoverned."